The Legend of the Firefish

THE LEGEND OF THE FIREFISH

George Bryan Polivka

HARVEST HOUSE PUBLISHERS
EUGENE, OREGON

All Scripture quotations are taken from the King James Version of the Bible.

Cover by Left Coast Design, Portland, Oregon

Cover photo © Greg Pease / Stone / Getty Images

This is a work of fiction. Names, characters, places, and incidents are products of the author's imagination or are used fictitiously. Any resemblance to actual persons, living or dead, or to events or locales, is entirely coincidental.

THE LEGEND OF THE FIREFISH

Published by Harvest House Publishers
Eugene, Oregon 97402
www.harvesthousepublishers.com

Polivka, Bryan.
The legend of the Firefish / George Bryan Polivka.
p. cm.—(Trophy Chase trilogy; bk. 1)
ISBN-13: 978-0-7369-1956-2 (pbk.)
ISBN-10: 0-7369-1956-2 (pbk.)
I. Title.
PS3616.O5677L44 2007
813.'6—dc22

2006021727

Printed in the United States of America

07 08 09 10 11 12 13 14 / LB-SK / 10 9 8 7 6 5 4 3 2 1

For Jeri, Jake, and Aime

Acknowledgments

I offer my grateful thanks to Hugh Smallwood for his generous help with the many details of tall-ship sailing as it was known in the past of our own world. Heartfelt thanks to John Patterson for his unwavering friendship and support on the long and sometimes perilous journey. Humble thanks to John Russell for helping me launch this ship. Delighted thanks to Tom Hawkins, who survived the Firefish, and who stood by me in my hour of peril. And wholehearted, full-and-by thanks to my beloved family for their understanding, patience, and unwavering support; for being my anchor and my safe harbor.

Contents

A Personal Note from George Bryan Polivka...

C.S. Lewis believed that the longings we all experience for something greater and deeper are captured in Myth, where the great truths of the universe shine out from simple stories. I hope you will find in *The Legend of the Firefish* a mythical story of that order.

The kingdom of Nearing Vast is a seafaring land without modern technology or science and, much like during our own history in such eras, tales of great sea monsters are told and retold. But in Nearing Vast the legends are true. There are monsters in the Vast Sea. These solitary, predatory beasts are as long as a sailing ship, snakelike in appearance, and capable of tremendous acts of destruction. But they are also highly desirable—legend has it that the meat of the Firefish bestows considerable powers upon all who consume it.

And so *The Legend of the Firefish* is the saga of a few brave and sometimes foolish souls who seek to discover and exploit the secrets of these beasts. Their individual quests for honor, love, power, riches, and redemption all revolve around the great sailing ship, the *Trophy Chase,* and its pursuit of the Firefish.

In *The Legend of the Firefish,* Packer Throme takes up the sword and goes to sea in order to redeem himself and restore the reputation of his father. Panna Seline sets out alone in a hostile world to find love and fulfillment. Scatter Wilkins seeks riches and glory at almost any cost. Talon, sworn enemy of all that is holy, is bent on proving that raw, ruthless power runs the universe and that no God exists to protect the weak and helpless.

Although the kingdom of Nearing Vast is mythical, it is not magical. Like our world, it is populated with people who have very real limitations. The world, the flesh, and the devil press in, and threaten destruction. But here, as in our world, there is power in faith, and all people have hope for redemption. This is not a "sword and sorcery" tale, but one of "sword and spirit." There is no magic...but there are miracles.

It's my prayer that anyone in search of something more, something greater...anyone who faces trials and troubles on the journey, anyone who has ever walked with trepidation among enemies or sought a conquering faith alongside true believers...will find a home in Nearing Vast.

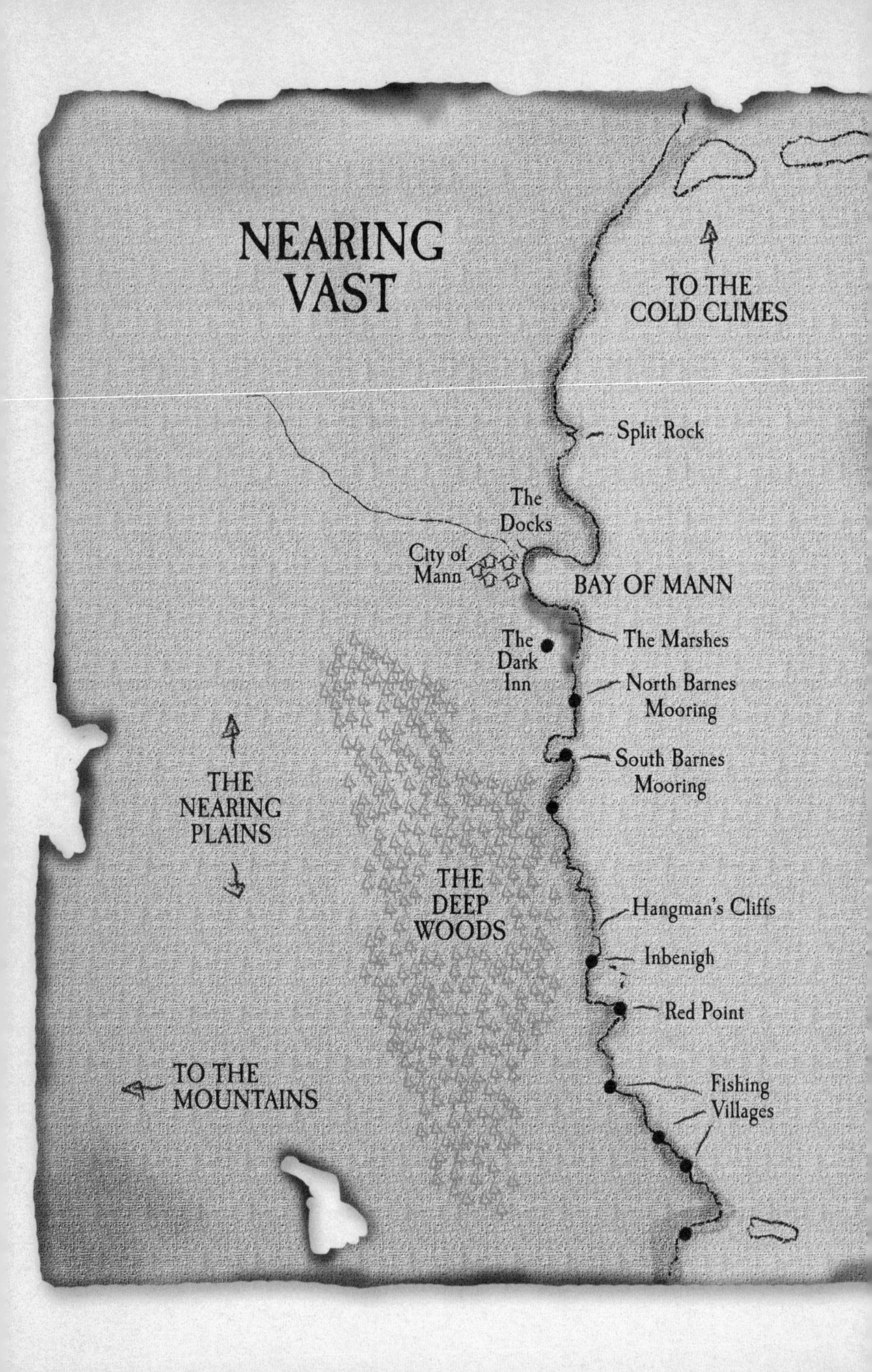
NEARING VAST
TO THE COLD CLIMES
Split Rock
The Docks
City of Mann
BAY OF MANN
The Marshes
The Dark Inn
North Barnes Mooring
South Barnes Mooring
THE NEARING PLAINS
THE DEEP WOODS
Hangman's Cliffs
Inbenigh
Red Point
TO THE MOUNTAINS
Fishing Villages

TO DRAMMUN

Scale in miles

0 10 20 30 40 50

Thy great deliverance is a greater thing
Than purest imagination can foregrasp,
A thing beyond all conscious hungering,
Beyond all hope that makes the poet sing,
It takes the clinging world, undoes its clasp,
Floats it afar upon a mighty sea,
And leaves us quiet with love and liberty and thee.

—George MacDonald, *Diary of an Old Soul*

Chapter 1

The Chase

"You deaf, boy?"

Packer Throme didn't answer. The last thing he wanted now was a fight. Dog Blestoe was a big man, bigger than Packer by three inches and thirty pounds, and Packer's elder by thirty years. Leathery, gray-headed, lean and muscular from a lifetime of hard labor, Dog stood across the table with his hands knotted into fists.

Packer stayed seated and silent.

Dog snorted. He had made sure Packer had left town humiliated four years ago. He would make sure the boy returned the same way. He rammed the table with his thigh, sloshing the mug of ale sitting on it. Packer caught it before it tipped.

"Say something!"

Packer didn't look up.

Dog grabbed the back of a wooden chair and tossed it aside, clattering it across the plank flooring, where it nearly shinned one of the regulars. "Disrespect!" he seethed, nodding around the pub at the undeniable proof Packer had just offered them all.

They did not nod back. These fishermen had come with their usual intentions, to talk and drink and smoke their pipes and do some modest complaining after a hard day at sea. Not to witness this. Not again.

"Stand up, boy!"

Packer studied his ale. Cap Hillis, the pub's friendly proprietor, had set the dark, white-capped mug there just moments ago. The modest complaining today had been about the pirate, Scatter Wilkins, and the rumors flying around that the feared outlaw had turned fisherman, and was now using harvesting techniques like those of their rivals across the sea in the Kingdom of Drammun. In so doing, Scat, as almost everyone called him, was helping to empty the sea of fish and glut the world's markets. In the process, he was also helping himself to a fortune, and making the fishing villages—like Hangman's Cliffs—all poorer by the day.

Dog believed the rumors. They gave him a specific target for a deep, general sense of discontent.

"The *Trophy Chase* wasn't built to catch cod," Packer had offered, the only full sentence he had spoken since arriving.

"I said *stand up!*" Dog now ordered. Packer did not comply.

Dog eyed Packer carefully. The boy had grown some, gained some weight. His pimples had turned to pockmarks. His mop of blond hair was even shaggier, if that were possible. But he was still the same spineless kid who wouldn't speak up, who couldn't look a man in the eye.

"They teach you this at seminary?" Dog sneered. "How to mock your elders?" He leaned on the table, his big, hard hands now splayed on the worn wood, his eyes locked on Packer as though they could burn through him. He dropped his voice. "Oh, no—I forgot. They didn't want you there, either."

Packer grimaced. He closed his eyes again, letting the pain, and then the anger, pass. Everyone in the village knew he had been expelled after less than a year at the seminary, rejected as a priest. But he was not prepared to have it flung at him the moment he returned.

Dog saw he was getting to the boy. He kept pushing. "So why'd you come back? You don't like hard work. That's what we have here. No books. No tea parties."

One groggy old fisherman, head hung over his ale, looked suddenly perturbed. "Hey, I got a book," he countered thickly. He was called Fourtooth, a nickname he'd earned after losing a run-in with a jib boom as a young man. Having had his say, he let his mug work its way back toward his mouth.

Packer took a sip of his own ale, careful to do it calmly and deliberately. It was cool, and his mouth was dry, and it felt good going down. He closed his eyes, and his mind returned him to where he'd been just this afternoon, standing atop the Hangman's Cliffs, the rugged precipices after which this village was named. He had been looking down on the inlet below, down on the great, sleek *Trophy Chase* shining in the sun, with her two escort ships beside her. Basking in the wrinkled blue water.

Packer alone knew of the pirate's ship hidden in the inlet below… and he knew he had to be aboard that ship. He wished he were standing on its forecastle deck, facing the Vast Sea, right now.

"You're cow dung," Dog sniffed, bringing Packer back to the moment. "And the only thing worse than cow dung is cow dung with no respect."

Packer tried not to imagine how a respectful pile of manure might behave. Would it salute? He tried to take another sip, but Dog must have noticed that he had let a trace of a smirk slip through, because the older man slapped him hard across the mouth with the back of his hand. The cool drink went flying, and the mug skittered across the floor.

Packer stroked his stinging jaw, but didn't respond, didn't look up. The innkeeper, round and red-faced, scrambled over, recovered the mug, examined it. It was made of sterner stuff than it appeared. He mopped halfheartedly with a rag at some of the puddled ale on the floor but was immediately distracted. It would soak into the open grain soon enough, absorbed like a thousand spills before it.

"Dog, lay off. Why not just hear him out?" a voice from the back of the room suggested. "Find out what he knows." Others echoed agreement.

"But he has nothing to say," Dog countered. "Do you, boy?"

Packer drew a line with his finger down a rough scar on the tabletop. The gash looked to Packer like it had been carved carefully with a knife, artwork made to look like an act of violence.

"Seems to me he's about to head right back out of town, now that he's finished his ale. Isn't that right, boy?" Dog snorted his disdain, pondering whether the lad needed hitting again. He decided against it and allowed himself half a smile. "Just as well you broke your promise to Panna. Marrying you would have ruined her."

There were a few oohs, and a whistle. Dog was hitting low.

Packer's jaw clenched just slightly, as Dog's words sliced through him. But this, too, was a familiar pain—the truth was, he couldn't

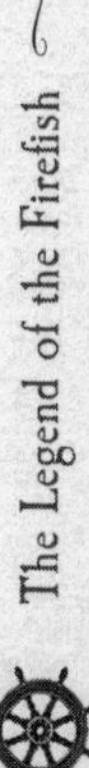

disagree. A more honorable man would have come home to Panna after the seminary rejected him and settled down to the quiet life of a fisherman. But Packer had not.

Dog laughed and turned away to pick up his chair. "Go ahead, try to act like nothing bothers you. If you want us to think you're turning the other cheek like some holy man, it ain't workin'. We all know you better than that. They sure knew better at your priest school. Like I've always told Panna," he continued casually, "you're just a worthless dreamer. Good for nothing." Dog stood over Packer now and delivered his final blow in a whisper. "Exactly like your daddy."

Audible breaths were taken and held.

Packer's face revealed nothing. But he stood up slowly, his blue eyes cold. Dog straightened, hands still clenching the back of the upright chair. Packer now looked Dog in the eye, a direct challenge. The fisherman smiled broadly. "What, you don't like me talking that way about your old man?"

Packer was smaller than Dog, but at just a shade under six feet, he was bigger than almost everyone else in the room. His shoulders were usually slouched some, but now he put his head back, squaring himself to the older man. He didn't look quite so soft, suddenly.

Dog was unimpressed. He looked for something else with which to bait him. He found it on Packer's belt. "Look at this! What do you know, boys! Did you see? He's a swordsman! Is that how you protect yourself from all us old fishermen?" Dog pantomimed a little loose-wristed swordplay, gaining laughs from around the room.

Packer's heartbeat quickened, but his cold gaze didn't change. He waited a moment longer, wrestling with his conscience, knowing he should walk away, not wanting to. Dog had crossed a line.

Dog's moment of mockery turned to disgust. "You're not fooling anybody. Your daddy was an embarrassment, and so are you. Tuck your tail and get."

Packer made his decision. He unbuckled his belt and gently laid it, with its scarred and stained leather scabbard, on the table. It was a dueling sword, a thin, straight, double-edged rapier. When all eyes were resting on it, Packer looked at Dog and spoke softly. "I'm sorry if this frightened you."

Dog's face went red, and the room erupted in a flash, amazed, gleeful. Packer had some fight in him after all.

"Draw it!" Dog demanded. Then without looking away, "Give me your iron, Cap!" Everyone knew what the innkeeper kept behind the bar for protection.

"No, Dog," Cap protested, his high voice strained. "Not swords!" But it didn't slow Dog or the others. One of them, a dark-spirited man named Ned Basser, reached behind the bar, and with a wild grin tossed Dog the barkeeper's sword. Cap tried vainly to intercept it, but his short, thick arms flailed uselessly as the rusted blade sailed over his bald head. Dog snatched it out of the air by the blade, proving to all who cared to notice just how dull it was. "There you go, Dog!" Ned called out. "Sic 'em!"

"No, leave him be!" Cap warned Dog in a shrill voice, grabbing at the big man's elbow. The innkeeper leaned in, stood on his tiptoes to speak into Dog's ear. "They say after he left the seminary he studied swordplay at the Academy…let it go, Dog."

But Dog's slitted eyes were now drilling into Packer's. He shook the barkeeper off his arm. "They can say what they like. I know what this boy's made of, and a few lessons in a lace drawing room can't change that."

Packer took his sword and scabbard from the table and looked at it, weighed it in his hands for a moment, and then suddenly unsheathed the blade. The oiled steel hissed as the blade flashed into view. It was a gleaming, finely crafted piece of work, with ornate detail engraved a third of the way up its length.

The older man's eyes widened almost imperceptibly. This was truly a swordsman's sword, the kind that Hangman's Cliffs had rarely seen. How Packer had gotten it and whether he knew how to use it were questions that only now formed in the older man's mind. He couldn't keep from looking down at Cap's sword, to which he had paid scant attention until this moment. The darkened thing looked like a fireplace poker by comparison. The blade was slightly bent, the tip rounded and dull, the hand-guard little more than a loose crosspiece of bent metal. He frowned. No matter. This was about manhood, not armor.

Dog gritted his teeth. "Come and get it," he croaked. But his voice didn't boom now. The words came not from the belly, but from the throat, more smoke than fire. Still, there was no chance he would back down. He turned sideways and raised his sword, pointing it so that the tip was inches from Packer's heart. The others stood and cleared a small space, moving chairs away and the table from between them, so the two could face each other properly.

Packer stood still, not taking his eyes off Dog. Rather than raise his guard, though, the younger man lowered his sword casually, resting its point on the rough flooring. Dog prodded a few times, brandishing his sword menacingly, actually poking Packer in the chest twice.

"Come on!" he demanded. His voice was now nasal. The room grew quiet again. The fishermen were suddenly worried Packer might not fight after all, even now. Last time it was fists, and humiliation. With swords, Packer might end up dead.

Packer had no such concerns. He shook his head casually, pulled on his earlobe. "You need to relax," he instructed his opponent. "You can't fence when you're tight as a drum." Dog looked sour—but more surprised than angry. Packer spoke with a casual authority the older man had not expected.

Now Packer raised his sword and stepped back, his body melting easily into a perfect guard position, eyes focused and ready, his blade just touching Dog's. "But most of all, Dog," he said, with a sudden, burning energy that seemed almost joyful, "try not to show so much fear." And he smiled.

This drew howls from the audience and a loud curse from Dog. The elder took a great sweeping hack at the younger. Packer reacted as though he expected exactly that move, as though he had meant to provoke exactly that move. He met the blow effortlessly, with the ring of steel on steel. In the same motion, his blade slid down the length of Dog's, sparking as it went, until its tip sliced across the knuckles of Dog's sword hand, easily missing the useless hand guard.

As Dog winced, a second flick of Packer's blade, executed so quickly it was almost imperceptible, sent the old sword flying across the tavern. Before it came to rest on the floor, and before the fisherman could grab his bleeding right hand with his left, the sharp tip of Packer's sword was pressed, cold and unyielding, into the sagging skin of the older man's throat.

Dog grabbed Packer's blade instinctively with his uninjured hand, closing his fist around it, but Packer quickly slid it out of his grasp, slicing Dog's palm and fingers as he did. And then he put the point right back where it had been, at Dog's throat. Dog held his two hands up, both of them now bleeding. He stepped backward reflexively until he stumbled into an open chair.

There he sat, hands now balled into bleeding fists, eyes wild, neck held back in a futile effort to stay away from the point of Packer's sword, which felt like it had already bored an inch into his throat. The room went quiet again. Dust swirled in the lamplight.

Packer's face was flint, but his voice went soft. "Now would be the appropriate time to show fear."

No one drew a breath. They all heard Dog's throat gurgle. His head didn't move, but his eyes darted around the room, vainly looking for help. He was having trouble grasping that there would be no help; it was already over.

Packer read his eyes, his expression, waiting for the moment when the obvious question arose in Dog's mind. And as soon as Packer saw it, he spoke. "Apologize to my father."

Dog's pride warred with his instinct for self-preservation. His mind spun, searching for another option, any option but apology or death. Apology was shameful; he had been ridiculing Packer Throme and his father, Dayton, for years. To simply retract it all in a moment would be to crumble completely, to admit cowardice as well as defeat. And yet to die at this boy's hands would be more shameful yet, giving Packer the last word, proving Dog wrong—and forever. Worse yet, Dog would be dead.

He very much did not want to be dead. But would the boy do it? Packer saw that question forming, the arrogance returning to Dog. He pushed just slightly on the blade and nodded, so there would be no question that he was willing.

Dog believed. From deep within him came a roar, full of anger and passion born of fear and pain. His teeth were bared, the strings of his neck taut and visible. He was a wounded, cornered animal, screaming his fury and his terror.

Packer's face didn't change, his blade didn't move. And then the rage in Dog was spent, and the roar rose to almost a shriek, petered out to a whimper. Dog closed his eyes, wrenched them tightly shut. He was breathing heavily, and looked like he might cry.

Still Packer waited. He knew Dog's moment of decision had not yet come. Dog had not yet decided to live with this moment branded into his memory, and into the memories of all these men; neither had he decided to die and be done with it. The choice would be

made now—now that the anger was gone. How deep did Dog's pride run?

The moment hung in the balance for what seemed like an eternity, Dog unwilling to choose, and Packer unwilling to choose for him. But it was Packer's resolve that crumbled. As his own emotion bled away, Packer suddenly saw himself—in this moment, detached from the events that had led to it. What if Dog were to choose death? Would Packer really kill him? A seated, helpless, unarmed old fisherman? Right here, like this? What was he doing? What would Panna think when she heard about it? And she would certainly hear. He looked around at the shocked, fearful, amazed expressions of those around him.

He had no idea how long he'd been standing here, the point of his sword poised to kill—but he couldn't continue, not another instant. He withdrew his sword, and sat down in the nearest open chair, his back to Dog. He laid his blade on the table in front of him.

Dog put a thumb and forefinger to his own throat, found the pinprick, was relieved to find so little damage. Then he looked around the room, assessing the much greater damage done to him in the eyes of his friends. Those few who would look at him seemed sad. He looked at Packer's back and forced a crooked smile.

"Well, boy. It's just as well you got kicked out of seminary. You'd sure make a lousy priest. No need to turn the other cheek when you can handle a sword like that."

There was scattered laughter, general agreement. But Packer hung his head, closed his eyes. It was a thrust to the heart.

Cap rushed up with a bar towel and began to bind it around Dog's bleeding hands. Dog rejected the help, snatched the cloth from the barkeeper. "I better go tend to these little scratches. I got work to do tomorrow." He eyed Packer with a cautious look. The younger man didn't see it. But when Dog said, "I'll see you later, Packer Throme," Packer heard the dark promise in it.

Hangman's Cliffs, the village Packer called home, was little more than a spot of lamplight perched above the ocean, the Vast Sea. A half-dozen storefronts huddled together on a rough cobblestone street, and a few dozen wooden and stone houses gathered around them. A small stone church stood at one end of the main road, facing the tavern at the other.

The church had no sign out front, but a cheerful hand-carved *Welcome* graced the doorway. At the other end of the town, above Cap's tavern doors hung a crude painting of a sea monster with a snake's body and a dragon's head, lightning coming from its mouth. It was the beast the locals called Firefish, and it was the name of Cap's pub. The main road ran east and west, so that the sun rose on the front doors of the church and set on the stoop of the tavern.

Behind the church at the western end of the unnamed main street were woods that stretched up and down the hills for miles, part of the timbered, rocky land that surrounded this warm circle of humanity. Beyond those woods were the Deep Woods, and beyond them, the Nearing Plains, which stretched nearly forever, north all the way to the Cold Climes, where few men dared to live, and south and west as far as the Great Mountains.

A stone's throw east of Cap's little pub, behind it, the ground rose up a few dozen feet. This rise was part of a long, rocky, tree-strewn ridge that ran parallel to the coastline along the top of the cliffs. When the ridge dropped off on the other side, it plummeted almost straight down into water. The small fishing village sat perched almost five hundred feet above the ocean. The fishermen trudged or drove their mule carts more than five miles each day around these cliffs, winding through switchbacks, to and from the ramshackle docks of Inbenigh, an unpleasant little spot that was named, or so the story went, after the carefully heeded advice to be "in by nightfall." And so, the elevated haven of Hangman's Cliffs was a fishing village hidden from the sea.

Packer had been born and raised here. He knew the terrain as only a local boy could. He had climbed and played and hiked during endless summer days, fall and spring, year after year, all along the rocks, clambering closer to the cliffs' edge than his parents knew or ever wanted to know.

He loved this place, and back then he had assumed he would always be here, as much a part of the landscape as a tree or an outcropping of rock. Going to sea with his father in their small fishing boat was as far from home as Packer ever thought he'd go. He would sit perched here beside his father, an eight-year-old boy watching the ocean, listening to its distant thunder. Saying few words, the fisherman taught his son about the enormity and the power of the created world, things seen and unseen, secrets known and deep secrets kept by God and the sea. If God could create all this, what couldn't He do? And a God who would choose to create all this, intricate in its beauty, perfect in detail, enormous in power, detail upon detail on such a grand plan, well...that was a God worth serving.

As Packer grew older and the work of fishing drew him in, he found himself fighting the inexorable flow of his life. The fishermen constantly scraping for subsistence, alternately praising and cursing the sea for what it yielded or refused to yield, somehow did not seem right. As the numbing and thoughtless repetition of their life dragged on him, he began to understand that he was connected to the created world, and the Creator of the world, in ways others around him did not seem to be or care to be.

Dayton Throme understood the longings within his son's heart. He told Packer there was a path for people who thought such thoughts and felt such things as he did. On this path, he could dedicate himself to God and to helping others love this great Creator. Packer's mother was thankful; she wanted her son to be anything but a fisherman, to live anywhere but Hangman's Cliffs. She felt keenly the scorn that was heaped on her husband for his strange devotion to the legend of the Firefish—certainly more keenly than Dayton did, who simply shrugged it all off with a laugh.

And then there was Panna Seline.

As far back as Packer could remember, Panna was always there. Panna, the daughter of Will Seline, the beloved village priest. Panna and Packer, playing, her silvery laughter rising up to the sun, the unceasing smile that teased behind her eyes always. The two of them had spent many hours talking about the world and everything in it, the sea and everything in it—sea monsters, pirates, the glorious life of the tall ships. And the God who created it all. Then, with a path to the priesthood opening up for Packer, their growing affection began to turn to love. And love grew into dreams for the future...and plans.

But so much had happened since those days. Dayton was gone, lost to this world years ago, his name now on the list *Taken by the Sea*—etched onto the marble memorial that stood in the cemetery amid the clearing in the woods. With Dayton gone from her life, Nettie Throme couldn't stay in Hangman's Cliffs. The day after Packer left for seminary, she moved back to her family in the Cold

Climes. In Packer's mind that awful plaque read, *All Dreams Shattered—All Hearts Broken.*

It had been two days ago in the City of Mann when Packer had heard that the *Trophy Chase* was headed to Hangman's Cliffs. For months he had tried to locate her, following whispers and tips up and down the coast, but she was always one day ahead or one town away. Then, following a rumor, he'd found himself at a pub in Mann called Croc-Eyed Sam's. There he found an old pirate signing up sailors for a dangerous, secretive mission. But no strangers, and especially no fishermen, were welcome. Among the whispers that night, however, he heard the name of his own village uttered more than once.

It was a sign, a good omen. Packer knew exactly where a captain would take a tall ship if he had reliable information about the coves and tides and inlets near the village.

The cliffs themselves ran north and south as a whole, winding in and out along the shoreline for two or three miles like a corrugated piece of tin bent in a series of sinuous, eel-like "S" shapes. The result was a series of naturally formed bays that, had there been any way to dock or get ashore, might have made excellent ports of call. They would certainly shelter ships from any storm.

It was from above one of these small bays a mile-and-a-half north of town that Packer had found the *Trophy Chase* and her sister ships at anchor. The three vessels stood on the water, motionless. They looked as if they could have been painted on a blue background of sky and sea. Only the occasional flutter of the skull and bones above the *Chase* hinted at her true nature, like the revelation of dagger claws in the lazy stretch of a cat.

She was as perfect a vessel as Packer had ever seen, smoother in line and turn than he could have imagined a ship being; long, lean, as though in motion even when still. To Packer, she looked as much a part of the ocean as a dolphin, as a seagull. She looked like she could fly as easily as she could sail. The *Chase* was every bit the equal of her reputation. He drank in the sight. And he determined more than ever that he would put his new plan in motion, right here at the Hangman's Cliffs he knew and loved so well. It would be a

new beginning; his new calling would start where the old one had, looking out over the ocean.

"*Trophy Chase*," he said aloud, just to hear the sound. The name rolled into the pounding of the waves below, into the salt sea air and the cries of the gulls. He said it again.

The words had barely left his lips when a puff of smoke flew from a cannon portal facing him. Packer dove for cover. The cannonball crashed just below him, sending shards of rock high into the air. "*Vigilance*," he said with respect as dust and debris rained down on him. "*Vigilance and precision*." He knew these words—they were two-thirds of the motto by which Scat Wilkins sailed his ships.

Packer scrambled back down the far side of the rocky ridge, taking care not to be seen again.

"Today?" Fourtooth asked, his wet eyes unblinking. "You saw the pirates *today?*"

Packer nodded. He was sitting at the center of the pub now, where Dog had been, with all eyes and ears riveted to him and his message. He had come here to warn them, but now, after his skirmish with Dog, his heart wasn't in it. His words seemed flat and hollow, like he had to squeeze them from his chest. "Scat Wilkins and his escorts are anchored off the Hangman's Cliffs just north of here."

Fear darted into the eyes of the old fisherman. He hunched forward as if a pain had shot through his belly. "What do they want?"

"He's here for supplies," Packer replied. "No doubt he'll send a party into town tonight."

"Here?"

Packer fought irritation. "Yes, here. Hangman's Cliffs, and every other village for ten miles up and down the coast."

"But why?"

Packer took a deep breath. He knew they needed more. He forced himself to concentrate on these men, on the faces around him. They needed to understand. "Well, that's how he works. He won't dock the *Chase* in just any port in the kingdom. I guess he thinks he'll be boarded, or infiltrated. So he comes to small towns and scrounges."

"For what?" asked Cap Hillis, staring from his place behind the bar.

"Everything. Canvas. Lumber. Clothing. Food. Water. Ale."

With this final statement, the reality finally hit Cap over the head. "You mean…you mean, pirates might be coming *here?* To my pub?"

Packer's irritation dissolved with the sudden fright he saw in the old tavernkeeper. He felt warmly toward him. "No, Cap—I mean pirates *are* coming here. Tonight. If the town is locked down tight, they'll knock on a few doors, make their deals, and go away; so I'm told. But no one should be out until morning."

More silence. Then Ned Basser spoke up, still stinging from Dog's poor showing. "You better hope you're not lying."

Packer was silent, trying to untangle the logic of that statement.

Fourtooth stood up slowly. "I gotta get outta here," he said wide-eyed. Then another thought crossed his mind, and he sat back down heavily. "But first I gotta have another drink." He reached for a pitcher of ale, but his neighbors already had him under the arms, helping him up and out of the tavern.

Packer watched them all go. He took a deep breath. His message had been delivered, and believed. He felt some relief, but not enough to penetrate the dark cloud brought on by his duel with Dog.

Cap, alone now in the pub with Packer, picked up the half-empty pitcher of ale that Fourtooth had coveted and put it down between them. Then he slapped a clean mug in front of Packer, eyed and selected an empty mug from a nearby table for himself, wiped it dutifully with his towel, and poured ale for the two of them. He kept an eye on Packer, trying to assess him.

Cap was plenty nervous about the approach of Scat Wilkins, but he could see that Packer was not. So long as this young swordsman was around, he figured, maybe there was reason panic might be delayed.

"You were a fearsome foe here tonight," he said finally, testing the waters. He wanted to know how deep this new steel ran in his good friend's son. The boy had always had more backbone than he'd showed, but it was generally hidden beneath a sensitivity that never really fit in well here. The priesthood had seemed right for Packer. But was that soft heart now gone?

Packer shook his head, slouched back in his seat, and toyed with his mug. What if Dog had sworn at him, stood up, called his bluff? What if he had simply decided to die, and leaned into Packer's sword? This quiet moment would now be utterly hellish, with the priest summoned, a body on the floor, Dog's wife arriving to find herself widowed, weeping uncontrollably, hysterical, cursing Packer. Panna would never look at him again. There would be a sheriff's deputy called, and even if Packer were vindicated, he would live with that moment forever.

Would he have done it? Could he have killed the old man? He felt sure he could have. His skills came not from a few odd lessons, as Dog supposed, but from three grueling years of the best training in the kingdom, perhaps in the world. And to what end? So that Packer could draw his sword in anger and nearly kill an unarmed man in his very first duel? His swordmaster would be gravely disappointed in him.

Packer looked at the tables and chairs, still pushed aside for the duel. He stood and began dragging them back together, erasing evidence. Cap watched for a moment and then took a deep drink. "You'd have been within your rights to kill him, you know." He refilled his mug to the brim. "He struck you. He provoked you. He called for the duel, and he drew on you."

"No," Packer answered softly. "I shouldn't have fought him at all."

Cap rubbed his red face with a pudgy hand. He felt relief that the old Packer had not been completely swallowed up in the swordsman. "Well, I disagree. I think you taught him something he needed to learn. Had it been another man he picked on, one without your skill or your heart, we'd be burying Dog's bones tomorrow."

Packer paused, thought about that. He could see some truth in it...that the outcome might actually help Dog live a longer, wiser life. But it didn't mean Packer had done the right thing. He went back to arranging furniture.

No need to turn the other cheek when you can handle a sword like that. Dog's words and the scripture they pointed to weighed on his mind. "But I say unto you, that ye resist not evil: but whosoever shall smite thee on thy right cheek, turn to him the other also." The whole point of that doctrine, as far as Packer could tell, was that only those with the heart to let themselves be wronged could be shed of evil themselves. "Vengeance is mine; I will repay, saith the Lord." And that's because only He can wreak vengeance without malice, without impurity of heart. Those who retaliate on this earth, regardless of their motives, somehow join the ranks of the evil.

Packer had had the heart, four years ago, to "resist not evil" when

Dog had slapped him around. What good had it brought, though? What had changed for the better since then? It had clearly had no effect on Dog—if anything, it had stirred him up more. Packer knew that the only Man who ever lived without retaliating, not even once, not even in his heart, was the Man who had first uttered those words. But how is it possible to do good when you aren't that Man? When your efforts to do good are always mixed in with poor motives?

Cap watched Packer move chairs around, reading a troubled heart easily enough. "Well, I say the whole town's indebted to you for keeping us righteous."

Packer stopped and looked at Cap. "Righteous? What do you mean?"

Cap shrugged, as though the answer were obvious. "You saved us all from having to stand over his grave and lie about him."

Packer laughed out loud. "He's not all that bad."

Cap raised his mug in tribute. "'And he's one whale of a fisherman!' See how little it takes?"

Packer laughed again, then sat down across from Cap feeling genuinely relieved. He drank the toast, studied the innkeeper's smiling face for a moment, then turned somber. "Cap…I have to ask you to do a favor for me. And for my father. And for Dog and the rest of the fishermen."

Cap wrinkled his brow. "What kind of favor?"

"A risky one."

Cap scraped his chair closer to Packer. "Ask away."

Chapter 2

The Mission

The night sky was brilliant, and Packer imagined that it looked just this way, right now, to those out on the open sea far from shore. Packer was lightheaded and exhilarated. Maybe it was the ale, he thought to himself. But there was no reason not to be energized. He hadn't killed Dog, after all; the old salt probably took worse scratches on an average hike through the woods. Packer had taught him a good lesson, like Cap said, and it was one he'd surely needed to learn. Leave the rest to God.

And now the town was locked up, safe from the scrounging pirates. That was all good. Of course it was. Packer had done it; he'd done well. And best of all, Cap had agreed to help Packer get on board the *Trophy Chase*. This very night! And that was his true goal. Good had come of it all, and more good would come yet.

No, it wasn't the ale, he told himself—it was that everything was finally going to change. This was his new mission, his new calling—important enough to cut his training short and say goodbye to his swordmaster. He was taking the great risk for the great reward, the enormous opportunity ahead that would finally prove his worth, to himself and to everyone else. Especially to Panna.

Panna Seline. Even the thought of how he'd let her down couldn't break his mood. If he could just get aboard that ship, he could bring Scat Wilkins' new enterprise to Hangman's Cliffs, to these humble doorsteps. Surely this great new market would change everything. The village would prosper. His father would be vindicated. And he, Packer Throme, would have done it. Even Dog would look back and thank him. And Panna would be proud. He would be worthy of her love.

He walked the deserted streets in the direction of his father's cottage, where he had stashed his few possessions on the way into town. The place was boarded up and had fallen into disrepair, which Packer hated to see, but without the money or the time to rescue it, there was nothing to be done. He needed his knapsack, that was all, carefully packed with the few items he thought he'd need tonight, and his Bible and, of course, his father's diary.

Packer walked slowly, drinking in the elation he felt. Just where he should have turned up the winding path that led to the cottage in the woods, he looked instead at the church spire, now off to his left. It rose like a spike, a pylon driven from the earth into the sky by poor humans seeking a foundation in the heavens, yearning for meaning.

He walked toward it, drawn.

His was a hopeless dream if God wasn't in it. Packer's footsteps echoed on the dark cobblestones. But surely, God *was* in it.

"So he's a swordsman now," said an angel's voice from above him. Packer was jolted to the moment, and looked up. Panna stood at the upper porch railing of the parsonage.

He felt a lump like a piece of coal in his throat. "Panna."

"You were going to be a priest the last time we spoke. And now you are—what? One of those pirates, come to buy a little ale? Maybe kill a fisherman or two?" Panna Seline asked it softly, but the words pierced deep. She was more beautiful than ever, here in the moonlight, with her long dark hair pouring in soft swirls down her shoulders, dark eyes piercing him in familiar, painful, pleasant ways.

"No. No, of course not." The news had traveled like lightning. Why had he come up this street? He had been determined to avoid this encounter. He wasn't ready. But now in the starlight her cinched bodice outlined the form of a woman, more woman than the one he remembered leaving behind. He wanted to run, just turn and run away.

"You didn't kill Mr. Blestoe. But sooner or later, swordsmen either kill or die. Isn't that right?" Her voice was sweet and powerful and right on point. He was no match for this sword.

"Usually both." Packer's face flushed. His soul felt bare and raw. "How are you, Panna?"

"How am I? Oh, it's to be polite conversation, then? I see. I'm quite well, thank you, sir." She paused, and he could not speak. She spoke for him. "'And what have you been doing since we last spoke, Panna?' 'Well let's see, it's been so many years…I've done a lot of wash, and I've helped father with a lot of sermons. The wash and the sermons both smell of fish, but after so many years I barely notice.'"

Packer finally detected playfulness, and he felt relief. But the point of her sword was perfectly placed; he was struck through the heart. As he always was with her. "So," she concluded, "my life has been as grand as I could hope. And how have you been, Mr. Throme?"

Packer laughed. She made the sun shine in darkened places within him. He felt himself falling in love all over again. "You haven't changed," he whispered.

"Disappointed?"

"Oh, no. Never."

"Maybe I should have changed. Maybe you'd have come to visit a different girl. Or maybe…" her fingers played across the wooden railing in front of her, "maybe you *have* been visiting a different girl."

"No, Panna!" he blurted out, feeling panicked. Somehow it never occurred to him she'd think such a thing. "No, there's no one else."

"*Else?* Hmm. Well, if that's true, then what you mean to say is, there's no one at all. Because if you say there's no one *else,* that assumes there's me. And clearly, there's not me, since you couldn't possibly have known if I was even alive or dead. But I am alive, as you now see."

"I do see that. And I'm glad." He kicked himself. He was telling her he was glad to see she wasn't dead. Could he have said anything more stupid? No, not with a week to plan it.

But she responded with a smile. His voice was so very Packer. It was gentle, and earnest beyond reason, and hearing it again shook dust she didn't know existed from memories she had thought were fresh. Here was the boy she loved so much.

"Panna," he said, ready to pour his heart out to her, here and now, standing below her, looking up at her where she deserved to be, from where he deserved to be. "You deserve so much more." She leaned toward him.

"Says who?" bellowed a gruff voice behind her, breaking the

moment. The voice was quickly followed by its owner out onto the tiny porch. "Who's passing judgment on my household now?" The village priest emerged, a big bear in a gray robe, looking fierce. But Packer could easily read the playfulness in this man.

"Hello, Pastor, I didn't mean—"

"Well, well…Packer Throme, the prodigal returned," the priest interrupted, not interested in Packer's apologies. "We have no fatted calf, if that's what you were hoping. But we do have coffee freshly brewed, and plenty of cake." He patted his stomach, raised an eyebrow. "Too much cake. Come in this house and relieve me of some of it…this one here won't help me a bit!"

"I really—" Packer began, but the priest cut him off again with a wave of his hand.

"I know all about the pirates on their way. The whole town is buzzing like flies at a picnic. But the blaggards aren't here yet, and I say it's God's will that you obey your priest just one last time before we're all overrun and our village burned to the ground and our bones hung out to bleach on some creaking yardarm." He grinned. "But I'll have the last laugh—there's not a yardarm made that'll hold me!" Packer laughed, but the priest's grin disappeared. "Or am I no longer your priest?"

"Oh, you are, sir," Packer said quickly. "Definitely you are. And I'd be honored."

"So. When do you apply for readmission to seminary?"

Packer stopped mid-bite, the fork between his lips. This pastor had sponsored his admission; Will Seline knew more than anyone outside the seminary, and likely more than many within it, about what had happened. He knew how impossible it would be for him to go back.

Will's face was inscrutable, though. He sat across the table from Packer, patiently waiting, his bushy, graying beard jutting out, his hands resting on his proud girth.

And it was indeed proud. The less his parishioners could afford to put in the offering plate, the more they tried to pile on his dinner plate, bringing him food or inviting him and Panna to dine. Will Seline's view was that if supper was all they could give, then it would be uncharitable not to partake. And so their pastor's belly gave the village a common sense of accomplishment.

Packer chewed the cake, and sweet though it had been a moment ago, it now seemed dry and tasteless.

"Excuse me," Panna said, rising from her spot beside her father.

"No, no," the priest responded, waving her back to her place. "This should concern you as well, since you were at one time betrothed to this sword-brandishing vagabond."

"Father..." she began, but left it at that. It was a warning.

"I'm not...called back to seminary," Packer said slowly.

"No?" A big eyebrow floated up, then back down. "And to what, then, are you now called?"

Packer wasn't sure how to answer. "Well. Commerce, I suppose." He said it a bit more glumly than he intended.

The priest feigned admiration. "So God has called you to riches?"

Packer spoke softly. "Pastor, I've seen a lot of commerce, but not many riches. I'm not sure the one very often leads to the other."

The priest considered this and smiled. "Well said." Then he leaned across the table toward Packer, his face and voice suddenly intense. "Packer, my boy—what happened? You leave here with a vision for the priesthood. You return a swordsman, picking fights with old men in pubs. I've spoken to the dean of your seminary. The young man they dismissed did not sound to me like the young man who left here with a full and eager heart."

Packer took the pause as an opportunity to look down into his coffee cup. He was not willing to talk to Pastor Seline about these things, and certainly not with Panna listening. He glanced at her, and saw some combination of anger and concern he couldn't sort out.

"And you couldn't even come to see me," Will continued. "Or this young woman here, as true a friend as you'll ever have, who loves you in spite of yourself." The priest's voice dropped to a whisper. "You couldn't come see us until you'd had your ale at the local spigot and proven your manhood with steel."

"Father! It's not your place!" Panna's anger was searing. Will Seline winced at the sudden attack from his flank.

"Not my place? I could dispute that." But the priest relented. He could argue with her, but she was his daughter. He couldn't win. And she certainly had the greater claim on Packer. He softened. "No one can force a young man to do..." He trailed off. "I pray you change your mind, and reapply."

Packer's shoulders slumped. He was asking the impossible. Why would Will pretend there was any hope of his returning to seminary after what he'd done?

Panna now spoke. "It's your path, Packer. No one else's." She shot an accusing look at her father. Packer glanced at her, but when she looked at him he saw only pain and forgiveness, and the beauty of the two together.

The priest looked hard at him. "When you were turned out of the seminary, you turned to the Academy...and you were schooled by the Swordmaster of Nearing Vast. This is the rumor," the priest said. "And after your encounter with Dog Blestoe, I must assume the rumor is true?"

Packer nodded.

"What brand of commerce comes of such a trade? I haven't seen swordsmanship for sale in the local market."

Packer looked at him closely, softened, then looked at Panna. "I'm going to sea."

Panna misunderstood, was about to ask him what he expected to see, when the meaning hit her. Packer saw her stricken look and closed his eyes, buffeted by the storm within. He saw suddenly, standing before him, Senslar Zendoda, the small man with the crimson beret, the perfectly groomed white beard, the sparking eyes. Packer remembered perfectly their conversation at the end of a series of mind-numbing drills. He'd been tired—but not just tired, frustrated. Even angry. The swordmaster lowered his own sword, stood casually, and asked Packer, "What will you do with your life?"

The question caught Packer off guard. "My life?"

"I have taught you swordsmanship. You may be the most gifted pupil I have ever had. But your heart, Packer. Where is it leading you?"

The young man looked at the wooden floor, his eyes drawn to the spot where his sword tip rested on the grain. "I don't know."

"But you are driven to it, regardless," Senslar said. Packer looked up at him, into those dark, fiery eyes. He took a deep breath. This was the sort of discussion he usually ran from, but somehow Senslar's tone, his voice, his spirit did not allow escape. "Swordplay to you is like a well to a man crossing a desert."

Suddenly, Packer realized this wise little man might help. "Do you know why?"

Senslar smiled, always a glittering thing in Packer's memory, but this smile carried more light yet. "No. No, I do not. But I do know of a sea turtle that lives in waters of the Warm Climes, and grows to be three hundred pounds. It is a sea creature, but it is born from an egg that hatches on dry land, far from the shore. At first, it knows only its shell. After a great struggle, it frees itself of that prison, and then it knows only air and sand. But it hears the ocean. It smells the salt in the air. It feels it. And it is pulled in the direction it must go. It does not know why, or what it will find there. It is drawn by an inescapable desire for something it cannot describe and has never known, but that it must, must find. Or it will die."

Packer knew what it was to crawl across that dry sand toward a welcoming sea. He understood this to the foundation of his soul.

"Only one thing can put such drive in a man's heart as the drive I see in you. God has made you for a single end, and even though you do not know what that end is, you know what direction you must go to find it."

"To the sea?"

Senslar laughed and shook his head. "You are not a turtle, Packer. You are a man created in the image of God. The sea will be too small for you."

"What do you mean?"

The swordmaster grew serious. "The deep longings of your heart may take you out to sea, but the sea itself will not fulfill them. Only the calling that God has put within you can do that."

"And what is that calling?" Packer asked, desperately hoping this man was wise enough to answer, to stop the bleeding caused by his severed call to the priesthood.

"I cannot tell you. That is why I asked."

Packer fought back disappointment. Senslar Zendoda knew no more than Packer did.

The priest also saw his daughter's stricken look and decided not to press further. He would leave it to Panna to question Packer on his intentions. Will Seline stood. "Well, then. God bless you." The words were somehow harder to say than he ever remembered. Then he turned and left the young man with his only child.

As he climbed the stairway, he could make his heart feel nothing but a great sorrow. His wife dead and gone these past eight years, his parishioners falling into poverty, and the one great joy God had left him—his Panna—wilting, it seemed, even as she bloomed. Knowing as the pastor did the depth of his daughter's love, her devotion to this reckless young man, the future seemed bleak, at best.

But Will Seline believed in God. He believed God cared deeply. And so he would continue to pray. His heart would cry out to God. And God would hear; He always heard. And eventually, He would answer.

The dark-haired young woman, her heart aching, stood and walked around the table. She snuffed the oil lamp on the way, so that only a single candle on the table lit the room. She sat close to the young man she loved, close beside him on the wooden bench.

"I've missed you," she said simply. What he heard, what he saw, was far more complex.

"I often think how things might have been different." Her voice was liquid silver, flowing like a stream. "How we could have had a cottage, and a child—maybe two by now—running to the door to welcome their father home each night."

Packer couldn't look at her. She should be scolding him, forcing him to answer hard questions about where he'd been, why he hadn't returned home, what he really felt about her. These were questions he dreaded, but they were questions he expected.

This was unfair. She touched his face, turned it toward her. Her beauty was overwhelming. Completely unfair. He was self-conscious for only a moment, knowing his face to be marred, like his heart. But he forgot that quickly, lost himself in her eyes.

She was infinitely beautiful. He saw again those things in Panna he always remembered when her face came to his mind. The small shelf of her cheekbone just under her eyes. The roundness of her forehead as it swept back to her hairline. The tiny, intricate lines creasing her full lips. He loved all these things. But mostly he loved her eyes, loved the light that shone from them. And here they were right now, deep, dark, soft as evening, drawing him in, more pleasant and powerful than he could have remembered or dreamed. There was gentle urgency in her. A delicate, powerful passion.

She spoke. "You know that I love…that faraway place inside you." Her voice was a stream over stones, clear and perfect. Exactly as he remembered it, but even more so. "I love that place," she told him, "the one you're always trying to find. I always have. Even though I can't ever seem to go there with you."

You are that place, he thought.

"If you were to settle here in this town and fish while that place still beckoned you, or become a priest, I'm afraid it might mean that place would one day be gone."

Packer didn't understand what she was saying. She moved her body closer to his. She put a fingertip to her lips, and then touched it to his. This he understood. He felt inadequate, clumsy...and powerfully, inescapably drawn. His pulse raced as his defenses crumbled.

"You will do great things," she was saying. "And I don't ever want you to settle for anything less. I just want to be with you, where you are. That's all I've ever wanted."

Looking into her eyes, he couldn't avoid one great, simple truth. He knew now why he had come up this street. He knew why he was here. So he said it.

"I love you, Panna."

She smiled sadly and said, "But you're leaving again...aren't you?"

He was so glad she believed his admission of love. But he was crushed by her sadness. He couldn't answer.

"When?"

He shook his head, not wanting to say the one word that was the only truthful answer, knowing what it would do. But he had to say it. "Tonight."

Her face fell, and she sat back. She looked away. "When will you be back?"

"I don't know."

Packer least expected Panna's next response. She placed her hands on either side of his face and turned him to her. "Take me with you, Packer. Anywhere." Her hands were firm, and warm. Her brown eyes were intense. Her face was everything of value in this world, and most of the next—searching, and caring, and hopeful.

"I can't," he said, as though from a great distance. "Panna—I'm going to sea on the *Trophy Chase.*"

Her eyes widened. She dropped her hands. "Scatter Wilkins' ship?"

He nodded. "Look, Panna, I shouldn't tell you this—you can't tell anyone, even after I'm gone. Not your father, not anyone. It could be dangerous for me and...others...if it gets out."

She was still searching. "Of course it's dangerous. Packer, he's a pirate." She sat back and looked hard at him.

"He's not now. At least, not like he was. He's turned to fishing… and…a lot more." He had to tell her everything. He took a deep breath. "Panna, he's going after the Firefish. And I can help him."

Her face was blank. "The Firefish? But they don't exist."

"They do, Panna. I'm sure of it."

She knew the stories, of course—everyone did. But they were only stories…of the great sea monsters large enough to take down a whole ship with a single lunge. This was Leviathan, from the book of Job. This was legend.

"If they exist, why aren't they seen more often?"

"Panna, how many ships simply disappear, fishing boats that never return? It happens every year." The unspoken memory of Packer's father's fate in just such a way hung between them.

"Packer. Even if there is such a beast, what net could hold it?"

Packer looked intently at her. "The *Trophy Chase* is fast, a fighting craft. I think they aren't fishing. It's more like whaling. They're… hunting them."

"Them? But how many Firefish are there?"

"I don't know. But more than one. Many, I suspect."

She thought a moment. "What makes you believe all this?"

"I've pieced it together, Panna. Talking to a lot of sailors, even a few sea captains. The *Chase* is always at sea, and one of her escorts, the *Camadan,* is a regular at merchant ports all over the kingdom, and the rumors have it that Scat—"

"Rumors? You're risking your life on rumors?"

"More than rumors, Panna." He looked at her hesitation, took a deep breath. "Panna, my father believed the Firefish could be taken. He believed the meat has some kind of extraordinary power. And whatever Scat's doing, I think it's something local fishermen can learn to do. My father believed it. It's in his diary. He found their feeding waters, or at least thought he did. If I can help Scat Wilkins find them, it will change everything. For everyone."

"But—they're *pirates,* Packer. They're dangerous people. Bad men."

He felt exasperated. "Panna, I can take care of myself."

"By the sword, I suppose?"

"I've thought it all through. I've planned this for a long time. I'll be safe. Panna, I have to find out. If for no other reason than for my father's memory."

She sighed. True or not, she could see why he couldn't resist it. This was so much like Packer.

He took her hands. "Panna, I'll come back for you. If you still want me then, we'll get married."

Her eyes widened, but this time in fear. "Don't say that, Packer." These were words she longed to hear, but not this way—words said to make her feel better as he left her.

"I promise you—"

She put a finger to his lips. "I love you, Packer. But listen to me. I'm not holding you to a promise you may not be able to keep. You've only now come to see me, and I'm not sure you were meaning to come see me at all."

Packer lowered his eyes. Yes, he had planned to avoid her…and now he was pledging his future to her. But this was right. This was true. He looked back up at her. She was a part of him in so many ways. "I *will* come back, Panna."

He pulled her gently toward him and kissed her.

And then, from somewhere far away, a sound reached him. The clatter and clop of a cart pulled by a single horse on a cobblestone street. It took a moment longer for an image to form in his mind: sailors from the ship *Trophy Chase* in search of supplies.

Panna knew that the moment, somehow, was over. "Packer?"

"Shh!" He sat straight up, listening. He couldn't let this happen—couldn't miss this chance. "It's them. Panna, I have to go."

"Packer…"

"I have to, Panna. I have to go. Now."

And he was gone before she could say more.

The single candle lit only the drab, familiar dining room. Was that the last look she would have of him? She held the image in her mind: his pain and joy and excitement fully commingled. There was love there. It was a worthy look, worthy of him, worth holding forever.

Forever? Packer was gone. He might never come back for her. Panna slumped to the floor and wept.

Upstairs, Will Seline heard the door close, then heard the sobs of his daughter. He prayed for Panna. And he prayed for the grace not to hate Packer Throme.

CHAPTER 3

The Stowaway

Cap Hillis had no sooner shut up the storeroom than he heard a knock on his tavern door.

"We're closed!" Cap called out as cheerily as he could manage. He was sweating, quite sure he wouldn't remember the details he was supposed to be able to recite with confidence.

"Well then, open!" came the gruff answer back. "We've got gold coin and we need drink, and plenty of it. We'll pay top price."

Cap walked closer to the door. "Who are you?" he asked, trying to sound appropriately suspicious.

"Cash customers. Two gold coins for each barrel of ale. Are you interested, or do we go elsewhere?"

"That's a good price," Cap told them, genuine surprise in his voice. He started to open the door, but then didn't want to seem too eager. He leaned into it, hand still on the knob. "Why don't you come in daylight?"

The voice was irritated. "Just open the door."

Cap opened, as he correctly assumed all other businesses in the village either had or would.

Two men in leather forester's clothing entered. They didn't look like sailors. They were followed by a woman, a foreigner, also in leather jacket and leggings, though hers were dark, a dull black. She had shiny, jet-black hair pulled into a braid that went from her left ear to her shoulder in the customary way of Drammune women, thick by her high cheekbone and deep-set eyes. The braid paralleled the slash of a deep scar that stretched from the corner of her left eye down to her jaw and reappeared on her neck. A warrior's scar, made by a blade. She held a drawn rapier; a black-powder pistol was tucked into her belt beside the sheath of a long knife. Her eyes scanned the room with the cold vigilance of a hawk.

"Where's your storeroom?" the first man demanded. He wasn't tall, but he was built like a block, square from shoulders to hips, with beefy arms and big paws for hands. This cubic torso was held up by thick legs that seemed too short for him. He had almost no neck; his sullen face started with a round chin at his chest and rose up to a thick, bony brow.

He was called Ox.

Cap pointed. Ox opened the storeroom door, and the other man went in quickly. This one was bowlegged, taller than Ox but spindly. An old head injury left his right eye half closed and the right side of his mouth carved into a permanent smile, a winking mockery of a carefree disposition. Everyone called him Monkey. The two animals, Ox and Monkey, rolled out both of Cap's untapped barrels on a wooden hand truck, neither speaking another word.

The woman kept an eye on the innkeeper between glances out the window. Cap Hillis had never heard of a swordswoman, but he had no doubt he was looking at one now. She was the smallest of the three, but struck Cap as the most dangerous. And though she said little, he got the distinct impression she was in charge.

"Two barrels. Four coins." Ox dropped the coins on the bar. "We need more," he grumbled. "How much is left in that one?" He pointed to the barrel lying on its side, on a pedestal behind the bar, already tapped.

"Not much. Check for yourself."

Ox jostled it easily with one hand. "Is there another tavern in town?"

Cap shook his head as he picked up the coins, hefting them in his hand.

"Ask him if he's hiding anything," Monkey suggested in a nasal voice, as though Cap couldn't hear him. "They always try to hide something."

Ox squinted at the barkeeper suspiciously. "Do you have any more ale somewhere?"

As Cap shrugged, the woman walked over to him and looked him directly in the eye. He was terrified by the dark promise he saw in her, the threat implicit in her look. This was as cold a pair of eyes as he'd ever seen. He could see death there; he could feel it. He glanced sideways at the storeroom. There were two empty barrels, and one covered one, back in the corner.

"Fools," the woman said, pointing her sword. "There's a barrel under the blanket." The woman spoke in a thick accent, with hard, rolling R's.

"Oh, that," Cap said quickly. "That's not something I thought sailors would want."

"Who said we were sailors?" The woman's eyes pierced him again.

Cap shook his head, afraid to speak, then glanced at the two men for help. Cap grinned painfully at Monkey—a reflex before realizing that Monkey's disarming expression was frozen on half his face while the other half frowned. The barkeeper's smile vanished as quickly as it had appeared.

"Who told you we were sailors?" she repeated.

Cap flushed. "No one said it, ma'am. I just…there were rumors, and well, I don't…" Cap completely foundered, and put a sharp laugh where the rest of his sentence should have been.

"Rumors." The woman eyed him menacingly, but could see no danger in him. She jerked her head in silent command, and the two animals went for the last barrel.

Suddenly, Cap very much did not want Packer to go through with this. It was wrong; it was dangerous. Cap was foolish to have agreed to help. He felt panic, not knowing how to get himself, and Packer, out of this jam without putting them both in greater jeopardy yet. "Wait, wait!" Cap tried, but Ox and Monkey were already rolling the barrel out the door to the waiting cart.

Inside the barrel, Packer fought back his own surge of panic. He pressed his knees tightly against the staves, pushing with his shoulders, pulling on his wedged sword to steady him, praying that nothing would rattle or knock from within. He was sweating; he felt completely out of control. After all his careful planning, he had rushed everything, running here from Panna's house, leaving his knapsack behind. He had drilled Cap with instructions as the barkeeper gathered up the few items he would need. And now it was going badly; how then could it not *end* badly?

"It doesn't feel full," Monkey offered after they had hefted it into the back of the cart.

"One coin," Ox said flatly to the innkeeper, who had followed them nervously out into the moonlight.

Cap was impressed with Packer's plan in spite of himself. The boy knew they'd want everything, and holding out on them would only make them want this barrel more. He now remembered his instructions, to ask a high price for this "special ale." But he couldn't do it. He didn't want them to take it. "You're right," Cap said. "Something wrong with it, no doubt. You should probably just leave it."

Packer had trouble hearing the words clearly, but he was quite sure the words "wrong with it" and "leave it" had been uttered by the barkeeper. He held his breath.

Cap's words had an equally alarming effect on the trio of pirates. They looked at him, then at one another. Then Ox narrowed his eyes suspiciously. "What's in here? Why isn't it full?"

"Nothing. Nothing in there but ale. It's just bad ale. Probably."

Cap was a terrible liar, and they all knew he was lying, and he knew they knew. His chin started to tremble.

"It's a new barrel. Ask him how could it go bad," Monkey said to Ox. "Ask him what he has in there." Monkey rapped on the barrel with a knuckle.

"Tap it," the woman ordered, and her disgusted tone suggested she had resisted adding the phrase "you idiots." Her voice was deep, angular, impatient.

"No, wait!" Cap said, almost shrieking.

"Tap it," she repeated. "Then we'll know."

Before Cap could think of any reason to stop them, Monkey tipped the barrel so it lay on its side and then left it to find a hammer and spigot. As soon as the sailor looked away, the barrel rolled a quarter turn across the back of the buckboard all by itself, as its contents found a center of gravity. Cap's eyes widened, but no one else seemed to have noticed. Monkey rummaged in a leather sack behind the wagon's seat, produced the needed items, and went to the barrel.

Cap was in a state of near panic as the man started pounding the point into the cork of the bung. Cap's heart fell. There was only one thing to be done now. He walked back into the tavern, toward the bar, where his sword had been replaced after the goings-on earlier in the evening. He wasn't much of a swordsman, in fact he wasn't a swordsman at all, but maybe he could distract them long enough for Packer to get out of the barrel and fight. How had Packer talked him into this? A nice mug of ale and a few stories, that's all he'd wanted from Packer. Not pirates and swords and lies and bloodshed.

The spigot bit into the wood of the cask, deeper and deeper. Cap's hand shook noticeably as he reached across the bar and found the steel blade. As his hand closed around the cold rusted metal, he looked back at the door. The hawklike woman was staring at him, her own blade poised casually in her hand. He froze.

"I need a mug, Ox!" called Monkey, as ale splattered onto the street.

Cap was startled, but instantly let go of the blade, reached instead for a mug. He squeezed past the woman with a quick, "Excuse me, ma'am," avoiding the cold look in her eye. He was sure she could hear his heart pounding. He handed the mug to the shorter man, who turned the spout back on and began to fill it. Cap scratched his head. *How did Packer…?* But then he knew.

One of the items Packer had insisted on taking with him into the barrel was a winebladder full of ale, mixed with water and a shot of whiskey. Cap didn't understand why Packer had wanted it, but now it was obvious. Inside the barrel, Packer had waited until the point of the spigot penetrated the barrel lid, and then he pushed the wineskin against it, puncturing it. The mug was a quarter full when the man turned off the spout.

First one, then the other man tasted it. The woman declined with a shake of her head. "Strange," said Ox. Monkey made a disapproving face.

"It's light, but it kicks like a mule," Cap offered, thankful that he had also remembered that bit of the story.

"It's awful," Ox said. "Something wrong with it."

"Then leave it," the woman instructed.

Packer heard this clearly, and he fought back a surge of disappointment.

"Oh, thank God," Cap said aloud. He felt genuine relief.

Ox and Monkey stopped short once again and stared at Cap.

Ox walked over to Cap and grabbed him by the shirt collar, pulled his face so close that the barkeeper couldn't avoid his breath,

beef-and-cabbage. "Why don't you want us to take this? Tell the truth now or I'll crush your bald skull."

Cap's lips trembled. He looked off into the darkness of the night, not wanting to make eye contact with any of them. "Take it. That's fine. Or leave it. Either way. It's just the Fall Festival, that's all. All those, um, foreigners, you know. They'll be disappointed, coming so far for such a famous ale." Most of that story came from Packer's instructions, but the foreigners he added himself.

"Foreigners?" Ox asked.

"Famous?" asked the Monkey.

"Well, a 'course," Cap said, deadly serious now. "It's…Hangman's Ale." He kept not looking at Ox or Monkey or the woman or at his now-prized barrel.

Ox released Cap, who straightened his collar, then his apron. The two supply men looked at one other. Then they looked at the woman. She nodded her head, almost imperceptibly. Ox turned back to Cap and sighed. "We'll take it."

Cap was glum.

Ox gestured, and Monkey quickly helped him right the barrel. "Two coins," Ox said to Cap, seeing that he was crestfallen. He handed the money to the barkeeper with a sly smile.

Cap looked at them. There were three. "But—"

The big man leaned in. "The extra's for the trouble you'll have with a crowd of angry Drammune. It's tough enough with just one." He said it with a wink, cutting his eyes toward the woman.

Cap was looking at the coins and didn't see the woman's eyes narrow. Then the two men hoisted the barrel into the cart and climbed aboard. The big man shook the reins, and the cart creaked away. The woman walked beside it, sword still drawn.

Cap looked at the three coins in his hand, suddenly feeling his breath come back to him, as though he had not been breathing for the last five minutes. He glanced up at his tavern's shingle, the sea monster writhing through the waves. "I hope it's not blood money, Packer Throme," he said aloud.

The cart turned a dark corner ahead.

Packer was thankful they had tapped the barrel. The air had quickly become too thick to breathe, something he somehow hadn't anticipated. His back ached already, and he wished he had insisted on some cloth to soften the hard wood beneath him. All that he could ignore. Air, however, he needed. He pulled the hatchet that Cap had given him from his belt, and gently tapped out the cork that Monkey had hammered in. The fresh air was an immediate relief.

With the cork out, he found he could hear snatches of conversation over the creak of the cart and the thudding of the horse's hooves on the dirt road.

"They find the Firefish, and our backs won't fear the lash," Ox was saying. A chill ran through Packer's spine. They were, then, hunting the beasts.

"That's true," Monkey replied solemnly. "An extra coin for a famous ale means nothin' to the Captain if the money's rollin' in." Packer's heart raced. It was true. It was all true.

Ox just grunted.

"But another week without a score, and it'll come straight out of our hides," Monkey continued. "You know how he gets when the revenues are down." Packer was amazed. They *didn't* know where to look for Firefish! And that meant they needed the one piece of information he carried with him. They would listen to him. They would have to.

The woman snarled. "I hope we never find another one of those stinking fish." Her voice was very near as she walked beside the cart; her exotic accent was unmistakable and her sullen anger frightening. But it was what she said, more than how she said it, that cut into Packer.

He knew who she was. He'd learned about her from his swordmaster. This was the woman who served as Scat Wilkins' enforcer, the security officer of the *Trophy Chase,* and she was one of the best hands with a sword alive. "Maybe then we'll return to the old ways," she said.

Packer knew when he chose this path that he would have to face Talon eventually. It was through a breach of security he meant to gain passage on that ship. But he certainly didn't anticipate that she would hate this new venture of hunting the Firefish. He pondered it. The information he carried in his head about the great beasts was his only real protection. If it was Talon's trust he must gain in order to preserve his life, he was in deep, deep trouble.

He lowered his head farther, between his knees, and fought back a sudden riptide of fear. Talon stood between him and his mission. It would be impossible to fight her and win, and now it seemed it

would be impossible to side with her. He was not prepared for this turn in the road.

The very real possibility of death upon discovery now weighed on him. Talon was merciless; she would follow the pirate's tradition and execute her stowaway on the spot.

Was Packer prepared to die? No, he realized. He was not. He was suddenly very much afraid of dying. So what had he been prepared for? What had he expected? And suddenly he couldn't conceive of why he was taking this kind of risk, when a full life with Panna, and with a home and children like she had described, was waiting for him. Why was he doing this?

And as he asked himself that question, dark answers began to come to him. Was he really doing this for the fishermen of the village? Or was that just something he told himself to help justify this…this what? This blind ambition. This substitute for the priesthood. This need to prove himself, to vindicate himself and his father's dreams. Was Will Seline right? Was he no more than a sword-brandishing vagabond, fit only for humiliating old men in pubs?

He tried to calm himself. No, no. It wasn't that simple. He did have a mission. *This* was his mission, and an important one.

No…*mission* was not the right word. He was no missionary. A missionary would not get into a barrel in order to join up with pirates like Scat Wilkins and Talon. And there could be no doubt now, these were still pirates, some of them at least. His resolve faltered again. If this was no mission, then how was God in it? How could He be?

Fear begot fear, and his sudden loss of confidence multiplied, collapsing in on itself. If the very first sign of trouble caused this kind of doubt, if one statement from Talon was all it took to put a hole in his hull, how could he expect to survive when he had to face her? Or a whole ship full of her fellow pirates? Suddenly he was sweating like a prisoner in a hangman's noose.

And then he felt the burning weight of shame. How utterly foolish to think he could succeed at this. He was an ignorant peasant who had grown drunk on his own ambitions. He was the gutless boy Dog believed him to be. He was the rogue Will Seline feared him to be.

What must God think, looking down from heaven on such a person? *If God is not in it,* he thought, *I will never survive this.* And what if God were not in it at all? What if all this was but his own elaborate attempt to recreate something God had so clearly taken away? The prophet Jeremiah said it: "The heart is deceitful above all things, and desperately wicked. Who can know it?" Those words moved him from shame to despair. To be cast aside by God was worse than anything Talon could do to him.

Packer's past came to him now as nothing more than a long series of failures and sins. The worst of them was, he had attacked a priest. The fact that Usher Fell wasn't a good priest, or even a good man, was beside the point. No matter what the man had done, how could there be any hope for someone who had it in his heart to do that? Being thrown out of seminary wasn't nearly punishment enough.

Then Packer had added to that shame by studying swordplay, with a vengeance. Hour after hour, day after day, as though it would save him, cramming the hollow places within him with this substitute calling, forming it into a new kind of mission, a new passion, ignoring all else.

Senslar Zendoda, the Swordmaster of Nearing Vast, had tried to school him in what he called "the Heart of the Warrior"—his whole servant-warrior philosophy, the old man's claim to fame. But Packer had never really followed that. Not really. He listened, he thought about it, but in the end he just learned to move his hands and feet in a way that would effectively kill an opponent, and he learned to exploit any weaknesses of will and of mind. Master Zendoda showed great patience with Packer, knowing and respecting Packer's first choice, the seminary. But Packer's drive was such that he simply took advantage of the good opportunity he had been granted, and learned to fight.

And now he had abandoned Panna once again. And he had talked a good, simple barkeeper into risking his neck to load him into a keg of ale and sell him to pirates. And not just to any pirates, but to the one pirate who beyond any shadow of a doubt could destroy him at swords!

What could he do now? Nothing. He was helpless. He could do nothing but carry it out to the end, whatever the end might be. He could not turn back. To call out, to break out of the barrel now, would be death. They would kill him, and then they would go back and kill Cap.

Packer had no control over the outcome. God could save him or let him be killed off. He could protect Cap or not. Packer realized he had thrown himself, quite literally, on the mercy of God.

And then, just as suddenly as he had been overwhelmed with guilt and shame and fear, a wholly unexpected peacefulness settled on him. It came from a single, simple thought, which he discovered he believed, absolutely: *God will choose the outcome. No one else.* It was truly, truly that simple. God had not vanished. God was here still, holding him in His hands, as surely as if this barrel were His fist. God could crush him. Or not. But either way, it would happen because God wanted it. Either way, it would be a good thing, the right thing. What God wanted.

Packer had given up control of his destiny by climbing into this barrel. He had handed his life over to God on a platter, and if God wanted to take it, He could have it any number of ways. And He would! Packer felt it, knew in his heart that God was there, and that He would choose. And the peace now began to grow into joy.

You will choose the outcome. That thought, spoken as a prayer, filled him with a joy totally inappropriate to his circumstances. He suddenly wanted to laugh out loud, to sing out, to dance with the sheer, weightless immensity of it. Packer Throme was free, and unconstrained.

The truth of his current state stood in stark opposition to the harsh reality of his circumstances.

Chapter 4

Keelhauled

Captain Scatter Wilkins was not a big man, but he wasn't small, either. No one who met him in armed combat, as Packer Throme was about to do, had ever judged him less than a giant. He stood five-feet-nine and weighed two hundred pounds. As a pirate, he had always stayed in excellent physical condition, and his endurance in battle was legendary. The past years of this commercial venture had lessened his opportunities, and his ardor, for physical exertion. He had let himself go. But he was not the least afraid of making the first move, and making it count.

Most who had heard of his exploits and then met him face-to-face were surprised by his age. At forty-four, the Captain was the grand old man of the pirate clan, due to the carnage and infamy that had spread in his wake from his youth. Scatter's peers were all dead now or gone into retirement, forced or otherwise. Belisar the Whale had disappeared, rumored to have been murdered. Conch Imbry was hanged gloriously. Skewer Uttley and Fishbait McGee had fled to the Warmer Climes, where, word had it, they drank rum and told lies—a couple of old, toothless sharks hand-fed by those who, but for the grace of God, might well have been their victims in years past.

Only "Scat" remained, brashly flying the skull and bones, continuing to build his legend, though in a slightly different line of work.

Now Scatter moved lithely and quietly from his quarters and

into the Captain's saloon. He looked around him. What had his steward said? Stowaway? Where? Had he misheard? No, that was the word. The jumpy, fearful man had yelled it while running the other direction.

Stowaway.

Now Scat walked slowly through the saloon. Table, benches, wire-screened cupboards. Nothing. He walked across the floor to the storeroom. He had requested a taste of that new ale the supply team had scrounged. Had the steward discovered something amiss while filling that request?

Unseen to Scat, Packer stood only a few feet away, with his sword drawn in the center of the small storeroom, listening to slow, steady footfalls amid the creaks and groans of the great wooden ship. Once he had freed himself from his barrel and discovered himself locked in this storeroom, he had climbed up on a row of four other barrels of ale and found a small shelf of wood behind them. Wedged there out of sight, he had fallen fast asleep. And so he had missed his opportunity to face the Captain's steward rather than the Captain himself.

Deeter Pimm was a man with no stomach for bloodshed, which was why Scat trusted him to be around when the Captain was sleeping, and otherwise vulnerable. The steward had taken one look at the remnants of Packer's deception, a barrel upended and empty on the floor, and had slammed the door, bolted it, and gone running off in search of the first mate. He had chosen not to awaken the Captain, not for fear of his master, but for fear that an assassin's evil deeds were being perpetrated even now behind that door. Running for help was a course of action Deeter Pimm had always found preferable to confrontation.

Now Packer heard the easy, finely-oiled click of a pistol's firing pin as it was cocked and made ready. It was a fine piece, a wheel-lock pistol. Such a weapon rarely misfired, and rarely missed at close quarters.

Packer flattened himself against the wall. He breathed shallow, quick breaths as he was trained to do, preparing for battle. He thought about speaking up, about warning whoever it was that he was no threat. He considered surrender, then decided against it. God would certainly choose the outcome. Still, he liked his odds better with a rapier in his hand.

The iron bolt of the bulkhead door slid against its wooden runner. Packer felt it as though it were sliding within him, bone against bone. And then silence. He saw the door swing slowly inward. He heard its iron hinges creak as the wedge of light widened across the planks of the flooring. The door stopped when it hit Packer's boot. The light exposed the empty wooden barrel, dust hovering around it.

Then Packer heard a hoarse whisper say, "Stowaways die." This voice had no anger. It had none of Dog's vanity, none of that masked fear. It had confidence, and credibility. This was the voice of a man who would kill him.

The gleaming steel muzzle came into view first, and then a finger pressed close on a trigger, and then the hand that held the weapon, gripping a mother-of-pearl stock.

Packer never thought about what he would do. He just did it. It was easier for him than much of his training had been. Senslar Zendoda had always demanded pinpoint accuracy in swordplay, and in that regard, Packer had been a prodigy. In one quick, silent motion, Packer slipped the tip of his sword through the trigger guard just behind the trigger. He didn't do it cleanly; he grazed the underside of Scat's finger, but then Packer backed the thrust with speed and strength, driving the point of his sword into the wooden wall behind it.

In the moment it took the pirate to glance down to see what angel or devil had stopped his pistol in midair, Packer's free hand caught Scat Wilkins on the mouth with a hard left hook. The Captain went down, leaving his pistol behind. In one more motion, Packer pulled his sword free of the wall, and the gun free of the sword.

As the Captain's head cleared, he found himself looking up into the blue eyes of a young man, hardly more than a boy, holding a fancy dueling sword in his right hand and Scat Wilkins' own favorite pistol in his left.

"I'm sorry," Packer said quietly. "I don't mean any harm to you, or to this ship."

"That's one cussed poor way to prove it," the bewildered Captain replied in a ragged voice, staggering to his feet and wiping away the blood that trickled from his lip into his salt-speckled beard. "You'll die for this."

"I'm sorry," he repeated. "I'm not here to cause trouble. I just want to meet the Captain of this ship, and tell him my business."

"That's half done, boy. Better tell me your business before the first mate arrives and blows your head clean off your shoulders."

Packer's face showed its first sign of confusion. The man was dressed almost casually. Except for the boots and the vest, he could have been any crewman. But Packer didn't doubt. Even now, unarmed and facing two weapons, this man was a hairsbreadth from attacking Packer.

Footsteps now came from outside the saloon, men running down the alleyway, and Packer saw the light of Scat's intentions glow. "State your business. And you best do it quick, or you'll die unsatisfied." The pirate smiled; he'd already won.

The footsteps were all but in the saloon. Again without a conscious thought, he dropped to a knee and spun both the pistol and the sword around to offer the less deadly ends to Scatter Wilkins. The Captain quickly snatched both weapons as they were offered and put the barrel of the pistol to Packer's forehead. His finger was against the trigger as Packer spoke.

"I have come to help you find the Firefish." His voice was soft, his eyes hard and purposeful.

Scat did not fire. First mate Jonas Deal burst into the storeroom. Packer lowered his head.

Had he looked at the first mate, he'd have seen a rabid vision of a man. Deal's brown and black teeth were bared, his eyes almost invisible under a thick brow pinched downward in a brutal scowl. The stubble on his head did not hide a lumpy skull. In his grip was the largest pistol ever manufactured in Nearing Vast, weighing almost eight pounds, with a barrel almost an inch across. It was known as the "Hand Cannon." But as he saw the relative posture of the intruder and his Captain, his murderous look turned into one of glee.

Jonas Deal laughed from deep within. "You see this, gents? Here's yet one more tale they'll tell of Scatter Wilkins!"

Scat lowered his pistol, still staring at the boy. The grizzled sailor took this cue, tucked his enormous weapon into his belt, grabbed Packer by the collar and hauled him to his feet. "That'll teach you to cross Captain Wilkins and the *Trophy Chase!*" Deal shook Packer violently, as easily as he would shake out a rag, and grinned at his Captain. "What'll we do with this weasel, Cap'n? The yardarm or the plank? Or do you want his blood shed where he stands?" Jonas looked at Packer hungrily, clearly pleased with any of these options.

The sailors who'd followed the first mate into the saloon whooped their approval. Not one of them noticed the uneasiness in their Captain, nor did they hear the faint hesitation in his reply. "Keelhaul him."

"Aye, aye!" This was a highly satisfactory order.

Packer now took his first good look at Jonas Deal, and was appropriately shocked by the man's appearance. But even more unnerving was the unabashed joy on his face. He relished this order. It was not only certain death for Packer, it was a brutal death. Deal jerked Packer toward the saloon door.

"Jonas!"

The first mate turned, surprised by the Captain's urgent tone. "Aye, sir?"

"Give him a fighting chance."

Jonas looked quizzical. "But Cap'n—"

Scat glared back, not to be questioned. "Let him swim." Jonas grumbled obediently and turned a disdainful look at Packer. Scat Wilkins turned away as the first mate angrily shoved his prisoner ahead of him. A long string of invective trailed down the alleyway, leaving the Captain to his thoughts. Then he turned his gaze to Packer Throme's sword, holding it, staring at it. That worried Deeter Pimm.

"You want that taken to the master-at-arms, sir?" Deeter asked.

Scat was focused on the craftsmanship of the weapon. "What? Oh, no. Jimmy Legs won't know what to do with the likes of this."

The steward nodded and turned to leave.

"Pimm!" Scat's blood was returning to him, and the steward already regretted being alone to experience it. "When the first mate finishes with his fun, you tell him I want to talk to him."

"Aye, aye, Cap'n." The steward hurried to leave. But Wilkins had another thought, and turned on him again. "And find that witch, Talon. I want to know how she managed to let a swordsman onto this ship in a barrel."

"Aye, aye." Deeter was afraid to turn again to leave.

"Well, get out of my sight!"

The steward nodded dutifully, and happily obeyed.

Alone, Captain Scat Wilkins swung the sword a few times, listening to the pristine hiss of its blade. An elegant rapier, perfectly balanced. And handed over to him by a man who knew how to use it. He relived the previous moments in his mind. The boy could have killed him, three or four ways.

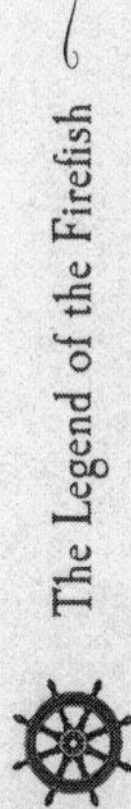

The force of the events weighed on him heavily. The *Trophy Chase* had been boarded. Scat Wilkins had been tried and found wanting, and by a mere lad at that. It was only by the miscreant's own choice that the ship and its Captain now sailed on as if nothing had changed. He cursed aloud, and threw the sword across the saloon. It clattered to a stop in the corner. Such an event did not bode well for a good voyage. It was a bad omen for a superstitious captain.

News traveled even faster aboard ship than it did in a small village like Hangman's Cliffs. By the time Packer reached the deck, shoved along roughly by Mr. Deal, the sailors were already gathering at the forecastle deck near the prow of the ship. Ratlines were descended as those in the rigging made their way down for a better view. Buckets, mops, and holystones were abandoned by those swabbing and scrubbing down the decks. Sailors not on duty were pouring up from their berths like a steady stream of insects. The buzz of their chatter grew like the approach of locusts.

Packer watched with amazement, forgetting for a moment that all this was about him, as he took in the color and the spectacle of this mass kaleidoscopic motion. He had seen many ships come ashore and put out to sea, merchant ships and Royal Navy vessels, but he had never seen a crew like this, where the shipmates were quite so energized, so full of motion and high spirits.

They were a colorful bunch. Not one of their outfits was actually identical to that of any other, but somehow on the whole they still seemed matched, as though, given perfect freedom to dress and outfit and adorn themselves however they saw fit, these sailors nonetheless managed to stay within a few basic themes that gave them a very particular look.

The men wore short sleeves, no sleeves, or long sleeves rolled up; all had sun-darkened skin, some black, some almost black, most emblazoned with tattoos. Some of the artwork was fresh and colorful. Many had their ears pierced and wore gold or brass rings; many wore tight leather necklaces with stone and bone and lumps of metal. They were bald-headed, bareheaded, long-haired, ponytailed, wearing kerchiefs or soft cloth hats. All wore loose-fitting breeches, most all coming to at least below the knee, with pant legs frayed or hard-cut or poorly hemmed at virtually any point after that, occasionally with the right leg actually matching the length of the left. All were barefooted.

As different as these outfits were, they had marked similarities. Earrings were small hoops, tight against the lobe. Bone, ivory, and other materials were reserved for the leather necklaces, which were universally taut enough to keep from being caught accidentally in clothing or rigging. There were no bracelets, no armbands, no anklets, no finger rings of any sort with the exception of the gold band worn by married men. Hats or kerchiefs were all pulled close against heads so they could not be blown off. And while the color of their wide array of clothing was varied, it hovered around a central theme, a fundamental shade of bleached gray-green. This was apparently the color of destiny for any material worn in the sun for work and then to bed at night for sleep, constantly drenched with sweat and washed in seawater, bathed in salt and algae along with its owner, sun-bleached, sea-drenched, and washed again, day in and day out.

As the buzz grew around him, Packer could overhear quite a few of the mutterings and whispers. Who was he, what did he do, why did he risk it, what was his goal, where did he come from, who found him, how did he get on board, who did he kill, why wasn't he killed on capture?

Soon enough, Jonas Deal had Packer Throme at the foredeck, just behind the prow. Deal stood at the rail, speaking to the crowd gathered.

"Here's a stowaway needs a lesson!" he sang out.

The sailors called back full-throated, "Yea!" "Teach him!" and other like phrases.

"Watch what we do with such as this on the great *Trophy Chase!*"

"Let's see!"

"Hang him!"

"Feed him to the sharks!"

Then Jonas sang out, "Gather up now for the keelhauling of a sneak and renegade!"

"Keelhaul him!"

"Shove him over!"

Packer's amazement quickly turned to dismay. Without a hearing, without a clue as to his actual identity or intent, they would all, to a man, gleefully kill him off. The bright eyes, the grins, their evident joy was unnerving.

"Spies and stowaways get a bellyful of seawater for their trouble here!"

"Aye, aye!"

"Keelhaul him!"

Deal's voice fell, and he looked down at his feet. "Now, mates, the Captain has ordered that we give him a fighting chance."

"No!"

"Boo!"

"Scrape him! Scrape him!"

And then the chant took hold. "Scrape him! Scrape him!"

Jonas quieted them down with a motion of his hands. "Cap'n's orders, cap'n's orders! He's won a bit o' luck, and we'll grant him his fighting chance. We won't be scrapin' him across the barnacles today."

There was grumbling. Someone sang out, "He's soft as cheese! Let's grate him!" There was laughter.

"Aye," Mr. Deal acknowledged. "Too soft to swim the depth of this ship...or its length!"

A great howl of laughter and applause greeted this revelation. They would let him try to swim under the ship if he could, but not from port to starboard, as was customary, but rather from prow to stern. It was a death sentence, and they knew it.

"On with it, then!" Mr. Deal sang out, to a joyous, guttural response.

Deal turned Packer around so he was facing the open sea ahead, speckled white from its blue horizon back toward them. Packer's heart beat loudly in his chest, and he could feel his pulse in his neck, hear it in his ears. The foam and green-blue water rushed under the ship thirty-odd feet below him. Even if he survived, how could he ever join this crew?

He shook his head, feeling sorrowful again about the choices he had made, wondering what Panna was thinking even now, wondering if perhaps she was praying for him. He hoped she was. He asked God to comfort her. How long before she knew he was dead? Would she ever know for sure? That thought shot through his heart, and almost crumpled his legs under him. The crew laughed, seeing him wobble.

Packer's arms were jerked out to his sides and held there as silent crewmen put a loop of rope from a coiled mooring line around each wrist and pulled it tight. He looked into the eyes of Jonas Deal, who relished the moment, reveling in Packer's anguish. The first mate smiled, shaking his head. His blackened teeth were unveiled in the grin.

"You've got an iceberg's chance in hell, sonny boy. I've never seen a man survive this." And he laughed again. "Not once!"

Jonas checked the knots. The mooring line tied to Packer's left hand ran under the bowsprit and was then held by a crewman on deck. The line tied to Packer's right was held by another crewman, standing to his right. Coils from these ropes were made ready by others. Once Packer was overboard, they would let the lines play out, and then walk them back toward the stern of the great ship.

When Jonas was content with the knots, he stepped up to Packer and pushed him back against the rail, just starboard of the bow, and turned him back to face the crew. Packer now stood with the back of his thighs pressed against the rail, the only thing between him and the cold blue sea. In a loud voice, Deal bellowed the command "Last words!" and looked down at his feet.

Packer was surprised by this protocol, which Deal obviously didn't like but followed obediently nonetheless. Packer looked at the men, who looked earnestly up at him. There were dozens of them. He had never spoken to so large an audience. And they were deathly quiet, waiting. He could hear seagulls, and the chop of the bow plowing the waves beneath him. The light breeze was cool, salty. He had not noticed before what a perfect spring day it was. His fears turned to sadness.

"Last words!" Deal demanded.

"Yes," Packer said, clearing his throat, but with no idea what he might say. "I just want to tell you..." He looked around him, up at the sails, billowing full. He spoke clearly, gently, loud enough to be heard but soft enough that the men almost in unison leaned forward to hear. "You have a beautiful ship." The men waited. "I know that I came aboard in a way that makes me seem like an enemy. But I'm not. I have wanted to stand on board this ship for a very long time. Though this is not exactly how I imagined it."

There was laughter. Packer smiled, relieved in spite of himself.

"Finish it!" Deal hissed.

"If I survive, somehow, by the grace of God, then I hope my debt will be paid. And I hope your Captain, and you, will think of me differently. And then maybe I can join you."

The sailors seemed frozen where they stood. Mouths were open. No gulls squawked. The wooden ship creaked and the canvas flapped. Packer wondered if he'd said something wrong.

Then anger moved Jonas Deal. "Join this!" he said, and he planted an open hand on Packer's throat, pushing him backward with a great heave.

Packer toppled over the short railing. He heard the roar of the men, and then smacked into the water on his back, thirty feet below. The sudden impact of cold water dazed him, and then he was overtaken by the speed of the ship, overrun by the vessel.

The lines played out through the hands of the sailors, who let them uncoil from the deck as Packer's downward and sternward momentum took him.

The men on deck rushed to the rails to get a look, but they were subdued now, their task emptied of some of its fun by the earnestness of the young man they had sent deep into the murky waters below them. Several of them hoped aloud he'd make it. The sailors walked the lines backward, hand-over-hand past the ratlines and rigging, over the cannon and cannonballs, toward the stern of the ship, where they would fish Packer, or his body, from the brine.

Packer's youth had been spent fishing, in almost every form of that endeavor. He'd spent many hours on board his father's boat, casting and trawling, hauling the big tuna and powerful blackfish aboard in carefully woven nets. He'd spent countless more hours on the docks with his homemade rod, catching seacat and flounder. And he'd spent many more hours yet diving from docks and boats and sandbars, gliding along the shallow, sunlit ocean floor looking for clams and swiggets and mussels. These shallow dives had helped expand his lung capacity considerably, until he could hold his breath for more than three minutes; more than enough time to make the voyage under the *Trophy Chase*.

But it had been years since he'd swum like that. And Jonas Deal had dealt him a foul blow, choking him just when he should have been filling his lungs. And just as he started to take air in, he had crashed into the water, losing more air on impact, a second blow that almost stunned him to unconsciousness. So as the great ship cast its dark shadow over him, turning the bright blue warmth of the sky and the shimmering yellow ball of the sun into cold darkness, Packer already felt the pangs. He needed to breathe.

Talon didn't wait to be summoned. She took one look at the stowaway as he was being led to the deck and then wound her way astern to the Captain's quarters. She passed Deeter, who saw the blood in her eye and flattened himself against the alleyway wall as she passed.

She burst in on the Captain, who was lying back on his bunk, hands laced behind his head. As the hatch banged open he greeted her with his pistol, unholstered in an instant from where it hung beside him, and aimed at her heart.

"Why is it you're the only one on this ship who considers it an indignity to announce yourself to the Captain?" he asked her, holstering the pistol again.

"Not the only one today," she answered evenly.

He stared at her a moment. He sat up, drank the last dregs of a pint of ale he'd been contemplating, then walked her to the saloon. He opened the storeroom hatch and showed her the barrel in silence. Her eyes flashed.

"I want someone's head on a platter, Talon."

She nodded.

"Who sold you the ale?"

Her mind grew dark as the lies of Cap Hillis were replayed in her ears. "An innkeeper at the Hangman's Cliffs," she said in her cold accent. "A tavern under the sign of the Firefish."

Scat paused, as though there were meaning in it. "You couldn't tell he was lying?" There was a trace of suspicion in his voice.

She nodded. "I knew he was lying. But I was deceived as to why."

Scat Wilkins eyed her again. He had rarely seen her deceived so thoroughly.

She glared at the barrel. "Within three days from the moment we dock again, I'll find out who sent the assassin, and he will send no more."

"This was no assassin."

Her look said she doubted him.

"Sure as I'm standing here," he told her, "that boy did not come aboard to kill me." He stared at her until she understood. And the understanding enraged her. It was Talon's responsibility to keep the ship secure; that was the reason she personally escorted the supply carts. She had failed.

She pulled the long knife from its sheath on her belt and held it out to him. "Take my head. I have failed you."

Scat considered the offer. The razor-edged blade she proffered would easily do the job. He wasn't about to lose her, but even so...he wondered if he could. Would she really let him? Yes, he decided. She would let him.

He suppressed a smile. He'd seen more blood and had been in more fights than most men could imagine, but if he could pick just one of all the fighters he'd ever known to fight beside him, he'd choose Talon. He'd seen her use this knife she offered, and her sword, and her pistol in battle, and had yet to see a man her equal for quickness, for action and reaction, for sheer cold-blooded focus. She wasn't the strongest, and didn't have the most stamina. But ice water ran in her veins. The choices she made, the chances she took without blinking—and always they paid off.

He had come to believe she knew death intimately, understood it somehow in ways others couldn't, as though death were on her side, or she on its. She might die of her own will, but not anyone else's. He couldn't imagine someone taking her life. "Put that away," Scat said, almost gently. "I want to know who sent him. And why."

"I want the lad," she said, sheathing the knife. She could not believe she had been beaten by an innkeeper and a mere boy. There was more here. There was something deeper behind such a scheme.

The Captain studied her. What she wanted, he knew, was permission to torture the boy without interference. "He said he could find Firefish."

She stared a moment, and then laughed. "So he knows your weaknesses already? That is a sure sign that he was sent."

Scat had to admit this was true. He sighed. The kid had signed his own death warrant when he climbed into the barrel. And if he wanted to help, he had already done it by improving the ship's security. Scat waved a hand. "If he lives, you can have him."

Talon noticed the blood on his hand. "Let me see the wound," she said.

"It's a scratch," he protested. But he offered it up to her anyway.

She looked at it, then at him. "A puncture."

He nodded. "My trigger finger."

She looked shocked.

"Yes," Scat said. "He's that good."

She snorted. Another sign there was a conspiracy here. She took a bottle of rum from the storeroom shelf and poured alcohol on the cut.

The Captain swore at her and pulled his hand away. "That's my good rum!" He took the bottle from her, read the label, then took a long pull.

Talon wrapped his finger with a handkerchief from her breast pocket. "Close your hand and squeeze, like so, until the bleeding stops," she ordered. He obeyed. Her knowledge of the healing arts was part of her dark magic, springing, he believed, from her alliance with death. She could make a man die or make him live, as she chose.

"Where is his sword?"

Scat pointed. It still lay in the corner of the saloon, where he had flung it.

She picked it up gently, turned the blade over in her hands as delicately as if it were made of silk. "Only one forge in the world could have created this." She drew her own rapier and held it side by side with Packer's. They were dissimilar in many regards: Talon's was shorter by several inches, and her hand guard was so small as to be almost nonfunctional, designed as it was to be easily concealed. But both were of the highest possible craftsmanship, gleaming, polished, detailed, balanced, perfect. "It was made in the forge that created mine." She showed him the maker's mark. "The ovens of Pyre Dunn."

"Pyre Dunn? How could a stowaway rat afford his work?"

"We know nothing of this boy. Besides, Pyre works for more than money. He wants his swords in the hands of those who can bring him honor."

"But if he's good enough with a sword to get Pyre Dunn's attention, he may be of use to us," the Captain ventured.

"It only means he is very dangerous."

Scat met her gaze, wondering why a boy would flaunt such a thing if it was a sure giveaway he was a conspirator. Why not carry a lesser blade? But Scat acquiesced. "Do as you see fit," he told her. "But I want to know what he's doing here," he warned. "And while you're at it, find out what he knows about Firefish." He didn't want the boy dead or useless before he gave up his secrets. Talon was known to get distracted when she started in at that sort of work.

She smiled, nodded, and left quickly.

The last thing Packer saw was the great rudder rushing toward him. He had swum downward as hard as he could, knowing that the ship's keel plunged deep below the surface. It was against nature, contrary to every impulse, to force his body away from the air it needed so desperately. But he couldn't keep up with the speed of the ship, so the only alternative to a downward plunge was to be dragged against the wooden hull and its barnacles.

It seemed to Packer that the keel went on and on, lower into black, cold water than could be possible, deeper than he had ever been. His ears ached, his chest pounded. The effort burned what air his blood carried, and he was lightheaded as he turned, finally, to swim again for the surface. He swam hard, with a desperation born of the growing realization he would lose this race. Black spots appeared to both sides of his field of vision, growing as he focused on the rudder, which was now, finally, silhouetted against the shimmering blueness beyond. Another stroke or two and he would be clear of it…but his body would no longer respond.

The huge wooden rudder loomed before him. He could do nothing to get past it, he could not muster the strength to swim below it. He could not make his arms or his legs move at all. He had given it his best, but it wouldn't be enough. A searing pain, like regret multiplied to an infinite number, racked his chest and heart. *Why wouldn't it be enough?* The question gave way to peaceful acceptance. He quit swimming and knew, finally, that he would die. It was a relief to know. It was a relief to be done with it all.

Packer closed his eyes and gave himself up, repentant, humbled, pained, entirely yielded. God would take him, and this time it was forever. It was a good thing, a deeply sad thing, but a sadness that had joy written all through it. He felt a sorrow about Panna. Dear Panna. He prayed for her, prayer without words, like a flame released from a burning soul, a soul shed of its body, flowing upward. The bright sun grew brighter until its pure white light engulfed him.

Chapter 5

The Promise

"Pull!" ordered the first mate when it became clear there was no resistance, no movement at the other end of the lines. Had the boy gotten loose? The sailors holding the lines complied.

Beneath the ship, the limp body of Packer Throme responded, a puppet on two strings. Packer's head missed the rudder by an inch, but his left shoulder slammed into it. The force of the blow and the pull of the line on his wrist yanked the bone of his left arm out of its socket. Packer's unconscious body drank in seawater, seeking air that would not come.

"He's caught on the rudder, Mr. Deal!" cried one of the men, pulling fruitlessly on the line.

The sailors all looked at the first mate, waiting for his instruction. Deal smiled, in no hurry. He picked his teeth with a fingernail, studied the scrapings. Finally he sighed. "Well, then, I guess you better give 'im a little slack."

"Aye, aye," they said with knowing grins.

They played the lines back out, and within a few seconds, the limp body was visible just below the churning waters behind the ship. The sailors began hauling the line, dragging Packer back toward the ship. The force of the water created by the speed of the ship made it a difficult task. Packer's head broke the surface facing backward, away from the ship, with his chin driven down into his chest by the water rushing around his head. His head bobbed up, then went under, then came up again. It was hard to tell from the deck whether he had survived.

The two line-handlers, joined now by several others, finally hauled him clear. His left shoulder was grotesque in its angle, disfigured with the injury, and his back slammed into and scraped along the barnacles attached to the dead-work of the hull. Then his lifeless body banged up the wooden stern of the ship.

Captain Wilkins heard the banging against the wood and the glass, saw the pale body hauled up outside his windows. He just shook his head. Deal had made him swim the length of the ship. What sort of keelhauling was that? Well, so much for the stowaway's promise to help find the beasts.

The crewmen were silent when they finally pulled Packer in over the rail and laid him out on the deck. They'd seen this before. The boy's young face was ashen gray, his lips white, his chest unmoving, his wounds gaping but not bleeding.

He was dead.

Mr. Deal pushed at Packer's head with the toe of his boot. "Such is the price paid for stowing away on the great *Trophy Chase,* young pup," he growled. It was as close to a eulogy as Deal could get. He turned to the crew. "And let no man forget it!" They murmured their agreement, but did not turn away.

And then Talon was kneeling beside the body. "So get the men back to work, Mr. Deal," she said without so much as looking at him.

The first mate's face contorted with hatred and disgust. He spat.

Now she turned to look at him, calm eyes deadly. "He's mine now."

Jonas felt nausea, his stomach churning at her necromancy. He knew she'd already visited the Captain. That's what gave her such audacity. Why Captain Wilkins wasted so much of his time and energy on this witch, Jonas could only guess. But however good she was for the Captain, she was equally bad for the ship. She undermined discipline. She had no respect whatever for the first mate and didn't care who knew it. And now she wanted the boy's body? It was disgusting. She was a cancer he would dearly love to excise.

Talon studied Packer. He was young, younger than he'd seemed as he walked to his death. A strong body, and a face innocent and calm. She straddled him, putting both hands on his chest, her fingers splayed outward. The crewmen watched with morbid fascination, with looks of confusion. She pushed hard on his chest, and water came out of his mouth and nose. She did it again. And then again.

And then, to audible gasps, she opened his jaw and put her mouth on his. She held his nostrils shut and breathed into him, and his chest rose. The crew was shocked, each man certain he was witnessing some dark necromancy. She pulled away, and his chest fell again, the air leaving him.

"Bah!" Jonas Deal walked away from the scene and stood beside two huntsmen just arrived from below decks. "Black-magic voodoo woman. She'll lead us all to the devil."

Talon continued her efforts to revive Packer for several more minutes, until finally the young man gagged, vomited, coughed once, and began to breathe. The crewmen grumbled loudly, fear in their voices. Threats against Talon were audible, and the men moved in toward her menacingly.

Packer slowly regained consciousness to find the leather-clad woman standing above him, still straddling him. She was looking around at the crew, glaring at them until she cowed them. She didn't draw her sword; she didn't need to.

Their weakness and superstition disgusted her. "I have brought him back from death," she told them simply. "You have witnessed it. Take care, or I will send you to the Dead Lands in his place." The men backed up involuntarily. She smiled.

Packer tried to focus, tried to understand what was happening. The woman standing over him was Talon. She must be. The ship... now he recalled being shoved overboard. But he couldn't remember why. And then his left shoulder blazed in screaming pain. He looked at his right hand—the rope was still tight around his wrist. Suddenly it came back.

He'd been keelhauled.

And he was alive! Talon bent down and loosened the knots at his wrists. He looked at her fierce, determined face, the scar down the left cheek. She did not meet his gaze. She stepped away from him.

He tried to sit up, but the stabbing pain in his arm and shoulder stopped him cold. Without a word, Talon grabbed his left hand, put a boot against his ribs, and yanked hard. His dislocated shoulder

popped loudly back into place. Packer shrieked out in agony, but recognized the improvement almost immediately. She took a step back and drew her sword, putting the point to his neck. "Stand," she ordered.

He felt sick; his shoulder ached. His head throbbed, and his back felt like it had been flogged. He dragged himself to his feet, staggering slightly. He looked around at the sailors and saw a depth of fear and horror he couldn't comprehend. But he didn't have time to sort it out. Talon grabbed his left elbow and moved him toward the main hatch, taking him below decks. His shoulder screamed again, but this time the pain was more manageable. He gritted his teeth and stayed silent, following her lead.

"And now he breathes the witch's breath," Jonas Deal said quietly, but audibly enough, as they passed him.

Two huge men, bearded and unwashed, held Packer Throme's arms pinned behind him. They stood in a dark, wet room, far from the sunlight. Rivulets of sweat ran down Packer's forehead. Fear and defiance were in his eyes. One of the men yanked Packer's arm upward behind him, and he gasped. The brute yanked again, and the bone cracked. Packer whimpered, but did not cry out. Then a woman with long, dark hair falling across her shoulders walked close to Packer and looked him in the eye. He was afraid of her. She laughed at his fear. She stepped back, drew a dueling sword, and put the point of it to Packer's heart. And then she drove it home.

Panna sat up, gasping for air. Sweat soaked her nightgown. She closed her eyes and prayed it was just a dream. But something...its vividness, its feel...something told her there was truth in it. It was more like a vision. She quickly got out of bed, quietly got dressed, momentarily paused at her father's door to listen for his snoring. Satisfied he was asleep, she descended the warped boards of the creaking staircase. The wooden clock in the hall ticked through the minutes just past midnight.

It had been all she could do to force herself to stay behind, telling herself that all was as it should be, that God was in heaven looking out for them. But her prayers seemed not to leave the confines of her troubled mind, and her heart ached in ways she hadn't thought possible. And now this dream. It was too much.

She wrapped herself in a cloak and left the house.

Packer sat on a rough wooden bench built into the ship's wall, his back pressed against the inside of the angled hull. He felt sick and broken. He was deep below deck, where he had been led six hours earlier by Talon. She had put a salve in the wounds on his back that burned like fire. She had fastened iron manacles around his wrists and ankles, chained him to the wall, and tightened the chains so he could not move his feet or his hands. His arms were crossed in front of him. His right arm, crossed over his left, held the injured shoulder secure.

When Talon had chained him to her satisfaction, she delivered this message: "You died in the water. I have resurrected you. You belong to me." Then she left him to the darkness and the sickness and the pain.

His head still pounded, but the ache had moved from the back of his head to his forehead. His lungs felt heavy and leaden. His wounds seemed to be almost numb now, but his shoulder was, if anything, worse. The smallest movement caused excruciating pain to shoot through him, like a musket ball at close range. If he kept still, it was a manageable throb, but he couldn't keep still in a ship that rolled ceaselessly on the waves.

Worse than the physical discomfort was that his mind whirred, and he was unable to calm it. Packer did not know what Talon had meant. He had died? She had brought him back to life? Those were lies, of course. Had to be. No one could bring someone back from the dead but God. Was it a bald lie, or had something happened? God could have done it, and she might be claiming responsibility. He now remembered falling, hitting the water, and turning himself downward to swim away from the air. Then nothing. He certainly didn't die. And what did the first mate mean by "the witch's breath," and what were those dire, fearful looks he got from the crew?

He had no way to know what really happened until she returned, and he didn't want her to return.

He tried to put himself back into that place of peace he had found while hiding in the barrel, where he had felt such great freedom. But he could not. Nothing was right here. He thought of Panna, and what would have happened if he had stayed there, in her kitchen, and let the pirates come and go. Why hadn't he done that? What was wrong with him that he would try something like this? His mind drifted in and out of unsettling thoughts until he finally found unconsciousness once again.

But sleep was no better. He dreamed he was falling from the Hangman's Cliffs, falling toward the blue water, and then toward the *Trophy Chase,* anchored peacefully below. He saw the crew looking up at him as he fell. They were aghast, fearful. There were Captain Wilkins and Talon, grim-faced, and the first mate grinning up at him, holding out a rope. The others were crowding the decks, looking at him, pointing. Then they started laughing. He was falling toward Talon; he was trying desperately to avoid her, to land in the ocean, but he kept falling toward her. Suddenly he was tangled in rope; it was wrapped around him, then around his neck. It was a noose. Talon smiled a horrible smile as he crashed onto the deck at her feet, landing on his shoulder.

He came awake amid a torrent of pain and terror. Talon stood before him, her right arm outstretched. In her right hand she held her long knife, her dirk. She had pressed it against his left shoulder, triggering once again the searing pain. A lantern she'd brought with her lit her from behind and to the side, leaving her dark eyes black and empty, like sockets. Her hair was wild, unbraided now, falling around her shoulders. The fear more than the pain threatened to overwhelm him. It was hot and dank here; he was sweating, but his mouth was dry as dust. It hurt when he swallowed. There was a sharp, pungent smell of urine, and something else…a spice.

Seeing he was conscious, Talon spoke. "You stink. You have let your water go, like an animal," she said. "Like a pig."

Packer realized this was true. Somewhere in the night he had made water, right where he sat. He felt ashamed, could not help but feel ashamed, though he knew there was little he could have done to avoid it.

She took a pail of water and threw it at him. It was cold, but there was something in it to neutralize the odor. This was the spice he had smelled.

She stepped back toward him and put the point of the knife under his chin. She brought her face close to his. He couldn't see her; with the light coming from behind her she was little more than a dark presence. But he could now smell the leather of her jacket, her stale breath. More than that, he could feel the evil of her intent. Her voice was sinuous. "Shall we begin?"

The tavern lights were out. The door was locked. Panna knocked softly, glancing up and down the empty street. No answer. She knocked louder. No answer again. She banged on the door with her fist. The shutters opened above her.

"Panna, is that you? Land sakes, child, what do you need this time of night?" asked Henrietta Hillis, the innkeeper's wife. Her round, ruddy face peered down, her cheeks bouncing as she spoke.

"I'm sorry, Hen. I need to see Cap. I have to find out where Packer went."

Henrietta was silent a moment, chewing her lower lip. "Cap's gone. He went to the Nearing Plains to buy more ale. He won't be back for several days."

"But he told you what happened," Panna said flatly, undeterred. "You must tell me where Packer went."

She shook her head. "Cap made me promise…"

"I know he was going to sea. I know he was going aboard that ship. But I need to know where it is."

"Lordy, Panna—I don't know where any ship is!"

But she knew more than she was supposed to tell. Henrietta Hillis was a tireless worker and a font of wisdom in child-rearing and family matters, but she did not deal well with inner conflict. And at the moment, she felt a great deal of it.

"You must tell me what you know. Come down and open the door."

Henrietta hesitated.

Panna fought back a strong welling up of despair. "Please, Hen," she begged. "Please…"

Hen's maternal instincts won out. "You hold on, child." She looked up and down the street. "I'll be right down."

Talon stepped back and sat on the packing crate a few feet in front of him, leaning forward with her elbows on her knees, her knife still in her hand. Packer now noticed a number of large crates behind her, a wall of cargo. They were in the ship's hold.

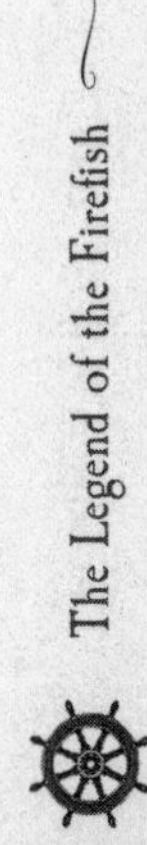

He could see Talon's eyes now, but this was no improvement. The black, empty sockets had been unnerving, but the sharp focus of her dark eyes, crisp, crackling with purpose, were worse. He was struck by the effect of her wild hair on her hard features. It made her look both fierce and feline.

"Why are you here?" she asked.

He opened his mouth, but nothing came out. Then he said hoarsely, "I just want to help."

She stood, her eyes flashing with anger, and he saw a deep, burning fire, a consuming hatred out of all proportion to the crimes of one stowaway. Packer felt sweat forming on his hands, his forehead, under his arms. Dog's bluster was a child's tantrum in comparison to this. He had never encountered such a seething cauldron within human flesh.

This vision of her lasted only a moment, and then her hard features returned, as though she had pulled a hood down over her emotions. Her tone was now easy, even friendly. "I want to know who sent you," she purred. "I want to know the reason you were sent." She approached him, knife held away from her, out to the side, as though it might cause harm of its own volition. She brought the knife in a quick, slashing motion to his throat. He felt the cold point against his skin, just below his left ear. He closed his eyes. She gently traced the point of the blade down under his chin, barely grazing the skin...brought it across his throat and up by his right ear. Then she put her left hand behind his head, grasping his hair with a grip like iron. Her voice was smooth as oil. "You do not yet fear me as you should."

She pulled his head backward sharply; his neck popped and a hot pain flashed down his spine. He cried out. She put the point of the blade into his shoulder, and the pain, the musket ball, shot through him again. She whispered in his ear as he struggled against his chains, trying to escape the agony she caused him. "I will take you apart with such precision that you will beg me to let you die. But I will not let you die. I will be vigilant, and keep you alive, awake, and alert."

She put the knife to his throat again, pressed on the blade until he felt the razor edge slice through the skin below his left ear. "You did not come here to help. Do not lie to me again. Who sent you?"

Now she saw what she wanted to see. Now she saw fear. He

swallowed a dry, sharp lump in his throat, felt himself trembling. "No one sent me. I serve no one." That didn't sound right. "No one but God."

She stepped back, laughing out loud, a ringing cry. "Ha! You serve God!" She laughed at him again. "You climb into a barrel and sneak into a pirate's lair! These are the orders of your God? He sent you here, to be in the darkness with me, bound, in pain, in your own stink?" She put the knifepoint into his belly, just above the navel. "What kind of God would send you here, for this?" And she pushed.

He swallowed hard, forcing himself not to look down at her knife. His hands, knees, all his extremities trembled violently. He couldn't tell how badly he'd been cut. He just knew how badly it hurt. But even so, he didn't regret saying it. "God's ways," he managed, in a tone that came out with more confidence than he would have believed possible, "are not man's ways."

She pulled the knife away. There was no blood on the tip of it. She snorted, half smiling. "Ah. You are a true believer, then."

He nodded, confessing it with fear.

"You have the words of a missionary." Now she placed the knife tip at the center of his chest, just below his breastbone. "But do you have the heart of a missionary? Shall we take a look?" She jabbed the knife delicately into him; this time he felt the point break through, felt the razor slice him, felt the ragged sharpness cleaving his flesh, the pain flashing like lightning through his body. He whimpered, trying not to breathe, because with every breath he felt the blade cut deeper, felt the knife's edge saw his flesh. But his breaths came anyway, in short bursts. He felt the warm blood flowing down from the pain, covering his belly, soaking his shirt. Sweat poured from him everywhere else.

She continued speaking as though nothing had happened, as though she were having a simple conversation. "I have killed missionaries. But I have always found their hearts to be like all men's hearts." She saw his reaction. "If I cut yours out, will I find God inside it?" She smiled serenely as she watched him writhe.

She pulled the knife out and held it up to show him his own blood, which covered an inch or so of the knife's tip. "You have the words of a missionary." She nodded, as though certain of herself now. She wiped the blood from the knife onto his forehead, tracing as she did the pattern of a cross. "But you carry a sword, and not a crucifix. This tells me that you trust your sword and not your God. Why is this? Is this because you know He cannot protect you?"

She saw the fear in him turn to anger. She smiled. "The Son of God, you call him. This is your God?"

He nodded, eyes ablaze with anger, pain, and fear.

She continued. "He died in shame, and in pain. Naked, no doubt, for all to see. And your holy book says the power of God brought him back from the dead. But you see, *I* brought you back from the dead. So who has the power of life and death?" She put her face in his and looked him in the eye.

He wrenched his face away. She laughed out loud again, this time a cold, hollow laugh that grated to his bones. He closed his eyes, trying to get away from her words. In the darkness, with his eyes clamped shut, it came back to him. He didn't want to remember it now, but he did, he remembered rising up toward the rudder, the blue water shimmering behind it. He remembered he had stopped swimming. He remembered giving up. He remembered taking in the ocean, swallowing it all, and knowing, without a doubt, that he was dying. He remembered the darkness turning to light. He remembered rising up into that light, and into that joy.

His heart beat faster, and he felt sicker. Tears stung his eyes. He had died! What in God's name had she done?

"I brought you back," she answered, and he opened his eyes, saw her certainty. Now he believed her, and it terrified him. "You gave up on your weak God and you trusted in your sword." Packer grimaced, his pain no longer physical. How did she know these things? "So He gave up on you. He abandoned you. To me."

Packer struggled wildly against his chains, panicked, crying out, but he could only writhe helplessly. She laughed again. He could deal with pain, but not with this. Not with the abandonment of God. He felt everything within him crumbling; he was unable to hide from her words. What had happened to him? He couldn't find any peace here, could not find his way back to God. What had she done? Who was she? Who was he?

She continued smiling, an evil leer. He was in her grasp, the fly in the spider's web. She was the predator and he was prey, behaving like all prey everywhere. She leaned in close again, this time putting the knife under his chin. He shook uncontrollably.

Her teeth were bared. She reached behind him, found the deepest cuts on his back, and dug her fingernails into them, creating a stabbing pain that felt like multiple knife blades, like swords thrust through his back, through to his chest. It was as though she touched all his wounds at once, to manipulate him like a puppet on strings that connected directly to his most vital points of raw pain, both physical and spiritual.

He arched his back, struggled to shake free of her claws, trying to avoid her, but he could not. The more he struggled, the more it hurt. She surrounded him, infiltrated him, in his body and his soul. Pain was everywhere. She was everywhere. His chains rattled and the manacles bit into his wrists, but they held him fast. He was a mouse pinned by a cat.

She spoke slowly now, her face inches from his. She eased his pain just slightly, so that he could focus on her words. "Now you understand. I can kill you. I can resurrect you. I can hurt you..." She did, and he winced against it, tears running down his cheeks. "...Or I can heal you." She eased his pain, and he took several gasping breaths. "Do you understand who I am now? Do you?"

He found himself nodding, pleading, helpless. Tears flowed in rivers down cheeks. Sobs began to come up from deep in him.

"Tell me you understand."

"I understand. Please, yes, I understand."

He was losing control, abandoning everything, everything he knew, everything he had trusted, in order to comply with her.

"There. That wasn't so hard. Now tell me. Why are you here?"

He hated her. But he feared her more than he hated her. He had to tell her. He had to pour it out. That was the only way to stop her, to keep her away. And yet it wouldn't keep her away, it would only invite her in more deeply, only open the door to everything that was within him, everything and everyone who mattered to him. He knew this, but he spoke anyway, the words coming however they would, and though they were his, he did not recognize them and could not stop them. It was as though she had pried the lid off his soul, had taken away his protection, had gotten inside the doors of his own will, and no secrets would be withheld. He was weak.

"I came to find the Firefish. I know where they feed. I know where to look. My father knew about the feeding waters. He was a fisherman." Sentences came out in a rush, each one true, but barely

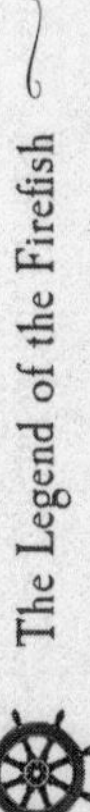

connected to one another, as though he couldn't disclose things fast enough. "I tried to sign up with you, on the *Trophy Chase*. I wanted to learn how it's done. But you wouldn't have me because I was from the fishing villages, so I stowed away." The sobs now interfered with his speech, unwanted, unavoidable. She hated Firefish. He had heard her say so as she walked alongside the cart. But he could do nothing about that. He hated her, and feared her, and he was powerless against her.

"But you are a swordsman. How does the son of a fisherman become a swordsman?" She seemed patient, and suddenly he was thankful to her, appreciative, lapping up her lack of anger as though it were kindness.

Talon let him talk. She had done this many times, had seen this many times before, and knew she would soon know everything he knew. The boy had broken easily. She was even a little disappointed. She had hoped for more sport.

"I'm not a swordsman or a fisherman," he continued, confessing the uncertainty at the root of his soul. "Or a priest or a missionary. I don't know what I am. I'm nothing. I'm a dreamer." He could hardly speak for the sobs, but he spoke anyway. "Dog was right. I'm a dreamer. I should have stayed with Panna, should have married her, should have learned to fish. But I'm nothing. I'm a peasant who studied swordplay at the Academy and I thought I could do something I can't. But I can't. That's it, that's all."

She pulled away, and stepped back to look at him, as he sobbed like a baby. "Who are you?" she asked bluntly. "What is your name?"

He was surprised by this abrupt shift in her demeanor. "My name is Packer Throme," he told her quickly.

"Packer Throme." She said it as though memorizing it. "You have lied to me, Packer Throme."

"No!" Her words terrified him. How could she say this? He was speaking only the truth, with nothing covered, nothing hidden. Could she not see that?

But she was baffled. How could he be lying to her? He was broken. And yet he was lying; he must be. "Fishermen of your realm do not attend the Academy of Mann, any more than do pirates. Either you are not a fisherman's son, or you did not attend the Academy."

Thank God, he thought, she just didn't understand. "You're

right. I wasn't enrolled. My father saved the life of a nobleman's son. Fished him out of the ocean. He'd been adrift. The king secretly arranged for my education in gratitude. Whatever I chose. I chose seminary, but was expelled. Then I chose swordsmanship. But I couldn't enroll in the Academy. Just as you say. So I was tutored."

Talon waited. "By whom?" she finally asked. Packer did not hear the tremor in her voice.

"Senslar Zendoda. The Swordmaster of Mann."

A shudder went through her. "The Traitor!" she hissed.

Packer recognized now, far too late, what this meant to her. Senslar Zendoda was Drammune by birth. Of course Talon would see him as a traitor to her people. Not that he could have withheld it, even if he had foreseen her reaction. But he felt all hope drain from him. She would kill him now. And then he realized he would welcome that; he should be dead anyway. By all rights, he should not be alive. God wanted him dead. It was Talon who wanted him alive, so she could read him like a book.

But now he was afraid she wouldn't kill him. She would keep him alive and in this hell. His heart felt like it died within him.

She stared at him. "Schooled by Senslar Zendoda." She said it softly, as though letting the words out to take a look at them. Then she said it again, with a venom that made it sound like a curse. "Schooled by Senslar Zendoda." She leaned in toward Packer, now taking his neck in her bare hand and squeezing. Her fingernails, already stained with his blood, bit into his skin. Packer heard a gurgling sound from his own throat, much like he had heard from Dog's. He let it happen.

His hatred for her was gone. She could torture him, kill him, resurrect him, kill him again. It didn't matter. He felt relief, relaxing into the inevitable pain, the inevitable living death. And now that he was free of fear, he could see her as she was, controlled by hate, by a deep, passionate hatred completely unveiled. He found he could even feel sorry for her. He wouldn't fight her any longer. She would do as she pleased. Whatever God would let her do, that is precisely what she would do. Yes, that was true. God had let her bring him back. God had let her torture him. He might let anything at all happen. Anything at all. So be it. So be it.

She clipped the words, spitting each one out in her hard accent the way tin snips cut bits of wire. "I have a duty to this ship, and you have violated that. I have a duty to my Captain, and you have violated that. I have a duty to my native land, and you have violated even that."

She stepped back, and he drew a gasping breath as she released her grip on his throat. She pulled her sword from her belt and placed the point of it to his throat, pushing his head back against the boards behind him. He recognized the angle of her blade. With one thrust it would penetrate through to the base of his skull, and he would die instantly, collapsing without so much as a twitch. It was the exact manner in which he had threatened Dog. He smiled. This was right. He deserved it. He knew that she would not hesitate as he had. He found himself hoping she would do it soon, and do it quickly.

A loud, urgent knocking filled the room, knuckles rapping on wood. The noise startled Packer. Talon bared her teeth angrily, but did not move the tip of her sword.

Chapter 6

Banished

"You're not really thinking of following him, are you, child?" Hen Hillis asked, alarmed. She and Panna were seated at a table just inside the inn door, the same table where Packer had sat after thrashing Dog so easily the previous night. The innkeeper's wife feared she had told this girl too much. "That's not why you're asking, is it?"

"Of course not," Panna lied. She was accustomed to telling the truth, had rarely felt any need to do otherwise, and so she was surprised at how easily and with what force she spoke falsely.

"All right, then." Hen spoke in an urgent whisper, leaning in close. "He left in a barrel." She waited for that to sink in. Panna's eyes widened slightly. "Cap put him in it so's no one could tell. I have no idea why Cap would do such a thing, even though I'm sure Packer asked him politely." In fact, she feared Packer had threatened him with a sword. "And then the pirate's cart took him away."

Panna nodded, her alarm tempered by the simple fact that this was good, helpful information. "Took him where?"

"Toward the docks, I guess. That's all I know, child."

Panna fought a tremble. "Tell me about the woman. What did she look like?"

"I don't know. All Cap told me is that she was a woman, and she brandished a sword about."

"Did she have dark hair?" Panna's dream was still real to her, burned into her memory as if she had been there. Her heart beat wildly.

"I don't know. I did watch out the window at them as they left, but it was dark and I thought all three of them to be men until Cap told me otherwise. I just don't know." Hen's eyes searched Panna's. "Child. You won't go off after them, will you? They'll be at sea by now, far out at sea. So it's much better to stay behind, and be the support here that Packer needs."

"Of course you're right." Panna smiled gently. "I…just needed to know."

Now that Panna seemed to take the news well, Henrietta felt much better. She was glad she had found someone who needed to hear this secret as badly as Panna did, so she could stop keeping it to herself. Hen's inner conflict was resolved, her burden lifted. "That's a good girl, then. You need some rest. You'll go home and sleep, won't you?" She patted Panna's hand.

"I'll try."

By the time Panna had said goodbye and started up the street, she had already worked out exactly what she would need to carry in her knapsack and what she must leave behind. If she could get back into the house and out again without waking her father, she would be gone within the hour.

The knocking grew more insistent. Talon turned her head toward it, looked back at Packer with disgust, then reluctantly lowered her sword. "I will kill you," she promised. She sheathed her blade and left the lantern behind as she walked around the packing crates.

Captain Wilkins closed the small wooden window in the adjoining room, the peephole built so that he could view the questioning of prisoners unnoticed. The room was located just behind the packing crates, which were not actually crates at all, but walls.

"You said he was mine!" Talon hissed at the Captain as she entered.

"You were going to kill him. You haven't even questioned him."

She narrowed her eyes. "I brought him back from the dead. His life is mine to take as I please."

He waved her off. "Don't try me with your witchcraft. He said he can find the Firefish!"

Talon was furious, wishing she could shake some sense into him. He didn't understand. It was exactly this story about Firefish that would make the Captain believe, want to believe, everything the boy said. Who could come up with such a perfect path to Scat's confidence but the Traitor?

"Nothing this boy says will be what it seems, whether he lies or not. He carries the poison, and the plans, of Senslar Zendoda. He could spy against us, sabotage us a thousand ways, all of which would require the trust of the Captain, not his death."

"Nonsense." It all seemed absurdly conspiratorial. "I will trust a man until he proves himself untrustworthy." He shrugged. "Then I'll kill him."

Talon was unmoved. "That is beyond foolish."

Scatter Wilkins rubbed his temples. Foolish? He would have laughed at her, had he not known how furious it would make her. "It's easily tested. We go where he says there are Firefish. If he lies, he dies."

"It will be a trap."

"Who wants to trap us? We have a deal with the King of Nearing Vast. Your own emperor, the Hezzan, expects shipments. There are no pirates left but me. Where are our enemies? Who are they?"

She clamped her jaw. "You make your money from enemies who hate one another. Is that not enough reason to hate you?"

"But the Swordmaster of Nearing Vast? What does he care?"

Talon bit her tongue. He couldn't see it. Five years ago, even two years ago, the boy would have been dead already and the Captain would be thanking her. But Scat had changed. He had grown so soft that now he thought he had no enemies simply because he couldn't name them. She had met the king. She knew the Hezzan. The two were a knife's edge away from war, and each had a hundred reasons to plot, to use a venture that traded in the dark gray markets between them. But Scat saw no shades of gray. He saw only shades of gold. "You have charged me with the security of this ship. And I tell you he is dangerous, and should die."

"And I am the Captain of this ship, and I say not yet," Scat replied evenly.

She trembled with rage. She opened her mouth to speak, but her teeth remained clenched. Her right hand moved almost of its own accord toward her sword hilt.

The Captain's visage grew dark, and one eyebrow rose. "Talon."

She caught herself, lowered her eyes.

Scat laughed now, low and rumbling. "Woman, do you know what I think? I think you need to kill somebody. It's just been too long." He studied her. Then he spoke words of command, softly, but in a tone she knew better than to challenge. "Here's what you're going to do. You're going to find the innkeeper who sold you the ale, and question him. Follow your theory wherever it takes you. Take your pleasure of vengeance on shore. It'll do you good."

"When we return to shore, I will do as you command." She stared hard at him, but the Captain was shaking his head.

"You'll do as I command *now.*"

Talon was stunned. He was sending her away? Putting her off the ship?

"Take whatever boat you want. Take whatever supplies you need. Take your two animals with you. You'll find them confined to quarters, nursing wounds from Mr. Deal's lash."

Her eyes flashed. Ox and Monkey had been whipped? She had not been told they were to be disciplined. She said nothing, but her insides wound into a knot. Flogging her subordinates was Scat's way of telling her she deserved punishment herself. Well, she had offered her head. He had refused it. He would never have that chance again.

The old times were gone, never to return. Suddenly, she wanted off this ship immediately.

Scatter Wilkins continued. "We'll let the boy soften in chains a while, see what he tells us about the big Fish. In thirty days we'll make port at Split Rock. By then he'll have outlived his usefulness. You'll rejoin us then."

"You will keep him in chains?" she asked darkly.

He nodded, but did not meet her eye.

She did not back away. "His spirit has been among the dead," she said in a hoarse whisper. "Trust him at your gravest peril." Then she bowed, a shade excessively, he thought, and left.

Talon walked straight back to Packer Throme, grasped his hair and slung his head back into the wall, banging it painfully. He looked at her from the corner of his eye, wary but listless. She held his head tight in her grip, and spat in his face.

Then she spoke to him again in a hiss, not wanting the Captain to hear her words. It was barely more than a whisper, and all venom. "Know this, Packer Throme. I will find the one who has schooled you, the one who sent you, and those who have harbored you. I will return to the innkeeper. I will find this girl, your Panna, whom neither you nor anyone shall ever marry."

Now Packer eyed her fearfully. She smiled. "Yes, you did not tell me everything. But you told me enough. I will find them. I will kill them all. I will not rest until you, and all whom you love, are dead. This I swear to you."

She banged his head once more into the wooden wall, and left. He closed his eyes and waited, numb. He did not pray. He could not. Though he had believed she could do him no more harm, her words now crushed him further. Master Zendoda, and Cap Hillis. Panna Seline. His heart, all that was in him, emptied like a burst wineskin, leaving a hollow shell, emptier and more useless than he had ever dreamed possible. There was nothing he could do about any of it. Not even death promised rest now.

Scatter Wilkins took a deep breath. He couldn't tell what she had said to the boy, but he assumed it was devastating. She could do that to a man, more quickly and more thoroughly than he could comprehend. He hoped she hadn't broken him completely. He hoped she'd left enough so he could get one more bit of information out of him.

He sighed. This was her witchcraft, this ability to destroy a man from within. It had protected him well while buccaneering. But neither her wiles nor her sword seemed necessary now. She didn't have any appreciation for what was at stake; instead she and her enchantments were always getting in the way. Perhaps it was time to part ways with her permanently. He wasn't sure how to do that, how to rid himself of her and keep his own head on his shoulders. Well, getting her ashore was a good first step.

The Captain looked again at Packer, whose head was hung down now, his body still quivering with each breath. He was crying. A mere boy. Yet he'd beaten the Captain at arms, survived Jonas Deal's justice, and now had lived through Talon's torture. Scat closed the peephole door. The boy was turning the ship upside down. Well, so what? If he could find Firefish, it was well worth it. Had anyone ever, in all of history, Scat wondered for the thousandth time, hoarded a million gold coins?

A million in gold. It was an inconceivable sum, but Scat Wilkins now believed it was possible. Piracy hadn't brought in more than a thousand a month, perhaps a little more in a very good month. And there had always been the risk of capture or death. But the Firefish, now...this was a realm of riches beyond reckoning, uncharted glory. This was the land of legend. And the only risk was death, effectively cutting the possibility of ill fate in half.

Last year Scat's enterprise had earned nearly two hundred thousand gold coins in one season, and they had done it by sailing the seas, for all intents and purposes, aimlessly. Their only methodology was to head for deep water and hope a Fish would take their bait. But this idea of knowing where the Firefish fed...of feeding waters...

Scatter Wilkins would investigate. And Talon could sink into hell if she didn't like it.

All hands were on deck or in the rigging as the small boat was lowered over the side, into the black darkness of the shadow cast by the ship as it sailed under the light of a pale moon. Talon was all but invisible, wrapped in a dark cloak against the chill night air. She sat in the stern of the shallop, manning the tiller. The boat settled into the water with a gentle slap, and Ox and Monkey unhooked the lowering blocks. "Good voyage!" one of the sailors above them called as others rewound the windlass, pulling the heavy lines back up.

"Yeah, it'll be great," Ox answered sullenly, grabbing an oar. Pain shot through the torn flesh of his back with the sudden movement.

Talon was silent. This promised to be a long, arduous row back to shore, with no means of propulsion beyond human muscle and sinew. Talon faced the stern and watched the *Trophy Chase* and her two escorts, the *Camadan* and the *Marchessa,* recede. She did not pay attention to the two men as they made ready the oars, as they struggled in pain. She felt no trace of pity for them.

By her feet was her duffel, heavy with clothing, provisions, and weapons. For this trip, it was imperative that the boat be small enough to hide, and so she had chosen the shallop rather than the sail-equipped jolly. She would have preferred the longboat of the huntsmen, but two men, let alone two idiots like these, could not handle such a craft.

Her two henchmen glowered at the back of their dark mistress's head. She didn't care about the task ahead of them, they knew, didn't care about the lash wounds that ripped at their backs in the salt spray. She had not offered them salve—none of the healing arts they knew she possessed. She had done nothing to even acknowledge their pain.

She, of course, had received no punishment for allowing the stowaway onboard. And she, of course, was solely responsible. It was their task only to negotiate, buy, and haul goods. It was hers to protect the ship.

"I say we'll be gone half a day with a good wind," Monkey said softly to his mate. "We'll row twice, maybe three times that long getting back to shore." And with little rest, he didn't need to add. The boat was wide enough that neither man could row it by himself, and there was little chance Talon would volunteer a turn.

"Aye," Ox answered hoarsely, "but only if we make a straight line of it. Row otherwise and we row ourselves to Hades."

Talon turned toward the two men. With the moon behind her, she was a dark form, hardly more than a shadow. "You have more pressing business, perhaps?" Her voice was cold enough to damp a fire.

Ox just glared at her.

Monkey panicked; he never spoke to Talon. That was Ox's job. But Ox wasn't speaking. "Barring a storm, this is just a fine way to spend the hours." His voice cracked, went falsetto. He attempted a smile that caused her to roll her eyes. Did he think her as stupid as he was himself?

"I'd welcome a storm," she said, and turned away from them.

The two men glanced at one another. Even a minor squall would swamp their boat. Something had happened aboard the *Chase*. She'd had it out with the Captain, certainly, over the stowaway. And now she didn't care whether they lived or died.

But Talon knew what they didn't. The *Chase*'s course had been a zigzag as the Captain swept the seas for Firefish. The row back would be less than a day. Anyone who understood sailing would have known it. But she was in no mood to lighten the load of men too ignorant or too lazy to have learned the basic navigation of their own ship.

These two feared a storm! If they had been paying any attention to the ship's mission during the past two seasons, they would fear something much harder to predict...and impossible to survive. In her duffel was a Firefish lure she dearly hoped she wouldn't have to use. And if she did need to use it, she dearly hoped it worked.

"It'll kill us before it dies," the huntsman said, dropping the large brass box that was a Firefish lure onto the wooden table of the engineer's small cabin. "The fuse is too long." Stedman Due crossed his arms, daring disagreement.

Lund Lander forced a smile. Then he took his spectacles from his pocket and placed them carefully on his nose. "How much too long?" He picked up the lure easily, a brass container that weighed almost twenty-five pounds, and set it on end. He first examined a dent that had pushed the plating inward a full inch on one side. Then he looked at the top end, at a small door beside the box's most outstanding feature, a large brass ring. The little door was covered with a thick wax seal. He took a knife from his desktop and peeled away the seal, opened the door, and peered into it.

"How much too long?" Lund repeated.

"I don't know," Stedman answered.

"Guess."

"Maybe four or five seconds."

"Tell me why you think that," Lund demanded in his quiet, intense way.

The huntsman glared. "I just guessed." Talking to Lund was always like this. They called Lund "the Toymaker," an ironic nickname that stood in stark contrast to both his calling and his demeanor. "It's too long," the huntsman explained again. "The boys are worried. I'm worried. We've had some close calls."

"You want me to adjust just this one, or all of them?"

The huntsman shrugged. "All of them," he said softly.

Part of the reason Lund was intimidating was physical. The Toymaker was a big man, six-feet-four, lanky, strong, a sailor who could get drunk and get in fights and win more than he lost, even when paired against the huntsmen. But most of the intimidation came from the way Lund made Stedman feel. Like there was always something he knew that others didn't.

Now Lund looked across the table, one eyebrow raised. It wasn't that he disliked the man before him or didn't appreciate his role. Lund respected the difficulty and danger of the huntsmen's job. But what respect he did manage, the huntsmen always seemed more than eager to undermine. And this particular huntsman, the experienced, respected Stedman Due, was their leader. He should know better.

"Has there been even one incident in which the fuse was actually too long?" Lund knew the answer.

Stedman shrugged again.

The Toymaker nodded his understanding. "Each fuse," he explained patiently, for what seemed like the hundredth time, "has been calibrated based on what we've learned from all the encounters with Firefish that you and your men have ever had. Every time you use a lure, we recalculate the average time to strike." Stedman glanced around the room, trying not to show his irritation. Lund noticed it, but pressed on. "That's why an engineer accompanies every longboat. Some lures have detonated too early, as you know," Lund shot Stedman a sharp look. Early detonations had cost thirteen lives to date, but Lund didn't need to say it. The tally was universally known, a baker's dozen who ended as quarry, in the bellies of their prey. Three were Lund's own men, who had died with their timepieces in their hands and pages of notes in their laps.

Lund let the silence speak for him. Then he continued. "We adjusted the calibration. They don't detonate too early any more. And so far, none have detonated too late. So tell me. Should I go by our calculations, by what we know about Firefish strikes, or should I go by...something else?"

The huntsman stewed. He pulled at his ragged beard. Then he spoke softly, imploring. "Listen, Lund. The boys are concerned you went too far the other direction, that's all. You don't know these monsters like we do."

Lund's eyebrow shot up again.

"Oh, you know all the numbers. I grant you that. But these things..." he swallowed, trying hard not to show any fear. "You can't predict what they'll do."

Lund waited.

"They...they *change.*"

Lund was unimpressed. Stedman saw he was getting nowhere. Anger crept into his tone. "I'm telling you, Lund. We're the ones out there baiting those killers, trusting your fuses and your explosives and your fool calculations. But while we're studying them, they're out there studying us."

Lund stared harder. Could Stedman Due be losing his nerve?

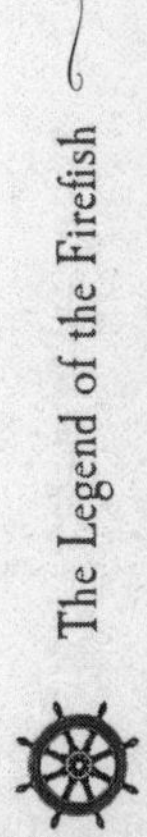

These were beasts, forces of nature, certainly intelligent as far as animals went, but their patterns were unmistakable. Lund Lander and his team had reduced the hunt to simple calculations. Human fear on the part of the huntsmen was, of course, part of the equation—expected. Complete loss of nerve, however, would make the hunters unpredictable, not the beasts. The Captain needed to be aware of this. "Very well, then. I think I understand your concern. I'll look into it," he said, smiling. "Anything else?"

Stedman had gone as far as he could. He knew Lund would do nothing. But there was something else—there were problems with getting the fuse to ignite when it got wet. But Stedman didn't particularly want to answer questions about how and why the fuses were getting wet, because he didn't know the answer. The Toymaker was extremely proud of his water-resistant fuse. Once it was lit, you could drop it to the ocean floor. But Lund had told them again and again it wouldn't ignite in the first place if it went past a "saturation point," or some such malarkey.

Stedman sighed. He and his men were hunters. They were tracking the most dangerous prey in the world. And they weren't accustomed to being held captive by calibrations and calculations and saturation points and other mathematical gobbledygook. It hurt morale.

One of Lund's engineers burst into the cabin. "Beggin' pardon, sir, but the witch is gone!"

"What?" Lund asked, startled.

The engineer nodded. "The Captain's put Talon off the ship."

"What?" Stedman asked, incredulous.

"She's been put off the ship and is being rowed to shore by her two goons."

Stedman smiled at Lund. Lund smiled back. If the witch was gone, many things could change. Suddenly, they were partners, brothers in arms.

Talon sat hunched in the shallop as Ox and Monkey pulled rhythmically at the oars. The small craft moved slowly along, an eerie image as it made its way down the glimmering silver path that was the moon's reflection.

Talon knew what the talk would be among the crew. The Captain would explain her departure as a necessary mission to learn how the boy got aboard, but the crew would read it the way they wanted to read it. She was being punished. Banished. They would all rejoice.

Well, let them. She would never return.

The vast silence of the ocean seemed to swallow the tiny shallop. Ox and Monkey had both long ago grown accustomed to Talon's demeanor; they knew that she was cold as winter. But now she was colder than ever. What had happened? They had been told nothing. It wasn't hard to guess that they were headed back to Hangman's Cliffs, to get their money back. And then some.

But trouble ashore was generally left ashore until the next port of call. Putting Talon off the ship was highly unusual. And Ox and Monkey were simply supply hands. If she were going on a manhunt, a security mission, why not take a swordsman or a musketeer instead? These thoughts played in their heads, shared thoughts left unspoken.

Monkey tried to think of something else, something more pleasant. But Ox let the possibilities play out in his mind. Maybe Talon had been stripped of her commission. That was a terrifying thought. If Talon were free of the Captain's orders, then she might do anything. Maybe she planned to kill them as soon as they reached shore. And once that thought lodged in Ox's brain, he had trouble plucking it out. It stayed there and festered.

So this is where it all leads, the Ox thought. *This is what comes of taking orders from a foreigner, and a female at that.* For endless hours he and Monkey would row in pain, not even knowing why, and for endless hours she would sit there, silently. Endless hours on a huge, featureless ocean, days perhaps, far from the reach of captains, or first mates, or the law, or God.

In the thick, tangled growth of Ox's brain, images began rising like mists, images he couldn't fend off and had little desire to try. He could see Talon slumping over, collapsing from a pistol shot to the head. He saw her cloak-draped body splashing over the stern of the boat. He had no pistol, of course, but that didn't stop his imagination. Somewhere, in one of those hours, would be a moment, a second or two is all it would take, and he could rid the world of her forever.

Talon turned suddenly and looked into his eyes. Ox quickly looked up at the moon, then down at his hands as he pulled on the oar. *She saw nothing,* he told himself. *No one can see a man's thoughts.*

But she did see.

Chapter 7

The Bargain

Packer blinked in the darkness, squinting. Someone was there. The scratch of a match turned the darkness bright, and lit the face of Captain Wilkins as he puffed a cigar-tip red. Smoke swirled. He put the match to a lantern, and set the lantern on a crate beside him.

How long had it been since Talon had left? Packer didn't know, but he'd been drifting in and out of consciousness for what seemed like days.

The Captain was in no hurry. Packer watched him through empty, half-shut eyes. Scat smoked, considering the boy carefully. Packer's belly had quit bleeding. The cut below his ear was starting to scab. The dried blood was still visible on Packer's forehead in the shape of a cross, a particularly creative touch on Talon's part, the Captain thought. He sighed. "You're not easy to kill."

Packer understood the words and could sense that the Captain meant them, but he could not grasp their meaning. He was infinitely weak, in body and in spirit. He had been crushed, killed, resurrected, crushed again, inside and out. He was sick, hurt, damaged, in pain, hungry and thirsty, and drained of both the will to live and the desire to die. None of it had been in his power, none of it in his hands. The idea that he was hard to kill had no meaning.

He tried to speak, to ask the Captain to explain, but he could not. His mouth and throat were like parchment. He was desperately thirsty. He tried to clear his throat, but only managed to gag, and bring a pounding pain to his head. He closed his eyes.

Scat picked a piece of tobacco from his tongue, examined it, flicked it away. "It's not every day we keelhaul a stowaway."

Packer tried again to speak, to ask for water, but his tongue wouldn't work. It seemed stuck to his teeth. Scat watched, chuckled. "Cat got your tongue, I see. Well, she'll do that." He looked at Packer a while longer, then picked up a wooden bucket that had been sitting at his feet. He stood and splashed about half the contents, cool, clean water, into Packer's face. It felt like mercy itself; Packer was able to wet his tongue and mouth, and even swallow a little.

Scat sat back down, surrounded by the soft blue haze he had created around himself. "We've seen none of the big Fish."

Now Packer nodded. Scat had come to hear his information. Well, fine. Packer would tell him everything. "Feeding waters," he croaked.

Scat sat silent, waiting for his pulse to slow. He did not want to seem eager. "Do you know where they are?"

Packer shrugged. He didn't know if his information was accurate or not. He was finished with this voyage. He was finished with everything.

"Tell me," Scat commanded evenly.

Packer nodded and closed his eyes, ready to give up the one hope he'd had of surviving. But nothing came to him.

He couldn't remember. His brain wasn't working. He tried to recall his father's diary, tried to remember all the times he'd thought about the location of the feeding waters. But his mind was completely blank...every path that led to that piece of information blocked. His brain seemed as empty as his heart. The whole reason he was here, the reason he dared attempt this mission. And he couldn't remember it.

This was his final humiliation, he thought. The Captain would think him mad, an imbecile, the village idiot who hid in a barrel and found himself in chains. A jack-in-the-box.

And then this absurd situation suddenly struck him as humorous. Packer let out a laugh, surprising himself as much as Scat. It wasn't much of a laugh, more like a half a smile and a partial grunt, but it felt good. It was more refreshing even than the cool water.

Scat's eyebrows went up. Then he nodded. The boy was smart, he thought. He wouldn't give up his information cheaply. It didn't

occur to Scat that the boy would simply be unable to remember. Scat's lust for a million in gold did not allow for such mundane possibilities. He read his own desires into Packer, saw his own reflection, and respected what he saw. "So tell me what you want in exchange for this information."

Packer was confused. "What I want?"

"How much," Scat answered. "Name your price."

Packer closed his eyes, understanding now that Scat thought he was driving a bargain. He did not want the Captain to misunderstand. *The truth,* Packer thought. *No matter now. Just the truth.* "It's not that." He worked to summon more moisture into his mouth so he could explain.

Scat took a deep pull on his cigar, blew out a great swath of smoke. He was in no hurry. He remembered what Packer said under Talon's interrogation, decided to prod. "You came to learn how to hunt Firefish."

Packer nodded.

"Is that what you want in exchange?" Scat was hopeful.

Packer closed his eyes. He wanted nothing in exchange.

Now it was Scat's turn to laugh. The boy had come up with something bigger than Scat had even imagined. It was, in fact, precisely what the Captain had been trying to avoid by refusing to put fishermen on crew, or dock in busy ports. The boy wanted to take away Scat's monopoly. "You don't know what you're asking."

Packer opened his eyes. He wasn't asking anything.

"And why would you risk all this for a ragged lot of fishermen? What good would Firefish do them?"

Packer thought for a moment, quite sure he really didn't know. "They're poor," he said at last.

He said it with such simple honesty that it drew Scat's respect. Scat had been poor as a young boy. He knew what it was like to be hungry, to steal to eat, to grow tired of being poor. Now the boy's mission made sense to him. One of the poor fishermen learns a little swordsmanship, and so they send him on a dangerous mission, hoping to bring back a whole new economy. Not a bad plan. Desperate, foolhardy, and without half a chance to succeed. But not bad. "Feeding the poor." Scat smiled. "Maybe you are a missionary after all."

This statement struck Packer like a slap. If only it were true.

"How do you know your father's information is accurate?"

"I don't."

Scat frowned. Then he smiled. He respected honesty. "Where did he learn it?"

"I don't know."

Scat sighed. This was not good. Likely there were no feeding waters. So whatever he gave up to the boy, it probably wouldn't matter. But he had to play it out. "You've asked a hard thing. But I'll do it."

Packer looked confused. He did not understand that he had asked anything at all. "Do what?"

"I'll teach you to take the Firefish, and you can take that knowledge where you like."

Packer then understood. Scat still thought he was bargaining. "No. I don't remember."

Now Scat was alarmed. "You don't remember what?"

"The location. The feeding waters." Packer saw a flash of anger cross Scat's face. It came and went, and was replaced again with the blank look.

"I've given you my word. I want the information, son."

Packer closed his eyes, helpless. He opened his mouth to speak, to tell Scat once again that he truly couldn't remember. That was the truth, and he needed to say it again, make him believe it regardless of the consequences. But Packer's mouth had dried up again, and he couldn't get his tongue to work. Scat snorted, but picked up the bucket of water and eased a mouthful into the boy.

As the cool water went down his throat, the image of his father's diary came back to him. He was reading the page again, as easily as if it hung before his eyes. A sense of joy grew in him. It was as if God had given it to him, now that He had completed the bargain. God had done this. For the villages.

"Thank you." Packer closed his eyes. "Sail to the Freeman Reef."

Scat looked disappointed. He sat still, puffed his cigar again, and then chewed it rather severely. "I know it well. There's no school of Fish there."

Packer shook his head. "Sail north-northeast thirty-nine leagues from the reef."

Scat blinked. "That's well inside Achawuk Territory."

Packer nodded.

The Achawuk. Scat had no desire to sail in among their islands. "I've found Firefish in deep water all across the sea."

Packer nodded again. He had said all he knew.

Achawuk. The Captain's thoughts went dark.

From below, in the dark, the bottom of the lumbering rowboat looked like the underbelly of a great, fat, slow fish. The oars dipping below the surface were skinny little fins, comically inadequate for any evasive movement.

But it had seen this before, and remembered. Years had passed, but the memory was vivid and timeless, visceral and tactile…crunching through a hollow shell that burned and crushed easily, but that splintered painfully and tasted of dry land and bottom weeds. There had been a small, meaty morsel within it, which would have been quite tasty by itself. The memory of disappointment roiled through the brain of the great predator, this prehistoric cousin of shark and eel, giving it pause. This prey was surely a shellfish.

So rather than simply attack, it moved off in search of more satisfying prey. Anything that was soft and meaty and easily caught, easily devoured. Like a whale, or a shark.

The Ox and the Monkey were unarmed. This made Ox's designs on Talon more difficult, but not impossible. He had a goodly piece of oak in his hands, tooled into the shape of an oar, and he harbored a deadly hatred. His hands were blistering, his back was raw, and he had grave doubts they would survive this trip, doubts that grew with each passing hour.

Talon's apparent lack of interest played upon Ox's misgivings. Four hours gone, and she had yet to produce a compass. She had barely glanced around her, and had scanned the skies only once that he had seen. And he had been watching. A rowboat, he knew, was notoriously easy to turn, and it would be a simple thing for them to row in large circles for days on end. He didn't know what provisions she had brought, but her duffel wasn't big enough to be very promising.

Once, Ox had purposefully begun pulling harder on his oar than Monkey did; not enough to notice, he thought, but enough to steer the ship away from him, to starboard. He watched Talon's hand on the tiller, looking for some course change to counter him. He saw none. And that clinched it. Believing she cared nothing about living, and they therefore would die anyway, he very much wanted to see her die first. And the sooner the better, while he was still strong enough for a fight, and perhaps a lucky row to shore.

Talon, for her part, was far more at home on the sea than Ox or Monkey could have guessed, neither one being a sailor. She knew the stars by sight and would need a glance at a compass only once or twice during the night, and then only for confirmation. The shoreline of Nearing Vast was not far off, and she wasn't concerned about landing anywhere in particular. She could hardly make a mistake so long as they headed west.

She also knew the feel of a boat on the water and could tell which way the boat was headed, pull by pull. It was a skill learned during her years navigating the slave galleys of her homeland. When Ox began his test, she felt it, and compensated with each pull. When he tired of it, she felt that, too, and compensated back. Ox's inconsistencies, and the reasons for them, didn't concern her. Her mind was occupied with Packer Throme.

She should have killed the boy, she knew. She should have ignored the knock, pretended not to hear it, and run her sword up to its hilt into his soft flesh. The Captain would have been displeased, angry even, but he would have gotten over it. Why hadn't she done it? What had stopped her? She didn't know. Perhaps she was growing soft too.

No, no…it was Senslar Zendoda. It was the Traitor in Packer. The boy's clear blue eyes pleading up to her, filled with tears, as though he was just a child, scared and hurt. That was a mind trick, she now knew, a trick he'd undoubtedly learned from the Traitor. Yes, it was Zendoda who had stopped her. On some level she had fallen for his tricks, even before she heard the Captain's knock. She cursed herself, remembering how she had been disappointed that Packer had broken so easily. But perhaps he hadn't broken. Perhaps he had beaten her. She gnawed on that thought for a while.

Then she grew determined. Ultimately, she would triumph. Packer would die. Zendoda would die. Such mind tricks came from their religion, she knew, from this God of theirs who supposedly allowed himself to be tortured and killed. She understood, even respected, the deceit in it.

What had really happened to this man they called the Son of God, whom they crucified, was that he had been brought back to life by someone who knew the healing arts as she did. Their Son of God was no more special than Packer Throme, who had also been to the Dead Lands and returned. The power of the lie was that this Jesus claimed God had done it, that therefore all he did and said was directly from God, and could not be questioned.

So therefore, all people must humble themselves before him, worship him, and...here was the great deceit...become weak like him. His return from the dead was somehow proof that such weakness was actually strength, they said, that God was strong within them. The leaders of this religion could preach that people should be meek, should follow like lambs. And thereby, the leaders could amass all the power.

It was an obvious lie, once it was exposed, but a powerful and seductive lie when it was not. Packer Throme's pleading eyes, his sobs, his show of weakness were all a part of that lie. Whether he had truly broken or simply pretended to be broken didn't matter. There was no God who would protect such sheep, who would step in to help such weaklings. No God would usher them into some glorious realm as a reward for their humiliation. She could have killed him with a thrust. No God had stopped her. Scat Wilkins had not stopped her. It was her own weakness that had stopped her blade. Never again.

She spent the hours, as Ox imagined a world rid of Talon, imagining a world rid of Senslar the Traitor. She would relish his destruction, of course. But then what? She was finished with the *Trophy Chase* and its gold-blind captain. She let her mind wander out into the future. For a Drammune native to kill the Swordmaster of Nearing Vast, to assassinate him, could be considered an act of war, if it was done properly. If it was done by a Drammune warrior, a spy. She smiled.

She could return to her home, to the Kingdom of Drammun. She could find a way to help her homeland destroy the entire Kingdom of Nearing Vast, and its crucified God. That was a goal worthy of her abilities.

Scat took the cigar out of his mouth and chewed the inside of his lip. He was silent for only a few seconds, but during that time a flurry of thoughts led him to a single conclusion, which was in fact foregone, driven by the power of a million gold coins. He would go. Of course he would go. He would brave the Achawuk.

Among Scat's thoughts were some truly discouraging realities. Scat didn't have nearly the firepower to handle the Achawuk. He'd hidden in their territory twice, and had once watched from a cove while they attacked, boarded, and destroyed the ship that was pursuing him. It had been a gruesome, ugly sight, etched deeply into a memory scarred by a lifetime of ugly sights. The warriors had been oblivious to his presence, or he wouldn't have escaped either.

Efforts to appease them were useless; Scat knew that. They cared nothing for money. Unless the Captain went back for more men and arms first, he'd need to attempt the trip from the reef in one night, hoping to remain unseen by the natives in the darkness.

Of course, he wouldn't need to *hunt* the beasts. If he could see them—more than one of them, anyway—he could run, regroup, and return for a bigger score. He'd need a good wind, and some luck. But for a million in gold…

"You look like a rat's last meal," Scat said to Packer, as though just now noticing. "Get some sleep." And with that, he took the lantern and left.

Packer doubted he would ever live to see village fishermen taking Firefish. If there were no Firefish at the location he'd just given to Scat, Packer would be killed. If there were Firefish there three-hundred-and-sixty-four days a year, but they weren't there the one day that Scat and the *Trophy Chase* arrived, Packer would be killed. If there were a thousand Firefish there that day, Packer might be killed anyway, no longer being needed. Or they could all be killed by the Achawuk. Or they could all be killed by the Firefish. Many possibilities, one common result.

Well, God would choose the outcome. That phrase came back to him, but with a very different sense now. It wasn't hope, but resignation. There was some strange faith in it, a kind that lived on just the other side of despair. He had been useless, hopeless, emptied, and yet God had stepped in and bargained for the villages. God had chosen the outcome.

"Resist not evil." The words fluttered around in his brain like birds in an empty house. Is that what he'd just done? In fact, it was.

He had not resisted, though he'd wanted to, had tried to. Undoubtedly, what he'd done was not at all what Jesus meant. Jesus did not want all His followers to go find an evil person, a Talon, and submit. But perhaps somehow, some way, when evil is there, when an evil person is ready to kill, to destroy, when evil is overpowering and inevitable, when the choice is to flee or to fight, perhaps there is a third path, one that Packer hadn't taken but that he might have, a path of submission to God that is also, somehow, submission to the will of the evil one.

Isn't that what Jesus did on the cross? Packer marveled at the thought. Didn't Jesus submit to the will of the evil one, who very much wanted him humiliated, tortured, and dead? And if such passivity were practiced in obedience to God, as Jesus had done, without ever folding, as Packer had done, then certainly God would take over. Wouldn't He?

Ox's palms were sweating. He had to strike first, that he knew. That would be the only way to beat her. Her head was down, bobbing with the movement of the boat. He was sure she was at least half asleep. This killing seemed to him more than justified. This would be a completely upright act; he would be commended for it. Many would applaud him. And since the Captain had banished her, as Ox now believed, and they were therefore doomed to die, only a coward would stay his hand. And Ox was no coward. He was a strong, brave man.

Talon was deep in thought, but she was not asleep. She sensed, before she heard it, that something was amiss. The oar came up out of the water awkwardly, Ox shifted in his seat oddly, just enough to set off an alarm within her. Then she heard the soft clink of the oar's pin coming up out of the socket, and she knew. She heard, as she ducked her head, the whoosh of the air around the oar.

Idiot! she thought. It was Talon's feel for the sea that saved her. Her ability to sense changes and keep her bearings, even in a tiny pod skittering on a massive ocean, was something Ox couldn't fathom. It was what led him to believe she was careless with their lives, and what led him to be careless with his own. The wooden beam passed over her harmlessly.

But in the half second it took Ox to recover his balance and to stop the oar before it struck Monkey, Talon had pulled her knife from her belt and lunged, swinging her blade backhanded. For a moment, Ox just looked at her where she crouched, coiled now for an inevitable second attack. His eyes were wide, afraid of what might have just happened, afraid of what might yet happen. And then, as the blood began to pour from his neck, he dropped the oar and pawed at his throat with both hands. As he felt the damage done, he began to understand what she already knew. She sprang again, sinking the knife deep into his belly, up under his ribs. Using it like a baling hook, she took him by the collar with her left hand and, with a short, quick thrust of her body, dropped him over the side of the boat.

She had pierced his heart, and he was dead before he hit the water. He sank like a stone. And so, not five seconds from the moment he'd swung the oar, he was gone, swallowed by the sea.

Monkey stared, slack-jawed, at the dark spot in the water where his partner of seventeen years had simply disappeared. Talon quickly lashed the rudder true, then sat down next to Monkey. She put the oar back into its place. She stirred her knife through the water a few times, and wiped it dry on the black leather of her pant leg. She looked at Monkey as she returned the knife to its sheath.

"Row," she said quietly.

Monkey obeyed.

The two rowed for shore with a renewed sense of purpose. Monkey was unable to stop shaking, unable to hide from the images of what he'd just witnessed, as they played again and again in his mind.

Talon didn't give it another thought. She was already planning her approach to the inn, and the methodology she would employ with the innkeeper to learn more about this boy swordsman, and his betrothed. She now wished she had probed Packer further about this Panna. But Talon knew her, without knowing her. She was some pretty thing with no ambition and a strong back.

Talon would relish wringing Panna of information and then taking vengeance on her. And a greater pleasure still would be that through her, she would find her way to the Traitor. Talon smiled. This was the course for her now. Their God had spared Packer Throme? Fine, let them believe that. But because of that, and only because of that, Packer would be the death of his own true love, and then of his swordmaster, Senslar Zendoda.

Panna's knapsack included some food and a few extra articles of clothing. She wished, as she made her way up the darkened street, heading for the wagon path that led over the hills toward the docks, that she had a man's clothing. She wished she had a weapon, any weapon, and some skill at using it. She wished she had spent more time listening to her father's talk about his own travels, his seminary days, and his various adventures.

She was a woman, alone on a darkened street heading out of town, her peasant dress billowing in the breeze under clear, moonlit skies, signaling to all who might happen to look that here she was, female, vulnerable, and traveling alone. She had taken her father's floppy fishing hat, which he seldom wore, and had tied her hair up under it. But that did little good without some similar disguise for the rest of her.

She had been foolish, she now knew, to keep to woman's work and woman's ways, to the exclusion of even the most rudimentary survival skills that might be needed in the greater world. She could mend shirts and serve supper, even sing solos for the church choir. But how did she choose an inn in a strange city? How much did room and board cost? How would she know who to trust?

What had she thought—that having long hair and lovely eyes, a soft voice and a way with a washtub, would win her man? That all it would take would be one kiss, and he would melt, swear undying love, and stay with her forever? Yes, she supposed, that was exactly what she had thought.

Well, he hadn't. Instead, he'd cared more for his pirate adventures, dropping her like a wrung rag at the sound of the outlaws' cart on the cobblestones, leaving her to stay behind in helpless agony or follow in hopeless pursuit.

What was she good for, without him? Washing her father's undershirts, scrubbing floors, and listening to endless women's prattle about husbands and children and all their shortcomings—or settling for some other suitor who'd soon turn her into yet another prattling wife, a full partaker in all those numbing daydreams of patterned porcelain plates.

She had been utterly without backbone. Her father, a good and kind man who loved her dearly, had not helped. He was as much to

blame as anyone for her predicament; he had not schooled her in anything but what would be useful in marriage. She could see that now. He meant well, of course. But he was a passive man, nothing like Packer. Even his sermons were full of "wait upon the Lord," and "humble yourself before Him," and "Let God fight your battles."

All that seemed terribly inadequate now. What battles would God fight for you if you never went to war? A life of dreams and prayers and waiting was fine for him; porcelain plates were fine for all the hens of Nearing Vast. No, she would do whatever it took to find Packer, or she would die trying. This was the right thing to do; she felt it deep in her soul. It was what Packer chose, what he valued.

And besides, Packer needed her. Why else would God send her such a dream? Packer needed help, and no one else cared, no one else knew. If she didn't try to help, who would? Why would God put all this into her heart and her head if He didn't want her to take the step of faith it took to go after Packer, to trust Him in the midst of all that was out there, all the unknowns of the world?

She was energized by these thoughts as she paused by the last house at the edge of town. She turned behind her. The soft, flickering light from the two streetlamps gave the little village a warm glow, a sense of safety she could almost touch. But it was an illusion. It was a trap.

An owl hooted in the trees, startling her. She looked up. The great bird's wings flapped as it rose slowly from the wooded grove, a silhouette against the sky. When she looked back down, she saw something else flapping in the wind. Hanging on a clothesline not four full steps from her, across no fence or border whatever, was Mrs. Molander's wash.

Mr. Molander was a cobbler, a man whose most important characteristics at this moment were that he was just about Panna's height and weight. His pants, his shirts, his socks, they were all there, waving in the wind. She smiled. He had other clothes. It was doubtful he'd miss these. Mrs. Molander, forgetful enough to leave them out all night, might not even miss them for a day or two.

Panna looked at the cottage. It was dark. She looked at the street. It was empty. She looked at the road through the trees toward the hills. It beckoned.

Five minutes later, a figure under a floppy hat, wearing a cobbler's clothes, plodded up over the hill and down toward the docks.

A peasant dress lay hurriedly buried under rocks and twigs in the woods. And a young woman with a purpose born of passion walked quietly into a world she did not know, which she had only begun to dream about.

Scat Wilkins stood on the quarterdeck and scanned the night sky above the dark, white-capped ocean. Beside him the helmsman kept the great ship's course. Above him, the sails were sheeted to port, the ship being on a starboard tack, and thousands of square feet of white canvas billowed firm. The mainsail and the mizzen had just been reefed another six points, the wind having freshened a knot or two, and crewmen were descending the ratlines, their task completed to the bosun's satisfaction. The captain nodded his approval to Mr. Haas.

Sailing was a great joy to the Captain. A clear night on deck with a good wind was as close to heaven as he figured he'd ever get. He was a demanding captain in most ways, but particularly in the precision of sailing, of adjusting the square footage of canvas to exactly match the wind's velocity, and the angle of the sails to match its direction. After all his years at sea, all he'd seen and done, he had never tired of this, never tired of demanding such perfection, and getting it, from his crew. He could feel the wind and the water as though he were part of the ship, as though the hull and sails were his own skin. The waves against the bow, the wind pressing, heeling the ship, the sheets hauled just so, now forty degrees, now forty-five, creating precisely the maximum efficiency, as the ship plunged and rose, cutting the ocean like a keen blade through tender steak. There was nothing like it on earth.

And Scat Wilkins loved the *Trophy Chase* like he loved nothing else on earth, human or otherwise. He loved her not for her superior accoutrements, the iron-capped planks in her decks, the mahogany furnishings, but for her perfect, powerful movement through the water. She was so solid and so tight that no energy seemed lost between sail and keel. Running with the wind or sailing across it, she moved like a cat pouncing, jumping forward, it seemed, each time a sheet was hauled to better a sail's angle.

But sailing into the wind, as she was now, she was nothing short of spectacular. She used the laws of nature as though they had been invented just for her. All sailing ships labor greatly as they beat to windward, their great square rigged sails losing draft as they are trimmed closer on the wind. If their destination was directly into the wind, as it was now, ships like the *Marchessa* and the *Camadan* needed to tack through a full eighty degrees. This meant the best they could do was to set a heading forty degrees to starboard of their target, run as far as they dared, then turn into the wind, powerless until they were on a heading forty degrees to port of their goal. During that turn they were in irons, losing speed.

But the *Trophy Chase* was different. She needed to tack through only fifty degrees. She could remain under full sail at speed when on a heading only twenty-five degrees from her appointed goal. And her turns were so quick that she lost almost no speed even in irons, giving her the edge on any pursuers. Or any prey. She could chase the Firefish at hull speed through two-hundred-and-ninety-degrees of seas.

The *Chase* changed the game. Her designers, John Hand and Lund Lander, made her longer, narrower, and deeper in proportion than any ship ever built. Her sleek hull and deep, long keel simply refused to allow her any significant sideways drift. Her masts were also taller and nimbler than those on any other ship, giving her more canvas to catch the wind, and more opportunity to take advantage of every change in its direction or speed.

The combination of these design features, handled skillfully, made it such that any wind that could fill her sails could force her forward with amazing speed. With the wind pressing from the bow, only twenty-five degrees from head-on, and with her sails close-hauled and her lee rail down, she was a sight to see. Tonight, in twenty knots of breeze, she was doing twelve knots to windward under reefed main and mizzen. The sensation was extraordinary, even for a lifelong seaman like Scat Wilkins. She shot through the water like a grape seed squeezed between the finger of the wind and the thumb of the sea.

The Captain looked astern. Behind the *Chase,* off the port side, was the *Camadan,* and off the starboard, the *Marchessa.* They were both good ships, steady and strong, faster than all but a handful of Vast ships. But in comparison to the *Chase,* they were aging, plodding bulwarks.

"They're struggling now!" the Captain announced, clearly pleased

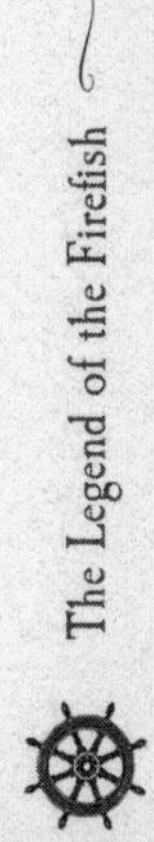

to see his flagship putting distance between herself and her escorts, despite the severe angle at which both ships were heeled, sails full, fighting, not to catch up, since that was impossible, but just not to lose ground so quickly that they would risk Scat Wilkins' ire.

"As usual, Captain," Andrew Haas responded, smiling. Captain Wilkins would rather fly ahead and turn back, running literal circles around them at full gallop, than slow his course in order to keep ranks. "A ship is made to sail, boys," he liked to say, "and the wind is free."

The *Marchessa* carried most of the huntsmen—slayers of Firefish—and all the longboats except the one assigned to the *Chase*. The *Camadan,* though fast, was an illusion, a well-equipped and well-disguised packing plant, a whaler in which Firefish were processed for sale. But the *Chase* was the standard-bearer, the point, and the enforcer, with every sailor a swordsman, a marksman, and a cannoneer.

The Captain looked up through the darkness. High above the sails, in the crows' nest, was the lookout. His job was to scan for Firefish, first and foremost, and for any possible threat second. Scat saw him now, telescope jutting, examining the horizon. Here was the second point on which the Captain was excessively demanding. *Vigilance.* If a ship or a shore were ever spotted by an officer or crewman on deck before the warning came from the crow's nest, the officer was rewarded and the offender flogged.

If the crew were vigilant and the sailing precise, then the ship had a good chance at fame and fortune, two results which, when combined together in large doses, equaled glory. *Vigilance, Precision, Glory.* This triune motto was inscribed around the carved and painted image of the pouncing lioness mounted below the bowsprit, claws out, mouth agape, head cocked to one side as though some invisible prey were already in her grasp. Together, the bold words and the bolder image stated unequivocally the identity of the *Trophy Chase.*

The Captain had changed headings after his visit with Packer Throme. No one had questioned it. Why would they, after years of wandering the seas aimlessly? But still, the Captain wondered, would the crews of his escort ships go willingly into the Achawuk waters? Would his own? Soon it would be obvious to the navigators and officers of all three ships that the Achawuk lay dead ahead, and then he would find out. Morale was low, as it always was when revenues were down, and many on board the *Camadan,* and most on the *Marchessa,* were not experienced in warfare.

The *Chase* could outrun anything afloat, Achawuk canoes no exception. If, that is, she had any wind. And if the Achawuk didn't simply appear from nowhere, surrounding her as they had the *Macomb* all those years back.

The *Macomb* had been a fast ship, too. But the Achawuk warriors, armed only with spears and torches, had materialized in legions of canoes, filling the sea. Cannons, pistols, swords—nothing was enough to deal with the sheer numbers. The Captain let the image play out in his mind, looking for some advantage, or some defensive action not taken by the *Macomb.* He found none.

The Captain's thoughts turned to the source of his present mission. What if the boy was a spy after all? What if he led them into a trap? Wilkins had heard of suicide missions. Perhaps Throme was on one. Achawuk on the left, Firefish on the right. What had Talon said? "Trust him at your gravest peril." And rightly so. He didn't yet trust the boy, but here he was anyway, sailing his ships, and all his hopes, into the two gravest perils he knew.

Chapter 8

Mutiny

The docks groaned as the fishing boats bobbed up and down in their moorings, leaning into and then away from the wooden posts, stretching lines taut, releasing them slack again. Panna stood in the darkness of the woods, behind a tree, peering out from the shadows at the warped boards of the docks and the jumble of boats, all gray and haphazard in the moonlight. The place smelled of rotting fish, and a fly buzzed around her face. There were a dozen or so small boats here, none bigger than perhaps twenty-five feet stem to stern. Panna could see lights shining from under the canvas, or within the tiny cabins, of several of them.

During her walk down the switchbacks from the village, she had concluded that if she were to find Packer, she would need three things: a boat, a sailor, and information about the *Trophy Chase.* But she didn't know how to go about acquiring any of them, or what they might cost her. The two gold coins she carried were all the money in her father's house, saved scrupulously by the priest over many years. They would buy a lot of flour and meat, but the price of things like boats and guides was a mystery to her.

She didn't feel guilty about taking her father's money, a fact that surprised her a little. He had always said it was being saved for a special reason only God knew. She couldn't imagine a more significant one than this. But she didn't want to squander it, either.

Now Panna heard voices from within the lamp-lit boats, then a burst of laughter that startled her, made her pulse race. She took a deep breath. Fishermen were drinking and playing cards, nothing more. Perhaps in some of the darkened boats other men were sleeping off the effects of having done the same. The place seemed to be unguarded, despite the pirates who'd been about just last night. Apparently, danger had passed quickly and completely.

She knew she needed a plan, but her mind could not seem to form one. These were not heroic men in general, these fishermen, but they were not usually cowards either, and she was not anxious to be caught. Any man here who spent an hour on Sunday in her father's church would put a quick end to her journey. Or at least try to.

The small inn was clearly visible from her spot in the woods. It was an unpainted and uninviting ramshackle wooden building with maybe four rooms above a saloon. A lamp burned inside the closed front door. Did that signify it was open for business? Would the door be locked? Panna didn't know. She did not want to stand outside and bang on that door, calling out to awaken some groggy innkeeper from his slumber. The more she looked at the inn, the less she liked it. How could anyone trust a place that would let any random person enter and stay the night just because he had money?

She pulled her hat down farther over her eyes, and looked at the other two buildings. One sold fishing supplies, nets mostly, and the other, she couldn't tell. Both were dark. She tried to recall conversations, any scrap of a recollection that would help her make a decision. But topics like this were precisely the ones that were unimportant to a woman's work in a woman's world.

She remembered that Mr. Sopwash had been hit over the head by a scoundrel who then stole his money and his boots. The next day, Danny Strewn had given up his day's earnings and all his clothing to the brigand, who had been living in the woods for months. Dog Blestoe had been outraged, organized a group of armed vigilantes, and caught him the next day. It turned out the scoundrel was wanted in the City of Mann for several robberies.

Panna swallowed hard. She had to find a safe place. She was angry with herself for taking so long to make a decision. She did not want to be weak. And so Panna made her choice: She would brave the boats. She steeled herself and stepped out of the woods.

But no sooner had she passed from shadow to moonlight than the choice was made moot. She came face-to-face with the silhouette of a man standing less than five paces away from her, a dark shape in the moonlight, with the inn's single lamp behind him. Panic seized her. Where had he come from? How long had she been watched? She groaned silently, her mission over almost before it began.

The lantern swayed crazily, casting shadows that grew and shrank, grew and shrank. Packer squinted past it, trying to see who held the lamp.

"Alive now, are you?" the sailor whispered, finally holding the lantern still. His breath smelled of garlic and ale. "You hardly look it." He was a stoop-shouldered, glint-eyed, leather-skinned man with a large chunk of his right ear missing and a gold earring in his left. His age was impossible to determine; he could have been less than thirty, weathered and withered from a hard life, or he could have been a well-preserved and healthy forty-five. He wore a greasy blue bandana tied around his neck.

The sailor held up a large gray iron key. "Bet you'd like to get out of them manacles, now wouldn't you, sonny?" He set the lantern down and, with a smile that was almost gleeful, unlocked the iron bands around Packer's wrists and ankles.

"Thank you," Packer managed as the last iron clanked and dropped from him. His mind still felt numb, and his newly freed limbs were aching and stiff. His arms moved with such difficulty he would not have been surprised to hear them creak. His left shoulder shouted in pain. How long had he been bound? It seemed to him like years, but in the darkness of this hold, how could he know? The stiffness, though, was almost welcome. He realized that for the first time since he'd left Hangman's Cliffs, he felt rested.

"Delaney's my name," the sailor said, reaching out a hand. Packer took it; it was hard, and strong as a wooden vise. The sailor pulled Packer painfully to his feet. His head spun; he almost blacked out. As he rocked unsteadily, Delaney caught him at the elbows, causing a slicing pain through his left shoulder, which was still wailing its grief over having been wrenched from its socket.

"Bad arm, eh?"

Packer nodded, rubbing his shoulder.

"Take 'er easy. Maybe you better sit."

"No, thanks. Been sitting."

The sailor backed away cautiously, watching Packer get his legs under him. Delaney was a smallish man, but he was wiry and strong. The knotted muscles of his thin chest and shoulders were outlined through his ragged shirt, a piece of clothing that had long ago reached its faded, gray-green color of destiny. He had two swords tucked in his belt, one at each hip.

He also sported a recent tattoo on his upper left arm, an enormous blue and red cross with the vertical piece from shoulder to elbow, the horizontal piece covering a knobby bicep. Decorative swirls surrounded the crucifix, and a banner of some sort draped it, with a single word tattooed in fancy lettering. Packer couldn't read it.

"You have a knack for stayin' alive," the sailor told him. He picked up the wooden bucket Scatter Wilkins had left behind. "That's a good gift to have around here." He sniffed the bucket, raised his eyebrows. "Thirsty?"

Packer nodded, accepted it, brought it to his mouth, and poured cool water down his throat until he gagged. As he spluttered, the sailor laughed. Packer felt his body absorb it like a sponge.

"Let's see what else I've got here." He took a small package from his shirt, unwrapped a piece of dried white fish from its sheaf of brown parchment, and gave it to Packer. It was strong-tasting, like squid or ray, and required a bit of chewing, but he ate it ravenously. "Thanks," he mumbled around it.

"Pleasure."

The ragged sailor's easy smile showed more gum than teeth, and his eyes sparkled with mischief. Packer searched his memory for this face, trying to find it on deck as he walked to or from his death sentence. He couldn't.

"Did the Captain send you?" Packer asked. His voice still sounded ragged, not much more than a croak.

The sailor just kept grinning, and he drew one of his swords, turned the handle to Packer. "In a manner of speaking. Here. You'll need this."

Packer accepted the weapon without hesitation. "Is there trouble?" The blade was a two-edged broadsword, short and straight

and heavy, a no-nonsense weapon for hacking and slashing and stabbing. A pirate's tool.

"Oh, yes. Lots of trouble. For the Cap'n, anyway." Delaney's smile showed even more of his red and black gums.

Packer stepped back, and as he did the room spun again. He closed his eyes for a moment while he processed the words. "What are you saying?"

"Mutiny!" the sailor whispered with glee, leaning in close. "Most of the boys are with us, and some officers too. But what's left can fight. We need every swinging blade." He waved his own broadsword through the air twice, showing great confidence, if not much grace. Then he motioned for Packer to follow him. "Come on, sonny, let's go!"

Packer stood still, the sword in his hand, feeling baffled. "Go where?"

"You there! State your business!" a gruff voice called from the silhouette.

Panna didn't answer.

"I said, state your business!" There was tension in the man's voice, an urgency that cut through her, electrifying her with fear.

Panna lowered her head to be sure he couldn't see her face. She didn't dare speak. She considered answering in a gruff voice of her own, trying to bluff her way past him. But she knew such a ruse wouldn't work. Her clothing might fool him, but her voice never would. How many people had told her over the course of her life that hers was an angel's voice, that she sang like a dove? The gift for which she'd been most thankful was now worse than useless.

So she turned to run back into the woods.

He caught her easily, almost instantly, by the wrist. He was strong; his grip was painful. She was helpless. If he hadn't figured it out already, in another instant he would know for certain she was a woman. He would laugh at her weakness, and her quest would be over. He'd send her home. That would be it. He would send her back, where she would be the focus of talk and gossip about how Packer Throme had left her again, how distraught she was, how out of her mind she was with pining for him. Poor girl.

Pining. She despised that word.

So she rejected it. She felt a determination rise in her that she had never felt before; she could almost hear the locking and clicking of her will as her body tensed to take the required action, which she now knew she would take. She *would* find Packer. She would not return home. This man would not stop her. He would never know who she was, would never guess, would never believe she was a woman, even if someone told him. He would never know what, or who, had hit him.

Her fear and her anger and her iron resolve now flowed together into a volatile mix, kerosene and fire. She knew she must fight like a man, so she balled her free hand into a fist and drove it into his face to block his vision, and her legs drove him backward. When she wrenched her wrist from his grip, his forearms went up to shield himself. She kept him moving backward, kept pressing the attack. She didn't know how hard to hit; she had never hit anyone before. She just knew it had to be hard, so she backed each blow with every ounce of strength she had, aiming instinctively to punch through him, following through in case he stepped backward. She did not want to miss.

She did not miss. She heard and felt the crack of sinew beneath her knuckles, something breaking. She didn't know if it was her hand or his nose, but she didn't care, couldn't worry about it now.

He tumbled backward, and she followed, driving, pushing, still striking as hard as she could. He hit the ground hard, gasping as though he had landed on something; she fell with her full weight on top of him, knees into his stomach. His eyes were wide, fear in them; his body groaned with the sudden escape of breath. She could smell the alcohol he'd been drinking, and could see now the wrinkles around his eyes, the white in his hair and beard. She didn't know him, but all she could think was that he might recognize her, that he must not recognize her, that she must close his eyes so he could not recognize her.

She didn't know how many times she hit him. She wasn't thinking about anything except her own aggression, fearing it was too little, too puny to be manly, forcing more and more ferocity from somewhere deep within, from the seat of her frustration, her years of loneliness, her newfound anger, and her fear. She didn't notice when he started to moan, or when he began to cry out in a high-pitched whimper; she didn't recognize these sounds, being unprepared to believe they meant what clearly they did mean. But finally, after many blows, she realized he had ceased to resist. The rain of fists slowed. And then she heard him. He was sobbing. Her hands were wet with his tears. She heard footsteps and looked up, saw men running up the docks toward her, heard them shouting at her. She jumped up and bolted for the woods, for the darkest spot she could see. They called after her, shouting for her to stop. Someone fired a pistol, and she heard the ball strike wood just ahead of her.

She ran uphill into the woods in a full panic, avoiding trees that appeared from nowhere, knowing she was being chased, afraid to look back, fearing another iron grip from someone, some man who would catch her just as easily as she had been caught once already. She willed speed and strength into her legs and kept running, unwanted tears now blocking her vision. Cool air tore in and out of her lungs. Branches whipped at her. She cursed her own blindness as she crashed through shrubs, tripped on roots, her knapsack bouncing painfully, throwing her off balance. She could hear her pursuers behind her, crashing through the same branches at almost the same time she did. She ran uphill all the while, her legs burning, moving far too slowly, a nightmare of flight in which she grew slower and slower, when she needed more and more speed. Finally, she topped a rise, her enemies upon her, and she stumbled and fell headlong, tumbling down a steep ravine, coming to rest at the foot of a large tree. She lay there in tears, unable to catch her breath, ready to surrender. She could run no more.

But nothing happened.

When her breath began to come more evenly, she sat up. She wiped her eyes and peered up at the dimly lit slope she had rolled down. There were no signs of movement, no sounds. Nothing. She shook her head, trying to understand what had happened. Had she somehow lost them? They had been on her heels. Hadn't they? She should have been caught. But she could hear nothing.

She stood and looked around her. The tall trees waved their leaves in the wind high above her, allowing rare moonbeams through to the forest floor. Insects, katydids and cicadas, buzzed and hissed. She was alone. She must have imagined them behind her, so close as to be able to touch her. She must have heard her own footsteps, the rustle of leaves and branches she herself had disturbed. She laughed silently at her imagination.

And then the reality of her actual predicament crept up on her. She was in fact alone, deep in the woods, deep in the night, with no idea where she was, and only the most general idea which way she had come. And that was the one direction she could not go.

Monkey had grown numb. His hands were blistered, and his muscles were knotted and cramped with the effort of rowing. The wounds on his back had torn open, bled, and then stayed raw under the chafing of his sweat- and spray-soaked shirt. His throat was parched and his tongue was swollen. But he hardly noticed any of it. His mind wandered pitifully, uncontrolled, until he was barely conscious.

His heart had been gutted by the sudden, bloody loss of the only person he considered a friend; in truth, his mentor, protector, and guide. Ox had said they might row straight to hell, and Monkey believed it. And so he rowed in great agony, unable to escape, or to quit, or to rest, or to die, enslaved by the devil beside him, sent to torment him.

Talon was a tormentor, perhaps, but she wasn't the devil. The devil would have greater power than she. The devil would have the strength and the will to destroy them both in a single blow. He would be cunning beyond their imagining, and would desire their destruction simply to satisfy his own unending and ravenous appetite. He would be a predator of mythical proportion, but one who promised life and riches and power, seducing men and women to their own destruction.

The devil was about to pay them a visit.

"Are you with us or agin' us?" Delaney's eyebrows rose, the glee fading.

"And if I'm against?"

"Sonny." Delaney took on a fatherly air. "You been keelhauled by the Captain and tortured by the witch. You're a prisoner, not a sailor. You owe nobody nothin'."

Packer closed his eyes, trying to come to grips with this.

"What'll it be? No time for discussin'." Delaney's voice was still light, but his visage was noticeably darker.

Packer wished he knew more about what was happening, but he knew for certain that mutiny was a crime punishable by hanging. "I made a bargain with the Captain. I can't fight against him."

Delaney's dark look brightened. "That's easy then. You'll fight against me!"

Packer shook his head. Not another duel that he did not seek. "I didn't ask to be freed. Put me back in irons. I'll take my chances."

"That's not in the cards, sonny." The man's look was flint.

"And if I refuse to fight?"

"Then you'll die here." He grinned.

He meant it. Packer did not doubt that the man had killed before. This was a pirate ship. Packer took a deep breath. Fight or die. He looked at the blade in his hand. He hefted it, turned it around. It felt awkward, too heavy to use. It made him feel weak and small, as though the only sword he knew how to use was a child's plaything, and this was a weapon for grown-ups.

Fight or die. Suddenly he realized he was facing another opportunity to "resist not evil," presented this time without any ambiguity whatsoever. Here was the choice, stark and brutal, and in so many words. Retaliate, or turn the other cheek. Now Packer smiled. God had given him another chance. This one should be easy.

Packer paused only a moment, then held the sword hilt toward Delaney. "I hope you came prepared to kill."

Delaney blanched, as though it was the first time it had occurred to him that Packer might actually not fight. "You're a young man, with a life ahead of you. You'd die for the Captain, just like that?"

Packer shook his head. "Just doing what's right."

Delaney scratched his head. "What's right? Captain keelhauled you. Witch tortured you." Another thought occurred to him. "Oh, you're scared of them, I bet. Well, there's no need for that. Captain's captured. Lund Lander, Stedman Due, they're with us. And Talon's gone. Just a few officers yet, like that miserable Jonas Deal who shoved you overboard."

"Talon's gone? Gone where?"

"Captain put her off the ship."

Packer's scalp crawled. His head buzzed as though a swarm of locusts had enveloped him. "Off the ship?"

"Sure, no need to fear her now."

Packer felt panic. "But where did she go?"

"Easy, sonny. Gone back to shore. That's why we made free to take over. Without her sword and her witchcraft, why, we got this thing about done."

"But why did she go ashore?" Packer demanded. He felt the ship move under him.

"Who cares? Captain sent her on some mission or other."

Packer stepped backward, sat hard on his putrid bench, oblivious to the pain that shot through his shoulder. Talon had sworn an oath to kill everyone who mattered to him. Panna! He had to stop Talon. But how? What was the best path?

"You all right?"

Packer didn't answer. He needed to think. Should he join up with Delaney and his mutiny? Would that help? No, Captain Wilkins was likely the only person who could command Talon. Packer closed his eyes. How could he make all this stop? It was as though he had started a boulder rolling down a mountain toward his own village, and toward Panna. He hadn't meant to hurt anyone in the village; he'd meant to help. But the boulder was rolling downhill anyway, and he couldn't stop it.

He could not stand the thought of Talon leering at Panna, as she had at him. Talon hurting Panna. It was Packer's fault, irrevocably and absolutely.

"Sonny. There's a mutiny on here."

Now Packer smiled at the sailor. It was a resigned smile, because he knew what he would do. He had been willing, in the barrel, to live or to die, however God intended it. When he was keelhauled, he had been willing to let God take him as he drowned. He had been willing to die at Talon's hand, when God stepped in and bargained for him. And all those years ago, he had been willing to be humiliated by Dog. In each case, though, he had had little choice but to submit.

But in every case where he had had any power, he had used it. He had fought against the priest who had tried to hurt that girl. He had faced down Dog. He had not surrendered to the Captain in the storeroom, not until death was imminent. And now, now he had another chance. He had the clearest choice God could possibly put in front of him. Fight or die. Resist, or resist not, evil. It was obvious what he should do.

But it was equally obvious that he would not do it. He would not submit now, not with Talon loose. Could God stop her? Yes. Would He? Perhaps. But how could Packer not try? How could he not fight for her, stay alive for the chance to save her?

No, he would not let himself be killed. He would resist. He would fight Delaney…for her. Because with all the punishment he had taken, with all the weakness he'd endured in chains, he still wanted to return a hero. Her hero. He didn't want to die here, even if God would know, even if God would smile down on him for it. God would know, but she would not. And she would weep.

He wanted, more than anything, to go back to the bench in her house, back to where he left her, hold her close again, kiss her again, and never let her go. If he laid down his weapon now, spread his arms wide, accepted Delaney's sword, all manner of things would change, certainly for him they would change for the better. He would be in heaven. But one thing was sure beyond the slightest doubt…there would be no more kisses.

And in a blinding flash, as though the sun shone on his very soul, Packer knew exactly what it meant to "resist not evil," and why it was absolutely required. It meant choosing God over all else. It meant sacrificing all things for God, and God alone. It meant trusting that the outcome would be God's doing, and not one's own; it meant there would be no doubt that whatever the result, it was God's hand at work and *only* God's hand. It was laying down this life and taking up the next.

"You 'bout done thinkin'?"

"Yes. I'm ready." Packer now understood Adam in the Garden, with Eve and her apple. Eve was there, in great need, in great danger, with the juice of the forbidden fruit still dripping down her chin. She was alone, completely alone, and frightened. Adam had to make a choice: separate himself from her forever, or separate himself from God. He knew he should refuse to eat the fruit. He should choose God above all. But he also knew that such a choice would crush her, completely. She would never understand why she was condemned to a living death in a fallen world without him, in isolation and in pain, while he lived on in glory.

Packer, as Adam, would choose to separate himself from God, would choose his own personal mutiny, in the dim hope that he might bond for a short time more with Panna, in living death perhaps, but in love. Packer would not have holiness. Not just yet. He would not have heaven. He would have hardship and trial and struggle and pain. But if he could just see her once again, he would most certainly also have the kisses of the one he loved.

Perhaps in Adam's mind, as in Packer's now, even as he bit the apple, as he stood and lifted his sword, feeling its balance, preparing to use it, there was hope that God would forgive, would somehow make it right anyway, would show mercy, even through fire and flood and pestilence.

Packer looked at the sailor carefully. "I don't want to kill you," he said simply, because it was true, and he felt it deeply. What was left unsaid, but what was said most clearly, was that he certainly would kill Delaney if he had to.

Delaney grinned. "Not much chance of that, sonny, though you're welcome to have a go!" Here was a man who loved a good fight. The sailor moved into his fighting stance, his sword tip tracing little circles in the air.

Somehow, Packer felt better, seeing Delaney's appetite for the contest. Packer nodded, appreciative.

It was better now than it had been with Dog. The odds were all stacked against Packer this time, rather than against his adversary. This felt good. Packer had an unfamiliar blade, a bad shoulder, and a very long time in chains with no food and little water. He had an unknown adversary who was strong and willing, and who knew how to kill.

There was a very good chance that Packer would die here. Packer found comfort in that thought. He would give it all he had, for Panna, and if it wasn't enough, so be it. Death would come from the hand of God, through Delaney, and it would all be over. Or Packer would win, and there would be one more chance to return to Panna's bench. And perhaps, one more chance to know God's overriding mercy.

Delaney continued to grin. He stepped away, providing Packer a reasonable space to engage in combat. Packer nodded his appreciation. Then Delaney swung his sword several times through the air, and advanced on Packer.

As Delaney closed in, Packer turned and assumed the familiar guard position. His left shoulder screamed at him as he lifted his left hand behind him for balance. The sword in his right hand felt slow and awkward. This heavy, hacking tool, this cudgel of a blade, the stiffness of his body, the searing wounds at his back, his chest, his shoulder, all conspired against him. So be it. And as Delaney approached, Packer focused only on the fight at hand; it was a gleaming, bright thing in his mind now, pure in its own way: the duel to the death.

Delaney swung at him twice; both strikes stopped quickly by Packer. Delaney's eyes grew colder, harder, recognizing the skill he faced. Packer, too, knew this would not be easy. The man hit hard, and quick. He was difficult to read, not easy to predict. He moved almost awkwardly, but with little or no signal of what his next move would be. Packer's own parries seemed horrifically slow to him. The second parry had allowed Delaney's blade to glance into Packer's hand-guard.

Delaney swung again, and then again. He was an unschooled swordsman, a self-schooled one, but very good. Packer deflected both beats and started to feel some control, even though his left shoulder was still hot with pain. He also started to gain some respect for the pirate's weapon of choice. The stronger and quicker the man, the better advantage he would have with this short, heavy blade.

Packer felt surprisingly strong at the moment, but he didn't know how much he had in him, how much endurance. Delaney was on the offensive. Slash, slash, thrust, slash; Packer deflected them all, and waited. Delaney wondered. Cut, thrust, cut, cut, thrust. Packer parried these as well. Frustration grew in Delaney's eyes. Cut, cut, slash, thrust, hack, hack. Delaney was already losing patience and technique. Packer calmly and carefully defended each blow, apparently with greater and greater ease.

Packer waited again. Then he saw the opening. He now knew how to defeat Delaney. Whenever Delaney tried a thrust, the sailor lunged too far forward, requiring a small step with his lead foot before he could recover. As he stepped, he was off-balance. All Packer needed to do was to bring his own blade across Delaney's from underneath, right to left, effectively pulling Delaney forward at the instant he was off balance, then counter back beneath the thrust. It would need to be timed well, of course, but for a fraction of a second Delaney's entire midsection would be exposed.

"Fight!" Delaney demanded. His guard was up; his eyes were wild. Packer shook his head. Delaney then lit into Packer with a furious series of blows, each of which Packer parried neatly. The second and third parry, however, Packer mistimed by a fraction of a second, and caught too close to his hand-guard for his own comfort. It was not something Delaney would likely have noticed, but it was a sign to Packer that he was nearing the end of his own stamina; he might err at any time now, and the battle would be suddenly lost. It was time to end this. At Delaney's next break, Packer would make his move.

Delaney slowed, breathing heavily. Then he stopped, clearly frustrated. During all his hacking and swinging, Packer hadn't budged, had barely moved his feet.

Packer appreciated the earnestness of his opponent, his complete lack of pretense—now in his frustration as in his previous delight. So Packer struck not with steel, but with words. His voice was quiet, his face grim, his tone a warning, but not without compassion. "Delaney. You're a good swordsman, but you know I'm better. When I begin to fight, you will die."

"Easy words," Delaney countered defiantly.

Packer needed a way to prove it to him. Then a thought occurred. "I'm guessing you've already got a scar or two on your belly from blades you've crossed."

Delaney's eyes went wide. He put a hand to his chest. "How do you know…?" but then he realized how Packer knew, and his heart sank.

Packer nodded. "You leave it exposed. I've seen the way in."

Delaney could not doubt Packer now. The younger man had not been toying with him, but studying him. Delaney swallowed hard, and glanced around the room as though looking for help, or a way out.

Packer didn't relax yet, however. Now was Delaney's moment of decision, and Packer took full advantage. "I don't want to kill you. Put down your sword, and we'll talk. Swing it again, and they'll bury you at sea today."

Delaney was trapped. If he fought, the boy would kill him. If he surrendered…He broke out in a cold sweat, unable to move.

Chapter 9

The Beast

The Firefish had smelled the blood in the water from more than a league away. It moved at full speed, snaking its body through the water like an eel, its ninety-foot length moving in serpentine fashion at almost forty knots. It came to feed. It found only a snack, the body of the Ox, and it devoured that in one bite. Its electrified teeth snapped down on the bloody corpse, sending its signature flash across the ocean.

Dawn was breaking. Talon and Monkey faced directly into the rising sun. Its first rays reflected deep orange and red in the water, obscuring the beast's brief underwater show of lightning, which was now far behind them.

The thing swallowed its morsel undetected, circled once, and easily picked up the scent again. Ox's blood had been spattered on the oar of the shallop and across the hull on Talon's side where he had gone overboard. These minuscule droplets were all but invisible, but to the Firefish, they were meat sizzling on a spit, wafting an open invitation to dine.

"Surrender or die," Packer pressed. But something in the man's eyes told Packer he wouldn't quit. "Drop the sword," Packer implored. "Live another day."

Delaney shook his head. His face softened, grew sad. Then he smiled, a gentle look that surprised Packer. "We're all born to die."

Packer saw and felt that Delaney held him in high esteem; the man who would take his life was to be respected. Packer wanted to return that respect. "Sir. There's no shame in admitting defeat when you're beaten fairly. I'll accept terms. You've got no reason to fight me to the death."

"Ah, but I do." He smiled again, content with his choice. He raised his sword. "If you're ready."

Packer swallowed hard, then lowered his own sword. He was not ready. He felt a bond, a strong bond with this man, who had fought fairly and well. "You're a good man," he told Delaney. "Why end it with bloodshed? I'll put you in the shackles."

"It must end as it must, sonny. But I thank you." The sailor lowered his sword and took on the air of a teacher. "I don't hold it against you. It's but one life you take, and I know my rest. Now, I trust you know how to end this quickly."

Packer shook his head, an involuntary motion. But Delaney was not going to waste any time about it. The sailor drew back his arm for one more thrust of his sword. He did it with gravity, but without any defensive protection, and little offense. He was not fighting any more; he was giving himself to Packer's blade. He had made his choice to die in battle.

As Delaney's blade plunged toward him, Packer knew what he had to do. He brought his blade across, from underneath, drawing the sailor forward, just as he had planned. Delaney stumbled, off balance. And then Packer hit him hard in the head, slamming his hand-guard to the man's left ear, hard enough, he hoped, that there would be no opportunity to keep fighting, and therefore no shame. Delaney crumpled to the floor.

Packer knelt beside him, tossing his own and then Delaney's sword aside. "Why not surrender?" Packer asked the groggy man irritably, not expecting a response, as he looked around for something he could use as a compress. He untied Delaney's bandana from around his neck, folded it, and put it to the man's bloody head. Delaney was semiconscious, unable to hold the bandage himself.

Packer knew little about the treatment of wounds, but he knew enough not to leave Delaney flat on his back, bleeding from the head. He managed to get the dazed man to sit up, but had to sit beside him to hold both him and the compress.

Packer tried to work out what had just happened. Delaney's situation wasn't hopeless. There were rules of engagement about these things, and Packer had offered an honorable end. Delaney wasn't rabid with rage, like Dog had been; he was an experienced fighter who in all likelihood had been taken prisoner before. Packer would have accepted almost any conditions Delaney suggested. But he wouldn't surrender, insisted on fighting to the death, though he clearly didn't want to die. It was as though he were under orders. But who could have ordered such a thing, if there was a mutiny aboard ship?

Packer pieced it together at almost the same time he heard the footsteps coming toward him. Scat Wilkins walked from behind the façade of crates, scratching his grizzled beard, a bright smile on his face. "You're a better swordsman than I have seen in some time." *Maybe as good as Talon,* he was thinking. And he liked that thought.

Packer's mind churned as he grasped the meaning of all this. The Captain had seen it all. He had been watching the whole time. That explained Delaney's actions completely. Packer stood up, keeping a hand on Delaney. "Help me get him over near the hull, if you would, sir," Packer suggested. When Scat Wilkins didn't move, Packer looked him in the eye. "Please," he added.

Scat considered the boy and his request. This wasn't begging, and it wasn't ordering. It was a simple request, and the boy seemed willing to wait for the Captain, as long as it took, for him either to help or to refuse to help. Scat smiled slightly. A smart young man. He helped Packer drag Delaney over to the side of the ship, where the two propped him up at an angle.

Delaney's bleeding had slowed considerably. "Do you have a surgeon on board?"

The Captain walked over to the lantern, picked it up, brought it near Delaney's face. "Aye," the Captain replied, pulling Packer's hand away from the sailor's head so that he could more clearly see the wound. "That was a nicely delivered blow."

Packer looked again into the eyes of the Captain. He could find nothing he wanted to say. The idea that Scat sent Delaney to fight to the death just to test Packer told him more than he needed to know. Scat had fully expected either his prisoner, with whom he had just struck a bargain, or his own sailor, an obedient man with a good sword, to die.

Scat read Packer's disapproval, smiled, stood up. He pulled a cigar from a pocket, bit off the end, spit it out, then walked to Delaney's lantern and lit it. He took several long pulls, examined the glowing tip. When he was satisfied, he said, "Not that it's any of your business, but I wouldn't have had him killed for taking the coward's way out. That was his choice."

Packer shook his head and looked at Delaney. He tied the bandanna around the sailor's head. He did not look at the Captain. "I might have killed him, and for no reason."

"No reason?" Scat laughed his low, rumbling laugh. It was disquieting. "I don't call my orders 'no reason.' He wouldn't have been the first to die for me. Wouldn't have been the last either."

Packer looked back down at Delaney. The bandage was doing its job. He picked up the two swords from the floorboards, put Delaney's at the sailor's side and turned his own sword-handle toward the Captain.

"The last time you offered me a sword, I didn't know you quite so well. Keep it," Scat said, and walked away, showing Packer his back.

"Sir!"

Scat stopped, turned back. Packer's eyes were suddenly bright and earnest. "Delaney said you've put Talon off the ship."

"So?" Scat knew exactly why the boy asked the question.

"Begging your pardon. I need to know if you've sent her back to the village...if her mission is about me."

Scat paused. "That's what you need, is it? Well, I have no corresponding need to tell you. But since you ask, I figure if she kills all the fishermen in all the villages, then I can keep my side of our bargain at little cost to me."

Packer blinked several times. Then Scat laughed softly. "Come on, son, I'm a businessman! That would be bad for business. No, she's on a different mission entirely." He put the cigar back in his mouth. Packer hesitated, their eyes locked. Packer wanted to believe him, but needed more assurance. This time it was the Captain who stood still, waiting. The boy would either have to doubt his word or accept it.

When Packer finally looked back down at Delaney, Scat spoke.

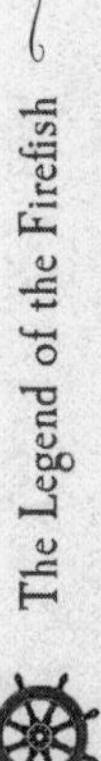

He was not displeased. The boy was smart enough not to question his Captain, but also insightful enough to doubt his word. "You can sleep well. Talon has strict orders to stick to her mission in the City of Mann," he lied. Finished with the subject, he turned away, spoke as he walked. "I'll take you to your quarters. You've earned a berth."

Even if the Captain was telling the truth, and Packer had no reason to believe him, would Talon follow Scat's orders? But there was no more to be said about it now.

"What about Delaney?"

"I'll send someone for him," the Captain lied again, already out of sight.

Packer went to Delaney, knelt beside him. The sailor was breathing gently and seemed in no danger. "You are a good man," Packer told him.

To his surprise, Delaney opened one eye. "As are you," he said in a whisper, with a ragged smile. "Better go on." Packer smiled back, clapping Delaney on the arm. As he did, he noticed again the cross tattoo. Now he could read the banner draped over it. Delaney winked and held out a hand, which Packer shook. "God bless you, for a merciful man."

Packer didn't know what to say. Delaney flicked his hand, gesturing for Packer to get moving. Packer smiled, then ran after Scat Wilkins, knowing something good had just happened, the first good thing since he had boarded this ship. He had an ally. And likely, he had more than that.

Delaney's tattooed banner read, "Brotherhood."

Panna shivered. She had not been cold at all during the night, wrapped in her winter cloak, but with the glow of sunrise breaking over her the air seemed suddenly icy, cutting through to her skin. She crawled out from under the pine tree where she had slept in the thick duff and, dragging her knapsack behind her, stood painfully. Her legs and back ached. She seemed sore from head to foot. While she wondered at so much pain, she couldn't find anything that would declare itself as an actual injury.

She looked at her hands; they were filthy. The knuckles of both her hands were dark and swollen, scraped and bruised, and covered with mud. It hurt to move her fingers. Her face was probably as dirty as her hands, she thought. She wondered vaguely how the backs of her hands got dirtier than the fronts. Perhaps rolling down the hill. Then she noticed that the dirt had a reddish tint.

A horror emptied her like the bottom dropping out of a bucket. It was not dirt that colored the backs of her hands. It was blood. She looked at her knuckles more closely. This was not her blood. It was the blood of the fisherman. Fear rose up from within her, and she trembled. What had she done? How badly had she hurt him?

The specifics came back to her in stark, terrible, relentless detail. Gouging at his eyes. Her fist to his nose. The cracking sound. She shuddered. The old man falling backward to the ground. The sick, pained gasp when he landed on his back. The fists to his face, over and over. The whimpers, the crying out. The wetness of his face, his body going limp. Now a remorse far greater than the previous night's fear threatened to overwhelm her. What if she had maimed him permanently? What if she had…

What had she done? How could she have done it? She was but a young woman, a girl, and he was a grown man, a fisherman. In her mind, that made her weak and him strong, a child fighting an adult. She had believed she needed every ounce of her strength, everything she had, just to stop him, just to fool him into believing she was a man. But now she realized she had been completely deceived. She was the stronger one, probably by far. He had fought back with all the fury of a feather pillow.

She held up her swollen hand in the light and turned it slowly around, seeing something totally foreign now, something she had never seen there before. Her hand was a weapon. She hid it beneath her cloak and looked around, fearful that someone was watching. She wanted to cut it off, throw it away, bury it.

Then she had a vision of herself. She was a figure wrapped in a dark cloak, hiding in the woods from villagers. She was the dangerous rogue. She had brutally attacked one of their own. Without provocation. Her face went white.

This cloaked figure in Panna's vision was an outlaw.

Panna knelt on the ground, crumpling with the weight of these thoughts. She had rejected a return to the village, but up until this moment it had been her choice. Now any return to the village would be followed by arrest, and disgrace. It would take her a while, she knew, to adjust to this. But she would adjust. This was not something she had foreseen. It was not the step of faith she had envisioned. But neither was it going to stop her. Just the opposite, she now knew she had to keep going. Now she had to find Packer. Now there were no other options.

The huge Firefish circled, its long, lithe, serpentine body squaring off each turn with a lightning-fast darting movement. Still stalking, still ravenous, it surfaced behind the shellfish, to avoid detection.

When the beast's head broke through the water, Monkey was in a dream state, very near the point of collapse. Talon was weary and angry, less vigilant than usual. She had spotted land off the port bow, and knew it to be a sparsely populated island less than a league from the shoreline, not far from Hangman's Cliffs. They had made good time. She was not interested in stopping, and she hoped to row past it without Monkey ever seeing it. She only needed three more miles out of him, and didn't want him whimpering about the need to rest.

He would never reach shore, of course. He was far too much a liability now, too much a blithering imbecile, too likely to say anything to anybody. She cursed silently. Monkey had been an ally, and a loyal crewman as far as his feeble capabilities let him. Doubtless, he was completely incapable of attacking her. But that didn't matter now. He would meet the same fate as Ox.

And Ox! Ox had proven to be a murderous traitor. She had known how much he feared and hated her, of course, but she had been unprepared to believe his fear could so easily have been overcome by his hatred. What could have moved him to such a suicidal plan? Likely it was the simple fact that she had been sent back to shore; likely he believed the Captain was displeased with her over the stowaway. *The stowaway.* This was Packer Throme's doing. Of course it was. Well then, Ox was the first death payment in her revenge on Packer Throme, the first body left along her bloody pathway back to the source of the poison, Senslar Zendoda. Monkey would be the second.

In Monkey's dream state, Talon had her knife out, and was calling his bunkmates on the *Trophy Chase* into her stateroom, one by one, behind a wooden door marked with gashes and blood. None of them put up a fight, all went obediently. None came back out. She returned each time with her knife bloodied and called the next one in. Ox would protect him. Ox had crushed the skull of the man who had battered his face, who had left him with his permanent wink and his miserable half grin. Ox, Monkey's protector, went last, but he was just as docile, and went just as easily. And then she came out from behind the door, her knife held downward, dripping blood from its tip. She beckoned to Monkey.

Tears rose in his eyes as he looked into hers. He had not been a good man, or even a brave one. She would kill him. She would have no pity. He deserved none. But she just looked at him and waited. Who could save him? Krendall Room didn't mean to be so bad as to deserve this. He just wanted to belong, to fit in. That's all he had ever wanted. He had mocked church, and family, and God. But he didn't really hate anyone. He just wanted to live another day. Who would help him now? Who would show him mercy?

There would be no mercy here, her eyes told him. Talon's eyes told him: Now is the time to go quietly, to follow his friends, to follow his choices where they all led. Those eyes! They were cold and cruel. They were yellow, wet, and unblinking. They were oddly yellow, and growing brighter. Almost like a…He cocked his head to one side, confused.

The Firefish was perhaps twenty yards from the boat, looking directly at Monkey, and Monkey was looking directly into its eyes. Talon would have seen the thing too, but she had glanced over at Monkey at just that moment. He was still rowing, but she saw the strange, quizzical expression on his face. She looked out over the ocean. She squinted against the rising sun. But she saw nothing. The Firefish was gone.

To the beast the twin mounds protruding from the top of the boat were certainly the shellfish's eyes. And one of those eyes was focused on him. So the Firefish had quickly slipped back under the water.

Talon looked back at Monkey. His mouth moved, but no sounds came out. She decided she had better give him some bread, and so she told him to quit rowing, picked up the duffel by her feet, and rummaged for the hardtack. Before she could pull it out, the beast broke through the water again, this time much, much closer.

It had watched from below for a moment, its long, snakelike body writhing to and fro as it held its place. It had seen the shellfish quit paddling its little fins. The shellfish wasn't running. No protective measures were being taken. It had seen its predator, and frozen. This could only mean the creature trusted its shell for protection and had no ability to defend itself otherwise. If it trusted its shell against even so great a threat, then that was all the more reason not to be hasty. After a few more seconds the beast rose again, closer now, to discover how it might consume the meaty part without crunching through the shell.

Talon saw it rise not five yards from her. She couldn't have missed it this time. Although in silhouette with the sun behind it, it was now light enough that Talon could make out its features.

The beast's head was a mountain, bald, irregular, and misshapen. It glistened with small, dark scales overlapping in no discernable pattern. Its enormous mouth, reaching across the entire base of its head, the rough triangle visible above the water, was like that of a deepwater devilfish, a sullen horseshoe frown set in a permanent grimace enhanced by a dramatically jutting jaw, with ragged, razor-sharp white teeth poking up like an array of knives. It struck Talon that, should it open its mouth, the effect would be like a huge sluicegate opened near her. Her boat would simply float in and down its gullet.

But she was most taken by its eyes. Bulbous and yellow, lidless and watery, positioned about halfway up and on either side of the triangle of its head, these eyes darted quickly, alertly, between her and Monkey. They were unlike those of any animal Talon had ever seen. While a shark's eyes were dull and distant, terrifying in their murky inscrutability, and a dolphin's were sharp and focused, disarming and accessible, the Firefish had eyes that were sharp, focused, and inscrutable all at once. This was an intelligent killer. As Talon watched, she was convinced she saw a smile behind its hunger, within its eyes. This thing delighted in the hunt. It loved the kill.

Talon shook herself, cursing her own lack of attentiveness. Dazed though he was, Monkey had seen this monster and could have warned her, could have given her the few extra seconds that might have saved them. She knew that unlike a shark, a Firefish could attack from a stationary position. Sharks needed to work up a head of steam, but the Firefish had a skeletal framework like a snake's, and could strike like one. This one she estimated to be at least eighty feet long. It seemed still, but she knew its body, every bit as wide as its head, was undulating through the water. It was ready, and could lunge forward ten, fifteen, perhaps even twenty feet in an instant. These beasts were quick, too, much quicker than sharks, with the lightning reflexes of a school of silverfish. Usually they snapped their prey, but she had seen one unhinge its jaw in order to engulf an entire longboat, like a python eating a pig.

She had no time. She looked down at the duffel in her hands. It contained her only hope of survival, the lure she had packed there, the Toymaker's brass box. But it would take her several seconds, perhaps half a minute, to retrieve it and set the fuse. Now she cursed out loud. Why had she not anticipated this? She looked back at the Firefish. The beast's dark, scaly skin was now glowing yellow, building the electrical charge that would in a moment flash across the sea. She looked at Monkey. He stared, mesmerized, unmoving. She needed time.

He would provide it.

With both hands, she grabbed Monkey's shirt at the collar, behind his neck, thrust her hip into him, and slung him over the stern, throwing him as far as her strength would allow, toward the beast. Almost before Monkey hit the water, she was pouring the contents of the duffel onto the boat's floor. She needed that lure.

The Firefish did not hesitate to accept the morsel as offered. The thing was surprised to see one of the shellfish's eye mounds drop into the water, but neither memory nor instinct allowed delay. The tasty morsel was eaten.

Talon fell to her knees on the floor of the boat, the large brass box, her only hope, now firmly in her hands. But she didn't have a chance to ignite the fuse. She did not hear the crack of the beast's electrified teeth as they snapped down on Monkey, hundreds of twelve- to twenty-four-inch knives backed by rocklike jaws, puncturing, crushing, and shredding him instantly, even as a thousand volts anesthetized him.

She did not feel the rush of water generated by the beast's lunge forward. She never felt the water as it spilled over the stern and propelled the boat forward. She was unconscious, anesthetized herself by the beast's power, as it prepared her to be its next bite with several hundred volts that discharged through the water toward her.

Having swallowed one meaty morsel, one eye mound of the shellfish, and feeling successful in its efforts, the Firefish rose again, hoping for more. It was disappointed to find that the shellfish had moved twenty yards away and that the other eye mound had disappeared. The beast immediately retracted its head and looked around underwater, thinking that perhaps both eyes had fallen into the sea and it had eaten only one.

Talon regained consciousness lying against the transom at the stern of the shallop, cold water sloshing around her. The lure had been pushed back under the wooden seat. Her joints ached with the residual effects of the electric shock, and her brain seemed to be buzzing. She cursed these symptoms, then ignored them. She had the lure back in her hands and was kneeling over it again almost instantly. The side of it was dented. She knew that this lure had been placed on a stack of lures to be reconditioned. She knew there was a chance it wouldn't work. She opened the small brass door beside the large ring at its top; the wax seal was already broken. Inside was the fuse. She poured water from the opening. There, next to the fuse, a flint wheel was mounted. She turned it quickly with her thumb. A spark jumped, but the fuse did not catch.

She felt the boat shift in the water, and heard the beast's head break through the surface again. She pinched the fuse, squeezing seawater from it. She turned the flint wheel again. A spark jumped again, but the fuse did not light. It was a futile effort. A shadow fell over her. She turned the wheel with her thumb a third time. The fuse would not ignite. She cursed out loud. Water dripped down around her, on her back, down the back of her neck. She looked behind her, and then up. The Firefish looked down on her, its huge head looming over her, the water dripping off its protruding teeth, its smiling eyes fifteen feet above the stern of the boat. It was craning its neck down on her, pleased to find the other eye mound.

This time Talon was not just impressed, she was stunned. The beast was probing, hungry, seeking, brooding, ready, and studying her intently. It was absolutely pure of purpose. It wanted to kill, to kill now, and to devour its prey. But it approached its quarry with skill and craftiness in order to defeat it, and with utter disregard for it otherwise.

What stopped her, what prevented her from setting the lure, what kept her from the one act that could save her life, was that these were the traits she respected above all others. This giant, meticulous killer had absolutely no capacity for remorse, or fear, or pity, or self-doubt. It didn't care whether its victims fought back or not. It was calm, almost joyous about its business. Perfect in design. She was astonished to see her own ambition achieved so perfectly. So triumphantly. On such a magnificent scale. She felt she was looking into the eyes of a superior being.

The beast had needed to raise its head quite high to find this eye mound, which had apparently been retracted into the shell. But there it was. The Firefish waited, giving this morsel a chance to drop into the water as the other had. But that did not seem to be happening. The remaining eye mound watched, but the shellfish again took no defensive action. It was frozen again; a desperate and silly attempt on the part of prey to avoid detection even when cornered. But there was something missing. All these behaviors were expected. An uneasiness grew. The beast sensed no fear. There was a calm presence, not threatening, with intelligence all out of proportion for a fleeing shellfish. Its instinct was to attack, now.

Talon saw the yellow glow begin, growing out from the eyes. The Firefish's jaw unhinged, dropping, stretching the scaly skin so that it seemed to be melting downward, pulling on the eyes and making them droop. The rows of teeth framed a gaping jaw so huge she could have stepped into it standing up. It would kill her within seconds.

The thought jolted her. She looked down at the lure and was surprised to find she was still kneeling over it, surprised further to see that her thumb was still on the flint wheel. She turned it, a spark jumped, and the fuse ignited. She grabbed the ring and with all her strength threw the lure up, deep into the beast's throat.

Immediately, the jaws clamped shut, and the Firefish submerged. Again, the electric shock knocked her to the floor of the boat, unconscious.

Something deep within the dark predator's brain told it that it had made a grave mistake. Another morsel had been offered, but this one had no substance whatever. It had eaten not what it wanted, but what the shellfish offered. And it was not meat. The intelligence of the shellfish, the lack of fear...the beast's instincts now buzzed danger, triggering rage; and with that came the demand for retaliation.

The Firefish dove deep. The shellfish must be destroyed. At two hundred feet, it turned and swam straight up at the shellfish as fast as it could, its body writhing and undulating in a frantic attack. Its eyes were ablaze, its scaly skin glowing bright yellow. This time, shell or no shell, the creature would be consumed—utterly, wholly, immediately.

Talon lay in the frigid, sloshing water at the stern of the boat, this time on her back. She blinked twice, looking up at a red morning sky. *Storm coming,* she thought. For a moment, she didn't remember where she was. Then she felt an odd turbulence below her, a deep rumbling. It was at that moment, as she remembered what had happened, and realized what was about to happen, that the Firefish hit the boat. This time, her quick reflexes would not be enough to save her.

But something—her quickness, or her intelligence, or her lack of fear, or perhaps her intimate knowledge of death and the kill—something had already saved her. She had bought herself enough time; she had lit the fuse in time, and tossed the brass lure into the beast's maw in time. And true to Lund Lander's calibrations, the fuse had burned down in time. As the Firefish struck the boat from below, its huge jaws wide, its swordlike teeth visible to Talon on either side of the hull, the explosive detonated. The beast's gullet burst, blowing out its jaws, incapacitating its electrical organs, shattering its brain.

The blast killed it instantly, but the speed of its carcass, carrying tons of hurtling flesh, was not significantly diminished. The remains smashed into the boat from below. Talon—her back still flat against the wooden flooring, with pieces of boat, oars, teeth, skull, and flesh flying around her—rose twenty feet in the air. The long, sleek body of the Firefish pushed up from below like a pylon, like a spear driven from beneath the sea, before all crashed again into the water.

Talon was barely conscious as she surfaced, gasping for air. Involuntarily she pushed away huge chunks of white meat and gray brain matter and grabbed the largest piece of wood she could find. She knew she should start swimming for shore, for the nearby island Monkey had never seen, and never would see. But she couldn't make her body respond.

Around her floated the grail of Captain Scat Wilkins' quest, the hope of Packer Throme for the fishing villages: thousands of coins' worth of Firefish meat. But the meat, like the quest of the Captain and the hope of Packer Throme, disgusted Talon. It occurred to her that its legendary strength-giving capacity might be of some help, but she was repulsed by the thought of eating it. She was dazed, her whole body throbbing from the explosion. She couldn't seem to focus and was afraid she had suffered a blow to the head. She kept bobbing under the cold water as she held onto her small piece of wooden planking. It took great effort for her to return each time to the sunlight. She knew she had little energy left. Panicked, she opened her eyes and saw a larger piece of the shallop, with part of the seat still attached. She swam toward it, seeing it now as a lifeline. She had to reach it, to pull it under her, to climb onto it.

Panna walked toward the sea, hopeful that just the sight of it, the sound of it, could soothe the troubled thoughts that flowed through her mind. Out there, somewhere, was Packer. She needed him; she needed to be with him. He would understand, if she could just hold him again, if they could just be together.

It would never be like it was, like it could have been. He now served on a pirate's ship, and she was a fugitive. They were both outlaws now. But if they could hold one another, none of that would matter. She caught a glimpse of the sea through the trees, shimmering red with the morning sun, and it gladdened her heart, lightening her burden.

She did not know that at that moment, someone was struggling to get ashore, on a mission to find her. And it was not Packer Throme.

Chapter 10

Brotherhood

Packer awoke to the sounds of voices and footsteps nearby. He kept his eyes closed. He heard the creak of the ship, and recalled that he was aboard the *Trophy Chase.* Slowly, his multiple failures settled into his chest like a dull pain, and into his stomach like a sickness. All the trouble behind him, and all the trouble yet to come...all his fault. Transfixing it, holding it all together, like steel claws piercing through every layer of the fabric of his life and deep into his flesh, was Talon in flight, headed to shore.

Packer listened to the creaking of the ship. It occurred to him that he felt no movement, no rocking. Were they at port? His heart beat quicker. He opened his eyes and saw the polished ceiling planks of the small stateroom moving slowly above him in the dim light, left to right, then back again, right to left. They were not at port. He was in a hammock. His moment of hope faded again, and went darker yet.

He closed his eyes, wanting to return to the oblivion of sleep. But what came to him was the face of Talon, swearing vengeance on all he held dear. And then he saw the face of Panna; saw fear in her eyes as she watched Talon approach with that long knife drawn. His heart cried out, pierced as surely as if it were skewered by Talon's blade.

He wept before God, as a child weeps to his mother.

Will Seline had given up conversing with the crowd of well-meaning visitors packed into his living room. He was their pastor, and they were his flock, but he couldn't speak with them. He was sick at heart, and their consolations only made him feel worse. Too much conjecture, too many guesses. He left them talking, chattering to themselves, gathered like sheep huddled together for safety, and climbed the stairs to his room.

He locked the door behind him and sat on the bed, his heart raw and aching, his mind clouded and thick. Panna was gone. Gone into a cloud of unknowns, with no warning, no note, no explanation. Gone on a night when some violent brigand was known to be loose, someone who had beaten a simple fisherman senseless. Almost anything was possible, of course, but he was sure Packer was involved somehow, that only her love for him could have pulled her away like this.

He thought of his wife, Tamma, of her illness, of losing her so slowly over those months that stretched into years. He had thought anything would be preferable to that long agony, but now he was not sure. What if he never knew? What if Panna was just gone, forever?

He put his head in his hands. Almost involuntarily, he slumped to the floor, turned toward the bed, and buried his face in the quilt. He would pray. He could go looking for her, but he would not. He would stay here, locked in his room, with God and God alone. There was nothing he could do that God could not. No human on earth could find her, keep her safe, bring her home, if God did not will it. No human on earth could kill her, or hurt her, if God did not allow it. And no human, Panna herself included, could keep her from walking back through his own front door if God wanted her to walk in that door. No, God held all the keys, as He always did. Will would spend his time where it mattered, dealing with the One who could, and would, determine Panna's fate.

Will would stay on his knees, on his face, for as long as he needed to, forever if necessary, and cry out to God. He would plead. He would beg. He would listen. He would read Scripture. He would offer up all he had in this world and the next. He would do all these things, and whatever else came to his heart. He would prepare himself to die, he would offer Panna up in his heart, a sacrifice like the

one Abraham made with Isaac. He would offer himself to God in Panna's place. But he would leave it all to God, and do nothing else, unless God told him, in a Voice that could not be questioned, that there was something else he must do.

Suddenly there was a knock on the door that jarred Packer from his dark laments. "Yes?" Packer wiped his eyes quickly. He knew he sounded as startled as he felt.

"We've come to see you!" the voice said. It was a familiar voice, a welcome sound.

"Come in." Packer dabbed his eyes with his sleeve. Delaney entered, followed by a young man Packer did not recognize. Packer tried to sit up, and winced. He had moved well enough last night, but now he was stiff and aching.

"What, sleepin' till noon?" Delaney feigned disapproval, and then the familiar grin appeared. "You'd think you were the one who got himself cold-cocked." He jabbed an elbow into his companion's side. "Look at him, like he needs to rest up, when it was him who sliced me to ribbons and then flattened me with a single blow, like I was no more'n a fly buzzing around his head!"

Delaney's companion—a boy, tall and slim, not a day over sixteen—laughed, but his eyes blazed with amazement, as though in the presence of some legendary hero. His hair was wild and thick like the top of a sheaf of wheat, and the color of amber ale. His face was freckled, sunburned and peeling, his clothing almost white. He was new to the ship, Packer guessed correctly, perhaps new to any ship. He carried in his bony hands a covered pot about the size of a loaf of bread.

"We brought you food," the boy said, holding the pot out. Packer had already caught the aroma. It smelled wonderfully like beef. Now Packer sat up, this time simply ignoring the pain, and threw his legs over the side of the hammock, losing his balance and almost falling. Delaney's hard hands caught him, then helped him to the floor. Blood had seeped through the bandages on Packer's chest and back and colored the hammock.

Delaney spoke gently, looking at the blood. "I kidded you, but forgot you were keelhauled. Not to mention tortured. All the more amazing what you did to me." He nodded at the boy again.

Packer liked the teasing better than the apology. "I'm fine. How's your head?"

Delaney grinned again and pointed to the red, swollen cut above his left ear. "No worse than last you saw it. Throbs a bit, but I've been hit harder."

"We brought you this," the boy said, again holding out his offering proudly.

"Sit, let's feed you," Delaney commanded, maneuvering Packer to a wooden bench built back into the wall. Packer sat and accepted the pot. It was warm. He put it in his lap. He took off the lid, and the sweet steaming aroma of beef stew rose up to greet him. His mouth watered as the extent of his own hunger hit him. He didn't know how to ask whether they had brought a spoon. He thought about raising the dish to his mouth and gulping it down, and would have if it hadn't looked so thick. He didn't want to waste a single bite by sending it down his shirtfront.

"It's not Firefish, this time," Delaney told him. "But it'll still help."

"This time?"

Delaney grinned. "What do you think I fed you last night? Crab cakes? Nothing puts fight back in a man like Fireflesh."

Packer absorbed that thought. Packer had felt better almost immediately after eating the morsel. So at least that part of the legend was true. He had now eaten Firefish.

"This here's Marcus Pile," Delaney offered up into the silence. "New hand, but shows promise. He's apprenticed to Cane Dewar, the ship's carpenter."

"I'm sorry about my manners, I'm Packer Throme," he said to the boy, holding out a hand.

The boy shook it happily. "It's my first real voyage. But I know a good bit about boatbuilding and carpentry already."

Packer nodded. "Well, I'm glad to hear it."

"Packer." Delaney repeated it to Marcus. "Told you he had a name; I just didn't know what it was." He looked back at Packer, satisfied, then put a thumb to his chest. "I'm Delaney."

"I remember," Packer told him. Delaney kept smiling, and so Packer put out his hand to Delaney as well. "Good to see you again." Delaney shook it vigorously.

"Why...why did you bring this?" It was all Packer could think to ask.

Delaney's smile vanished. "You don't want it?"

Packer laughed at the absurdity. "It may be the best gift I've ever been given." This restored Delaney's smile. "Captain Wilkins confined me to quarters, so I thought I wasn't supposed to have visitors."

Delaney nodded, then spoke in a confidential whisper, "Some rules was just made to be broke."

Packer looked down into the stew again, took a deep breath in through his nose, savoring it. "Thank you."

Delaney suddenly looked troubled. "Marcus, did you bring that spoon? How's he supposed to eat it?"

Marcus blinked, then started patting himself. He found the wooden spoon stuck in his belt. Packer no sooner had the spoon in his hand than it was in the pot, and in his mouth. It tasted every bit as good as it smelled. "Wonderful," Packer told them through a full mouth. Then he caught himself. "Want some?"

"No no, we've eaten. That's all for you."

Packer took two more bites as his benefactors watched with satisfaction. Then Packer's manners returned once more. "Will you sit, at least?"

"Why, thank you," Delaney said, and flopped onto the floor at Packer's feet. Marcus followed suit. They both sat, looking up at Packer and grinning.

As Packer began to eat again, there was another knock at the door. Marcus reacted with something akin to panic, but Delaney just stood, put a finger to his lips, and opened the door a crack. "What is it?"

"Excuse me," a tremulous voice said from the other side, "but the Captain gave strict orders. You must leave!"

"Must I?" Delaney asked, sounding baffled. "Or what will happen?"

"Well, the Captain will be notified," the voice said, shrill and parsimonious. The nasal tone was that of the Captain's steward, Deeter Pimm.

"Well, you just go on and notify the Captain," Delaney told him. "And you know what will happen then, Mr. Pimm?" There was silence. Delaney stuck his head far out the door, and spoke in an urgent voice not much above a whisper. "Here's what will happen. I will be flogged for bringing this poor prisoner some soup."

"You will have earned it!"

"No denying that, Mr. Pimm. At least twelve, no more than two dozen lashes, I'd guess. And you know where you'll be, Mr. Pimm, while Jonas Deal is raking my back with his cat-o-'nine-tails, and chunks of flesh are flyin' off a' me, and my blood is flowing in rivers onto the deck?" There was silence. "You'll be standing right by my side, a' course. As my accuser, that'll be your rightful place according to the laws of this ship. I will have earned it, yes sir, very true. And I won't think less of you for it. And there you'll be, standing so close that your shoes will be stained red, and your shirt spotted with little red dots. But I won't blame you. You're an honest man, taking an honest man's path. I'll respect that."

"Heavens," was all Packer heard. Marcus Pile grinned at Packer.

"So you do what you must," Delaney continued. Then he said, more gently, "Now, if perchance you don't tell the Captain, here's what happens. Absolutely nothin'. I wait till the boy finishes his bowl, take the empty, and go my way."

There was another long pause. "Well," Pimm said finally, with a sniff. "If I come back by here in thirty minutes and you're not here…Well, I'm not at all sure I could even remember this conversation. My mind isn't what it used to be."

"Ah, but your heart is good as it ever was," Delaney said, with genuine warmth. "Good morning to you."

"Hmmph." Pimm padded off.

Delaney pulled his head back into the cabin with an impish sparkle in his eye, and closed the door, bolting it this time. "Now, where were we?"

"Is that true?" Packer asked. "Would you be flogged?"

"Hard sayin'. Few lashes maybe. But I've had that before." Marcus looked worried again.

"You should go then. Why risk it?" Packer felt humbled and self-conscious.

Delaney looked shocked. "Why risk it? Mr. Packer, sir, if it weren't for you, I'd be dead! You saved my life!"

Packer was confused. "How did I do that?"

"Why, by hitting me on the head rather than killing me. That's a debt worth a few stripes, I'd say."

"But wait…if it weren't for me, you would never have…" Packer trailed off. The two stared at him, waiting. "I mean, if it weren't for me there would have been no duel between us to begin with."

Delaney frowned, as though Packer spoke nonsense. "But there was a duel. And you bein' what you are with a sword in your hand, I should by all rights be dead, except for who you are in here," he tapped his chest with his forefinger, "which is what saved me. And asides that, Captain sent me to kill or die, and I didn't do neither one, and yet Captain is perfectly pleased. That, sonny, is a miracle. No, I owe you. I truly do."

Packer smiled warmly. Delaney was wrong, of course, but he spoke with such certainty it was impossible to even want to debate him.

"May I ask you something?" Marcus addressed Packer hesitantly.

"Sure."

"Are you a Christian?"

"I am." Packer nodded, and kept eating.

"Told you he was," Delaney nodded. Packer looked at him quizzically. "I saw you eyeing my cross here," Delaney said by way of explanation, pointing to his upper arm. "Saw the light in your eyes. Sure did."

Marcus smiled at Delaney, happy and relieved. "So then," the boy asked Packer, "what happened after you died? I mean when you were keelhauled. Did you see Jesus?"

Packer coughed. He looked at Marcus carefully. "I don't really remember."

Marcus looked disappointed. "Anything?"

Packer realized this was very important to the young man. He thought. "Well, there was a lot of white light. I remember rising up through the water toward the light. I think there was more, but that's all I can recall."

Marcus nodded, seeming satisfied. "The boys say you went to the Dead Lands. I just wondered what you saw."

Delaney lowered his eyes. "Some of 'em say that. Not all."

"What are the Dead Lands?" Packer asked. There was talk aboard ship, then. Of course there was; he would be the biggest news of the voyage. He hadn't really thought about what they might be saying, but if he were to join them, it would matter greatly.

"It's what the Drammune believe. Another world much like this, but on the other side. Those who know how can pass back and forth. They think Talon knows how. After all, it was Talon who brought your spirit back, they say."

Packer took a deep breath. He set the pot down on the seat

beside him. "I don't know what happened. But I seriously doubt it was any of that."

"You still believe," Marcus asked in a tone that implied agreement, "you still believe in Jesus?"

"Yes, of course," Packer said gently.

"Then we're with you, no matter what." Marcus was determined, forthright. "It don't matter what they say about you. God's been with you. You can count on us to stick by you."

Packer was grateful, but his heart was pained. He didn't want them to have any trouble on his account. Then Delaney spoke, in a tone of gravity to which he was clearly unaccustomed. "I have been a believer only just a couple of years. I have nothing for me on this earth no more. Never did have too much to begin with. But it doesn't matter what they do to me. I'm with you, as you're with God."

"You shouldn't suffer on account of me," Packer told them both. "It doesn't matter what happens to me. I've earned it. I just don't want anyone else to be hurt on my account."

Delaney looked surprised. "Anyone else? Who's hurt? Not me." He touched his skull above his ear. "This didn't hurt me, it saved me."

Packer sat back. Delaney had an odd sort of faith, unsoiled somehow by his blind obedience to the scurrilous commands of a pirate captain. But even so, if these two knew who he was, what he'd done, surely they would not hold him in such high esteem. So he determined to tell them everything, in short order. And he did, starting with how he'd chosen Panna over God when fighting Delaney, then going back to how he'd completely caved in under Talon's torture and betrayed first God, then Panna, Cap, Senslar Zendoda, and who knows who else to their certain deaths, then continuing backward until they knew how he'd struck the priest, Father Usher Fell, and ending with the final danger to which he was subjecting them all: how he'd given the Captain the coordinates to find the feeding waters, in the Achawuk territory.

He unburdened his soul, making sure they understood his poor motives, his weakness, his bad judgment, his pride, all his stupidity. He held nothing back. Delaney and Marcus sat motionless, listening intently. Their faces were blank, then shocked, then deeply troubled. Then their demeanors diverged, Marcus remaining troubled, Delaney growing irritated. Packer pressed on. After ten minutes or so, he sat back and nodded at them. "So please. Don't add to the long

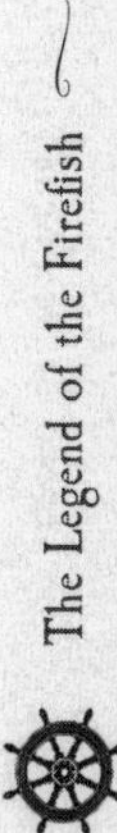

list of injuries I've inflicted by getting yourselves in trouble over me."

Then Packer and Marcus both looked over to Delaney, who seemed to be biting his tongue. "Well, say what's on your heart," Packer suggested.

Delaney took a deep breath. "I will, then. Now, I'm a blunt man, without much practice softening a blow."

"Please do not soften any blows," Packer said earnestly.

"All right, then. Here's what I see. I see a young man stowed away aboard the ship of the most famous pirate on earth, which it takes great guts or no brains to do, which this young man has brains. I see him survive a keelhauling, which thing I've never seen before, particularly if you consider he died or at least sure seemed to die, and then came back, with some help from a devil maybe involved, but I don't know nothin' about that. Anyways, he's alive to the amazement of all. He's hurt several ways, but not bad enough for the witch, who tortures him some more for good measure. He survives that too, which many a man has managed not to do. Not only he survives it, he does so while setting the Captain against the witch, which ends up the Captain gives her the boot! So this young man's now done the whole ship a service.

"Then, beat and bruised, he still manages to whip the second-best swordsman aboard, after Talon the witch, without hardly even trying, which is not a easy thing by no means. Not only that, he wins the confidence of the Captain while doing it and saves the life of that same swordsman, who is me. So…he's got the witch gone, the Captain all busting with excitement about finding Firefish, and the whole ship buzzing about being freed of the witch and wondering what miracles might happen next and are they from God or the devil. And all this in two days time."

Packer sighed. Those were all the externals, and none of that addressed the darkness in his heart. But Delaney wasn't through.

"Now, some way it happens that person can't see God is plainly working through him. And why? Cause he's got too much Woe is me, I'm no good, I should be dead, which is because of sins everyone who's ever lived has done, and which sins are all forgiven anyway, him being a Christian! So seems to me, beggin' your pardon for being blunt, that person, who is you, should quit thinking about the bad in himself so much and start trustin' God who done all those miracles I just mentioned, and quit thinkin' God will just flat stop, and therefore let everyone die a horrible death. If God is good, which He is, He won't let these horrible things happen. And if He does let them happen, what are you going to do about it anyway? He's got His own plan and you can't stop it."

It was not the assessment Packer had expected. But it was cold water to a dry soul. "Thank you," was all he could say.

"You're welcome," Delaney said with finality.

After a moment's pause, Marcus suggested cheerfully, "So let's pray then." And they all bowed their heads.

"Our Father in heaven," Marcus began, his voice betraying a slight tremor. "Our brother Packer here has been sent on this ship by Thee. We don't know what Thou art doing, as we hardly ever do know. But we know that all trials are from Thy hand, because Thou hast said so in the Book, and told us we are to take joy in such hard times because they're for a reason even if we don't know it. Which we hardly ever do.

"Forgive Packer our brother for his sins, and his faults, as he has confessed them here fully without hiding away or holding 'em back as far as I can tell, as true a Christian thing as I ever heard a soul do, and let him take joy in the pains Thou hast brought his way, rough though they have been for him to take, particularly in his shoulder. And protect his girl Panna and his friend the barkeeper, and all the others he loves, from the hand of Talon the evil witch, who hates about everyone as far as I can tell, and while you're at it please see if you can work your way into her heart some, though it's hard for me to figure how Thou might do that one. But Thou art God and we art not. And please God, by Thy grace, let Packer take joy in knowing that you art working in him, or, rather I mean to say, that *Thou* art working in him, and through him do Thy work. And let Delaney and me here do anything to help our good brother that we can do, at the cost even of our own lives, or of our own suffering, for we three are most certainly brothers, maybe the only ones on this ship, and we hope and pray he will do the same for us, which we know he will, push comes to punch, 'cause he already saved Delaney. We pray in the name of Thy Son our Savior, Jesus our Lord."

Delaney added a hearty, "Amen!" And then grinned through teary eyes at Packer. "He's a real good prayer, ain't he?"

Chapter 11

The Criminal

Panna looked out over the ocean and felt a great longing to be there, somewhere in the middle of that sea, where Packer was. But she was not there, she was here, and so she took off her shoes and socks, rolled up Mr. Molander's pant legs, and waded into the surf. She had climbed down to this small beach from the hill above. At this spot the cliffs had just begun to rise from the shoreline. They grew tall not a quarter of a mile north, where the beach dwindled to rocks and the cliffs sprang up twenty, then thirty, then fifty feet. She squatted down and began scrubbing her hands. Painful though it was, it was good to be getting them clean.

What amazed her, now that she had some time to think about it, was not that the events of the night had happened the way they had. Panna understood them better, understood herself better now. Her sheltered existence had deceived her about her own strength, her ability to defend herself, and that was that. The rest was predictable enough, given that simple miscalculation.

What amazed her most was the quickness with which it had all changed. Yesterday morning she'd awakened to a day exactly like a thousand days before. She'd washed, scrubbed, cooked, cleaned, and longed to be doing all those things for Packer Throme and their children, rather than for her father. She was a part of the village, loved and accepted, pitied by some, perhaps, but that was the warp to go along with the woof. One day later, she awakes a criminal, hiding in the woods from the same villagers.

She still felt concern for the fisherman she'd hurt, but not remorse. He was among those who had deceived her, keeping her sheltered from the society of men, convincing her she was helpless and small. He simply drew the short straw, and felt her fury when she learned otherwise. It was wrong to have let her, and thousands of other young women just like her, believe they had no power, no strength, and therefore could have no place or position. Now that she had found out she was strong, she was an outlaw. That couldn't be right. There must be a way for women to be strong within the law, and it was worth finding. If only she had been able to learn about her strength some other way.

Her father would be missing her by now, and within a few hours he would have spoken to Hen Hillis, and perhaps Mrs. Molander. He would likely not join the search parties. He would stay home and pray. That was like him. And she took comfort from the thought that he would plead with God for her safety.

Panna's raw and swollen knuckles stung, but they were at last clean. She glanced up and down the beach again, to be certain she was alone. Then she leaned over and splashed water onto her face, scrubbing that, too.

Here was the true source of her amazement: She wasn't going back. Somehow, in the span of a day, she had become far more the dark-cloaked criminal than the pining maiden. Maybe she always had been, and this is what it took to bring it out.

She finished scrubbing up and trudged back toward the woods. She stayed just in sight of the sea, just inside the woods, as she walked south toward Inbenigh. Once she reached the village, she would find a spot far enough up the beach to be safe, and there she would wait for nightfall. Then she would get a boat, steal it if she had to, and set out after Packer Throme. She didn't know how to sail, but she now firmly believed that if all these frail old fishermen could do it, certainly she could figure it out.

Henrietta Hillis beckoned him to lean down. She was stretching up on tiptoes to get within an arm's reach of his shoulder. She looked frightened. "I talked to her last night," she whispered.

Dog looked around him. No one else was paying them any attention. "What time last night?"

"Long about midnight, I suppose," she answered, and covered her mouth. She felt guilty about saying it, guilty about having done it.

Dog turned to face her, put his hands on her shoulders, and leaned down. He spoke gently but urgently. "Go into the kitchen and wait for me. Don't say anything to anyone else."

She nodded.

The crowd in Pastor Seline's parlor and dining room was still buzzing, growing in size and number, at mid-morning. They had a lot to talk about. Not only had Panna disappeared, but word had now come that the battered man was Riley Odoms, a fisherman from Red Point. Pirates and Packer Throme were the leading suspects in both cases, but Dog had been doing his best to make sure everyone understood who the better candidate was. Packer had clearly become unbalanced and dangerous, he told anyone who would listen. Many witnesses had seen how violent and unpredictable he had become, and for those who hadn't seen, Dog carried the wounds on his hands and throat, enough to convince them.

Hen Hillis trembled noticeably. Her hands, her knees, her chins all shook. Extracting details in a coherent and fruitful manner might be difficult. Dog closed the kitchen door and leaned against it.

"Now, Hen. Everything's going to be fine. Just tell me what happened."

"I didn't think she'd go! She said she wouldn't!" Big tears welled and flowed, splattering on her calico bosom.

He looked around, found a dishcloth, offered it to her. He smiled as gently as he could. She dabbed her eyes. "Everything's going to be just fine," he repeated. "I just need to know the truth. Tell me exactly what happened, and what she said, and what you told her."

She smiled back. "Well," she began. "I was sound asleep when I heard this banging on the door below..." she knocked on the counter. "Startled me out of the deepest sleep. I was frightened, and I always worry anyway, and this time I was thinking those pirates had come back. So of course I was having bad dreams..."

The floodgates were opened. Every detail would be forthcoming. Eventually. Dog nodded, impatient to get to the facts that would condemn Packer Throme.

The piece of ship that carried Talon washed ashore on a desolate stretch of beach. The waves were just large enough that when they broke over her, she opened her eyes. She heard and felt sand scraping wood, reached out with a hand to test the depth. How long had she been unconscious? She remembered desperately trying to work her way onto the board, on her back, as the ocean tried to suck her under. She had known she needed to lie on her back so her head would remain out of the water, but she didn't remember succeeding. Her hands were numb, but the sandy bottom was there. She turned over, off the board, and splashed face first into the saltwater. She raised her head and looked around her. The beach was empty.

She looked for the sun, but it was obscured by heavy cloud cover. The wind was blowing in cold from the sea, and the smell of rain was in it. She recalled the red sunrise that had promised a storm. When was that? She could hardly feel anything, hands, legs, or feet. She had to get warm and dry. With a huge effort, she stood up in the sand. She lurched forward, barely keeping herself from falling. The beach was rocking under her. She staggered toward the woods, toward a dry gray tree trunk lying just outside the woods in the sand, parallel with the shoreline. Her body was dragging her back into sleep. She fell over the tree trunk and lay down on the other side, concealed now from the wind and from anyone on the beach.

She needed rest. Her mouth was dry, and it occurred to her, vaguely, that she should be thirsty. But she didn't feel a great need for anything but sleep. She put her head on the sand and closed her eyes.

In the woods, a cloaked figure watched.

When it was obvious that the stranger was asleep, Panna crept closer. She didn't know who this person might be, but she hoped he was a sailor. Panna had spent all day here, half a mile or so north of Inbenigh, waiting for the cover of night. She had been praying, rather weakly, she thought, for some help from above.

It was astonishing to her, even miraculous, that a stranger should wash up on the beach within her sight, and collapse not twenty yards away. If this was a sailor, and one who could be persuaded one way or another to help, then this was the answer to her prayer. If she could assist the sailor somehow, bring him back to health, perhaps he would feel a sense of gratitude. She would have her guide, and would need only a boat. Regardless of who it was, what harm could possibly come of doing good, and coming to the aid of a half-drowned man?

"He may fight like the devil, but he's a good man," Delaney swore to his rapt listeners, one hand raised. The entire watch had gathered in the forecastle, awaiting the start of the evening shift, lounging in hammocks, sitting on the floor, smoking pipes, and hanging on his every word. "You've seen me swinging steel, most of you. You know I can hold my own."

"You're the best I've seen," one piped in. Others murmured agreement. No one mentioned Talon, though more than one thought of her.

"I swear to you, he hardly moved a muscle from his head to his foot except what was needed in his arm and hand to fend my every stroke, and all the while he looks at me with them deep blue eyes like the sea itself, calm as the eye of the hurricane."

Delaney did not fancy himself much of a storyteller, and rarely joined in the spinning of yarns that often passed the time in the dark, cramped world of the forecastle. He was glad of it now. That he wasn't a teller of tales made his words stick deeper, somehow, with more meaning. And Delaney was quite pleased with his words, the part about the eye of the hurricane particularly.

"He's got the devil in him," a sailor suggested.

Delaney let out a short laugh. "No, no. Less than you or me. He's just got a sword that don't allow for comparison. And a heart of compassion to boot."

"So how is it he's alive, except he's got the devil in him?" another asked. "We all saw him dead. We saw what the witch done."

"He's got nothing in him but the devil," said a low voice from the darkest corner, a voice so sure of itself that it seemed almost bored with the observation. "No heart, no soul. It's a devil in a boy's body." All eyes peered into that dark corner. "The witch breathed it into him."

One of the sailors grabbed a lantern and swung it toward the speaker so he could be seen by the rest of them. It was Mutter Cabe, the old sailor who, it was rumored, was part Achawuk warrior. He would never admit to it, but he didn't go far to deny it either.

Mutter's face was deeply lined, his limbs scrawny; he seemed ancient, but his strength was equal to that of men half his age. He had a dark presence about him that kept him from making friends, even among those who had sailed with him for years. Achawuk ancestry was an acceptable rationale for all of his oddities. Plus, as was often noted, he talked to himself.

"You don't know what you're talking about, Mutter," Marcus Pile blurted out. The room's attention, and the lantern, swung toward the young man. He was agitated, eyes fierce. "I talked to him. Me and Delaney did. We know him, don't we, Delaney?"

"Aye, we do. Seems nothing like a devil, just the contrary. He's a swordsman and a Christian."

Mutter laughed again. Attention, and the lantern, swung back his way. He smiled thinly. "Convinced you two, anyway." His look suggested that such a deception might not be too difficult. There was laughter.

Delaney felt his audience slipping away. "He wouldn't join a mutiny even though he was a prisoner. Who'd do that but a Christian?"

"Mutiny? What mutiny?" several asked, alarmed.

Delaney pulled on his mangled ear, wishing he hadn't mentioned it. "It was just the Captain's orders, to try him with a story, that's all. Just a false mutiny, to test his honorable intentions. Which he passed, as might not well you or I in the same irons with him!" There were several quizzical expressions. Delaney was sorrowful now about the way his words seemed to come out jumbled. His oratory powers had fled.

"Would the devil announce himself?" Mutter asked, again quietly, but not aimed at Delaney or Marcus. He was asking all the rest, convincing them that these two were in utter error. "Or would he act the part of a gentleman, to deceive you?"

In the silence that followed, dark wings spread in each man's mind. The boy, if he could swing steel against Delaney without effort, certainly had something supernatural about him.

Delaney grew defiant. "He could have killed me. He had the right. He chose to show mercy, and gave me this instead." Delaney pointed to his swollen head.

Silence followed again, and eyes shifted back to Mutter. "He

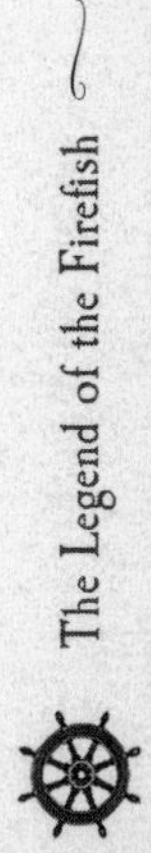

struck you down. Yet you swear allegiance. I want none of him, if that's what his mercy looks like."

Delaney could see that this was not going well. "All I can say is, next time, I want him fighting beside me and not against me."

There were a few murmurs of agreement.

Delaney turned on Mutter. "Mutter, you best not be speaking that way around the Cap'n. He hates that sort of talk, you know, spirits and whatnot. You'll find yourself keelhauled, and no witch will stop you from staying dead."

Mutter held up a hand, shook his head.

The issue had not been put to rest by any means, Delaney knew. Mutter was a talebearer, and the worst kind. But he and Marcus had done what they could, and at least kept the opinion of Packer from solidifying around Mutter's view. The debate was on.

The stranger was a woman. Panna fought back disappointment, reminding herself that not all women were as she was. Or rather, as she had been. This one was dressed as a forester, and carried both a sword and a knife. It passed through Panna's mind that before her might be the very woman who had accompanied the pirates to the inn, the woman in her dream, but she let that thought go. There was too much hope in it. That woman, for good or ill, would know exactly how to find Packer Throme. More likely, there were strong fighting women like this everywhere outside the fishing villages. Perhaps in all the world, women worked and rode and fought and sailed as men did, in all the world except the fishing villages of Nearing Vast. Panna simply didn't know. What else had they not told her?

This woman had a nasty scar on her left cheek, from her eye down to her jaw, and then down again on her neck. There was a story behind that slash, Panna thought. Perhaps she'd tell it. The woman's dark hair was knotted and braided alongside her head. She wasn't particularly beautiful, but she was exotic. Her sharp features, her olive-dark skin, high cheekbones and deep-set eyes...Panna's heart beat faster. A woman who knew the ways of the world might be the best companion possible. Better even than a man, a man who might do anything, try anything. A woman, even a fighting woman, would understand her. Wouldn't she?

Panna knelt beside her, reached out a hand and laid it gently on the castaway's shoulder. The leather jacket was cold and wet. She shook her gently. The woman didn't stir. Panna swallowed hard. Very carefully, trembling slightly, she put her hand on the woman's cheek. It was like ice.

Panna pulled her hand away. Was the woman dead? Fear rose. Was she breathing? Panna couldn't tell. She shook the woman harder, but with no response. Panna looked up and down the empty beach, as though help might be in sight. Then, still kneeling, she took the woman's face between her hands. "Wake up," she said softly.

Nothing.

Panna shook the woman's head. "Please," she said more loudly. "Please wake up. I need you."

Talon's face twitched.

"Good. Good—open your eyes now," Panna implored.

Talon struggled, but opened her eyes. She had trouble focusing, and when she succeeded, was confused by what she saw. It seemed to be a girl, smiling at her.

"Are you all right? You're so cold." Panna took off her knapsack and pulled her autumn cloak from it, laid it over the woman. "You must have been in the water for a long time. Was it a shipwreck?"

Talon tried to force her mind to work. She vaguely remembered being adrift. Was she cold? She didn't feel cold. An alarm rang deep within her. The healing arts in which she had been schooled worked through to her awareness. The numbness, the disorientation. She was suffering from exposure. "Fire..." she whispered. She was sleepy, and the single word came out without urgency, like a distant longing not likely to be fulfilled.

Panna shook her head. She had matches, and a flint. But she couldn't risk a fire; they'd be seen. "You stay under that cloak—it's the warmest thing I own."

Talon tried to reach for her flintlock, not thinking how wet it would be. She couldn't find it. She fumbled for her sword or her knife, but her fingers were too numb.

Panna didn't understand what the woman was trying to do. "I have some dry clothes, if that's what you need..." She had one extra peasant dress in her knapsack.

"Fire," Talon said again, even less urgently. The exhaustion was creeping over her, pulling her back in. She knew now it wasn't sleep that beckoned, but something permanent, unending.

Panna smiled. "You'll be warm in a minute or two."

Talon tried to focus on the girl, this stupid, happy girl who would let her die. But her mind drifted, and she closed her eyes.

Panna became alarmed. Unconscious, the woman looked lifeless once again. And her skin was still ice-cold. "Stay awake now," Panna said urgently, patting her hand. "Ma'am?"

Talon was in the water, warm water, floating face up, bobbing gently up and down under the moon and stars. Something was pulling her under, pulling her downward, and she longed to succumb, to quit struggling. But the voice, the sweet, angelic voice kept probing, asking her something, demanding she stay on the surface. There was light growing, light in the voice. Talon didn't want to go there, where it beckoned.

She let her head slide under the black water, let it overtake her. The darkness was cool, the sounds echoing, pleasant, reassuring. And then she was looking into those yellow eyes again, those huge, haunting, powerful, intelligent eyes—smiling, greedy, ravenous. The beast's mouth opened, its teeth crackled with lightning.

Talon surfaced in a panic. She reached a cold hand out to Panna. It rested on her neck, producing a chill that shot down Panna's spine.

Panna felt the urgency now, she couldn't miss it. "What do you need?" she asked fearfully.

The beast rose up from below the water, its teeth on either side of Talon, swallowing her whole. She could see nothing else. "Fire…" She could not complete the word, she could not name the beast. The single syllable was all she could manage. Her eyes stayed locked on Panna's for a moment, then they rolled upward. And then they closed. Her hand dropped.

Panna could not reawaken her.

"Strip down to your skivvies, Packer," Mrs. Throme had ordered, and seven-year-old Packer, wide-eyed and embarrassed, obeyed with tears. His mother had ordered him to lie beside the boy, whose clothes were already shed and whose skin was all ashen. Mr. Throme then wrapped the two of them together in blankets. Panna was there, and remembered Packer saying softly how cold he was, lying there with his back to the boy's icy stomach, and Panna remembered

Packer's shivers and blue lips, gotten from trying to warm the boy with his own body's heat.

Packer's father, Dayton Throme, had pulled the boy out of the water, a victim of a shipwreck, and sailed home as quickly as he could. The boy was wrapped in blankets when he arrived on a cart, Mr. Throme lashing the mule and yelling to Mrs. Throme, who ran out, took one look, and sent Packer to light the fire and heat some water. By the time the boy was inside the Throme house, the entire town seemed to be there as well, and several women went fetching hot water they already had boiling in their kitchens.

"Into the wineskins!" Tamma Throme had ordered as women arrived with their kettles of water. Packer's mother had directed the pouring of the steaming liquid into the wine flasks, the sealing of them, the placement against the boy's back. "Not too warm, now," she had said. She scolded her husband for bringing the boy all the way home, when fire and warmth were available in Inbenigh. "He's got the exposure. He'll die without warmth. But he'll die if he warms up too fast."

Panna opened her eyes, thankful for the memory. That boy had lived, and his father had rewarded Dayton and Packer by schooling Packer far above his station. Now Panna had to take a risk, or let the woman die. She couldn't heat water, but she could build a fire. She'd very possibly draw any search party's attention, but at least she'd be able to defend herself, or flee if necessary. Or she could avoid building a fire, and risk being found here, nigh on naked, trying to warm this woman with her own body, unable to run or to fight.

Panna would certainly save the woman's life. She hated what it might cost her, but how could she ever live with herself, or with Packer for that matter, if she sacrificed so basic a principle as this at the first opportunity? She may be an outlaw, but she was still a Christian. Which risk to take was not a difficult choice. Panna needed to be ready to run or to fight, or to go get help as necessary. She quickly entered the woods to gather tinder and kindling.

Dog Blestoe held the man's shoulders, looking closely at the bruises and cuts. Riley Odoms, the fisherman from Red Point, well known to Dog and others in Hangman's Cliffs, was a mess. His nose was broken, both eyes swollen almost shut, lips cut in several

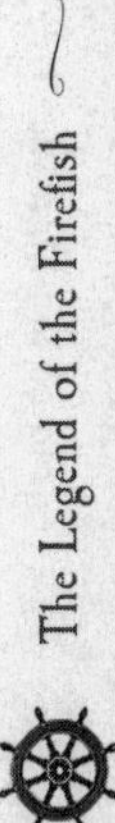

places. Dog nodded knowingly. "Was it Packer Throme who did this to you?" Dog had only just arrived here in Inbenigh, following up on the news given him by Hen Hillis.

"I don't know," Riley said, slitted eyes riveted on Dog as though he were both a judge and jury. Odoms was not much more than a wisp of a man even in his prime, which was a good decade past, and was not known for his backbone. He was altogether the wrong man to leave guarding boats, not only for his demeanor, but because he was prone to drink more than he could hold. Dog smelled alcohol on him now. "I don't think I ever seen him before in my life."

"But you didn't get a clear look at him."

Riley shook head. "Not really. I mean, it was dark."

"So it could have been Packer Throme."

"I...I guess. Coulda been anybody." Now Riley glanced at the other fishermen, those watching him. They stood on the creaking docks of Inbenigh—Riley, Dog, Ned Basser, and Duck Tillham, also of Red Point. These last two had yet to join the manhunt now underway throughout the woods because they had taken the time to return home for what they felt were the most necessary supplies, which they now concealed under their coats. The goings-on of the night before were still the only agenda of the day. Fishing could be done tomorrow.

"Did he have a beard?" Dog asked.

Riley paused, then shook his head. "No."

"Was he my height?"

"No, shorter."

"You're sure?"

"Well...yeah. He was standing uphill from me a little bit, but not much. He wasn't as tall as you."

"Old man?"

"No."

"Young then?"

"Yeah, I guess. Pretty young."

"Yellow hair?"

"No, I don't think so."

"Did you get a good look at it? At his hair?"

"No. Like I said, it was dark."

"So it could have been blond?"

"Sure, I guess."

"You know you've just described Packer Throme, don't you?"

"I guess. I don't know the boy that well."

"You're lucky. He cut me here, and here." Dog pointed to his hands. "And put his sword right here." He pointed to his throat. "And would have run me through if it hadn't been for so many witnesses to his murderous ways." The only eyewitness here present was Ned Basser, the man who had egged Dog on by tossing him Cap's sword. If he disagreed with Dog's assessment, he didn't show it.

"More to the point, Hen Hillis told me that Panna Seline left home last night to meet up with Packer. He lured her away. Now she's missing, and you're half killed. What does that tell you?"

Ned Basser cursed Packer Throme's parentage. "Come on, Riley. Let's us go a-huntin,'" he said quietly. His silver-tinged hair was swept back like he'd just stepped in out of a windstorm; his visage looked like he was aching to step right back into one. He opened his coat to show Riley and Dog his "supplies," the flintlock pistol he'd stuck in his waistband.

Duck, bigger and wider than Dog, though not as tall, showed off his pistol as well. Then he held out a sheathed hunting knife for Riley to take. "I brought this for you. For carving out some justice."

Riley was uncomfortable. Sympathy he'd take by the gallon, but he had no stomach for revenge. "Maybe we ought to let the sheriff handle it," he said weakly.

"The sheriff?" Dog scoffed. "He's got to come from Mann, if he cares to come at all, which I doubt. Which means even if he does come, he won't be around till tomorrow at least."

"And all he'll do," Ned chimed in, "is post a reward, and then the woods will be crawling with bounty hunters. You want some stranger getting your justice for you, walking off with a reward?"

That would suit Riley just fine, but he didn't say it. He shook his head. "I don't know, boys. My back's still hurtin'." He squirmed a bit, wincing, to prove his point. Then he touched his puffy eye and looked at the inn at the top of the docks. He felt suddenly dry. He longed to be inside its doors. "Maybe I'll just stay here and get a drink, if you don't mind. You know, heal up some."

Ned spat, angry. "You gonna sit around and moan while everyone else tracks him down for you?"

"Well, yeah..."

Dog stepped in before Ned let loose. "Riley should stay and heal

up. You and Duck'll move faster without him anyway. The important thing is catching Packer."

"How about you?" Ned grunted. "You coming with us? Seems like you've got as much reason to hunt the boy as anyone."

Dog hadn't considered traipsing through the woods himself. But now that Ned was leaning into him, there seemed little way to shake free of it. "I'll go with you some. I want to circle back here, though, now and again, see what the other groups have found. Mostly, I want to make sure he's caught."

The village fishermen were not woodsmen. Despite the best efforts of some of their number to organize into parties, or perhaps because of their best efforts, the fanning out, circling, and tracking down degenerated within the first hour into aimless wandering and the occasional shout, which brought any within earshot running. It was fortunate that so few had any weapons, since the strangers they continually encountered and accosted turned out, without exception, to be themselves. Then, once it was determined that all present were true and honest fishermen, handshakes and pipe-smoking commenced, flasks flashed and were passed liberally, until eventually it occurred to one or more that they had spent a good long while in one spot strategizing while the scoundrel they so valiantly hunted had perhaps moved farther afield, at which time they reluctantly returned to the search. What most of the villagers actually sought was their own safety, and they managed to find it everywhere they turned.

But those who sought danger found that as well. Dog, Duck, and Ned kept themselves apart from the larger groups, avoiding their peers, cursing them from a distance for ignoring and even running off the prey. Ned, Duck, and Dog also drank liberally from their flasks, but the same liquid that lessened their peers' keenness for the hunt had the opposite effect on them. As the day wore on, the three grew more and more bent on the heroic dispensing of justice that was certainly their right, they being the ones truly serious about the mission.

It was this agitated and armed threesome that, late in the day, flasks now fully emptied into bloodstreams, stalked their way through the woods toward the sea, a mile-and-a-half north of Inbenigh, toward the spot where a gray tree trunk lay just outside the woods, parallel with the shoreline.

"Once again John Hand is more vigilant than Moore Davies," Scat mused to himself. He had read the flagman's message, and was disappointed. He would always prefer that his huntsmen outperform his butchers, but it rarely happened that way. John Hand was as good a captain as there was.

Scat lowered his telescope. He sighed. "Signal this back," he ordered. "Coming about."

Jonas Deal looked askance at the Captain, but caught his return glance and quickly obeyed. Scat peered through the scope just long enough to see that his message was acknowledged. "It seems Captain John Hand has a question about our bearings. I'll be meeting with him."

"Aye, aye," Mr. Deal responded.

"Storm!" came the cry from the crow's nest, a hundred feet above them. "Starboard astern!"

Scat raised his telescope and looked at the dark line along the horizon to the south. They'd all felt the atmosphere changing, but hadn't seen evidence of what that change might bring. "Hmm," he said. "Not a small one, either." Before he returned to his quarters below deck, he said casually, "Bring her about, Mr. Deal. Then heave to on a port tack."

"Hard to starboard!" Jonas Deal commanded. "Reef the main four points! Strike the mizzen! Strike the top! Stand by to haul those sheets, ye swivel-yoked sea dogs! We're comin' hard about!" The bosun's mate, Dumas Need, piped the orders on his whistle. The entire watch was in motion; any inward grumbling at the sudden flare of activity so late in the shift quickly dissolved into the unified motion that was the muscle and sinew of the great cat, moving in synchronous, instinctive motion in response to the command from the sleek animal's brain.

The Captain was the mind of the cat, but the bosun was its instinct, its reflexes. Andrew Haas on the port watch, and his mate Dumas Need on starboard, forever peered anxiously at each sail, piping orders anew whenever something might be done better, faster, more completely. When the bosun needed a better view of a sail, he stepped into the bosun's chair and hauled himself up into the rigging using a series of lines and pulleys.

His orders given, his men busy carrying them out with all the energy they possessed, Scatter Wilkins was content to think about the future.

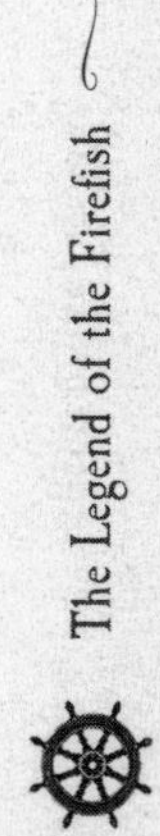

"So you're worried about the Achawuk, are you?" Scat asked with a smile when John Hand and Lund Lander had joined him in his saloon. John Hand, a full professor of Nautics at the University of Mann, had left his ivory tower to join with Scat and now captained one of the escort ships. It was a disgrace to the university, of course, but only served to increase the mystery around Scat's new dealings.

"Never saw a sane man who wasn't," Hand replied with ease. He was a big man, not as lean as Lund but broader across the shoulders, with a bushy head of graying hair and a gray-peppered beard to match. "Are we headed far inside their territory?"

"About twenty leagues." Scat's eyes were stony.

Lund's throat grew suddenly dry, and he threw a gulp of rum down it.

Scat Wilkins had been a little surprised to see Lund Lander follow John Hand into the saloon, but not enough to let it show. It bothered Scat that Hand always had someone in tow. Maybe it was the professor in him that made him always want to be teaching someone something. Or maybe it was the desire for counsel; Hand was a great one for talking everything to death before acting. Or maybe it was weakness; fear of facing the odds himself, alone. Scat Wilkins knew for certain only that John Hand was very different from himself in this regard.

"That's a long way," John Hand answered evenly. "All night in a good wind."

"We've got a good wind, and we've got all night."

"A good wind for sailing northeast." The same wind, of course, was bad for returning southwest. "What do you expect to find so far into the territory?"

"Firefish, Hand. Isn't that what we're out here for?"

"There are other places to look," Hand volleyed back.

"We've been looking other places."

"Why there?"

Scat squinted. "Don't like taking a little risk?" Talon was forever telling him the men were getting soft, and she blamed John Hand for it.

Hand stared hard and considered his answer. He was an easygoing sort, usually, but not when challenged directly. He knew all about Talon's messages to the Captain. She was not afraid to speak them in his presence. Finally Hand smiled. "If a little risk bothered me, I'd still be standing in front of a chalkboard."

"Making a living impressing students with your brilliance."

Hand's lips went taut. Scat was goading him; he liked to see John Hand angry. It comforted him. All three of these men knew that while the idea for hunting the Firefish belonged to Scat Wilkins, the course they had taken from idea to reality had been charted by John Hand and his chalkboards. Scat had had the idea, and had enlisted many a good man to the cause, Lund Lander and John Hand at the top of the list. Scat had hired the huntsmen, had staffed the *Marchessa* with a suitable captain in Moore Davies, and took great pride in their storied prowess.

But John Hand and his sketches, Lund Lander and his diagrams, blueprints, and equations, together had created the ships, the processes, the science, and the fledgling, hugely profitable and yet more promising Firefish industry. Without Lund's lures, Scat would have little to show but dead sailors and huntsmen.

Not that John Hand and Lund Lander didn't have great respect and admiration for Captain Scat Wilkins. They did. No fisherman or whaler or hunter or businessman had ever had the vision or the courage to do what Scat was doing. No one had thought of it; no one would have thought it possible. He was slaying dragons for profit. He was monetizing monsters. It took a pirate's guts and a pirate's greed to build this new world; and to John Hand, that was exactly what was being built. The entire economic life of the kingdom, of all known kingdoms, for that matter, would be turned upside down by this venture. That's what John Hand loved about it.

Hand was under no delusions: This was Scat's business top to bottom. The pirate was simply shrewd enough to stand back and let Hand and Lander make it work. The Captain knew they could succeed, had already succeeded, and would succeed more greatly yet.

But at what price in human life, if they were now to sail into the Achawuk Territory? The struggle between Hand and Wilkins was silent, but it was palpable, and Lund, for one, didn't want to see it escalate. So he spoke.

"Begging your pardon, Captain, but while no one on any of your ships is averse to a risk, the crew of the *Camadan* didn't sign on to face the Achawuk, and they aren't trained fighters. They're mostly tradesmen, and no match for those warriors."

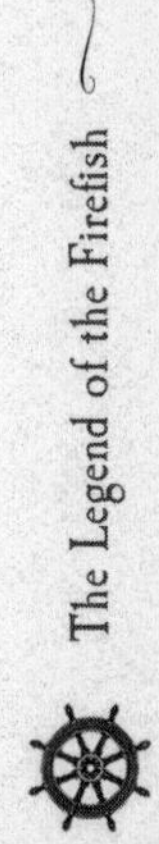

Scat turned on Lund, his voice cold. "You hired them."

Lund had indeed hired them. "To process the Firefish," he reminded him.

"How hard a job is that?" Scat asked with disdain. "Something a swordsman or a pistolier couldn't learn?"

Lund took a deep breath. Scat had always pushed John Hand to hire sailors, and fighting men, and then to teach them the trades they'd need. Hand had wisely held out for quality workers who knew what they were doing, the kind who could handle long voyages and demanding work below decks, who would put up a quality product worth buying. He didn't need a shipload of pirates deciding they had gutted enough fish. But all this was moot at the moment. The sterner fact was that it seemed Scat wouldn't hold them out of a fight just because they might all get killed.

"Take your licks when you've earned 'em," Scat said to Lund. "Then next time, you'll know better." Lund's face flushed. Scat saw it and was satisfied. Lund was smart, Scat knew, maybe a genius at designing things, making them work. That was useful. But the world needed more people with guts, men willing to gamble for the big payoff. Scat had seen plenty of smart men like Lund die with cold steel through the belly. Scat had put the steel there sometimes himself. He had yet to see an unarmed genius outduel an idiot with a pistol. He'd rather stand with half a dozen fighters who could swing a sword and weren't smart enough to know the odds than two dozen Lund Landers who could make a clock out of chicken bones and clothespins.

"What makes you think there's Firefish in there?" John Hand asked.

Scat shrugged. "Call it a hunch."

John was silent. Then he sighed and raised his glass. "Well, then, here's to your hunches—may they make us all rich." He drained it. Scat and Lund Lander locked eyes, both smiling through gritted teeth, and they both followed suit.

"Any possibility I could have a conversation with this hunch of yours?" Captain Hand asked.

Scat nodded. But it unnerved him that Hand knew about Packer Throme. He probably had sources of information aboard the *Chase* that Scat didn't know about.

Hand saw the suspicion, knew he needed to allay it. "Everyone knows about the stowaway. Talon took him below decks. Doesn't take much to figure out he told her something."

Scat rubbed his beard. "Pimm!" he called, not looking away from John Hand.

The steward entered. "Sir?"

"Fetch me Packer Throme."

Deeter nodded and left, looking slightly more pale than usual.

"I don't know if the lad knows where the Firefish feed. But he says he does. And I know that I sure don't."

A loud creak, followed by a howl, accompanied a leeward lurch of the ship. They all understood exactly what it meant, well before Jonas Deal burst in on them. "She's blowin' a gale, Cap'n," he said. "A true gale, and no lie."

Chapter 12

The Storm

Panna could build and stoke a fire; she'd done it for cooking all her life. She could keep smoke to a minimum: dry, dry kindling, and one piece of fuel at a time as it burned. Overload it and it would choke, producing more smoke than heat. The thin plume of black wood smoke, which now rose from behind the gray tree trunk, was almost invisible. It was the best she could hope for. Panna could warm the woman by keeping the fire very small, so that the woman could lie close to it, virtually wrapped around it. But the black clouds approaching from the southwest promised rain, and she could do nothing about that.

The woman's leathers were dry now, at least in front, and the tree trunk behind her served as a heat reflector, warming and drying her from behind. Panna had opened the woman's jacket and shirt, exposing more of her skin to the heat. The woman's temperature had risen steadily by Panna's reckoning, as Panna had checked it at the back of the woman's neck.

But now, the approaching dark clouds were more ominous. The smell of rain was in the air, and a dark wall loomed on the horizon. She had half an hour, maybe an hour at the most, and then she'd need shelter, some other way to keep the woman warm and dry. The simplest solution, and the only one that seemed practical, was to go to Inbenigh and bring back a stout piece of canvas, a tarpaulin like those the fishermen used to cover their boats. She couldn't buy one, of course, without being spotted. But if she had a knife, she could cut one loose. And the woman had a knife.

Panna spoke to her gently as she removed the knife from its sheath. "I'm just borrowing this. To help you. I will bring it back." She covered the woman's head and shoulders with her autumn cloak, leaving a clear airway. The fire might go out, but the woman would stay as warm and dry as possible, for as long as possible.

"I'll be right back," Panna told her, hoping she could return before the rain arrived. It was moving fast. She stoked the fire with an extra piece of fuel. The woman would have its heat for as long as possible.

Panna checked her hair to be sure it was still pulled up and tied securely. She pulled the hat down over her head. She looked up and down the beach to be sure it was empty and then headed south to Inbenigh, leaving her knapsack, her cloak, everything but the clothes on her back and Talon's knife.

The wind blew the rain into pellets, stinging the skin. Scat Wilkins, John Hand, and Lund Lander leaned into it. John and Lund were watching the *Camadan,* which had already been blown two hundred yards away from them. They could see the crew in the rigging, striking the sails. Hand knew there would be no return to his ship until the storm blew over. He was relieved; in fact, he had hoped for as much. Let the *Camadan* go her own way, and pray it was well out of Achawuk territory.

Scat scanned the running rigging of his own vessel, watching as the hands worked to strike the mainsail.

"Get it done, ye buzzards!" Jonas Deal screamed, his voice lost in the gale. "Get it done or say yer prayers!"

Six crewmen were spread across the yardarm, feet on the thin footlines, hands pulling on the heavy, drenched canvas. But six wouldn't be near enough in this gale. If they didn't get the sail struck soon, it would either shred or snap the mainmast. If the mainmast went, so would every man up there.

"All hands to the mains'l!" Jonas yelled, to no avail. "Where's the bosun?"

"Went up on the yard!" Lund screamed at him.

Jonas cursed and started roaming the slick, rainswept deck like a madman, clinging to the railings to keep from being blown overboard, grabbing anyone he could find by the shirt-collar and pointing up at the yard, forcing him to the ratlines. Soon there were twelve struggling to pull the canvas up, and two more leaving the foresail, which was already shredded and hopeless.

Every time they seemed to have sheeted the sail another point, a gust would blow it out of someone's hands before it was tied, then it would fill and pull away from all their hands, and they'd have to start again. The mainsail was struggling hard now, the ship heeling dramatically with it, the deck pitched at forty-five degrees and plowing through heavy surf, its starboard railings only three feet above the waterline at the height of the ship's lunge. The helmsman could do nothing but set the lock-timber in place so the rudder wouldn't be battered back and forth and break loose. And so the great cat ran with the wind to God knew where, wild and out of control.

Jonas Deal needed more hands. He climbed down below decks. "All hands! All hands to the mains'l or the mast's a goner!" The first mate ran through the ship as though leading a bayonet charge on the forecastle, where he would roust every last soul he could find.

John Hand quickly followed Jonas below. He still wanted to talk with this stowaway, and there was nothing he could do to help with the sail or the mast. As long as the outcome was in doubt, Scat would remain atop, he knew. He'd have the stowaway to himself.

Scat stood firm, both hands on the quarterdeck rail, teeth gritted as he looked up. He cursed himself and then his crew for letting this storm sneak up on them. He'd have someone whipped for it; he just didn't know who yet. He didn't want to lose the mainmast, but if it was going, he was going to be here to see it. This was his ship, his mistress, the dearest thing to him on earth, and he would make sure all had been done to protect her.

Lund watched the hands, scanning them through the storm, a close eye on their technique. Then he saw the problem. The sailor farthest out on the yard had clutched. He was bent over the yardarm as though working, but he wasn't. He was frozen. It was in that spot, farthest out from the mast, where the wind kept catching the canvas and blowing each man's work to naught. Lund inched his way toward Scat Wilkins and pointed up at the sailor. Scat couldn't understand what Lund was trying to tell him.

"He's clutched, Cap'n!" Lund screamed. With the wind howling and the rain beating into Scat's ears, the Captain couldn't have heard cannon fire distinctly. "I'm going up!"

Lund worked his way to the ratlines, careful to keep a good grip on something all the while—the railing, then the gunwale, then the lines. Scat looked up again into the rigging, trying to see what had gotten Lund's attention.

And then he saw it: the sailor, a young pup, good and strong, who had signed on at South Barnes Mooring. Dial, his name was, or Pile maybe. Not much experience, but a good way about him, knowledgeable and likable. Religious, yes, but not dangerous about it. He was clutched, that was a fact. Scat could see the canvas billowing out, pulling away.

Scat cursed. He reached into his jacket and pulled his wheel-lock pistol. With all its workings concealed within the steel wheel chamber, the flint and powder would stay dry for quite a while, even in a downpour like this. At no little danger to himself, Scat kept the mechanical spring wound tight so that all he needed to do was pull the trigger, and it would fire.

He cursed the sailor more thoroughly as he took aim, a difficult task with the ship pitching and rolling. Lund had climbed quickly up to the running rigging and was now working his way out the yard to the frozen crewman. Lund would spend three or four minutes trying to get the man working again, and most likely that effort would be in vain anyway. Once a man clutched, once terror set in, there was no reasoning with him. Three or four minutes could mean saving or losing the mainmast in this gale.

Scat waited for a moment when the ship reached the apex of its pitch, when he could hold the pistol true, and then he fired. At first, he didn't know if his aim was true. He thought he saw the boy's head jerk, but nothing happened. Then the boy's hands fell loose, and he tumbled limply backward, somersaulting into the pounding sea.

The sailors on the yard saw Marcus Pile fall, and assumed he had lost his footing. They all knew nothing could be done for him now, not in these seas, so they kept working, redoubling their efforts in order to avoid the same fate.

But Lund knew. He looked down at Scat and saw the Captain putting his pistol back into his coat. Scat stared hard at Lund until

the volunteer seaman went on with his work, taking Marcus Pile's place on the yard.

Undoubtedly he would have died anyway, Lund told himself as he began hauling on the canvas. Likely he would have stayed there, hugging the yardarm until his strength gave way, and the result would have been the same. Still, it was a cold-blooded thing to do, and Lund was repulsed by it.

His fingertips burned and his arms knotted up with the effort. He wasn't accustomed to this work anymore, not like he used to be.

Jonas Deal came up from the forecastle, leading his reinforcements, just in time to see Pile fall. He let go a stream of invective, hating to lose a man, not because he cared for any of them but because it was his job to keep them alive and working.

He worked his way to the gunwale, pulled out his knife, and cut loose a small boat, a shallop even smaller than the one Talon had taken. It would capsize, of course, but at least it would float. The odds were slim that Pile would find it in the storm, but at least he'd have a chance. Such an action was necessary more for the men left alive than for the boy, who would likely die regardless. They needed to know all was done for him that was possible, because none of them knew whether tomorrow he himself might be in the drink.

One way or another, the job was done. With more than twenty men across the yardarm, with the mast creaking like a great oak and the rigging whipsawing back and forth, they finally had the mainsail struck and tied, and worked their way back down to the deck with no further loss of life.

Now there was little to do but ride the storm out, and hope for the best.

The three vigilantes stumbled out of the woods about fifty yards north of the gray tree trunk. "What's that?" Duck Tillham asked, pointing to the thin plume of smoke.

Ned Basser cursed. "Some idiots decided to cook their supper, probably."

"I don't see anybody there," said Dog.

"Well, let's have a look."

Ned and Duck checked their pistols for the hundredth time. Dog unsheathed his dagger, but for some reason he had a strong sense of danger, a feeling he had not had all day. Something told him that this was the real thing. Duck and Ned could carry all the bravado they wished—Dog knew how dangerous Packer Throme was. And Dog didn't have a pistol or even a sword, just this short, dull hunting knife. He hoped the other two wouldn't notice how his hand trembled.

"I'm going to keep a watch on the woods," Dog announced. "You two have the pistols. You go. I'll keep an eye out, make sure it isn't a trap."

Ned and Duck looked at Dog blankly.

"He could have set the fire and seen us coming. Could be waiting," Dog insisted. "I'll yell out if I see anything."

Something, whether the force of the argument, the authority of his voice, or the alcohol they had consumed, convinced them. The two kept their weapons aimed at the tree trunk as they wound their way unevenly down the beach. Dog watched after them, ready to rush in and claim a part of the victory, or head into the woods for help, whichever was needed.

Duck and Ned were almost on top of the tree trunk before they saw the cloaked figure lying by the fire, head and shoulders covered.

"Is it him?" Duck asked in a whisper.

"I don't know," Ned whispered back. The waves crashing on the shore helped cover their voices, but it was their empty flasks that made them believe they were out of earshot.

Duck took aim with his pistol.

"What are you doing?" Ned asked hoarsely.

Duck looked at Ned like he was crazy. "I'm going to shoot him, what d'you think?"

"No! They can't find him with a hole in the back of his head, what would people say? Make him stand and face us."

Duck saw the reason in that. They could question him. Make him beg for mercy. Duck's heart thumped wildly. "All right. Let's see what he's made of."

"Up now, and be quick about it!" shouted Ned Basser, his pistol aimed unsteadily at the stranger's head. But the stranger didn't move. The two armed fishermen were standing with the tree trunk between themselves and the stranger. "You go around," Ned whispered to Duck, "and we'll surround him."

Duck moved slowly to his left around the fallen tree. "Hey!"

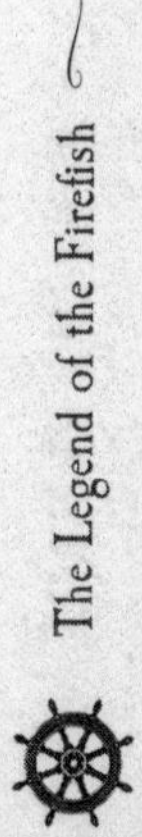

Duck said, eyes big, when he was close enough to see the stranger's face. "It's a woman!"

"No..." Ned responded. He lowered his pistol and followed his friend to the other side of the tree. "Is it the pastor's daughter?"

"No, someone else."

"Well, I'll be."

They looked at each other. Then they looked back at the woman. "She's foreign."

"Look, tracks!" Duck said, pointing to the footprints Panna had left as she went toward Inbenigh. "That must be him." But neither moved. They eyed the tracks for only a moment, then they were drawn again to the dark-haired woman asleep on the beach.

Up the beach, Dog watched in gripped fascination. He couldn't hear what they were saying, but clearly they had found someone. Was it Packer? They weren't aiming their pistols anymore. If they would just give him a sign. But something told Dog the danger had not passed.

"Wake her up," Ned ordered.

"You wake her up," Duck countered.

Ned stepped closer while Duck lingered back. "Hey. You awake?" Ned asked. There was no movement. He squatted next to the fire, at her head, his flintlock resting on his knee. He quickly lost his balance, almost put a hand into the fire. He cursed.

The single word reached Talon's brain, drawing her awake. But she didn't stir. She wasn't startled, but was pulled from a deep pool of dark dreams toward a bright surface filled with dangers. Her instincts and her intuition told her that she must wake up, quickly and carefully, but she found it hard, much harder than usual, to collect her thoughts, to fully assess her situation. But with great force of effort, she succeeded. Eyes still closed, she felt the heat of the fire, heard it crackle, sensed the presence of enemies.

"Well, if you swearing at her didn't wake her up, nothing will," Duck said with a laugh.

This voice was not much of a threat. Its owner was several feet away, off his guard, and stupid with drink.

"She's an outlaw, whoever she is," a nearer voice said, ragged and edgy. The man who owned this voice was more dangerous, close by and with a purpose. But he also was off his guard, and drunk. "She's in cahoots, is my bet."

Now Talon heard the rustle of clothing and felt the man's hand on her, pulling away a blanket, something heavy, that covered her. "Not a bad catch, eh, Duck?" His voice now had the edge of lust.

The man whipped the blanket off her, shook her shoulder. "Hey you, wake up. You have crimes to answer for." The voice was hungry now, aggressive. Talon wanted to reach for her knife, her sword, her pistol, but she couldn't risk it. Once this man knew she was conscious, he would be on his guard. Right now he felt in control.

"She's out cold," said the far voice, the one called Duck, almost gleefully. "What do you want to do with her?"

There was a pause—breathing. "Well. Let's take a closer look," said the near voice. "Then we'll decide." The aggressive, hungry edge was now in the fore, overtaking all else.

Talon still didn't know what weapons she had within her reach, but she clearly smelled the faint odor of gunpowder. The moisture in the air made it stand out. The man was likely holding a flintlock pistol. She had the element of surprise. She had no doubt about the outcome of the next few seconds.

Ned Basser reached for her jacket, his mouth working involuntarily.

The rain came in buckets.

From where he stood, Duck Tillham saw the first huge drops hit her face, and then he saw Talon's eyes open. He started to smile, thinking that this was good; she had awakened, and now they could question her. But before he could speak, or move, or take another breath, Ned Basser was dead.

As she opened her eyes she reached for her knife; it was not in its sheath. She saw at the same time, however, the flintlock pistol that her attacker held against his knee. She simply reached out and took hold of the pistol by its barrel, turned the muzzle toward the man's face, and pulled it upward. She didn't bother to take it away from him; she didn't need to. His finger was on the trigger, so the sudden movement caused it to fire.

Ned's reactions were slowed by drink, but they would never have been quick enough had he been sober. He never saw what killed him. The musket ball caught him under the chin. He fell backward, dead before his head hit the sand.

The sudden, blowing rain obscured his vision somewhat, but Dog Blestoe saw Ned fall backward, head jerking violently. For an

instant, he thought for sure he had heard a shot, but it was drowned in a clap of thunder, and he couldn't be certain.

Duck had enough time to quit smiling, but not enough to absorb what had suddenly happened to his friend. Talon was on her feet, sword drawn. Duck stumbled backward instinctively, trying to get out of her range, and as he did he raised the pistol in his hand. But the heel of his boot hit a root, and he went down. The pistol discharged.

Talon saw the smoke and fire, heard the crack of the powder and the whistle of the projectile. She slowed, knowing now that the wide-eyed man sitting before her in an ungainly heap had effectively disarmed himself.

Dog Blestoe saw a figure rise in an instant, as though appearing from the mist and the rain, and he saw Duck go down. He saw the powder flash. This time he heard the report clearly. The dark figure slashed at Duck's throat, and then plunged the sword blade deep into him.

Dog knew now that both Duck and Ned were dead. He was in the woods as quickly as his feet could move him, panicked that the swordsman would see him and come after him. There could be no doubt now about who it was. There could be no doubt now about who'd hurt Riley Odoms, who'd abducted Panna Seline, and who had now killed these two fishermen. Dog had seen it with his own eyes. He'd recognized the stance, the posture, the movement; he was sure of it. This was the swordsman who had humiliated and wounded him at the inn.

This was Packer Throme.

Duck's eyes, wild with fear, went dim, and he slumped backward and to his left. Talon let the man's weight pull her sword free.

She looked around her, up and down the beach, alert to any motion, any other sign of life. She looked directly at the spot where Dog had darted into the woods, but saw nothing through the heavy rain but leaves blowing in the wind. Confident she was alone, she moved quickly. She cleaned her blade on the cloak, and returned her sword to its scabbard. Then she rounded up items that would be of use to her. She examined both pistols, and settled for Ned's, the one that had fired true. She did not take the time to reload it, a useless effort in this rain. She tucked it into her belt. She buttoned up her jacket and slung Ned's powder horn over her shoulder. She tied his

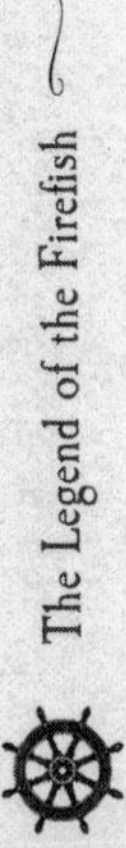

bag of ammunition to her belt. She stuffed half a loaf of his bread into her jacket. From Panna's knapsack she took only the wineskin, half full of water. Talon looked around again, hoping to find her knife. She quickly surmised that the strange girl had taken it.

She would leave these bodies to be found as they were. No one now alive had seen her, she was sure, no one but that stupid young thing who had almost let her die. Talon could not be connected to these deaths by anyone but that girl.

She looked at the tracks of the fishermen, but didn't take the time to sort them out. She wanted the girl. The rain had pelted the footsteps to pieces, but at the edge of the woods she found what she was looking for, a set of footprints, smaller and lighter, headed south. Without looking back, she followed Panna toward Inbenigh.

Captain John Hand entered Scat Wilkins' saloon to find the young man, yellow hair and blue eyes, seated at the table, gripping it with both hands. Packer stood as Hand entered.

"Sit down," Hand said quickly, and seated himself across from him. He noticed that the boy had a sword tucked in his belt. "You're the stowaway?" he asked.

"Yes, sir." The boy didn't look at all apologetic.

"Quite a gale."

"Yes, sir." The violent pitching of the ship made small talk seem smaller than usual.

John Hand looked him in the eye. "What are you up to, son?"

"Sir?"

"We're sailing into Achawuk territory on your advice."

Packer lowered his eyes, suddenly feeling ashamed. "I told Captain Wilkins that my father believed the Firefish feed there."

The wildness of the ship's movements were going to cut this interview short, John knew. It was hard to concentrate on anything else. Both men now gripped the table tightly.

"Is that true?"

Packer glanced up. "My father believed it."

"What's your name?"

"Packer Throme."

There was a pause as the older man eyed the younger. "I'm John Hand, captain of the *Camadan.*"

"Pleased to meet you."

"What do you know about the Achawuk, son?"

"Not much, sir."

"You're lucky."

Packer already liked what he saw in this captain. Here was a careful, intelligent man who was not quick to condemn, not rash, but not afraid either. He was clearly not the volatile sort that Scat Wilkins was.

"It'll be rough on the ship's crew until this weather blows over," Hand said. "But it'll be rougher when it does. I hope you can use that sword, son." He stood. "You can get back to the forecastle, I'm through with you."

Packer stood. "Sir, I've been confined to quarters."

"Get back to quarters, then. I'll speak to the Captain, get you assigned to Jonas Deal's watch."

"Sir," Packer said, clearly alarmed. "Jonas Deal?"

"What of him?"

Packer wondered if this was punishment, to be assigned to Jonas Deal. But he didn't know how to ask. John Hand deduced the problem. "Ah, the keelhauling." He smiled. "Andrew Haas, then."

"Thank you, sir." Packer stood firm, still holding the table for balance.

"Go on, now," Hand ordered. "And watch your noggin on the way. We'll all be needing clear heads when the weather clears."

"Aye, sir."

Panna arrived at Inbenigh as the rain did, a dark, heavy squall from the southeast that blew away anything not nailed or tied down. She was wearing only Mr. Molander's clothing, which the cold rain quickly soaked through. A piece of canvas, she thought, how hard could that be? Every boat was covered with a tarpaulin, and several were flapping at the corners, inviting her to help herself.

She looked up and down the docks, and at the pathway from them up to the dilapidated village. No one was in sight. Who would be out in this weather? She supposed that some of the boats might have fishermen inside them, but it wasn't likely. All would have sought the comfort of the inn by now, trusting the storm to keep prowlers away.

Panna picked out a boat about halfway up the dock, away from eyes in the village, but close enough that she would need to wrestle the canvas only a short distance up the pier. The canvas of her chosen boat was already flapping pitifully.

She looked at the knife in her hand. It occurred to her that she was about to commit another crime. It wasn't as bad a crime, true; stealing canvas from a boat in order to protect herself and another from the rain was hardly equal to smashing a man's face. So why was the pit of her stomach so empty?

She had no time for such thoughts; they only slowed her down. This was the path to Packer. She took a deep breath, steeled herself, and ran quickly to the foot of the dock, rocked by the wind-whipped rain. She was cold and wished she had her cloak, but of course she had needed to leave it behind. She moved slowly out onto the wet docks, leaning into the rain that now pelted her like sleet, being careful of her footing. Finally she squatted down by the chosen vessel. It was tied with its bow inward, on the north side of the dock. She looked around. The docks creaked and groaned, the boats tossed. But there were no fishermen to be seen.

Talon ran stealthily, catlike, along the edge of the woods. Her braid was coming loose, so she clawed at it as she moved, until it was undone and her hair was out of her way, hanging behind her.

She felt an elation she had not felt in a long time. She was in her element, on the hunt. Only now did the events of the afternoon return to her in their full power. She had defeated the Firefish.

She remembered its eyes, its intelligence, its delight of the hunt, its passion for the kill. And she had killed it. She had now also defeated two armed men, who had encircled her with weapons drawn while she was unconscious. And now she was tracking more prey, again the predator. The delight of the hunt energized her. Four corpses lay behind her in her trek toward Senslar Zendoda. The girl would be the fifth. She would die as quickly and as silently as had Ox, and Monkey, and the two drunken men on the beach. Packer Throme had set her loose, and she would wreak her vengeance with power.

Out on the dock, the wind swirled and kicked so that it was impossible to tell from which direction it was coming. The rain lashed at Panna. A sudden gust almost knocked her off the planks of the dock. She steadied herself against a post near the vessel she had

marked out, then grabbed the flapping canvas and peeked under it. Darkness. She took the knife to a rope-tie that held the canvas fast to the gunwale on the port side of the vessel, and was surprised, almost shocked, by how easily the blade slid through the hemp. It was the sharpest knife she'd ever wielded, sharp as the finest razor. She cut four more ties, all the while holding the canvas tightly, hoping that once it was loose it wouldn't be blown out of her hands.

But as soon as she had cut the last tie on the dock side, another gust of wind blew the canvas completely off the boat and into the water. The tarpaulin was held fast by the ties on the starboard side, but most of it was now submerged. She would need to get into the boat to pull it out of the water. She stepped over the gunwale and into the bilge. The boat rocked crazily. The aft of the vessel was open, the fore was decked, and an open hatch led to a small cabin below. The boom was tethered, but it whipped back and forth with the movement of the boat. If she wasn't careful, it would knock her down. She kept low, beneath it, and peeked into the cabin to be sure it was empty. It was.

The sailboat's mast gyrated wildly above her. She grabbed the tarpaulin and started to pull it toward her. It was hard work. She had to put the knife down in order to use all the strength of both arms and both hands, all the muscles of her back, knees pressed against the gunwale, to pull the wet canvas back into the bilge. When she finally got most of the canvas inside the boat, she couldn't find her knife. The rain picked up yet again, pelting her painfully, and the boat rocked like a seesaw. The knife was under the canvas somewhere; it had to be, on the planking of the bilge. She moved the canvas around, careful not to lift it high enough that the wind would catch it again. But she couldn't find the knife. Frustrated, she thought that perhaps she could untie the knots. She looked up at the gunwale, and was shocked to see, beyond it, the buildings of Inbenigh drifting away from her.

The boat had somehow come loose from the dock! For a brief moment she thought she must have cut the mooring lines instead of the tie ropes. But before she could check, a clap of thunder whirled her around. And there was the woman, the one she had left helpless on the beach, standing inside the boat with her, staring down at her.

"Looking for this, perhaps?" Talon asked in her deeply foreign accent. She held the knife aloft. Her long, black hair fell in a tangled wet mass, her thick scar all the more visible. Her black eyes were sharp and focused. The wind-whipped rain drenched her face. She stood wide-legged, easily balanced in the moving boat, just out of range of the boom. Her leathers were soaked. Her sword hung at her waist. In her hand was the silver knife blade, catching the reflection of the lightning flashing in the darkened sky behind her.

"Lord, you scared me!" Panna said, clutching her chest. But she was still terrified. This was surely the woman in her dream.

Talon smiled at the appearance of Panna's fear; fear, Talon's longtime ally. She lowered the knife, holding it underhanded, and took a single step toward Panna, who was still seated on the wet floor of the boat. The leather-clad woman stood over the drenched and frightened girl. The boom swung, and Talon stopped it easily with one hand. She hesitated only a moment, and then brought the knife across from left to right, backhanded, in a quick, perfect slash.

The light was brilliant, the heat intense. Will Seline was caught up in the flame, in a way he had been only once before in his life. That time, he had been on his knees at the deathbed of his beloved wife, as Tamma struggled for her final breaths, and then ceased struggling forever. Now Will was prostrate on the floor of his bedroom, his forehead flat against the rough planks, his arms spread out as though he were embracing the world. But he was not embracing this world; rather, he was letting it go entirely. His spirit was engulfed, offered up to the God who created the world and everything in it

This was the death of Will Seline. He was dying to sin, dying to this world and all its trappings, its cravings, its pains and its pleasures, its plans and designs and schemes and dreams, alive only to the Spirit of God. His heart ached with an ache greater than death, greater than life, as the Flame and the Light invaded his being, tearing open wounds, secrets, sins, and desires. He would let Panna go here, within this Flame, as he had let Tamma go. Of course he would; he was mortal, fallen flesh, and the God who claimed her was neither. But still, he would offer himself in her place, beseeching the holy, loving God whose power could stop the course of rivers, could split seas, could swallow cities whole. Will Seline pled with God to take him instead of her, to spare his beloved daughter, just as he had

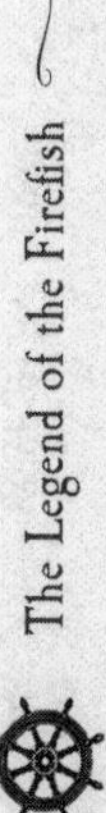

pled that He would spare his beloved wife, and that he, Will, would be allowed to suffer for her, in her place, so that she would be free of harm. He wanted to bear her burden, to carry her pain, if only God would allow it.

And as it had been with Tamma, so it was with Panna. Will's request was granted. Tamma had ceased to suffer at that very moment, and Will, the bereft husband, had carried with him always, from that moment, her pain, her anguish, while she was free and at peace. With Panna, he couldn't know the outcome. But he could know the pain, sharp as a knife slashed across his heart. He embraced that pain as it tore through him, recognizing it as Panna's, and as an answered prayer from God. The pain made him cry out in agony and in fear, and he knew it was her agony and her fear, and that she, wherever she was, would therefore not know such pain and terror. And he thanked God in tears for the grace he had been given, the mercy that the Merciful One had shown to Panna—wherever she was, in whatever danger, and whatever trial, to whatever end.

Talon had fully intended to slash Panna's throat, slice open her heart, silencing her and then killing her quickly, in her preferred manner. But just before she struck, she paused for the briefest moment as a thought occurred to her.

The girl might know Packer Throme. These were the docks of Inbenigh, the ones nearest Hangman's Cliffs. These were the boats of fishermen from small villages, where everyone knew everyone else. And so when she brought her knife across, her perfect backhanded slash instead severed the tie-line closest to Panna. Four more perfect slashes and the canvas was gone, sinking slowly into the dark water. Talon sheathed her knife and grabbed Panna by the arm, hauling her to her feet. And now Talon thought of another way the girl could be useful, stupid and naïve though she most certainly was.

"Steer," Talon commanded, putting Panna's hand on the tiller. Panna obeyed without hesitation.

Talon took hold of the halyard and hauled the sail up. As soon as it caught wind, it snapped full, straining at the brace. The tiny vessel heeled dramatically. Panna lost her footing, and had to pick herself up off the water-soaked bilge.

"Hard to starboard!" Talon cried, tying off the clew. She started

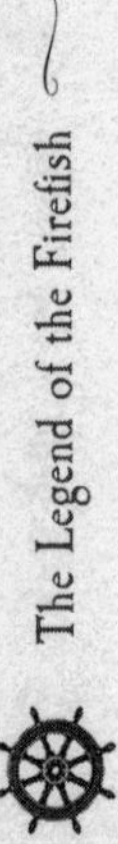

hauling the sheet on the port side to angle the sail. But Panna was frozen. "Move it that way!" Talon ordered, pointing to the trees. Panna's fear melted away as she poured herself into the task, straining at the tiller until it pointed toward the shoreline. Almost instantly, the fishing boat swerved northeast, on a starboard tack, and was running fast across the wind.

And now, contrary to all logic, Panna felt a surge of joy. Suddenly, she had her boat. She had her sailor. Now, all she needed was information about the *Trophy Chase.*

A single knock startled Packer awake. "Who is it?"

Rather than answer the question, Delaney entered the stateroom. He looked about as bedraggled as Packer had ever seen a man look. It wasn't just the fact that he was soaked through, dripping where he stood, with all his clothes and hair askew, with apparently no effort whatever made to dry off or straighten up. It was the sorrow lined into his face. He leaned against the doorframe, letting himself rock with the ship. To Packer, he seemed years older than the man who had visited him just hours before.

"He's dead," Delaney said.

Packer's heart fell. He sat up, rolling out of the hammock. "Who's dead?" But somehow Packer already knew.

Delaney looked at the wall, then the ceiling. He couldn't bring himself to say the name. "Just a boy."

"Marcus."

Delaney's chin trembled.

"How?"

"Fell from the rigging."

Packer felt stabbed through the heart. How could this be? He had for the first time aboard this ship felt real hope, hope that God was in fact doing something great, and all would work out. Marcus was part of that, part of the reason for it. More than that, he was a good lad, and Packer was looking forward to serving with him, to getting to know him better. *"He's a real good prayer, ain't he?"* Delaney's joyful words rung in Packer's ears.

And now he was gone. "How did it happen?"

Delaney couldn't speak for a moment. He seemed all bound up

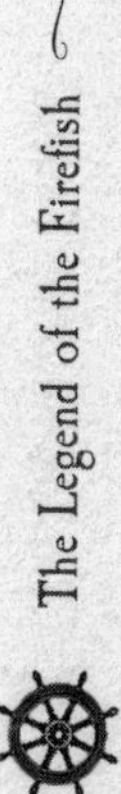

inside. "Who knows. God let him fall." He looked distant, cold. Angry with God.

"I'm sorry, Delaney."

"It ain't your fault."

It was a simple exchange, the kind that happens in moments of grief, but it had great meaning for Packer. He realized that no matter how much he thought it through, he would come to the same conclusion. Delaney was right; it was not Packer's fault. It was tragic, it was a great loss, and it was God's doing, for His own reasons. It was one tragedy Packer had not brought with him. Somehow there was great relief in that. Packer walked toward Delaney, wanting to find some way to express his concern.

Delaney held up a hand to stop him, to keep him away. "God is God and He does what He wants. He don't care whether it's what we want."

"I think He does care."

"Funny way of showing it." And with that, Delaney left, closing the door behind him.

Packer's sorrow multiplied. He climbed back in his hammock and stared up at the ceiling. "What is the point of that?" he asked, almost demanded. Packer's anger was not about Marcus Pile, who was in a far better place. He was concerned with Delaney, a young Christian with few brothers, now only one. Packer waited for an answer. But what came to him was a memory of his own choice, his own sin. He chose Panna over God, decided he would find Panna again, even through fire and flood and pestilence. Marcus's death was not Packer's fault, nor was it Delaney's, not directly. But in a world where every last inhabitant had at one time or another made Packer's choice, had chosen to turn his or her back on God, in a world that God had long ago cursed, how could there not be fire and flood and pestilence? How could there not be senseless, answerless death?

"Pastor?" Dog said in a soft voice. He was standing outside the priest's bedroom door, knocking.

Will Seline didn't answer.

Dog's mouth pursed into a frown. It was just as he'd been told

by the townspeople. Their spiritual leader, their priest, locked in his room and refusing to speak, to eat, to be comforted in any way.

"Pastor, it's Dog. Doogan Blestoe. I need to talk to you."

Not a sound. This just wasn't right. People had been bringing hot meals and taking them back home cold, or leaving meals spoiled with the waiting. Not right at all.

"I've got something to show you."

Still nothing.

"Has to do with what happened to Panna."

Will Seline rolled over on his back. He didn't know how long he'd been lying here on the floor. It had been some time since he had first felt the pain in his heart, but he didn't know how long. Though the pain was still there, lodged in his chest like a spike, he had felt a good deal of peace since then. He had even slept some, he thought. He sat up. "Just a moment."

When he came out of his room, Dog stood there waiting and walked with him down the stairs. A small, wet group of fishermen stood looking up at him with sorrowful eyes. On the table in front of them were Panna's things. Her knapsack, and her autumn cloak. Will was drawn toward them as though they were Panna herself. He picked up the knapsack gently, as he would a living thing, and held it in his hands. Water beaded and dripped from it like tears.

"It's hers?" Dog asked.

Will nodded. "Where...where did you find them?"

"On the beach," Dog said.

"And Panna?" He searched Dog's eyes.

He shook his head. "She wasn't there."

Will nodded, then picked up the cloak as gently as he had the knapsack, and held it in his big hands. It was soaked from the rain, and it smelled of wood smoke. But it was Panna's. He looked at it more closely, and saw the dark stain where Talon had cleaned her blade. He touched it, and the bloodstained water trickled from his fingers. He looked Dog in the eye. "Tell me."

Dog swallowed. "Duck Tillham and Ned Basser were found there, with these things. They're dead."

Will looked confused. "Dead? How?"

"Killed."

"How?"

"Murdered. By Packer Throme."

Will's brow furrowed and the pain in his chest increased. It couldn't be. The boy was reckless, but he wasn't a murderer. "How do you know?"

"I saw it, Pastor. I saw him with my own eyes. I was lucky to get away without him seeing me, or I'd be dead, too."

Will Seline sat down heavily on the bench where Packer and Panna had embraced only a few nights earlier.

"I'm sorry," Dog said stoically.

Will looked at the bloody cloak again. It couldn't be. And yet, Dog had seen it. Dog was a blowhard, and often a fool. But he was not a liar. "You're absolutely sure it was Packer?"

"It was at a distance, but yeah. It was him."

Will studied Dog's eyes. There was no doubt there, and a hint of defiance. But Dog could be wrong. Will sighed. "Thank you for bringing these." He stood, gathered up the articles, and turned to go back up the stairs.

"Father Seline," Dog said abruptly.

Will stopped, turned back, his face a blank.

Dog had meant to ask him what he was going to do, to ask him not to disappear into his room again, but he couldn't do it. "Is there anything I can do?"

Will nodded. "Yes. You can pray." He looked at the other fishermen. "We can all pray." His feet felt like they were made of lead as he slowly climbed the stairs again.

Dog and the others exchanged grim looks. How do you tell a grieving priest to quit hiding from his troubles, to stand up and take it like a man?

Chapter 13

Accused

When the winds abated just before dawn, the starboard watch was called to deck. The crewmen were, as a whole, in good spirits. A clear sky, a stiff breeze heavy with the recent rain, and calm waters were a tonic, as they ever have been to sailors, easing whatever ills they may be suffering.

These had lost a promising young sailor the night before. There was no memorial service for Marcus Pile. Andrew Haas gathered the men of the port watch and gave them the news, which to a man they already knew. Then he told them how Jonas Deal had cut loose the smallest shallop for Marcus, which to a man they didn't know, and were happy to hear. Finally, Andrew said a quick but heartfelt "May God have mercy on his soul," and ordered them all back to work.

"More should be said," Delaney suggested softly. "If he were here, he'd pray a prayer that would knock every man on his hindquarters."

"He would indeed," Packer said, relieved beyond measure to hear pain rather than anger in Delaney's voice.

And Delaney smiled, thinking back. "Like he said, we hardly ever do know why God does what he does." He took a deep breath, wiped the corner of his eye.

"To work, you two!" Andrew Haas commanded.

Delaney looked at Packer and nodded, thankful.

Most all the sails on the mainmast and the majority on the mizzen were quickly unfurled. The foresail was lost, so its tatters were cut loose and given to the sea. The ship carried plenty of spare canvas, and the men of the starboard watch went to work fashioning a replacement.

Scat's readings determined that the storm had blown them just inside the Achawuk waters, but much too far west, putting them still a good nineteen leagues from their objective. The wind blew with five to ten knots less force than it had the previous day, prior to the storm, and came now from the southeast. But it was gusting.

They headed northeast, directly across the wind. This was a stroke of good fortune that Scat took as a sign; sailing at ninety degrees to the wind provided the fastest possible progress. He maintained the best speed he dared by furling more sail and letting the ship heel to port so far that the deck was angled at almost thirty degrees. He might have taken an even greater risk but for the occasional bursts of wind that rocked the *Chase* as though she had been poked with a great stick. The Captain had been known to put the gunwales in the water when he wanted to make time, but he was loath to do it today with the wind so unpredictable. But the seasoned sailors paid little attention to either the slope of the deck or the rolling caused by the gusts, both absorbed by their legs with little effect on their activities.

They worked through the morning. "When are you going to prepare them, Captain?" John Hand asked finally, watching the sailors fly up and down the rigging without a care.

Scat was craning his neck upward, watching his newest sailor, the only one who seemed less than enthusiastic. Packer Throme was perched precariously on the footlines above the mainsail. "Soon as we get a good heading," Scat answered.

"Right." Hand knew this was an evasion. Scat was never satisfied with a heading; he would continue to fine-tune the set of the sails forever. He simply didn't like to bring the men down from the rigging. It slowed the cat's reflexes.

"Any sign of your escorts?" Hand asked.

Scat shook his head. "I've offered a gold coin to the man who spots one or the other of them today."

"That's safe money," Hand replied. Scat laughed. They both knew that the *Camadan* and the *Marchessa,* if they had also found themselves in Achawuk waters, were now headed out as quickly as possible. Only the *Chase* would be bound deeper yet.

Just then Andrew Haas approached with news. "The navigator reports we should be sighting land shortly."

Scat sighed. "Well, let's pay the piper. There's a dance to be danced. All hands a' deck, Mr. Haas," he said quietly.

Haas was a simple man with a gentler soul than Jonas Deal, but he was a rock of a sailor. He nodded without showing a trace of curiosity. "All hands on deck!" he bellowed impressively, but impassively. He quickly ran below to repeat the command in person to any members of the starboard watch not already on deck working on the foresail.

Packer was delighted to hear the command. Delaney had taken him under his wing and was showing him the trade as best he could, which of necessity took their minds off Marcus. But Packer's fingers and palms were hot where they were being chafed by the rigging, and his feet hurt from standing on the thin footlines. The good news was that his back and shoulder were hardly a concern. Whether it was the Firefish he'd eaten, Marcus's prayer, or that he simply couldn't afford to pay attention to anything else up here in the rigging, he didn't know.

Packer wasn't surprised to find himself high above the deck. He had heard enough about life on the big ships to know that a novice was always sent straight up the rigging at the first opportunity, so fears would have no time to settle in. And Packer understood sailing; his father had taught him the basics well. Even though he didn't yet know the names of all the sails or how they worked in unison with one another, he certainly knew the intended effect of every effort he was commanded to make. In this regard, his knowledge was equal to that of the most experienced hands aboard.

But he moved in the rigging like a great walrus compared to the nimbleness of Delaney and the other seamen. It was impossible for him to ignore, as they did, the exaggerated movement of the ship's mainmast. It was like an inverted pendulum in the sky, causing him to sway precariously, particularly at the extreme end of each pendulum swing. The occasional jarring movements caused by the wind gusts were devastating, feeling more like cannon shot than any natural occurrence, and these quickly became unnerving, causing him to tense up head to foot and squeeze the rigging in his hands until his fingers, hands, and forearms ached.

And to make matters worse, because the ship was heeled port, when Packer looked down he saw the sea rushing below him rather than the solid deck. His brain kept telling him he should be somewhere else. Anywhere else.

Within two minutes of Mr. Deal's orders, all the men but one were on deck and at attention before the Captain. Scat Wilkins stood on the quarterdeck. Packer's feet touched the planking just as Scat began his address. The novice ran as quickly as he could, but lost his balance and almost knocked Delaney over in his haste to fall in alongside him. Packer was very much aware of the looks, the sideways glances, the stifled laughter.

Scat ignored it all. "Men, you have shown me again and again the stuff of which you are made. You're a brave lot, as I saw last night in the rigging. My thanks." A murmur of pride and appreciation for the words rose and fell again.

"We lost a good man in Marcus Pile, and he'll be missed." Slight pause. "But considering the force of the gale, we're fortunate not to have lost more." Murmurs of agreement. Lund Lander, standing with the men, looked for any trace of discomfort from Scat, any sign of remorse or guilt for shooting down the very man he praised. The Toymaker looked in vain.

"We have the good fortune to have a replacement already aboard, a young man you've already met—or at least have seen, both fore and aft of our ship, and tied to a rope." Some laughter. Packer lowered his eyes, embarrassed. "Packer Throme has paid his dues for stowing away, and in any event will have to pay his passage from here out as a sailor. He should be accepted as such, on my orders. As your mate Delaney can tell you, he's also good with a sword. As good as they come." Some nods and grunts. A few stolen glances toward the boy. Delaney winked at Packer.

The Toymaker and John Hand exchanged looks. Good with a sword? How did Scat know that?

"And we'll need every sword this day," Scat continued, his tone growing somber, "as well as all the courage you can muster." The men cut glances at one another, questioning. "Odds are very good that before the end of this day..." he smiled a half smile and finished the sentence matter-of-factly, "…there'll be a fight." A cheer went up, led by the more experienced warriors aboard, Delaney among them.

Packer was amazed by their reaction. They didn't know who they'd be fighting, or why. But it was clear it had been a good long while since last they'd been called to arms, given their broadswords and muskets and pistols and powder horns, and ordered into the fray. They were delighted by the news.

Scat held up his hands to quiet them. When he spoke again, he was more somber yet. He leaned on the quarterdeck rail. "Listen to me, now. I've taken my readings, and the truth is simple. The gale has blown us deep within the Achawuk territory." Eyes grew wide and a few faces turned white as the blood thirst drained away.

"We have a good ship, the fastest ever built. We can certainly outrun canoes. The wind is sound, and the weaponry favors us. But the Achawuk attack in numbers. Great numbers. I have witnessed it, and lived. If you witness it, you will also live.

"Should we be attacked," and now Scat's guttural intonation came from somewhere well beyond this ship or this moment, from somewhere within the heart of man's most martial instincts, "I expect every mother's son of you to be as brave and bloody a man today as ever you will be on this earth."

The men were silent, but it was a fierce and deadly silence. Their Captain's words had hit their mark. "Vigilance. Precision. Glory. In that order. Now to the armory, Mr. Deal—and battle stations one and all until further notice."

Scat's own iron, his fire, had given them all strength. The men lined up at the armory, took their swords, muskets, and pistols, then moved quickly to their positions, all in silence. Packer ran to the stateroom where he'd been quartered to fetch his sword. Then, from the armory, he took a pistol, a weapon with which he had little experience. "Just tuck it in your belt," Delaney said with a nod. "You'll be glad you have it." The sailors stood mainly along the gunwales, although some men had positions in the rigging, and two were assigned to the crow's nest. Packer stood alongside Delaney on the port side, and watched, and waited. The creak of mast and flap of sail that moments ago had seemed vibrant sounds of the good life at sea now sounded ominous.

"Run up the battle flag, Mr. Deal," Scat ordered. He had waited

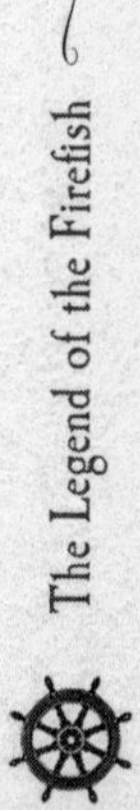

until all else was ready. This was a ritual for him his whole career, and one he was unwilling to give up simply because he was no longer a pirate.

Jonas Deal took this responsibility personally. He took the heavy roll of black cloth from the binnacle, draped it over his shoulder, and retied his belt over it, front and back. Then he climbed into the ratlines and up to the mainsail. The men all watched as he climbed past the maintop, the maintopgallant, and past the skysail to the crow's nest. From there he climbed up to the truck, the highest point of the mast. He then tied the grommets of the flag to the staff. When he let it go, forty square feet of black cloth, overlaid with a white skull floating above crossed bones, snapped full into the wind.

The crew, all but Packer Throme, cheered lustily.

Talon sat on the deck below the sail of her tiny vessel, watching Panna bail the bilge water over the side of the boat. They had ridden the storm most of the night, northward along the coastline. Talon was pleased with herself. Not many sailors could have survived a night running with those winds, especially with a green hand at the tiller.

It had been rough, to say the least, and dangerous. She had navigated by staying, as much as possible, within sight of shore. She had lost its outline in the rain and wind only a handful of times. With strength, luck, and courage, she had ridden the very brunt of the gale, avoiding both the rocks of the coastline and the unknowns of the open sea. She knew she was running far north of Inbenigh, toward the City of Mann, which was not according to her plan, but she had no desire to turn back. She had no desire to stop flying on the back of this storm until the storm itself deposited her wherever it would.

Talon felt like she had crossed a threshold. She had been freed from the power of Scat Wilkins, from the authority of any human. Since then she had defeated the Firefish; she had killed, and she had beaten death. She had ridden the storm, fearless before the lightning, the waves, the wind, and the rocks. Earth, wind, fire, and water were hers to command. She owned the elements; she felt as though she had been released into the dark power of the universe itself. She felt invulnerable.

Panna, on the other hand, had spent the night utterly terrified, once again feeling helpless and inadequate. The woman had not only kept them sailing through a horrible storm, but laughed merrily at the most dangerous moments, times when Panna was certain the boat would capsize, or run aground, or simply come apart with the stress. It was hard for Panna to believe this was the same woman who had been at death's door at sunset. It was as though the howling wind and danger that had caused Panna's heart to falter instead strengthened and energized this woman. Panna had counted the hours of the night in minutes, sometimes in seconds, as they climbed up a wave, dashed down the other side, and in between were thrown high into the air.

Panna's muscles had been knotted and burning within an hour, and after two hours she'd had no idea how she even managed to keep her grip on a tiller she couldn't feel beneath her cold hands. When it had become too much, when her shaking body simply gave out, there was Talon, screaming fierce words in a foreign tongue, manhandling her, slapping her, until Panna found the strength to continue for a few more minutes. And somehow, those few more minutes tallied up, until finally, light came from the East.

By the time the wind had finally died down, just before daylight, Panna was shaking like oak leaves in an autumn wind. And when she collapsed onto the floorboards, sitting in a foot of cold water that sloshed around her, she was finally beyond the capacity to care.

Talon just laughed. She ducked below and returned with a small wooden bucket. "If you must sit, at least bail." She threw the bucket into the water at Panna's side.

Panna was exhausted, cold, and hungry. She stared at the woman.

"Bail! You understand?"

Panna eyed Talon coldly. But with trembling hands and shaking arms, she filled the bucket from the seawater around her, and with a great effort emptied it over the side. The bucket was far too heavy, amazingly unwieldy, but Panna struggled until it was full again, and then emptied it once more.

Talon watched the girl carefully, as she had all during the night. There was much here to be admired. The girl didn't whine, didn't ask questions. She just did what was necessary. These were unexpected traits in a female whelp of Nearing Vast. A young woman with such strength was unusual enough in the Vast wasteland. More unusual yet, her knuckles were bruised and cut as they could only be if she had fought. A deep bruise along her left wrist showed there had been a struggle. And yet her face was unmarked. It was as though this young woman had inflicted a beating.

Stranger still, she was wearing a man's clothing. Not that this was much of a disguise. Her shirt and pants were long since soaked through, clinging to her. Her long hair was limp and lay wet across a bosom that was impossible to hide. This one would be very hard to mistake for a man.

"That's enough for now," Talon ordered in her thick accent. She was afraid the whelp's shaking hands might drop the bucket over the side.

Panna wiped a tress of wet hair from her eyes with cold and trembling fingers. She stared up at the woman, and waited sullenly for another command.

"You are an outlaw," Talon said simply.

Panna nodded, wondering how she knew.

"But you are not very good at it," Talon added, just as simply.

Panna looked confused.

"Tell me what you have done."

Some clarity returned to Panna, enough that she was aware of the danger that might result from her answer.

"I am not the law," Talon assured her. "I cannot help you if I do not know what you've done."

Panna's heart beat quicker. The woman wanted to help! "I…may have killed a man," she replied quietly, with more defiance than remorse. She felt horribly weak, but did not want to be seen as such. Talon raised an eyebrow. "I don't know. But I'm sure a lot of people are searching for me."

Two fewer than Panna knew. "If they are searching where I found you, then I believe you have escaped. You are a long way from there now." Panna nodded. This was certainly a true statement.

Talon drew her knife, looked at it carefully. "So. This man you attacked. Did you hurt him with my knife, with the weapon you stole from me?"

"No!" Panna was shocked by the charge. The wind gusted suddenly. Neither woman paid it any mind. "I didn't steal it. And I certainly didn't use it to…" Panna did borrow the knife, but only to get a piece of canvas. To steal a piece of canvas. She had borrowed the knife to steal…she closed her eyes, trying to get past the sudden confusion.

Talon watched with hidden satisfaction as the force of her simple accusation worked on the girl. Panna was ignorant of Talon's crimes, of course, she knew only the extent of her own. Panna had attacked a man; Panna was hunted; Panna had taken the knife; and Panna had tried to steal the canvas. With a single question, a verbal slash as quick and perfect as her knife strokes had been, Talon cut deeply into Panna's conscience, left her struggling to defend herself.

"I didn't use your knife to hurt anyone." Panna shook her head for emphasis, trying to think of a way to convince the woman. "I thought you were dying. I needed canvas to keep you dry." Her words sounded so empty.

"You are an assailant. You are a thief. Why should I believe you are not a liar as well?"

"I'm not lying." Panna said it with conviction, but knew she couldn't prove it to this woman's satisfaction. Instead, she looked at the water sloshing around her over the floorboards. "I'm not lying," she said quietly.

Talon nodded, the duel over. Panna was disarmed. The Drammune swordswoman toyed with the knife blade in her hand. The girl had the strength of her youth, but she had the naiveté of the Vast. That such a girl should be considered dangerous to anyone was absurd, another evidence of the weakness of this Christian kingdom.

Now, finally, Talon allowed an ember of empathy into her voice. "How did you become such a desperado, little one?"

Panna looked up quickly, jumping at the small spark, ignoring the condescension, wanting the ember to grow. "Yes, I am desperate, I suppose. If I've become an outlaw, it's because I'm searching for the man I love. I intend to find him, and to let no one stop me." Panna felt the power of her mission once again.

Driven by love. The girl's foolishness knew no bounds. And certainly, this was Packer's girl, Panna. How could it not be? They were perfect for one another.

Talon's half-smile was one of derision. "Who is he? What is his name?"

Panna was encouraged. "Packer Throme. He went to sea three nights ago. I believe he's in danger, and I want to find him."

Talon's smile vanished momentarily, then returned, slightly more genuine but also less friendly. Though she had expected it, the sound of that name was to Talon the sound of a curse. "Go on." Talon's voice showed no change of emotion.

But Panna caught the falter in Talon's smile. She didn't understand it, but it reined in her spirit. "That's all, really. And how did you come to be washed ashore?" Panna asked Talon instead.

Talon's mind worked behind blank eyes. She knew the ways of the Vast sheep well enough. Theirs was a peculiar but very powerful mythology of procreation, one that intertwined all their notions of fate, of faith, and of flesh. They called it love. It was notoriously easy to manipulate.

"That is my business. You are an outlaw," Talon answered without emotion. "I am asking you about yourself because I am not yet sure I can trust you."

Panna swallowed, recognizing again her own weakness, hating the feel of it. But she was exhausted, and out of answers. Tears rose to her eyes and she wiped them away ruthlessly, almost violently. The woman was right; she was no good at being an outlaw.

Talon smiled again, but this time she was genuinely entertained. "What is your name?" The ember of compassion glowed again. She sheathed her knife.

Panna wanted very much to fan the ember. "I'm Panna. Panna Seline," she said gently.

There was a pause. "I am...Talon."

Panna misheard it. In her ears, unaccustomed to the heavy accent, it sounded very different. "Tallanna," Panna repeated. "That's...a pretty name."

Talon suppressed a smile. "It is Drammune for...bird."

And the two women smiled at one another.

"You need rest."

The words were a featherbed to Panna's soul. "Yes," she told Talon. "I'm very tired."

"Go beneath. There's no bed, but there's a shelf where you can lie down. You may even find something dry. Fishermen of your country know how to prepare for the sea."

"Thank you," Panna said with all sincerity. "But where are we going?"

"I know where to dock. It won't be long."

Under the deck, the small cabin provided a welcome surprise. Bound up in a canvas, tied tight against the moisture, Panna found a blanket rolled around a few candles and a handful of matches. She stripped off her wet clothes, wound herself in the blanket, and was fast asleep within minutes.

Talon sailed on, looking for a particular cove she knew, near the Bay of Mann. Plans were already formed in her mind. A young woman attached to one of Senslar Zendoda's protégés could be granted access, under the right circumstances, and with the right story to tell, almost anywhere. Even to Senslar himself.

Scat ordered grapeshot into the cannons. Powder was loaded, shot rammed home, ignition powder poured. Torches were lit to provide the spark. Muskets and flintlocks were loaded. Seventy men stood ready, eyes scanning the seas. Within a few minutes, their vigilance paid off.

"Land ho!" Southeast of them, off the starboard bow, a small island could be seen. Men pointed, and whispered.

"Nor'east ten degrees, helmsman," Scat ordered. He did not order an accompanying change in the angle of the sails, a fact which went unnoticed by precisely no one. Clearly, the need for vigilance now outweighed the need for precision, in Scat's mind. *Vigilance. Precision. Glory.* In that order. Scat wanted to steer clear of all islands if possible.

"Land ho!" came another call. Another island was now visible off the port bow.

"Steady as she goes, helmsman," Scat ordered. He hoped the next island that appeared was not dead ahead. They'd find themselves surrounded, and by their own navigation.

"They overrun you," Delaney told Packer in a whisper. "Hundreds of 'em. They say they appear like ghosts." The two were leaning on the port rail, watching the sky where it met the horizon. Delaney's eyes darted anxiously, looking for spirits to materialize before them.

"What are their weapons?" Packer asked.

"Spears. No guns, no arrows, no swords. Spears and fire. That's all."

Packer took a deep breath. He wished it were swords. But if it was to be spears, he had the right weapon. His rapier would allow him quicker movements than this broadsword, but he would have trouble using its thin blade to block the thrust of a spear's shaft.

"You'll do fine," Delaney told him.

Packer only then realized how worried he must look. "I've never been in a battle."

Delaney smiled. "But God has been in every battle that's ever been fought. You know Him. You'll do fine."

Packer nodded. "I keep thinking of Marcus. What would he have made of this?"

Delaney nodded. "I been thinkin' about him, too. And I'm glad God spared him the Achawuk. I truly am."

"Land ho!" came the cry once again. A third island was spotted off the starboard bow, just where the first had been when it came into view.

"Steady," Scat said.

The wind kicked up, heeling the ship a few degrees. Scat studied the rigging, decided to let it stand.

"We get in a scuffle," Delaney whispered, "you watch the Cap'n. He'll be a madman. Never saw anyone fight like him." Delaney's eyes grew bright with memories. "You know why they call him Scatter, don't you?"

Packer shook his head.

"'Cause he scatters his enemies across the decks."

Cap Hillis was delighted to be back in the streets of Hangman's Cliffs, with a cart full of ale and two gold coins left in his purse. This would be a good year, thanks to Scat Wilkins and Packer Throme. He was even more pleased to see a horse tied to the post outside the Firefish Tavern. That meant a stranger, maybe two, looking for ale. Few fishermen owned horses, and he knew most of those sorry beasts on sight.

As he entered the front door, he knew immediately that this stranger meant business, but not for Cap's coffers. He was a lawman, wearing the badge of a deputy of the Sheriff of Mann, and he waited at the bar. Hen, serving from behind it, took one look at Cap and came running.

"Cap, Cap, thank God you're back. It's been terrible, just terrible! Panna's run off and Riley's hurt and Duck and Ned—"

"Ma'am!" the man said sharply, cutting her off. She put a hand to her mouth, but didn't take her eyes off Cap. "I told you I'd need to talk to your husband alone," the lawman continued. He was a square man, angular and defined, with a droopy mustache and a furrowed brow. His voice was deep and melodious. He looked fully the part of the competent, confident deputy. "I'm sorry to bark at your wife like that, sir, but I need to find out what you know and what you don't."

Cap looked from Hen's terrified eyes over to the lawman and back. The two gold coins in his pocket suddenly seemed heavy and leaden. His heart sank. "Well, don't you worry, Hen. It'll be fine. Just fine. I'm sure. You go on upstairs." He kissed her forehead. "I'll talk to him."

She searched his eyes, her chins trembling. She found some small comfort, smiled, and was gone.

"How long have you been waiting here, Deputy?" Cap asked lightly, pouring him a fresh cup of coffee. Cap had offered ale, as Hen had done, but the lawman preferred strong coffee, which Hen had brewed. Cap had closed and locked the tavern door, made a spot for the two of them to sit. He chose the same table where he and Packer had shared a pitcher of ale three nights ago.

"Oh, not long. An hour or so, give or take."

Cap nodded, setting the pot on the table. "So," he said, trying not to betray his nervousness, "how can I help you?" Whatever the issue, it was plainly obvious that nothing good had come of Packer's efforts.

"I'm Deputy Sheriff Marshall Bromley," the deputy said.

"Nice to meet you, Deputy. Or rather, Marshal."

"I know it's a mite confusing, but Marshall is my given name."

"Ah. Deputy Marshall."

Bromley sniffed. "Deputy Bromley. Anyway, we've got some trouble here, and the people of this town keep sending me to you."

"Is Packer okay? And Panna?"

"I'll tell you what I know. But first I wonder if you'd mind giving me a statement."

Cap didn't see that he had much of a choice. "Sure. I mean, no." Cap swallowed. "That is to say, I'd be happy to." Cap was not sure

what the deputy meant by "giving a statement," but he figured it out quickly enough when the deputy pulled a sheaf of parchment from his bag, and then a bottle of ink and a quill, and began writing down everything Cap said.

"Let's see, I have the date here. You're Cap Hillis?"

"Yes."

"That your given name, is it?"

"Caspar. Actually. Cap is what my parents called me since I was a tyke no higher than a down thistle. See, I used to like to wear—"

"Caspar. That's fine."

Cap nodded.

"You know a man named Packer Throme?"

"Sure I do. Everyone does. Least around here."

Deputy Bromley dutifully wrote each word. Then he looked at Cap thoughtfully. "If you could see your way clear to answer the questions with just a yes or a no, I'd appreciate it a lot."

Cap nodded sympathetically.

"When did you see him last?"

Cap thought a moment. "Yes. Three days ago." He watched as the deputy wrote, noticed he didn't write down the "yes."

"Did he say or do anything suspicious?"

"I…don't understand what you mean."

"I mean, did he yell at anyone, or fight, or make threats, or anything that might make you think he was dangerous?"

Cap rubbed his beard with his fingernails. "He fought Dog."

"Dog?" the deputy asked as he wrote.

"Yeah…" Cap had to think a minute to remember his real name. "Doogan. Doogan Blestoe."

"Who started the fight?"

"Dog did. Doogan."

"How?"

"He insulted Packer's father, said no one needed him around." There was so much more to it than that. "See, Packer's father died a few years back. He wasn't always one of the boys, if you know what I mean, and Dog—"

The deputy's look stopped Cap.

"Sorry."

Bromley looked down at the blank part of his page and grimaced. "I'm just going to write, 'Insulted his father.' That okay with you?"

Cap shrugged. "Sure. Fine with me."

"Swords, knives, pistols, or fists?"

"Swords."

"And who drew first?"

"That'd be Dog. Doogan."

"Anyone hurt?"

"Naw. Dog got a couple of scratches. Packer coulda killed him, but had mercy."

Bromley sighed deeply, wrote it all out.

"Sorry," Cap offered.

"And have you seen Packer Throme since the fight?"

"Yes."

The deputy wrote, didn't look up. "When did you see him last?"

"Oh." Cap took a deep breath, blew it out. "That same night I…closed him in a barrel, if I recall. And then, let's see, yes, then I sent the barrel with the pirates to Scat Wilkins' ship." Cap coughed, cleared his throat, sniffed, and waited.

The deputy didn't write. He put his quill down and looked hard at Cap.

"Is that too much to write down?" Cap asked hopefully.

"You mean you smuggled him?"

"No, no. No smuggling. He was…stowing away. That's all."

"Friend, do you know what you're saying?"

Cap sighed, nodded. "The truth, I'm afraid."

Now the deputy dipped his quill. "'Closed him in a barrel.' Whose idea was this?"

"Packer's."

The deputy wrote for a while, but Cap couldn't read what it said because Bromley put his hand in front of it. "And that's the last you saw him?"

"Yes."

The deputy sat back. He didn't look happy.

Cap squirmed, rubbed his beard. "Can I ask you a question you don't write down?"

"Go ahead."

"What happened? You know, I didn't think it was such a good idea for him to stow away, but he was determined to get on board that ship. I was a good friend of his father's and felt I owed it to him. I hope nothing bad has happened."

"Nobody's seen Packer Throme. Or Panna. But there's been violence ever since those two disappeared."

Cap shook his head. "What violence?"

Deputy Bromley shuffled through his papers. He found one and consulted it. "Man name of Riley Odoms got beat up next night, night afore last. Man name of Nedrick Basser, known as Ned, and a man name of Domm Tillham, known as Duck, got killed the following day. Yesterday."

"*Killed?* Ned and Duck got *killed?*"

Bromley nodded. "Ned was shot and Duck was stabbed while out in the woods looking for whoever it was beat up Riley Odoms. Panna Seline's belongings were found with them. Unless she's dead, or she did it herself, she's likely with whoever it was who killed them. Doogan Blestoe was a witness. Says it was Packer did the killing."

Cap was shaken, and shaking. His voice quivered noticeably. "Deputy, whoever it was, it wasn't Packer Throme did that. He wouldn't do such as that. And if he did, he was protecting Panna's honor or some such thing. And you can write that part down."

Bromley nodded, sympathetic. "I will. I know he's a friend of yours. But I got to tell you it looks real bad. People say the Seline girl would go anywhere, do just about anything for that boy. Is that right?"

Cap had to nod. "Maybe. But Packer wouldn't do that."

Bromley shuffled some more papers. "Says here Packer got in trouble in sema…sem…in school for attacking a priest." He raised his eyebrows and watched Cap's reaction. It was one of resignation. "And somebody took a fishing boat from the dock at Inbenigh, cut the tie ropes, rode it out into the storm last night. That had to be someone who could sail. He grew up in boats like that. And you're telling me he left here wanting to join up with pirates."

"There's a mistake, though. It couldn't be him. He was in a barrel."

"Well, maybe he got out of the barrel." Cap looked so glum that Deputy Bromley felt the need to help out. "Look, it's not a closed case. If Packer didn't do it, we'll find out. Eventually." He started writing.

"What are you putting down there?" Cap asked, trying to read it upside down.

"Just a minute…There." Then he read, "'Last saw Packer Throme when closed him in a barrel, sent him with pirates to *Trophy Chase*. At Throme's request. Not seen him since. Doesn't believe him guilty.' That okay?"

Cap nodded. Nothing was okay. "So what's going to happen now?"

Deputy Bromley stroked his mustache. "I'll take all this back to the Sheriff, and he'll decide. But I'm afraid he won't have much choice. He's going to have to swear out a warrant for Packer Throme's arrest."

"Warrant?"

"Yes, sir. For murder."

The winds were not steady, so the great cat did not reach the appointed waters until just before sundown. An island to the northeast was the only land visible, maybe a league away.

"Tell me what your daddy expected to see here," a tense Scat Wilkins asked Packer Throme after calling him down to the quarterdeck. Packer had not been looking forward to this exchange. He had no way to calculate the *Chase*'s position, but he knew they'd been inside Achawuk territory for a very long time, without a trace of Firefish. Sooner or later, they would have to arrive at Packer's bearings.

Packer looked around him. He shook his head. Why had he come here? Why had he done this? "Firefish, sir."

Scat was irritated by the reply. "Why here? What's so special about these bearings?" Scat bore into Packer with the question, expecting a significant revelation.

It was more than a fisherman's hunch, of course, which brought them all here. The idea that Firefish fed in these waters had been reinforced, or maybe even generated, by a visit Dayton Throme had paid to Packer's benefactor in the City of Mann years ago. Shortly after Dayton had returned home from that visit, he had begun talking about Firefish, and not long after that, about the Achawuk territory. Long before Scat Wilkins began harvesting the Firefish, Dayton Throme had been dreaming of it. Packer knew nothing for certain, but he had always believed that something or someone in the City of Mann had fired his father's imagination—something or someone extremely reliable.

Packer had nothing to hide. But none of this helped. None of those facts seemed solid enough to offer up to a snarling pirate looking for instant results. "We're thirty-nine leagues north-northeast of the Freeman Reef?" Packer asked instead. His voice sounded weak and puny.

"Yes. Yes." More irritation.

Then a thought struck Packer. "How big is the Freeman Reef?" he asked. The captain again stared hard at the boy. But he didn't back down. "I mean, north to south. How long is it?"

Scat spoke through clenched teeth. "About a mile and a half east to west and four north to south. Why?"

Packer nodded. "And are we thirty-nine leagues from the northern tip, or from the southern?"

"From the bay at the south, boy—that's the only navigable point. It's the only way to plot a course or measure a distance. If you knew anything about seafaring, or if your daddy knew anything worth teaching you, you'd a' known that."

Packer nodded. "My father didn't know much about plotting courses on the open seas. Maybe we should sail further, thirty-nine leagues from the northern tip."

The two held one another's gaze for a moment. "That'll buy you about half an hour."

Panna slept deeply and without dreams, waking only when she felt and heard the prow of the fishing boat scratch along the ground.

"Wake up, little desperado," Talon said in her heavy accent, rapping sharply on the wooden decking above Panna's head. "I am going to scout the area."

Panna hated to leave the comfort of sleep and the warmth of the blanket, but she struggled into her wet, cold clothes. She was shivering severely by the time she got out on the deck. Once there, she was quite pleased to find the small boat had been tethered in the sun among tall rushes. The air was warm, and full of the sound of frogs and katydids.

Panna reached down alongside the stern and splashed water onto her face. She tried to get her bearings. The image of Tallanna riding the wind, her eyes ablaze, and the ferocity of her commands, the force of the blows that had slapped Panna awake, these all seemed like a dream now. She had the strong sense that Tallanna was a dangerous person, but dangerous to whom? To her enemies, certainly. But Panna was not her enemy.

"I have found an inn," Talon announced from behind. Panna turned, startled. She had not heard her approach. "You will have a hot bath and fresh clothing. Do you have any money?"

Panna nodded before she thought, then swallowed hard. "Some."

"Good." Talon climbed aboard, sat down on the ship's stern, and looked Panna in the eye. "I have decided to trust you," she announced.

"Okay," Panna said, feeling relieved. Why did she fear this woman?

"I am a Drammune warrior. My ship was overtaken by the pirate, Scat Wilkins."

Panna looked shocked.

"Yes, it is amazing I am still alive. He takes no prisoners."

Panna's eyes were wide, her heart was in her throat. "The *Trophy Chase* attacked you?"

"Yes. Of course. He took all that was of value, and then burned our ship. He killed all aboard. It is his way. But I slipped into the water unseen and escaped, somehow making it to shore, where you found me."

"But I had heard that Scat, that is, that he wasn't a pirate. Anymore."

Talon laughed cruelly. "He would be glad to hear of such rumors. He likely started them. Such foolish talk makes his work easier."

Panna's eyes grew distant as her heart faltered.

Talon watched with satisfaction. "What is it? What is wrong?"

"That's where Packer went."

"Your lover? He went where?"

She looked Talon in the eye, desperate for help. "He believed…"

"What?"

Panna put her head in her hands. Tears welled up from within. "He went to join the *Trophy Chase*. He didn't think they were still pirates."

Talon stared hard at her. Finally Panna looked up, and saw something akin to sympathy in the warrior. Talon nodded. "Foolishness. But now we can help one another."

"How?"

"I am a Drammune warrior washed ashore in Nearing Vast, with no papers, no passage. I will be put in prison if I am found. They will believe me a spy. I need safe passage home. If you help me, I will help you find the *Trophy Chase*, and learn the fate of your Packer."

"Of course I will help if I can. Of course I will." Tears streamed now down Panna's cheeks. "But how can you help me?"

"I am not a spy. But there are Drammune spies in this land. They know people who are not…friends of Nearing Vast. Outlaws, you see, are drawn to one another. I will find those who may know where the pirates make port. Perhaps some who even know its charted course."

Panna had to believe that Packer was still alive, that somehow he had not been killed. He had known the whereabouts of the *Trophy Chase*. Certainly there were others who did as well. But hope was draining from her.

"Where will you find these people?"

Talon smiled. "The inn nearby. It has many guests who do not wish to be known. I will make inquiries."

Panna shook her head, very uneasy. "What kind of inn is this?"

"It is not what you might call a nice place. But do not worry. I will protect you." Talon's smile vanished. "But you must do what I command. Precisely. With no questions. Will you do this?"

Panna didn't answer.

"It is good you hesitate. Think hard about it. You must swear to me that you will obey me, no matter what I ask."

Panna couldn't breathe. Everything in her said this was not a good thing to do. But she felt she had no choice. She was an outlaw. She had no friends in this new, dark world she had entered. She had little hope of finding Packer, and all her hope rested with Tallanna. She had made her choices already. "I swear it." The words sounded hollow to her.

"Good. Now let us talk about what you can do for me."

Panna waited. Talon nodded and continued. "I need to find a person of rank in the City of Mann who will help me. I know of one Drammune native who will understand. You will take me to him. It will not be easy. He is, I believe, the Swordmaster of Nearing Vast."

Panna's eyes lit up. "Senslar Zendoda!"

"You know of him?"

"Yes! He taught Packer the sword! I'm sure I can help you find him."

Talon smiled. "There. You see. We can help one another. Now, let us go to the inn together."

Panna was trembling, but Talon took her by the hand. "Do as I say, and you will not be in danger. You will see."

Chapter 14

Achawuk

Darkness had settled on the water as the *Trophy Chase* turned for home. There were no Firefish. None had been seen all day. The extra league had changed precisely nothing. The wind was now out of the south, so the shortest distance out of the Achawuk territory was to the southeast, their current heading. Dead ahead, if they did not change course once they left the territory, was the Kingdom of Drammun. But Scat did not fear the Drammune nearly so much as he did the Achawuk.

"Sorry about the Fish, Cap'n," John Hand said to Scat Wilkins as they stood on the quarterdeck, looking out over the black water.

"A lot of bluster," Scat replied sullenly. No Firefish, no Achawuk, nothing but a tired crew ready to head home.

"What'll you do with the boy?" Hand asked.

"Nothing."

"Nothing at all?" That didn't sound like Scatter Wilkins.

Scat shook his head. "Nothing for now." He glanced at Hand, saw the disbelief, looked back over the waters. "I promised Talon she could have him. And so she'll have him."

"Ah." Hand's smile was a sad one. "He'd have been better off staying dead."

The ship sailed on, past many small islands that Scat continued to keep as far away as possible. The lookout was alert, vigilant as usual, but had seen no signs of life all day. Now darkness and cloud cover lessened their visibility considerably. Gradually, Scat had needed to decrease speed in order to navigate the islands, which tended to pop up at frighteningly close range. But they were just about clear of the territory, and all aboard knew that the Achawuk attacked with fire. The day's work was done, and done without a fight. By morning, they'd be in charted waters again, where the most dangerous threat to any and all was the *Trophy Chase* herself.

The crew looked forward to it.

A league away from the *Chase,* on the opposite side of a small island, three hundred canoes paddled silently through the waves toward the beach. Each canoe carried four warriors. Each warrior carried a spear. Each spear had a sharp, toothlike head on one end and a large loop of leather or crude twine on the other. Every sun-bronzed face was painted midnight blue, forest green, or deep crimson.

The birch-bark canoes never touched the beach. Before a prow could run aground on the sand, the warriors within it had stowed their paddles and splashed lightly into the surf, heaving the boat onto their shoulders without losing any speed, seamlessly portaging their canoes across the beach inland.

This nameless island was heavily wooded, but less than two hundred yards across. Twelve hundred warriors left their canoes in the underbrush and passed through the thick, tangled growth like floodwaters, emerging in a silent human wave on the other side. From that beach could be seen the lanterns of the intruder, the great ship, as it approached. Without hesitation, without a word or a gesture, they waded lightly into the waves. They had effectively passed through the island unchecked, the woods filtering out their boats and pouring armed warriors into the sea. With spears slung across their backs by means of the loops, twelve hundred warriors swam out to sea, out to meet their prey.

Only three remained behind. Gray-headed and regal, these watched from the beach. One, in crimson paint, standing between the other two, wore the tattered waistcoat that had belonged to the captain of the *Macomb.*

The dark shapes bobbed silently in the dark water. They spread out in a long, thin line, perhaps a hundred feet wide and a thousand feet long. They judged the speed of the ship perfectly. Once it reached them, it would run through their ranks for a great distance, unable to stop or turn quickly enough to avoid meeting virtually every one of them. The warriors waited as the great ship approached.

The two lookouts positioned high above the mainmast were scanning the seas for canoes. For torches. For Firefish. For other ships. Other islands. For anything familiar. But dark, bobbing shapes, the very colors of the ocean at night, were far outside their experience, and almost impossible to see even if they had been told what to look for. With the sun gone and night fallen, the Achawuk were invisible, black spots on a black background. But they were there, and they were waiting.

Scat Wilkins was still on the quarterdeck, and the starboard watch was in the rigging. Officially, all hands were on deck, at battle stations. But with the gravest danger now past, Scat had decided the need for precision outweighed the need for vigilance, and had sent half of the port watch, including Packer Throme and Delaney, up the ratlines to curry favor with the wind. He had less than half the ship's sails unfurled in a steady wind. Gusts were few now, but Scat wanted to adjust his canvas instantly, taking advantage of every breeze. He wished he could run faster, but among islands at night it simply was not wise. There was no need to risk it now.

Packer worked the mizzen. He had gained a little confidence in his footwork, enough so that even in the dim light from the lanterns and torches on the deck below him he could concentrate on the work rather than the danger. Delaney noticed it, and left him to it with the words, "I'll work the main."

Packer was glad to be off the deck, away from the Captain, relieved not to have faced instant punishment, and now, even thankful they had found nothing and were leaving these waters. He was learning more with every command from the deck, every shift of the wind. The triangular mizzen at the stern of the ship, he noted, mirrored the foresail at the bow. Hauling the mizzen sheets in careful concert with the fore, and especially with the spritsail in front of it, would turn this ship instantly—almost pivoting it in the middle. Packer felt a deep urge to be part of a few quick maneuvers, to help the *Chase* through her paces.

Then came the knocking, sounds like sticks hitting hollow trees, or hammers striking empty wooden barrels…many hammers, all at once. The sailors in the rigging stopped their work and looked to the deck below, but saw nothing. Crewmen stood frozen on deck, eyeing one another, afraid of what the sounds might mean.

But Scat knew. The memory rose instantly in his mind—Achawuk spears striking the sides of the *Macomb,* warriors climbing them like ladders.

"Stand and fight, men!" Scat bellowed. "The enemy is upon us!" He pulled his pistol and ran to the lee railing, cursing, baffled as to how they could have evaded his watchmen. There, below him in the dark, were the Achawuk. They climbed their own spears up the side of the *Trophy Chase,* grim and determined. Their faces were darkened, their expressions darker. The nearest one was ten feet below the railing, his spear raised, about to be driven into the hull. Scat put a musket ball through his forehead. The warrior fell but was immediately replaced by another. Those around the warrior showed no emotion, no reaction. They simply filled ranks.

Sailors flew across the decks and down the ratlines, gathering at every rail. Shocked into action, following their captain's lead as well as his orders, they unleashed a volley of musket and pistol fire, dropping about forty more warriors, splashing them back into the dark sea. Through the pungent powder and choking smoke the sailors watched as these forty were instantly replaced by sixty.

Packer stayed in the rigging. He moved as quickly as he could out the footline to the end of the mizzen yard. Hanging out over the ocean, he pulled his pistol from his belt. From this vantage point on the port side of the ship, he could see the warriors like barnacles, thick on the hull—and like seaweed, thick on the black water ahead of the *Chase.* If the first volley had felled any, he couldn't tell by looking. There were hundreds, hundreds of them, just as Delaney had promised, and the first of them were almost aboard. It would soon be swords against spears. Packer aimed and fired. He was unsure what, if anything, he had hit. Or what difference one musket ball could possibly make.

The sight was mesmerizing. What on earth drove these warriors to attack like this, he couldn't help but wonder. He could see even from here, in the yellow lamplight of the decks, faces of stone, actions measured and controlled. It was all business to them.

"Reload! Reload!" The sailors were already reloading their weapons when Scat screamed the order. They had at best half a minute to prepare another volley, Scat figured, and then the Achawuk would be over the rails in force. "Pull the cannon back!" he ordered. "Fire when they come over the rail!" The command was odd, and Scat got blank looks instead of action. He stepped to the nearest cannon, ordered those manning it, "You three! Pull it back to here, now!" He pointed at a spot on the deck ten feet behind the cannon's base plate. The men obeyed, lugging the heavy iron weaponry to the appointed spot. "You got grapeshot, men! Fire when you can take out half a dozen at once!" The sailor with the torch held it near the touchhole, a small vent in the breech of the cannon where the charge could be ignited. The other cannoneers looked, understood, and began pulling their weapons back.

Scat didn't reload his own pistol. He ran to the quarterdeck, pulling out his sword and his dagger. John Hand stood there with a loaded musket in his hands, prepared to aim at the first warriors over the rail. "Where the red blazes did they come from?" Scat asked him.

Captain Hand had been working on the same question. "No canoes and no fire. They just swam out to us."

"Hang them in hell for ignorant savages," Scat said through gritted teeth. But John Hand smiled wryly; the Achawuk had outwitted them. He knew there was deep respect in Scat's dark heart.

Scat squinted out, looking over the waters. Now that he knew what to look for, he could see them. More than a thousand, no doubt. Like lily pads covering a marsh. Even the speed of the *Chase* was no help now. He had sailed her into the midst of the enemy, and the enemy would be aboard before he could sail her out again.

Nothing to do but fight, and Scat knew how to do that. He pulled his sword and waved it over his head. "Come on up, ye monsters! Try the *Trophy Chase*! We'll send you back to the devil to learn some manners!"

The sailors heard the Captain's oath, and the fear in them caught fire. Scat Wilkins possessed that rare military gift, the ability to ignite men to fight without fear. *Back to the devil to learn some manners!* The words crossed the boundaries between laughter and tears, life and death, right and wrong, heaven and hell. Every man who heard them was filled with a dark glee, and a deep love for their Captain. A fight it would be, then—and if so, Scat was the man to follow.

A cry arose from the ship, deep and powerful and unvarnished, as each man let loose from within him the anger and excitement and fear that would carry him to kill, or to die, or most likely, both. It was the roar of the great cat. It sent a shiver down Packer's spine more powerful than any he had felt before. He knew its energy, but he did not join in.

The sailors' second volley felled more warriors than did the first. But the result was the same. The slain warriors were replaced immediately by others, ranks closing quickly with little effect on the whole.

The first Achawuk to reach the railings were unarmed, having left their spears in the ship's hull. This surprised the crewmen, stopped some of them with their swords raised. Here they were, face-to-face with the dreaded warriors they had heard so much about, eye-to-eye with painted, savage, legendary killers, who were tall and strong and muscular and fearless. And who had no weapons.

"Fire the cannon!" Scat screamed.

The first cannon boomed, a blinding flash, loosing its grapeshot as five warriors disappeared, limbs and torsos folding backward like paper dolls in a hurricane. Then the other cannon followed suit, twelve in rapid succession, some simultaneous, each cutting down four or five or six of the enemy at once, blasting away huge chunks of the *Chase*'s railings at the same time. The sweet, acrid smoke was so thick, the flashes in the darkness so bright, that no one on deck could see for a moment, and no one could hear for the ear-ringing aftereffects of the cannonade. And then the breeze took away the blue fog, gently clearing it from the deck, revealing more Achawuk yet, pouring up from the darkness, up over the rails. Still the warriors had no weapons. But each warrior who topped the railing alive reached for the nearest sailor, throttling him barehanded.

Scat saw his men pause, saw their uneasiness about attacking weaponless men, and knew the danger. Every alarm within him sounded; his men could not pause, not even for an instant. He cursed the brilliance of the Achawuk silently and ran to the gunwale himself, bringing his sword across the neck of the first Achawuk warrior he could reach. "Fight, every mother's son of you! The *Chase* is boarded!"

Another guttural cry rose from the sailors as now they waded into their attackers. Every crewman knew there would be no pause again until he lay down among the dead in defeat, or stood over the dead in victory.

But the crewmen found that killing even an unarmed Achawuk was not an easy task. These were strong men bent on destruction, their spirits unwilling to depart their accustomed dwellings without considerable application of force. It took several blows to fell one of them, and they kept fighting, killing armed sailors by strangling them, or by throwing them over the rails to the human piranha below. The effect on the sailors was profound: If the Achawuk were this hard to kill defenseless, imagine them armed with spears.

And very quickly, no imagination was necessary. Their ladder complete, they came each with a spear. Hundreds of hardwood shafts that blocked sword blows, and sharp white spearheads that penetrated flesh.

John Hand didn't leave the quarterdeck. He had fired his pistol once and his musket twice, and was reloading the musket for a third shot. His swordplay was suspect, he knew, and he didn't have the stamina of Scat or of the younger men on deck. He figured this was the best application of his limited fighting skills. But he could only shake his head as the Achawuk continued to pour onto the lamp-lit decks, rising from the darkness…and curse Scat's greed and Packer's information.

Wooden shafts and razor-sharp spearheads clashed and clanked against the sailors' swords, but the grim silence of the warriors as they fought cast an eerie pall over the battle. The great cat's roar was silenced now. The only constant sounds were blows and counter-blows, grunts, cries of pain, bodies thudding to wooden decks. The Achawuk men fought and died soundlessly.

John Hand pulled the ramrod from his musket barrel. At least the *Camadan* was safe, he told himself. That was his first duty. Likely his last as well. He scanned the deck again, looking for the most strategic need. He saw Lund Lander swinging a blade near the shot rack at the port railing, saw a warrior moving in behind him, spear poised. Hand leveled his musket and fired, dropping the warrior to the deck. He reloaded.

The Toymaker didn't notice, didn't pause. He had dispatched half a dozen warriors already, and had fallen into his own rhythm. But he was tiring. They were all tiring. Lund knew that the best-trained man could sustain this level of exertion for six or seven minutes at the most. And they had been at it for at least three already. Good men were falling all around him; the decks were growing slippery with blood, making it harder to stand and fight. Each new Achawuk warrior over the rail was fresh and strong. The sailors were better armed, and were better fighters, but they simply couldn't keep up the pace necessary to deal with the numbers.

The numbers. That was the problem. Lund's brain couldn't help but do the tally. They had seventy men, not counting Deeter, who was hiding somewhere below decks. Each sailor fighting for six minutes on average...averaging two warriors killed per minute, as Lund had done...adding up to eight-hundred-forty warriors killed, at the very most. And as sailors died, the curve grew steeper and steeper for those left fighting. Lund, like Scat, had estimated there were over a thousand of them; he had never heard of the Achawuk attacking with less. The numbers told him this was a losing battle. Numbers never lied.

Scat Wilkins calculated nothing. His face was set like a flint, his teeth were clenched, his eyes unseeing. In one hand was his sword, in the other his dagger. He stood still, dispatching foe after foe, dealing out death with the cold precision and lightning speed of a pit boss dealing blackjack. He was considerably better at the art of killing a man quickly than was Lund, better than anyone now aboard, with Jonas Deal running a distant second.

Scat could kill with such efficiency not just because his destructive skills were honed to a razor's edge, not just because he knew the exact placement of a knife or a sword that would inflict the most lethal wounds with the least energy, but because his skills were plied in the service of only one purpose, more emotion than thought, more lust than emotion. Put into words, which are invariably too precise for such a root and carnal drive, it might come out, *Die, you sons of Lucifer! Die!*

If Lund had made his calculations by Scatter Wilkins' tallies, if the average swordsman aboard the *Chase* could have destroyed six, or seven, or eight enemies per minute as Scat did, the crew could have fended off three times a thousand warriors inside six minutes. But they could not.

Packer stared down at the carnage, desolate. His momentary spark of energy had been drained before he could descend the ratlines, and now the carnage below him was gruesome beyond anything he had ever imagined. In minutes, the Achawuk would overwhelm the resistance on deck. He could see that. They were still

thick on the hull, still thick in the water for a hundred yards ahead. They had actually slowed the ship, creating a force of drag that was never figured into her design. And now they were thick on the deck as well, closing in and overwhelming pockets of sailors standing back to back, fighting for their lives. Those pockets were being squeezed down, then snuffed out like candles. Packer knew that his duty was to climb down into that horde, to kill and die with his shipmates. He was the only one left in the rigging. The thought occurred to him that he was being a coward, but it didn't stick. It didn't matter. Whatever he did now couldn't possibly matter. The outcome was not in doubt.

Still Packer watched. Scat Wilkins was cornered near the stairway to the quarterdeck. To his left was Jonas Deal, to his right was Mutter Cabe. They were holding off all comers, and a significant cluster of corpses surrounded them. Scat seemed to move faster and with more purpose than anyone else. He moved like a dervish, a killing machine. But even these three couldn't last; there were simply too many Achawuk.

Packer's heart felt like it was made of wood. He could feel his hands loosening their grip on the ratlines, but he seemed detached from that fact. What did it matter? He would die like those below would die. And if he survived, he would have to live as a survivor of this horror. What kind of life would that be? He felt as though he'd been sucked down into a whirlpool, as though the inevitable end of all he'd done, all his effort, his dreams, his mission, was this. It was not where he wanted to go, but where he must go, where he could not help but go. He had let the boulder loose, and it would smash what it would smash. It had been the destiny he couldn't see and couldn't escape, the deep darkness at the heart of it all, giving the lie to all his dreams.

But that was a selfish view, wasn't it? Delaney had chastised him for thinking it was all and only about Packer. No, it was bigger than Packer. This was not just his destiny. Death and destruction were the destiny of every man below, every sailor, every Achawuk warrior. None of them evaded it, and all of them played their part.

And then it struck him that this was in fact the destiny of men, across the entire world. Across history. He felt suddenly that he was looking at the world in miniature, a history told in wars and conflict and blood, playing out now on this one small stage. Here was the world's history, and its future. All dreams of glory—not just his, but all dreams—ultimately led here. Hoard gold? Change the world? Make a name for yourself? Gain honor, save your nation, your people, avenge your God? Every insatiable, noble, and heroic drive leads but one place, and this is it: Men killing other men with every ounce of strength they have.

It all leads nowhere else, it could lead nowhere else, because every mother's son on earth is a mutineer, every last soul is Adam in the garden, or Packer in the hold, raising a sword rather than submitting to God. Unwilling to die, we are therefore doomed to kill. And doomed to die killing. No one is spared this fate.

Why did Scat and his men kill? Because they were attacked. Why were they attacked? Because they had invaded the Achawuk territory. Why had they done that? Because they wanted gold.

The Achawuk were no different, no worse, no better. Why did they kill? Certainly there was some glorious reason. They had been invaded. It was pride, it was glory, it was honor, it was religion, it was something. They could no more turn the other cheek than Scat's pirates could. They wouldn't sacrifice themselves; no one would. Everyone had to stand and fight. That was the human way.

Packer had chosen not to die back in the hold. So now he would die on deck. He could have died turning the other cheek...when it would have mattered to God, when it would have been a righteous act, solitary and humble, where God alone would know and Packer's reward would have been eternal. But Packer chose to raise his sword. And now he would die where men would see and God would hide His face, he would die a brother in arms, as millions of men had died before him, and millions would die after, killing other men in a fight over a dream, a right, a principle, a lust, a passion, a truth, a hope.

Packer felt small, and infinitely unworthy, before a great and holy God who looked down on them all, who looked deep into Packer's heart and saw all the evil, all the sin of the whole world. And yet, Packer marveled, that same God, knowing all the ways of man, which from the beginning have been the same since Cain killed Abel, that same God sacrificed Himself. There was, after all, one Man who could do it. The thought gave Packer a shred of hope.

There was one Man who could turn the other cheek, who would "resist not evil," who could and would lay down His life rather than pick up His sword. That Man had come down from the rigging of heaven and joined the bloody fray on deck, but He hadn't fought. He became one of the ragged lot of cutthroats, but He didn't bloody His hands. He didn't defend Himself, or His land, or His dreams, or His country, or His gold, or His honor, or even His God. He allowed Himself, and all the things most valuable to men on earth, to be sacrificed. And to what end? So that people could learn a different way, could learn to lay down their swords, rejecting the ways of earth and taking up the ways of heaven.

Packer felt thankfulness well up within him. He looked up to heaven and asked God why, why He would care at all for such a horde of villains. The answer that came back was clear. It was not a question of men's worthiness, but of God's very being. The God Who is Love could do no other.

Humbled further, Packer found grace to ask God for mercy, not just for himself, but for his fellow mutineers as well. "Do not wipe us off the face of the earth," he pled. "Let us live, so that we can understand some shred of that love, and have a glimpse of the way it works in the Kingdom of Heaven."

Packer began the descent down the ratlines, sword at his hip. He did not know what he would do when he got to the deck, but he did not plan to draw his sword. Christ had descended to the melee, God as man, armed with a power He chose not to use. Packer knew he was not worthy of the comparison, but he was honored to walk in those footsteps anyway. He could die this way. He was following the path of his God at last.

Packer was a few feet from the deck when his eyes met those of an Achawuk warrior coming up over the port rail. *Is this the man who will kill me?* The warrior had his spear in his hand. He looked up at Packer without anger or pity or remorse, but with a very distinct purpose. Packer wanted to ask him why, why he killed, why he died. But the warrior's spear came up, its bone-white tip aimed at Packer. Packer put his hand to his sword reflexively, but he didn't draw it.

He put his foot on the rail. As he did, the great ship rocked. For a brief moment, Packer thought he had caused it, that his weight had jarred the ship. But the canvas overhead had popped at the same time; a great gust of wind had caught the mizzen and had then sustained its energy long enough to heel the ship to port. Packer had to grip the ratline tightly to keep from being thrown down into the water. The warrior in front of him had no line to hold; he lost his footing on the slippery deck and toppled back over the railing, into the ocean.

Packer looked after him: A great number of the Achawuk climbing up the hull, those nearest the waterline, were submerged. As the wind died away and the ship righted itself, he could see that many of the warriors had been swept away. Others grabbed the vacant spears and began climbing.

The wind and the sea had created a break in their lines. The sight gave Packer a small spark of hope that the sailors on deck would at least have a moment's rest from their fighting. But the Achawuk closed the lines quickly, and once again the hull was a single mass of climbing warriors.

As Packer stood on the rail and watched, another gust hit the sails, and more Achawuk were submerged below him. He saw several of them slip, giving the advantage to their adversaries. And then, suddenly, Packer knew.

Like cellar doors ripped away above him, sunlight shone into his soul. Packer could do nothing to change this outcome; he could do nothing but die. But God could do anything. If God would grant them wind…He looked up into the dark sky, asking God if He would grant them more gusts of wind. Patchy clouds scudded across the moon.

Energy arced through him like lightning. He looked around, saw Delaney's blade flicking red through the air. "Delaney!" he called, hands and feet already moving back up the ratlines. "Delaney!" The sailor looked up. "Full sail! Full sail! The wind!"

Delaney was puzzled. He glanced around him, and to his surprise few Achawuk were near at the moment. He looked back up at Packer.

Packer stopped, locked onto Delaney. "I need you!" he yelled. And then he grinned. "The wind!"

Delaney didn't understand the plan, but he understood the hope. He understood the man. He found himself climbing up the rigging before he could think it through.

"Full sail!" Packer yelled, reaching the mizzen yard. He raced along the footlines, hacking every tie-rope he passed, unfurling the mizzen sail completely.

John Hand heard Packer's call. He glanced up at Packer and Delaney as they scrambled around the ratlines, sails dropping in great unruly swaths behind them. It was a curious sight. But he ignored

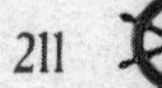

it. He looked back to the deck, saw Mutter Cabe waving his sword in the air, two warriors in front of him. Hand squeezed the trigger; a loud crack and a sharp plume of fire and smoke evened the odds. He looked back up as he reloaded.

Delaney was much faster in the rigging than Packer, and had unfurled the main and then moved above it, to the maintopgallant. Just then another gust hit, this time jarring the great cat significantly, poking it with a much bigger stick. More Achawuk slipped on deck. *Full sail,* Hand thought. He forced himself to pay attention to the wind and sea again, to the ship's heading and the cut of the sails. Then it dawned. *Yes, yes!* "Hard to port!" he cried out, only then realizing no one was manning the wheel.

Delaney had by now figured out what Packer had in mind, and when he heard John Hand's command he quickly understood what the two measures would mean combined, if only the wind picked up. He redoubled his efforts.

John Hand pulled the ramrod from his rifle, took aim at a warrior who was pulling his spear from a fallen crewman, a man the Captain recognized as Cane Dewar. Hand cursed softly, and apologized silently to Cane as he squeezed off his shot. Three seconds earlier and he'd have saved him; now he avenged him.

Hand turned his back to the fray and crossed to the wheel, kicking out the lock timber that held it steady. With great effort he spun the wheel counter-clockwise, trying to get the *Chase* heading east-southeast, at right angles to the wind. Adjusting the sheets was not an option; he was adjusting the course instead so that the sails would fill to their maximum. It wouldn't be precise, but it would have to do.

"Trim the main, I'll get the fore!" Delaney yelled to Packer as he descended toward the deck at the front of the *Chase*. "She'll pivot like she's caught in a maelstrom!"

Packer didn't say a word, but descended as quickly as he could. When he reached the quarterdeck, he quickly untied the main sheets and pulled the yardarm about so that the sail's angle was ninety degrees to the wind, then retied them. Delaney was doing the same on the forecastle deck with the foresail.

No sooner had Delaney tied off his sheet than another gust hit. It was no greater than the previous two, but because all the sails were now unfurled and angled more precisely, they now snapped with great drama. And the *Trophy Chase,* solid and tight as she was, the great cat that leapt with every small variation of sail, now exploded with fury. She rocked as though hit broadside by a dozen cannons, as though run aground sideways. At the same time, she turned hard. And Delaney was right; it felt more like a spin than a turn, the foresail and the mizzen working like the points of a pinwheel.

On deck, these efforts had exactly the desired effect. Every Achawuk engaged in combat lost his footing, and nearly every one of them fell, unaccustomed as they were to great ships such as this. And almost every sailor kept his balance, even on the slippery decks, fully accustomed as each man was to the *Trophy Chase* and her nimble ways. By the time the gust blew itself out, the ship's deck was angled at almost thirty-five degrees.

As the ship gathered way, she gradually righted herself to a less drastic heel and smoothed into about twelve knots of speed. By this time, the standing sailors were eagerly dispatching the fallen warriors. Moments later, the crew looked at one another, in wonder. Where was the enemy? The jolt had momentarily stopped the Achawuk who still climbed the spears on the hull, and had tumbled not a few of them back into the sea.

On the starboard side, the ship's hull had suddenly doubled in height, with the lowest spears well out of reach of those warriors left in the water. And the turning of the ship frustrated those trying to get new spears into the freshly exposed wood. On the port side, the warriors suddenly found themselves submerged, with a wooden hull above them and hundreds of spears, plus dozens of other warriors, blocking their path upward toward the air.

On deck, the crewmen panted hard and looked at one another. It was miraculous. The enemy had fallen. Chests heaving, blood and sweat dripping from them, they looked above them into the sails. They were unfurled. It was an awesome sight. Ghosts, white spirits, they seemed, billowing above them in the lantern glow with no mortal explanation.

At that moment, another gust hit the ship broadside, and the great cat rolled even more dramatically, listing now as though she would go down, with the deck pitched well past a thirty-five degree angle. And this time, the gust was followed by a sustained, powerful wind.

More warriors were rocked off the spears and into the sea.

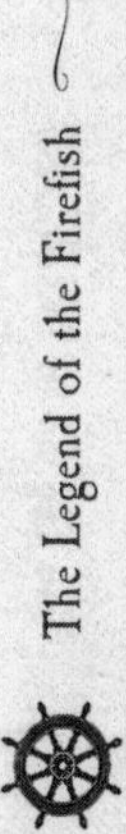

Others, who had managed to hold on, came up over the starboard rail, which was now high above the port rail. But then they tumbled down across the blood-slick deck. But most of the sailors kept their balance yet, even while sliding down the deck to the port rail. They hacked at the warriors as they went, or as they piled into other Achawuk now coming up from the water. But even these were not prepared to fight; they came up spluttering, hanging onto the port railing for dear life rather than climbing over it.

Then the sound came. It started low, with a few inarticulate grunts that were somewhere between deep laughs and vengeful growls. But it quickly grew. The tide had turned. The sailors felt it in their bones. Victory would be theirs. How could it be otherwise? Growls turned to whoops, and a few crewmen sang out in pure exultation. The sea, the wind, the sails, the deck, the *Trophy Chase* herself, all their most powerful, their most beloved allies had come to their aid. Allies summoned by God knew who, perhaps by God Himself, and welcomed down to their souls. And these reserve troops were now literally throwing their enemies down at their feet. The sound grew until the entire crew was cheering, shouting, howling, and singing at once, from their hearts and from their guts. It was a sound of pure joy of body and of spirit, pure internal, animal fire. The cat roared, the roar of a lion in victory. It continued to roar as it dispatched the last of its enemies. The crewmen's strength was renewed. They would not be defeated on this night.

John Hand turned to Packer Throme, saw eyes brilliant with intensity. "It broke their ranks, Captain," Packer explained breathlessly, and needlessly. "Coming up the hull."

Hand nodded. "Aye, that it did, and drowned 'em like rats on the other side." He clapped a hand on Packer's shoulder. He turned to the decks and bellowed, "Haul those sheets to starboard, anyone with an arm and a leg left! Let's sail!" A dozen men who suddenly had no enemy left to fight obeyed, and the *Chase* leapt away from the remaining Achawuk, leaving them to drift away in the ship's wake.

Scat Wilkins did not hear the command. His mind had been working on a level deeper and more visceral than those around him, further from consciousness, more focused, like a great athlete in a long race with the finish line in sight. He had heard the cheers, but couldn't expend the energy to wonder about them. He knew the deck had pitched, and he had used this to full advantage. But he didn't hear, or didn't comprehend, the orders coming from the quarterdeck above him. His focus was unaltered. He waded through the bodies, looking for any sign of life among the Achawuk and removing it. Finally, there was nothing left to fight. There were no enemy left to kill. He breathed heavily through clenched teeth as he looked around him, his eyes still wild, hands and arms drenched in blood to the elbows, boots wet to the knee, face, beard, and clothing bespattered.

Lund Lander had heard Captain Hand's message clearly and understood it immediately. The Toymaker stood dumbfounded, confronted with an amazing fact. There were no more Achawuk. The remaining number was zero. He peered over the rail. Spears stuck out of the hull like the quills of a porcupine. But they were empty. Achawuk floated away in the dark water behind them. *They can't reach us anymore,* he thought. He could hear a few thumps, as a few hardy Achawuk still attempted what was now a hopeless task. But most were now safely behind, thanks to the turning of the ship.

Lund's spirits soared. They were done. He didn't know how or why. They never should have escaped. The numbers never should have worked. But they did work. Something had changed the balance—in favor of the *Chase* and her men.

John Hand called out commands as he spun the wheel, angling for all the wind he could muster. The renewed strength of the crewmen turned from fighting for their lives back to the precision of sailing. They were already out of reach of those warriors left in the water. Now they would fly from these lands, at a speed no Achawuk would match.

It was over. The *Chase* and her crew had fought the Achawuk, and the *Chase* and her crew had won.

Finally, Scat's battle-scarred and blood-soaked brain understood that it was finished. He stood panting hard, blood and spittle flying from his mouth and nostrils with every breath, fire in his eyes. He looked around at his men, expecting to see the admiration, the worship, that was due him. Certainly no one had done more to win this battle, no one had killed more Achawuk than he. He had lived up to his legend once more, had once again proven worthy of his name. His enemies lay scattered at his feet. Instead, he saw all eyes on the quarterdeck—and the smiles, and the looks, the awe, were all aimed elsewhere.

Captain John Hand reached out and shook Packer's hand. "Well done, Packer Throme." He turned to men gathered on the decks. "He unfurled the sails!"

"Packer!" Delaney called out, rushing up the stairs to the quarterdeck, sword high.

"Packer!" the others echoed, many of them speaking the boy's name for the first time. Their bloody swords saluted him.

"Well, say something, stowaway," John Hand said with a great grin across his face.

"God bless the stowaway!" another sailor yelled, and they all cheered again. It was an odd cheer, though, from this group, full of light and thankfulness, as though they knew it was a miracle. Packer was amazed by it.

It had all started so quickly, and ended so quickly. He had been prepared to die, he had gone face to face with an Achawuk, unarmed, and God had chosen that he not die. Why? Certainly not out of merit. And now he was being cheered for it. God had blown wind into these sails and saved them all. They quieted, and waited again. Packer spoke up, thoughtful and obviously humbled. "God sent the wind. I just...helped it make a difference."

"God bless the difference!" someone yelled, and the others laughed.

"Packer!" Delaney cried again.

"Packer!" they roared again in unison. And then they began swiping their swords together, clanging them in celebration high above their heads.

Scat watched this scene with a growing sense of outrage, his chest still heaving. "Why are they cheering the boy?" he growled.

Jonas Deal shrugged. Mutter Cabe, standing on the other side of Scat, grew dark. "Not a drop of blood on him, Captain," Mutter said softly.

Scat's guts knotted up. Cabe was right. The stowaway hadn't even fought! Scat looked down at the Achawuk bodies that lay at his feet. He saw the blood that covered him, his hands, his arms. Deal and Cabe were spattered, soaked.

So why in thunder were they cheering Packer Throme?

There was blood in the water.

The recognition was instant, and the scent was overwhelming. As the beast followed, the scent grew stronger still. And within seconds the enormous, ancient predator was swimming at full speed, its mouth open, its whole being on fire with the craving for soft, fresh meat.

It was quickly joined by another.

And then another.

Chapter 15

The Feeding Waters

The women in the foyer stood and sat, talked and laughed, flirted with the men, as though unaware they were in varying states of undress. Panna blinked a few times, trying not to stare. Some of them were entirely in their underclothes. She realized her mouth was hanging open only when Talon put a finger under her chin and closed it for her. Panna was startled, but Talon just turned away to speak to the man at the desk. The music came from a room off the foyer; raucous, even dissonant music. The room was dark inside, and Panna couldn't see what was happening in there.

Talon handed the deskman Panna's two gold coins, and accepted no change. Then she took Panna by the elbow and walked her up the stairs. Halfway up, Panna realized they were looking at her. Odd smiles, raised eyebrows, whispering, nodding. She looked a mess, she knew, and tried to straighten her hair. Or maybe it was Talon they watched. Or both of them together. She blushed, and lowered her head.

Panna Seline did not like this place.

Scat Wilkins' blood-soaked boots stumped slowly up the creaking stairs to the quarterdeck, toward John Hand and Packer Throme. The crew watched in amazement, their celebration dying away before the specter he presented. He was breathing heavily, and made a chilling, bloody contrast to the unstained hero he approached. He reached the quarterdeck and stopped. He looked hard at Packer, then at John Hand. Delaney shrank away and disappeared down the stairs.

Hand could see the lack of comprehension, the fires of rage and death still burning deep within. "We shook 'em off us," he explained quietly. "Packer's idea, and a good one."

The Captain looked up at the sails. They were golden in the dim near the lamplight, ghostly blue in the moonlight above. Then he looked down at the bloody deck and the men, those fallen and those left standing, waiting. He rubbed his beard, felt the stickiness, looked at his hand. It shook. He wiped it on his shirt absently, without effect. "Shook 'em off us," he repeated, his breaths finally easing some. "Well. How 'bout that." His voice was quiet enough that the men below couldn't hear him, but Packer and Hand both felt its ragged, violent edge. "I gave orders…to fight."

Scat turned on Packer, eyes black and empty. He pointed his dripping blade, bared his teeth. "Where was that sword of yours, boy?"

Packer's words caught in his throat. "I…"

Hand spoke evenly. "He was cutting the yard ties with it, Captain. And you're lucky he was. Without the wind we'd have been overrun."

Overrun? Scat turned his look toward Hand. The very thought was mutinous. Scat's blade went up reflexively. The battle had been long and grisly, and the Captain's mind had been wholly immersed in death and dismemberment. Pride and anger moved him; fatigue clouded his judgment. His spirit had been running full speed before a gale and, unlike his ship, he was not capable of pivoting in an instant. So he raised his sword to John Hand, and as he did images cascaded before him unsolicited. They were images of his blade coming down, hacking across the neck and chest, images of the Captain of the *Camadan* falling to the ground.

"Scat!"

The pirate blinked, then swallowed. John Hand stood before him, alive, angry and intent, his wild shock of hair blowing in the breeze. Scat's eyes grew wide. He looked at his own sword, raised in his hand. What was he doing?

"Salute the men," Hand suggested in a hiss. "And then go get some rest."

The Captain lowered his sword, and turned. His men stood below him, questioning, uneasy, sweaty and bloody in the flickering light, each a mirror of Scat himself. The canvas snapped and the masts creaked above them. They hadn't heard his words, but they had seen the sword, and the anger. And they didn't understand it.

Scat's eyes labored in turning back to Hand. The pirate looked weary to the bone, small and vulnerable, and John Hand felt compassion for his old friend. "To victory," Hand whispered with a wink. Then he jerked his head toward the crewmen.

Scat raised his sword again, and turned to the men on deck. "Victory!" he bellowed. The men echoed a heartfelt cheer, though much of what their hearts felt was relief. After a moment, Scat dropped his sword onto the planking. "The quarterdeck is yours," he said quietly to Hand, and he descended the stairs. The men gave him a wide berth, but there was respect in their eyes, mixed with concern.

Scat nodded at a few of them as he made his way to his quarters. They had won, that was the main thing. The *Chase* was whole. She had been tried, and boarded, and had not been found wanting. All this was good. Scat entered his saloon. He needed a nap, a bath, a drink. And not in that order.

The bedroom was huge, as large as the entire downstairs of Panna's house. It was elegantly furnished, the centerpiece being a canopied cherrywood bed with burl cherry headboard and footboard, with matching side tables and an enormous armoire. A velvet-covered couch and chair stood just inside the door, against the wall. The ceiling was molded, the rugs plush, the walls papered with pink and gold flowers. But most appealing to Panna was the large metal bathtub that sat in the middle of the floor, on an ornate oriental rug. "Gracious," Panna said quietly as she looked around. "We're staying here?"

Talon shook her head. "Not we. You. Tonight you rest, and tomorrow we prepare. The next day, we travel by coach to the City of Mann."

"By coach?" Panna was surprised. "Why?"

"In the city, we will go unnoticed if you are a well-dressed and well-groomed young lady, accompanied by a servant." She paused, then curtsied.

Panna laughed. "I can't do that."

Talon was not amused. "You will do that, and more."

Panna nodded, feeling embarrassed. She had sworn. She just had not anticipated that the orders she would obey would be anything like this.

"Tonight you will bathe, eat, and sleep. Tomorrow you will wear what I tell you to wear, learn what I teach you, and the next day we will travel together as I have described. You will behave as though you are accustomed to privilege. I will guide you. There is nothing for you to decide. Do you understand?"

Panna felt her pulse quicken. She had made the bargain, but even had she not, this woman's commanding presence was impossible to refuse. Tallanna was as frightening now as she had been last night in the howling gale amidst the slaps and curses. "Yes. Yes, ma'am."

There was a knock on the door. Talon said curtly, "Now we begin. From this moment, whenever eyes are upon us, you treat me as your servant." Her voice and demeanor softened, like ice melting in the sun. "Now, if you would step behind the dressing screen, miss?" Panna couldn't help but feel relief, even though she knew this was a feigned sweetness. She obeyed.

Two women, both middle-aged and tired-looking, entered the room carrying four buckets of steaming water, one in each hand. The first was tall and distant, the second short and present. Each wore an apron and carried a thick white towel over a shoulder. They poured the buckets into the lukewarm water waiting in the tub.

"Time for your bath, miss," Talon said in the same sweet voice. "Are you ready?"

"Not quite," Panna said with a tremor. She had not begun to undress. She knew she looked and sounded scared. Serving this servant would be no easy thing to master.

She began unbuttoning Mr. Molander's damp shirt. Her knuckles were bruised, and still swollen. The women were not leaving. Panna did not know how this was supposed to work…were they to stay? To assist somehow?

"You can dismiss the servants," Panna said finally, a quaver in her voice.

There was a pause. "M'lady wishes to bathe alone," Talon told

them without a trace of disappointment, as though accustomed to taking orders from her.

"Very well," the tall one said, taking a small handbell from her apron. "Ring if you need anything at all; more water, towels, whatever." She sounded as tired as she looked.

"Here are some soaps, both bar and cream," said the shorter one, more sweetly. "This one's especially good for hair." She took the items from her apron and set them on the dresser.

"Thank you," Talon said as she ushered them out.

She appeared around the dressing screen, an angry scowl on her face. "You were born to privilege. You should not dismiss servants who are sent to help you."

Panna fought back fear, resisted the urge to swallow. She held out her hands, darkened knuckles out. "I didn't know how to explain this. I was afraid they might ask."

Talon's look softened. She nodded. "There is no explanation for that, not in a young lady of your position. You did well. I will get you gloves tomorrow, and you will not be seen without them."

"Yes, ma'am." Panna's eyes widened. "I mean…"

Talon raised one eyebrow. "We'll practice tomorrow. Bathe. You will find bedclothes in the armoire. I will have dinner sent up. Then sleep."

Only when Talon was gone and the door was locked could Panna begin to relax at all. The soaps were scented with lilac and were smoother than anything she had ever used before. The cream soap, just for hair, lathered wildly. The water in the tub had a smooth, almost oily texture, and smelled of honeysuckle.

When Panna did finally relax, she enjoyed the most wonderful bath she had ever taken in her life.

"Tie those sheets!" Hand called out when Scat was gone, as though nothing were amiss. And in fact, in his mind, nothing was. The incident was over and done. Scat Wilkins was a warrior, among the most skilled he'd ever known, and the blood frenzy in battle was his trademark. John Hand understood this warrior well enough to give him a wide berth. He would hold no grudge.

"Starboard watch, clear the decks of the Achawuk, count 'em

as they go over. Line up our own by the starboard rail. Port watch, swab the decks."

The crewmen were now feeling the effects of their exertion; the powerful energy of victory was fading, particularly as they began to consider the tasks ahead of them. They moved slowly across the lamp-lit decks. They had lost track of time, and with the darkness around them and the weariness within them, it seemed far deeper into the night than it was. They longed for their hammocks. But they knew that with their numbers diminished now, rest of any sort would be scarce until they could make port again. And sunrise would be a long time coming.

Captain Hand watched them, their heaviness now and again evaporating as they squabbled over an Achawuk spear. An instrument to be avoided at all costs only moments before, each now was a souvenir highly prized. "There's plenty more of those stuck in the hull, boys," Captain Hand told them. "Let's get to work."

John Hand picked Scat's blade off the decking where he had dropped it. He wondered if the savages would be squabbling over it at this moment, had the battle gone otherwise. Probably not. They'd have burned the *Chase,* and that would be it. It had all changed because the stowaway was in the rigging instead of on deck fighting. A man hardly more than a boy, now mopping up blood like nothing had happened.

"No, a circular motion, like this," Delaney instructed. Packer tried to imitate the technique, but his mind and his heart were elsewhere.

John Hand watched him, saw the sagging shoulders, the set jaw. He had defended the boy's actions to Scat, and with good reason. But the boy was a swordsman. Why wasn't he on deck swinging his blade? It was he, after all, who had led them all here. Then it occurred to Hand that the boy might actually feel such a weight of responsibility keenly. He had almost forgotten what conscience looked like.

"Packer!" Captain Hand called to him from the quarterdeck. "Can you cipher, son?"

Packer's eyes looked up, but he seemed far away. "Aye, sir."

"Haas!" Hand called to the bosun, who was preparing to help Jonas Deal flip an unseeing Achawuk warrior over the port rail. They had picked a spot where grapeshot from the cannon had obliterated much of the woodwork, to make the job easier. "Let Packer write the roll of the dead."

Haas nodded another "Aye, sir," and the two levered the corpse overboard with a grunt. Then Haas snatched up a warrior's spear he had claimed for himself. He stopped, thinking hard. "Delaney!"

"Aye, sir?"

"Go get the Captain's log. And take him this as a gift."

"Me, sir?" Delaney looked about as quizzical as a grown man can look.

"Something wrong?"

"No, sir." Delaney's questions turned to trepidation as he climbed the stairs. He had never been in the Captain's quarters before, had never been asked to go in, had never thought he would be asked.

Hand turned Scat's bloody sword around, looking at it. Then he looked at Packer with an odd gleam in his eye. "Shook 'em off us!" he called out, leaning over the rail. "What made you think of it?"

Packer stopped in mid-swab, straightened up. "Well, I wasn't thinking of it. I was coming down from the rigging." He recalled the moment clearly, seeing it again in his mind. "And the wind kicked up. I saw a few warriors go under. I saw what might be, and asked God if it could be."

"And so it was."

"Aye, sir. He—"

"Two captains and seventy crewmen, all seasoned sailors, all charged with sailing this ship," Hand interrupted with a smile. He wasn't interested in that line of discussion. "But the only one doing any sailing was the stowaway."

"I didn't think of it as disobeying orders."

Hand waved the thought away. "You didn't disobey anything. And even if you did, we can all thank God for it."

"Yes, sir. The Captain doesn't seem to feel that way, though."

"Forget that. You saved the *Trophy Chase,* my young friend. He'll think better of it when he's had a rest. He won't apologize, of course, but he'll think better of it." Hand laughed, swinging the sword through the air a couple of times. He was in good spirits, remarkably so considering the scythe of death that had just passed over, harvesting hundreds of souls around him.

Packer wondered how anyone could grow accustomed to such mayhem.

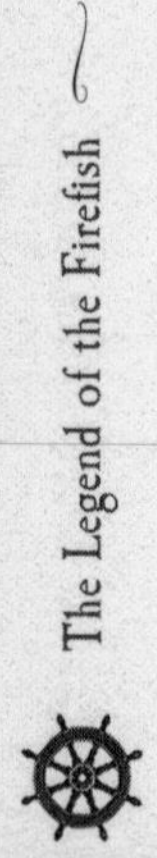

Captain Wilkins sat on the edge of his bunk in the darkness, with a mug of ale in his trembling hand, his head throbbing. His body was wrung and aching. His chest felt as tight as a drum. Nausea threatened to overtake him. He had the horrible sensation that he had breathed in too much blood, and it was still down there in his lungs.

He was getting old, he knew, far too old for what he'd just done. He'd pushed himself too far. The image he'd had, the hallucination—that told him so if nothing else did. What if he had swung the sword at Captain Hand? And the boy, the boy had done something well, which had shortened the battle. *Shook 'em off us.* Scat coughed, and wiped blood from his face with the sleeve of his shirt. He needed rest.

If Talon were here, she would know what to do. He cursed himself for trusting her as the ship's surgeon as well as its security officer. She didn't have assistants, either, except for Ox and Monkey, who occasionally held her patients down while she administered some painful curative. And they were gone too. He had no one left aboard to tend to the sick and wounded.

Where was Pimm? He had run off to get hot water, water to bathe off this red goo, now caking into chunks all over his skin. What was taking him so long?

Delaney knocked softly, entered humbly. "Beggin' your pardon, Cap'n Wilkins, but Cap'n Hand wanted the log to write the roll of the dead, if that's acceptable to you."

"On the table."

"Aye, sir." Delaney hesitated. The Captain hadn't washed up yet. His skin was still caked in blood, and his hair was matted with it. He looked terrible. "This is for you, sir, if you'd like it." He offered the spear, holding the shaft just under the tip. "Compliments of Mr. Haas."

Scatter looked at it a moment, then nodded and took it. The wood was smooth and straight as a gun barrel, the workmanship sturdy, but with no artistry. The twelve-inch tip was bone-white, serrated, and lighter in weight than he would have expected. He looked at it more carefully. "You know what that is?" he asked Delaney.

"No sir."

"That's a Firefish tooth."

Delaney opened his eyes wide in amazement. "No!" He touched it. "Well, I'll be."

"The Achawuk have killed the beasts, I'll bet my life on it."

Delaney pondered that. "They're strong men, sure enough."

"Nobody's that strong. How do they kill them without gunpowder?"

"I couldn't guess."

Scat didn't say anything more, so Delaney untied the lash that kept the huge captain's log in place, scooped it into his arms gently. "Thank you, sir," he said as he hurried to leave, cradling the book like it was a baby.

Scat called him back. "Delaney."

"Aye, sir?"

"The boy, Packer Throme. What did you see?"

"Sir?"

"Tell me what you saw him do during the battle."

Delaney blinked. "I didn't see anything, really. Just looked up when he called out to me. That was after the wind kicked us to port. He was cutting tie lines, unfurling sails. His idea completely. He did it himself, with only a little help from me." Delaney smiled. "Rolled the Achawuk right off our decks, it did."

Scat nodded, looking hard into the eyes of his best swordsman. "He never fought, though."

Delaney swallowed hard. Now he understood why Haas sent him on this errand. Scat was angry with the stowaway. And when Scat was angry he wanted agreement, not facts. But Haas knew, as Delaney did, that the whole lot of them would be dead by now without Packer Throme, and Haas knew that Delaney was not the sort to drop another man into the grease who didn't deserve it. And the Captain trusted Delaney when it came to fighting.

Delaney cleared his throat, put his chin up. "Cap'n, I saw many men fight with their steel tonight, and they fought bravely. Captain John Hand fought bravely using black powder and musket balls, though he didn't lift a sword. Other nights, other days, I seen men fight with cannon, knives, clubs, broken bottles, blackjacks, chairs, and fists. Even saw a man fight with a potato peeler once."

Scat snorted. "How'd he do?"

"He lost. But I believe Packer Throme is the first man I ever saw fight with nothing but God's own breath. He fought, sir. He surely did. Licked a hundred warriors, probably more, with no more weapon than the wind."

Scat coughed again, and then allowed himself a smile. There was logic in what the sailor said. "That'll be all."

"Hello, Talon." The greeting was almost warm, if reserved. The elderly woman could not see well anymore, but the presence in her room was unmistakable. She had heard that a Drammune woman had checked into her inn, and who else would simply enter the innkeeper's apartments unannounced? "So what brings you back home?"

Talon almost smiled. No one else would have the nerve to call this place Talon's home. Then again, no one else knew her past quite so well. "This is not my home, as you well know. I am here on business."

"Still serving at that pirate's beck and call?"

The question angered Talon. She let it go. "Not all women serve men as you do, Madam Lydia." Talon walked across plush carpet to where the old woman lay in her bed, and pulled up a chair. The woman was not so ancient as she seemed, lying bedridden and made up like a corpse. A hard life and lingering disease had taken a severe toll. Her dark eyes, once clear and sharp like a hawk's, were clouded, all but blind.

"How is your health?" Talon asked.

"Good enough."

"And business?"

"This business is always good. Who is it you brought me? Hank says she's pretty."

"She's not for you," Talon said flatly. "She's in my care."

"God help her, then." Madam Lydia chose not to ask Talon more questions along this line. "How long will you stay?"

"Two nights."

"And then what? Back to sea?"

"No. I am going into the city to find Senslar Zendoda."

The woman's mouth went tight. "Don't do it," she said coldly.

"It is time."

Madam Lydia was silent a long while, her thoughts her own. She could not bring herself to ask the question that burned in her, for fear of the answer.

Finally Talon said, "I need some things. Clothes, mostly. Some attention to the girl. Some tailoring."

"Hank will see that you get them."

Talon studied the old woman, feeling nothing. This was good. She didn't want to feel anything. "Be well," Talon said.

"Talitha."

Talon waited. She hated that name, hated that anyone knew it. It was her own, given her at birth.

"You belong in Drammun, you know," Madam Lydia told her.

"Yes." The bitterness of that truth never left her. "I am Drammune. After I visit Senslar the Traitor, I will go there. And I will never leave Drammune soil again."

The woman nodded, tears forming in her clouded eyes.

Then Talon was gone.

Lydia turned her head on her pillow. She coughed. She had thought nothing could touch her anymore, that there were no more emotions that could reach her. But she was wrong. She thought back to the time she had sent her six-year-old daughter to Drammun with a wealthy merchant of that realm, a man of strong lineage, who had fierce loyalties to Talitha's Drammune blood. She had expected, even hoped, never to see or hear from her again. She had wanted the girl to be absorbed into that foreign world, and to forget her true birthplace, forget her mother, and to forget her father.

The old madam shook her head. Some were born blessed. Some were born cursed. And there was no escaping whichever fate was pre-determined. She had lived almost sixty years on this earth, and this was all she knew.

Andrew Haas returned to the quarterdeck with the great black book, after Delaney had brought it up from the Captain's quarters. "Give it to Throme. He'll write the roll," Hand instructed. Haas nodded to Packer as he handed over the dark volume with two hands, a reverential gesture.

"Thank you," Packer said, feeling awkward about both the gesture and the assignment. It would be hard even to see using only the lamplight and the moonlight, much less to write.

"You did good, son," Haas told him with a hard look. He didn't want Packer doubting that point. "The Captain knows that now, I think."

"Thank you," Packer repeated, appreciative. Haas went back to work. Packer looked at the enormous volume in his hands.

The first Firefish to reach the battle site did not slow as it struck, but snapped its jaws on one, then another, and then another Achawuk body. The yellow flashes lit the dark sea, stunning nearby warriors who were still alive, knocking them unconscious.

Those warriors who could, and who still carried their spears, swam not away from, but toward the flashes.

The Captain's log was written in several hands, Packer noticed. It was a duty Scat Wilkins did not keep to himself. He couldn't identify the authors, of course, but something about the hard-edged, angular scratches of the most common one, the one that filled two of every three entries, looked familiar. The downstrokes were heavy, the upstrokes light, sometimes nonexistent. And at the bottom of each entry written in this hand was a single downstroke that looked like a dagger, a half-moon wide at the top, hooked to a point at the bottom. He guessed, correctly, that this was Talon's signature. He also guessed that, should she still be aboard, the roll of the dead would be her duty.

A page back from the last entry was a short one: "Lost sailor Marcus Pile overboard. Clutched on main yard in gale, relieved of duty by Cpn Wkns shot." It was signed "LL." Packer figured the LL stood for Lund Lander. But what did "by Cpn Wkns shot" mean?

Packer wrote the final lost crewman's name in the log, rubbed his tired eyes with ink-stained fingers, and handed the quill to Andrew Haas, who had been holding the book for him and dictating as Packer scratched the names down. The great sadness Packer felt went beyond these thirty-nine names, each attached to a body lined up at the rail. They had walked the length of the ship, name after name, body after body, recording with finality the score of the bloody contest.

It had been a difficult chore, more difficult with each line, each name. He had written names of men he didn't know, true. Garfield Just and Seval Carther and Lorne Beck and Onis Trill were not friends, hardly even co-workers. But each name belonged to a man,

one not much different than Packer himself. Each name represented a sailor with a home, a dream, a lifetime of years yet to be lived that would now not be lived.

Dumas Need, the bosun's mate, wore a wedding ring. So did Ren Malley and Skile Abadden. They now lay quiet and still on the deck, eyes staring out beyond the stars, unseeing, their wives and children somewhere under that same sky, unaware of all that had changed in their world forever. Barth Denton lay beside Westley Bead, who lay beside Amos Chath. Blue Garvey wore a silk scarf around his neck, a gift from his girl, probably. He lay between Chester Barnes and Wy Note. Each had someone, somewhere. If not a wife, then a fiancée, a sweetheart, a son, a daughter, brothers, sisters, a mother, a father.

Cane Dewar, the ship's carpenter, had the name "Sylla" tattooed on his forearm. Iggy Shupp had had "Gwenny" inscribed on his biceps, just where Dill Andrews had put "Janetta" and Big John Dell "Mother." Drumond Anse, Skiff Mulligan, Ricks Goodfellow, and George Callew all wore the double silver-stud earring of a second-generation seaman. And each man's father, each man's family had yet to learn that their son, husband, father, brother, or betrothed would not return from this voyage, would never return to them again.

Sander DeMotte, Ben Tigg, Carm Hogan, Jess Dunham lay in solitude, their last embrace of a loved one now long past. Packer felt pain for all who had yet to be hurt, yet to be damaged forever by this strange battle, this gory melee that Packer Throme himself had brought into existence by joining Scat's quest for gold. Boot Engler, Tiny Spokane, Kit Roan, Kipper Drake, Can Sethwall all carried nicknames that had worn so well their real names were lost to Andrew Haas. But they were well known to someone, somewhere.

By the time the task was half done, Packer understood that God had ordained this role for him; God had demanded he undertake these inscriptions so that he would know, deep in his soul, the price paid for his own presumption. Smithy Orr, Judd Talbot, Warn Pell, Angel Jibb, Lyle Stern. But why these? Why had these died, and the rest lived? John Hand stood on the quarterdeck and arbitrarily saved sailors by killing Achawuk warriors. Did God ordain it? Or was it random chance? Why Vern Killeen and not Andrew Haas? Why Ty Lumberton and not Smith Delaney or Stedman Due? Why did Northrup Walls take a spear while Mutter Cabe, Jonas Deal, Scat

Wilkins, and Packer Throme avoided them all, only to die another day? Was Zach Franks less worthy? It was not possible. No one was less worthy of surviving this than Packer Throme, who had caused it in the first place. Does the Angel of Death work blindfolded?

No, Packer concluded as he corked the ink bottle. *Not one sparrow falls from the sky without God knowing.* Every hair of every head is numbered. No one can kill a man who God wants alive. No one can save a man God wants dead. Of this, Packer was now certain. But it did not mean he understood why.

These truths created in him both comfort and helplessness. They did not mean he was destined to live through the night, much less live a long and prosperous life. He could die just as easily as any man; only God knew, only God had the power. These truths did not mean Packer was not guilty in their deaths, any more than they meant a man could murder another man and not be guilty of the crime. Perhaps God had kept him alive as punishment, so he could know and see the true nature of this battle he caused, so he could be weighted with this burden. Now that he understood, perhaps God would take Packer home to Himself this very night. Packer found hope in that possibility. God would do what God wanted, and it was fine with Packer.

Thirty-nine dead, four more missing. More than half the crew. Most of those left alive were nursing wounds of some sort. And that wasn't nearly the end of it. Did the Achawuk not also have names? Did they not also have wives and sons and daughters and parents? God had granted the *Trophy Chase* not victory over them, but escape. They had not beaten the Achawuk, only evaded being butchered to the last man.

And what achievement, what glory in all the world was worth this? Would Sylla Dewar rather have prosperity in Nearing Vast for a century, or Cane Dewar home again with her for one more night? He thought of Panna's bench, and how he longed to be there. Didn't Sylla have a bench, too?

Haas had been watching the boy's eyes; he saw and felt the respect, the honor, the pain with which the stowaway performed this duty. "It's a hard thing," he said softly. Packer was surprised by the bosun's gentleness. Haas closed the book, looked over the bodies along with Packer. "I loved 'em like brothers," he said thoughtfully. "But they all chose this life. They wanted a fight, remember? *They*

chose this fate, not you." He turned to Packer, winked, patted the young man's shoulder. "Let those who knew 'em grieve 'em." Then he looked up at the quarterdeck. "Any words, Cap'n?"

John Hand rubbed his beard. He owned no prayer book, and was not comfortable with these duties. Scat should be doing this, he knew, but Scat wouldn't. John Hand probably knew Scat Wilkins better than any man on earth did, and he knew that Scat hated, detested, probably even feared, the aftermath of battle. Scat's pride was wounded, true, but that would heal quickly. What would keep Scat below were corpses. As blithe as he was in dealing out death, Scat was anything but when it came to death's trappings, the bodies and burials and funerals. Hand believed it the warrior's burden; having no fear whatsoever of anything known, he was doomed to fear the unknown.

Hand studied the deck. Thirty-nine crewmen lined shoulder to shoulder, heads at the port rail, hands folded neatly across chests in the sign of the cross, all eyes staring at the heavens. Twenty-seven living crewmen waited.

Hand pursed his lips. "They were all fine crewmen," he said without emotion, and not altogether convincingly. "I wish I'd known them better. And I do wish they'd lived to know what they did here tonight." He stopped, thoughtful. Now he had found words worth saying. "They did something, as did you all, never done before, never in the history of Nearing Vast. They defeated the Achawuk." A grunting of agreement, mostly self-congratulatory, spread across the deck. "For that, they will always be remembered."

They had counted one hundred and sixteen Achawuk dead. But that number included only the ones slain on deck who remained after Packer's maneuvers, not those many who littered the decks before rolling overboard, or those who went down in the initial gun volleys. The actual count would have been much closer to three hundred. The pitching of the deck and the turning of the ship had saved the crew from facing better than eight hundred additional warriors. John Hand and Lund Lander were right. They'd have been overrun.

"We now commit their souls to God and their bodies to the sea," Hand said flatly. "Proceed."

Scat had been sitting on his bunk for some time, his blood-darkened boots up on blankets, when he first noticed the flicker.

He looked around his stateroom, confirming that it was not coming from a lantern. The light had come from the portholes. Not another storm…

Then he saw it again, and knew it wasn't lightning. He forgot his weariness in an instant and rushed to the stern portholes. Behind them he saw it, flash after flash. His face lit up with wonder. It couldn't be one Firefish. It had to be more. It had to be. He watched a moment longer, then rushed out through the saloon, back to the quarterdeck.

Jonas Deal and Andrew Haas had dispensed with ceremony after the first half-dozen went over the rail. They were too tired, there were too many bodies, and the burden of somberness was simply too much to bear. This was a chore, hard work for weary arms and aching backs, and not a church service after all. The last of their fallen comrades had been manhandled over or through the decimated railings, treated in death with roughly the same dignity they were afforded in life, when Scat Wilkins burst out the doorway from his cabin and ran up the stairway to the quarterdeck.

"Firefish!" he yelled. He didn't stop at the quarterdeck, but ran up and beyond it to the afterdeck rail.

The crewmen stopped, frozen. Normally the call would have sent them scurrying to ready the longboat for the huntsmen, and the sailors who doubled as huntsmen, but they couldn't imagine that Scat would send them after a Firefish now, at this moment. More likely, Scat was angry he had seen it first. That would mean punishment for someone. But he didn't sound angry.

"Great Scot, look at 'em! Just look at 'em!" He was pointing behind them. "Every man to the rail!" Scat called out, refusing to look at anything but the sea. "Ha-ha!" he exulted. "Just look! Every mother's son of you misbegotten sea dogs, come to the rail, and that's an order!"

The crewmen obeyed their captain, drawn by his enthusiasm as much as his words.

There behind them, half a league back in their wake, at the site of their agonizing battle, they saw a sea on fire. One flash couldn't die away before two more took its place, until the ocean glowed in teeming, liquid fire. It was as though a huge, sprawling city lay just below the water, burning, every building alight, the flames licking up through the churning surface. It was as though the sun had set into the sea and now burned beneath the waves, its rays reaching out through the white foam. The men stood in awe, dwarfed by the spectacle.

"Then it's true," Scat said at last. "The feeding waters."

Packer was close enough to hear Scat's words. "What now, Captain?" John Hand asked.

Scat didn't answer. He was mesmerized, joyously so, by what he saw. He saw, glittering beneath the waves, a million gold coins. It would take an entire fleet to sail back here, overcome the Achawuk, and bring home these trophies. He only wished he had that armada right now. If he had the *Camadan* and the *Marchessa,* he would turn for some of them, even now.

He looked at Packer. Then he looked quickly back to sea. The boy would be trouble, most likely. He would want a steep cut of those coins. Scat saw men's hearts through the veil of his own, and what he saw now in Packer was a pretender to Scat's new riches. The boy had stolen his glory…what else might he take? Packer was a young prizefighter who had landed a lucky punch and then expected the same honors given to the storied champion. Scat had dealt with such men before. Scat had been such a man before. He could worry about it later. Right now, he beheld all he had been seeking. He had found the end of the rainbow. His pot of gold. Nothing was going to darken it, or threaten it, not at this moment.

Packer watched Scat. The look the Captain gave him was not one he would have expected. It was brief, and then it was gone, but in it was no trace of gratitude, or congratulations, or forgiveness, or respect. Not even comradeship. It was the look of a greedy man shielding his prize. It was a warning.

Packer turned back to the sea. What he saw beneath the waves was quite different than what Scat saw. Here were the fires of hell, flames licking up from the pit. These beasts had lured his father to his death, and had lured Packer here, causing the deaths of half the crew in the process. Could such a power ever be harnessed to serve the simple fishermen of Nearing Vast? And if so, at what cost? It seemed little more than a fool's quest now, sure to bring more death and destruction before it could be accomplished. If it could be accomplished at all.

"Now there's a challenge," John Hand said quietly. The Captain of the *Camadan* saw a different kind of fire. He was watching his carefully laid plans go up in smoke. The designs of the *Camadan* and the *Marchessa* were not based on sailing into the midst of a feeding frenzy. He would need to rethink the entire venture. To deal with these volumes of product would take enormous numbers of men and ships.

"Captain," Delaney said with surprising urgency, and even fear. All those who heard him looked at him. His eyes were wide, seeing a fire the others didn't, not the Captain, not John Hand, not Andrew Haas, not Packer Throme. He saw a procession of torches below the waves that promised yet another battle. He said now in a hoarse whisper: "They're gaining on us."

All eyes looked back to sea. Off in the distance, Achawuk lights could now be seen on the surface of the water, and the golden glow beneath the waves was vanishing at its farthest points. It moved like a lava flow toward the ship.

The Firefish were once again following the blood scent, and their trail was made up of bodies buried at sea.

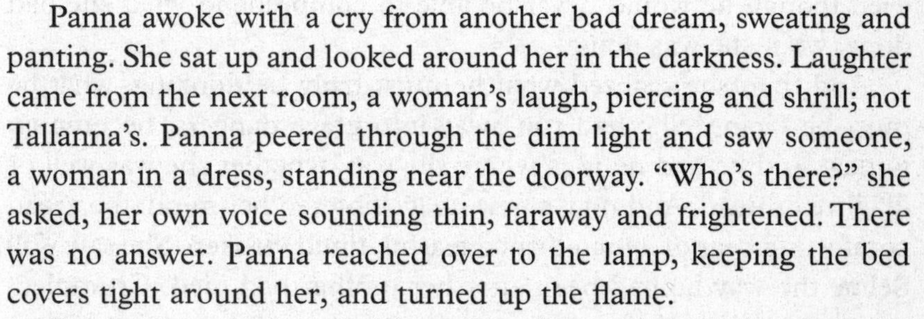

Panna awoke with a cry from another bad dream, sweating and panting. She sat up and looked around her in the darkness. Laughter came from the next room, a woman's laugh, piercing and shrill; not Tallanna's. Panna peered through the dim light and saw someone, a woman in a dress, standing near the doorway. "Who's there?" she asked, her own voice sounding thin, faraway and frightened. There was no answer. Panna reached over to the lamp, keeping the bed covers tight around her, and turned up the flame.

By the door hung a lady's spring dress, with petticoats and a bustle. Panna breathed easier. Tallanna had brought it for her. Panna sat back against the headboard. No one else was in the room. Beside her was the dining tray, the remains of her dinner of fish, cheeses, and fruits. She touched her shoulder and pulled up the strap of her nightgown. She could still feel the silkiness of the honeysuckle bath.

It had been a horrible dream. In it, Tallanna was the woman of the nightmare, and in this new dream she had killed Packer once again, and again he didn't fight back. She had then come for Panna, who ran, but couldn't escape.

Panna listened to the laughter from next door, and the music

down below. She was in a strange place, where women were used as property. She had been brought here by a woman she didn't know, a dangerous woman who frightened her, but who nonetheless would determine her destiny. Packer, the one in the dream, came back to her. His eyes had been black, and blank, and he had showed no emotion, as though he had already been dead before Tallanna killed him. What did that mean?

"Packer," she said softly, trying hard to bring back memories of his face as it really was. "Packer Throme." She couldn't. As much as she tried, the only images she could conjure were blurred or disfigured, and they quickly melted into the empty-eyed Packer of the dream.

"Oh, God," she said aloud, turning over. And now the image of her father came to her, the big, gentle smile and the dancing eyes, as he listened to her sing to him. It was comforting, warm; the love he offered was a father's love, lean on understanding but rich with emotion; unending, unwavering, protecting.

What would he think now if he knew where she was? It wouldn't matter to him, she knew, as long as she was safe. He would love her, even though he would never be able to comprehend what she had done, what she was doing.

And then she realized what he must truly be thinking, what he must be facing. She had run away into grave dangers, become an outlaw, and he had no idea where she was, whether she was well or ill, alive or dead. And now a new image entered her mind: the great, comforting bear of a man turned fearful, timid, broken. She saw Will Seline the way he had been after her mother had died. Crumpled, crippled by the pain.

What had she done? She had left him, left her home, left the village to follow Packer, and had cut herself off from every form of protection and comfort she knew in the world. She had indeed stepped outside God's appointed protection; away from family, friends, society. All for Packer, for a swordsman she hardly knew, a boy who went to join up with pirates, and whose face she couldn't even recall.

The laughter in the next room sounded ugly, the music hollow. What could she do now? Run away again? And where would she go? To jail, no doubt. They might forgive her in Hangman's Cliffs, but to the City of Mann she was just another criminal, just another woman with a dark secret hiding in an inn with other criminals, others with dark secrets, doing things unlawful, outside the bounds of society, of family, of friends.

There is nothing for you to decide.

How could Panna awaken from this dream? How was reality any better than the nightmare? She buried her head in the pillow and wept. The brute force of the world, the blank ugliness of it, the evil it carried with it in every sultry look, in every smug wink, was more than she could bear. Outlaws everywhere, dark purposes lurking behind every expression of every face of every person. How could she make it stop? What could she do to make things right, to wake up to a day that was not grim and lost and dark?

Chapter 16

The Ghost

"We need more canvas," Scat said aloud, without lowering his telescope from the waters receding behind them.

John Hand was the recipient of the command. He paused for half of a second, looking at his superior. Scat still looked like the aftermath of war; dried blood and sweat had left his clothes and hair caked and matted. He had wiped his face, or tried to, but it was streaked and drawn and pale. And he was clearly unwilling to take back command of the quarterdeck.

Hand looked to the stars to assure himself of their heading, which was now southeast, then turned to face the wind, which was still from the south. Sailing at a right angle to it, two points abaft the beam, with studding sails unfurled, would give them maximum speed. "East, then?" East was the fastest way out of the Achawuk territory.

"Maximum speed, Captain," Scat snapped out.

There was no time for debate. The yellow lava was growing closer every second.

Hand left Scat at the afterdeck rail and returned to the quarterdeck. "Aye, aye."

He turned to the first mate and pointed to each sail as he gave explicit orders. "Strike the sprits'l. Reef the main four points, the mizzen three. I want the fores'l full, the foretopgallant full—blast it, let all the others stand full. Trim her as she goes; I want hull speed!"

Jonas Deal was wide-eyed at the aggressiveness, not to mention the danger, of the set.

"We know the *Chase* can fight," Hand explained, clapping Deal on the shoulder. "Now we'll find out if she can fly."

"Aye, Cap'n. That we will. All hands!" Jonas went to work, relaying the orders.

The crew couldn't respond as quickly as they would have liked. There was confusion in the melding of the survivors from two watches. But Haas and Deal stood side by side on the quarterdeck, conferring briefly, barking orders as to which man should be where, who should do what, then conferring again. Inside of three minutes the orders were carried out, the canvas snapped full, the great cat leaped, and the chase was on.

"That maintopgallant is laboring hard," Andrew Haas warned Captain Hand, looking up at the moonlit sail. The wind had freshened now, up to thirty-five knots. The *Chase* was heeled just as dramatically as she had been during the Achawuk battle, but was moving now at a clip of better than twenty knots. The chains on the port side, just eighteen inches below the rail, were under water. Sea spray splashed onto the deck, soaking everything, washing clean what was left of the blood. Too much rudder to port under these conditions, and she would be laid on her beams, in imminent danger of capsizing. Too much rudder to starboard and she could broach, bringing her full broadside to the wind and waves, again in danger of capsizing. Even an ill-timed gust of wind could be disastrous. But the set of the sails was the Captain's charge, and Haas wasn't bold enough to break etiquette to question the overall danger of it. At least not yet.

"She's holding full," Hand said evenly, eyeing the canvas.

The Firefish kept coming, and they were gaining on the *Chase* despite her top speed. Scat saw the yellow flashes under the black water, lighting the night sky as they grew in intensity where the Achawuk had been tossed from the ship's decks. He couldn't take his eyes from the sight, his greatest fear and his strongest desire commingled there in a vision both wonderful and terrible. So he stood silently, watching the jagged dorsal fins in the moonlight, cutting the

water white behind them as the pursuers closed in on the burial site of the *Chase's* own dead. An occasional flash marked their location even more clearly, as an unfortunate dolphin, barracuda, or shark strayed into their path.

"They'll slow some in a moment," Hand said to Scat, walking up to him at the afterdeck rail. "When they reach our dead."

"You're sure of that?" Scat asked flatly.

When the yellow flashes came they were in tight succession, one after another like a string of fireworks on a common fuse. Thirty-nine lightning strikes in the darkness, barely discernible one from another, and the churning waters remained in pursuit, still gaining.

John Hand just shook his head. "Incredible."

"So what does a whole pack of Firefish do when they attack, Professor Hand?" Scat asked, not moving.

Hand let out a laugh. "They take us down. That ought to slow them some, don't you think?"

The Captain was not amused. He peered through his telescope. "We don't know what they'll do. Nobody knows what a pack will do." Alone, an attacking Firefish would always take the easy bait, the carcass with the lure thrown from a longboat. He looked closely at John Hand. They'd had close calls, survived some damage, but in all their battles, all their experience, they had yet to see the great Fish destroy a tall ship. "But they'll take us down if they want to, no doubt about that."

From below, in the dark, silhouetted against the shimmering white disk of the moon, the hull of the *Trophy Chase* looked like a bleeding, listing, silent animal. This prey was longer and wider than any Firefish, and extremely fast. It did not have the churning strokes of a land beast, or the paddling motions typical of an air beast in water. This was a sea creature.

In the lead, closest to the *Chase,* a massive Firefish sliced through the cold waters. This one was half the age but half again the size of the beast that had confronted Talon. A chunk of scaled flesh had been ripped from it just above the tail, and its right eye was gone. Great slashing scars like four strokes of a knife above and below the empty eye socket testified to the fury of the battle that had left it half blind. This was the lead Firefish, the alpha of the pack. Its decisions would be the pack's decisions.

The sleek prey it sought, despite its size, had shown no desire to fight. It simply ran. But it ran fast. Its appearance from below, with the one long, angled fin, suggested a shark. The one-eyed beast had seen this before, in prey not nearly this size, not remotely this fast. This prey moved without the oscillating, swiveling motion of a shark, or of any fish, for that matter. In the darkness of the beast's mind, it knew it sought a dangerous prey. Its speed spoke of sleek and supple flesh, but the rigid body spoke its opposite, a protective shell.

But the blood! The tasty morsels it left in its wake! The size and gracefulness of it, silent and focused, running, smooth, without effort! A great pain grew within the beast, an ache it did not understand and that it could not differentiate from physical sensation. It was a hunger, a lust, which grew stronger as it pursued. This prey was a prize. And the one-eyed beast would not be satisfied until this prize swelled and warmed its belly.

"We need Stedman Due," Hand said. "We need the lures."

Scat dropped the scope and looked at John Hand with a scowl. "There's two dozen Firefish back there if there's one. We've got one longboat and four dozen lures, and no bait."

"You'd rather do nothing?"

Scat took a deep breath. It wasn't in him to wait and watch. This was the *Trophy Chase* threatened. He would take almost any risk to save her. "We could try the cannon. We might get lucky."

"Scat—we know what a five-inch ball will do to those beasts." It would do precisely nothing. Round shot, canister, grapeshot, scrapshot, shell, all bouncing harmlessly off Firefish scales, was a scene often repeated and well documented in the early encounters, a scene that had led in great part to the development of the lures in the first place. "If we can kill one with a lure, maybe it'll distract the rest. Maybe we can even scare them."

Scat doubted it. But to see one die would be some comfort. "Well, Stedman and Gregor survived the Achawuk battle," Scat said with a sudden, cruel grin. "They have their role to play."

"We all have our duty," Hand agreed solemnly.

Scat pondered. The huntsmen knew how to set a lure lashed to a side of beef, and throw it into the path of an approaching Firefish. With the help of Lund Lander, they had reduced the exercise as near as possible to simple mathematics. But they had no beef. The *Camadan* carried the sides of beef, and the cattle, used by the

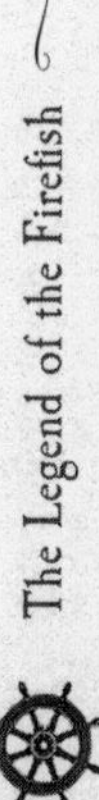

huntsmen in the longboats. How would they entice a Firefish to take a brass box?

"And what for bait?" Hand asked in a whisper.

"Use the Achawuk." Scat did not like the sound of the words as he said them, superstitious as he was about death.

"Already overboard."

Scat swallowed, still focused on the Firefish. "Then use..." his voice dropped off..."one of our men fallen in battle." Scat was trying to sound casual about it, though John Hand heard the tremor.

"Already overboard," John Hand said. And he and Scat looked one another in the eye.

"Blamed efficient of you, Captain."

Hand stared hard at Scat. "Maybe you'll get lucky, and one of your crew nursing wounds down in sick bay will die in the next few minutes."

Scat stared back. The idea of crewmen in sick bay was new to him. With Talon as healer, very few men seemed to get sick enough to quit working. He snorted. "We have no surgeon. Maybe one's dead already."

A man on a large gray horse entered the dark streets of Hangman's Cliffs at a full gallop. The horse foamed with sweat, throwing clumps of mud behind her as she ran. The man's dark cape billowed behind him. Pulling up short at the pub, under the sign of the Firefish, the man bounded from the horse, the steel scabbard of his rapier flashing in the lamplight. He was a small man, but strong and lithe. He took the crimson beret from his head as he went through the doorway.

Less than five minutes later, he was back on his horse, again at a full gallop, not back in the direction from which he had come, but past Mrs. Molander's wash, up the hillside toward the ramshackle docks of Inbenigh.

Lund ascended from the hold carrying a brass box in each hand. He was followed by a crewman similarly laden. Leaving the sailor on deck, Lund climbed the short rope ladder down to the longboat and quickly, carefully, placed his two lures inside it.

Scat watched in grim silence. None of the wounded in sick bay had cooperated. The huntsmen would go alone, without bait. This was a far cry from picking a doomed sailor off the yardarm with a pistol. This was ordering two men to jump with all the other men watching. Scat wasn't worried about losing them; he'd signed enough death warrants to have been long past losing sleep over the passing of another sailor or two.

And he wasn't worried about himself. Captains could outlive reputations; his own was testament to that. What he worried about was his ship. Ships had souls, and their reputations rarely changed. Once a ship had earned a bad name, she carried it with her to the end. Ships could be cursed, and dead sailors could curse them.

Long before the *Macomb* succumbed to the Achawuk, she had carried a dark shadow. That same ship endured an outbreak of smallpox at sea during one voyage, and two murders on her decks during another. Every sailor in the Royal Navy, every pirate, and every tall-ship sea dog, knew the *Macomb.* She had a reputation for killing her own. The Achawuk had played out their appointed role, and had surprised no one but the *Macomb*'s crew. Perhaps not even them.

Scat's own *Lantern Liege,* on the other hand, had a reputation of protecting her own, and his sailors knew it. But she also had the reputation of a pirate, and decks bloodied by piracy would never wash clean enough for Scat's new plans. Scat had scuttled her himself. She could never bring him the glory promised by the *Trophy Chase.*

John Hand's stomach knotted. He wasn't as superstitious about these things as Scat, or as were most other seamen, but he wasn't anxious to play this scene out either. Ordering men to certain death was never a captain's highest and best choice. He would dearly love another option. But what? They couldn't outrun the beasts. They couldn't outmaneuver them. Could they? "Haas," he called.

"Aye, sir."

"Get Throme into the crow's nest, will you?"

"What are you thinking?" Scat asked.

"He saw a way out of our last jam. Maybe he'll see a way out of this one."

"That was dumb luck," Scat said darkly.

"We could use more of that."

"Hmm." Hand had a point.

Haas scanned the rigging, unable at first to find Packer in the darkness; then he saw the yellow hair. He was working the foretop-sail, out of sure earshot. Haas sent a sailor up to deliver the orders.

Packer Throme. Scat pondered him. The boy had been an omen of a troubled voyage right from the start. A stowaway, besting the Captain. *Trust him at your gravest peril,* Talon had warned. But the boy had delivered. Scat Wilkins had seen the glow of a million gold coins. He looked up at the crow's nest. And who was this Packer Throme, anyway? Who was he to take on such a role, braiding his own reputation into that of the great *Trophy Chase,* like strands of a rope?

The men worked the rigging, those on the topsails working in silvery moonlight, those lower in yellow lamplight, but all stealing glances at the dark chop behind, catching glimpses of the lightning below the sea, trying not to think about what would happen when the beasts caught them. Their arms and hands and shoulders and legs were painfully in need of rest, aching and trembling as they clung just a bit too tightly, trying not to think about how far out over the sea they hung, how severely the ship was heeled, at what speed, and trying not to think about what would be their fate should they slip from the rigging into the sea with that devil's pack behind them.

They also tried unsuccessfully to ignore the activity below them: Lund, the lures, the longboat. But the meaning of it, the despera-tion of what was being done, shot through the crew like a dark elec-trical charge. The men on deck were morose, watching the whitecaps slide by the leeward side and splash over the rail, listening to the anguished creak of the masts, trying to discern the tone of the con-versation between the two captains, if not the words.

It took little time for word to spread that Packer Throme had been sent to the crow's nest; and it did offer a shred of hope. What-ever was true of him—blessed by God as he claimed, or a ghost made up of the witch's breath as Mutter claimed—he was on their side, wasn't he? Had he not brought the sea and the wind to their aid in battle? Surely if God had saved them once by Packer, He could do it again. And if it hadn't been God, well, then the devil had saved them once, and might do it again.

The lead Firefish surged forward, its want of its prey still growing. The sleek target ran in a straight line, which was always a sign of panic. But this one gave off no sensation of panic, none of the telltale sounds or smells or tactile offerings of a frightened beast. It showed no fear. But fear or no fear, the prey was wounded, running at full exertion, and would tire soon. When it did, the others would expect the leader to send a signal through the water, not much more than a grunt, and then they would fan out to surround the animal. They would attack. And then they would feast. But the lead beast was now working on a new idea.

It wanted the kill for itself.

A few of these Fish, the lead beast included, carried outer scars, chunks of fin or tail or flesh missing, that reflected deeper scars yet within, darkened memories of similar attacks, and vague, undefined hopes of even greater feasting.

The one-eyed leader wanted only to devour the *Chase*. The pack behind it wanted the *Chase* and more…these beasts were hoping for the orgy of carnage that was always associated with Achawuk canoes.

Packer accepted the telescope from the crewman in the crow's nest and put its leather strap around his neck. The pale seaman quickly disappeared, happy to work the rigging rather than sit and watch helplessly as the Firefish approached.

The crow's nest was tiny, a wooden barrel-top three feet in diameter circled by a brass railing eighteen inches above its outer lip. It wasn't a nest; it was a perch. Scat, in his insistence on vigilance, had ordered that the wooden encasement originally built there be removed. So now the barrel staves surrounding the perch, which would provide some sense of security and some protection in a sea battle, were gone. "I want a clear view for my lookout, and a clear view of him," he had said.

The one nod to caution, a short safety rope that ringed the masthead and was then hooked to the lookout's belt, secured Packer now. The deck a hundred feet below was pitched at thirty-five degrees, which meant the crow's nest was also pitched at thirty-five degrees—and hanging almost sixty feet out over the water. The sensation was mind-skewing. With the moonlit, whitecapped waves actually closer to him than the lamp-lit deck, Packer felt cut off from the reality of the *Chase* and her crew. He clung to his perch under the ruffle

and snap of the skull and bones as though outcast, as though his first duty were to the sea and the wind, and whatever demands they might make.

As he had seen others do, he slung his right leg around the masthead and tucked his right foot under his left knee, and then propped his left foot against the railing. Steadied thus with his legs, he had two hands free to hold and focus the telescope. He peered through it astern.

The Firefish were now five hundred yards back. He couldn't judge how many there were, but he guessed more than a dozen, probably less than two dozen, their jagged green dorsal fins cutting through the water and then dipping just below it, resurfacing a few moments later. He couldn't help but be awed by their size, their power.

He slowly worked the telescope around, three-hundred-sixty degrees. He scanned the waters ahead carefully. He saw nothing. The moon had come out overhead and now offered good visibility. No islands were near, no signs of life anywhere. He looked back at the Firefish, and watched.

The two bearded, brown-clad huntsmen who preceded John Hand onto the deck were dour and drawn, looking like prisoners at an execution. And in fact, hardly a difference existed between their orders and a death warrant. The longboat made ready and hanging from its hoists would be their gallows. Their nooses were the ropes tied to brass crossbeams, holding the boat above the water. The huntsmen scowled, eyes shifting back and forth among the witnesses.

They were unarmed. Huntsmen usually went proudly to their duty, somber, noble, their muskets over their shoulders, for show, mostly, but also for pride. But now the pride of the *Marchessa,* Stedman Due and Gregor Tesh, killers of Firefish, had been stripped of their weapons, along with their dignity.

"Dangerous maneuver at this speed, don't you think, Captain?" asked Andrew Haas matter-of-factly, as though making conversation for its own sake. He patted the thick hull of the heavy longboat.

Hand nodded. "Aye. But the water's up to the port rail. If we run the bow line forward through a turning block, then lower the boat from the davits stern first, it should work."

Andrew sniffed, nodded. It would be dangerous, nonetheless.

The plan was simple. Once the longboat was lowered to the

waterline, the bow line would become a fishing line, the foreward davit arm would become the rod, the windlass the reel, and the longboat itself the bait. The sailors would slowly let out line, sending the longboat backward to meet the Fish.

The *Trophy Chase* was about to go fishing.

"Hope you kill more Firefish than you did Achawuk," Jonas Deal whispered into Gregor's ear as he held the ladder for the huntsman. Gregor scowled but said nothing as he climbed aboard. Stedman Due followed, similarly silent, but now he raised his head, his shoulders back. He would go proudly. Quickly the two were seated uncomfortably in the boat, with all eyes focused on them.

"We all knew the dangers of our mission when we signed on," Scat said quietly, but with a rumble that carried his voice to all on deck and a number still in the rigging. "We thank you for doing your duty."

The two huntsmen nodded. Stedman Due opened his mouth to speak. But whatever words he thought of saying hung in his throat, and he looked instead at the faces surrounding him—some hard, some not, but all of them men worth serving alongside. When he caught Scat's eye he could see the Captain had no time for speeches. He nodded. "An honor, Captain," he croaked with a salute. When Scat nodded back, a dozen hands took to the windlass, ready to begin lowering the best hope of the *Trophy Chase* over the side.

"God be wi' ye," Jonas called to them, grinning. "Say hello to 'im for me when ye get there."

"Just do your duty, mate!" John Hand cut in gruffly. He turned to the huntsmen. "We'll keep the ropes taut, and reel you back in when you're done." He saw the doubt in their eyes.

"Aye, sir," Stedman said weakly. He knew what all the others knew. He would never see the deck of this or any other ship again. Hand knew it, or why not send all four lures at once? Hand wanted to save two, for use once the longboat was lost.

Packer watched the efforts on deck with a heaviness he couldn't shake. From as far away as he was, it seemed ceremonial, precise, slow. As though this were burial at sea.

Behind them in the darkness, the Firefish were now two hundred yards from the ship. And gaining. Through the telescope he could now clearly see the triangular scales on their backs, and the dorsal fins glistening in the moonlight. With an unprecedented sacrifice, the huntsmen might kill one of them. And then what?

Packer saw the lead Firefish surface. "Dear God," he said aloud. The beast's flesh was dark gray and slick in the moonlight, but as clear through the telescope as though it were on top of him. He saw the black socket of the eye, apparently clawed out with a single vicious swipe. But what was big or strong enough to do that, except maybe another Firefish? He saw the other eye, dark and cunning. The beast was measuring its prey for the kill.

What the Firefish saw as it surfaced filled its misshapen head with awe. This beast had never seen even a modest tall ship at full sail, had never encountered anything like the clouds of white canvas the *Chase* boasted. This prey was massive! It was much larger above the water than below. And those huge white...wings! They were wings, spreading across the night sky...

The beast's lust grew yet again. This was no sea creature. This was a creature of the air!

And then into the dark mind of the predator clicked an angering thought: The bird was trying to fly away. That was the reason for the straight line, the speed. For the first time, the Firefish felt urgency. It all fell into place in an instant. Only severe wounds, the wounds that created the blood trail, the morsels, could keep such a feathered, plumed, proud thing in the water. The Firefish scanned the creature, looking for signs of its injury. It was crippled, or it would have flown by now. Instinctively it looked for anything ungainly, anything unnatural or awkward. It saw nothing.

The wind gusted, the flag snapped, standing out at a right angle to the ship. The Firefish saw the face of the prey; black eyes on a white skull. And those eyes seemed to be locked onto it, the predator.

Packer was amazed at how intelligent, how human the beast appeared. It was little more than a hundred yards away now, but it seemed to have slowed its pace. Was it looking at him? He fumbled for better focus, and as he did his foot slipped from the brass railing. He let go of the telescope and grasped at the ring with both hands, but missed it. His knee was still firmly encompassing the masthead, so the services of the safety rope were not needed. But he found himself hanging upside down, his heart racing like a runaway horse.

He righted himself, replaced his foot on the rail, and quickly repositioned the telescope, which had dangled and banged the railing, but was kept from falling by its strap around his neck. But when he scanned the choppy waters behind them, the beast was gone, under the water once again.

The huge Firefish dove, increasing its speed to an all-out sprint. It did not send out the signal that would cause the others to surround this prey, but rather it sounded the soft, easy clicks that held them in pursuit while it stalked. The beast had seen the weakness, an ungainly fluttering just under the face, at the animal's neck. Surely this was the crippling injury—such awkward movement, obvious in the moonlight, in such a vital spot. The ancient predatory instincts, the beast's own memories and experience conspired, and a new strategy formed itself in its dark brain…

Lunging from below the surface…

Clamping powerful jaws around the animal's injured neck…

Pulling the animal, wings and all, down under the water…

Overwhelming the huge bird, turning it, rolling it, submerging it…

Ripping the soft flesh…

Killing it…

Feasting!

The strategy became a vision, and the vision became a need, and the need became a craving, and the craving a fiery lust, a lust that it would sate. Now.

The Firefish swam upward hungrily, measuring its own speed, watching the white wings shimmer through the surface of the water under the light of the moon, judging the distance to its neck.

It would be possible. It could reach the neck. The beast's appetite grew ravenous. Its whole being turned to fire with excitement for the kill, and its skin glowed yellow. It increased its velocity yet again, swimming now at an attack speed possible only when fueled by rage and hunger, upward, toward the surface.

It broke the surface moving much faster than the *Chase* herself, with easily enough momentum to carry it to the crow's nest. Water poured from it as it opened its huge jaws, baring uneven rows of jagged teeth, its yellow skin ablaze, its aim perfect.

This would be a satisfying, exciting, powerful kill.

The longboat's prow hovered eight feet from the rushing water. The huntsmen's eyes were astern, watching the Firefish behind, preparing for the rushing water to meet the prow. The beast broke the surface twenty yards away.

The two captains and the crew on deck stood at the railing, their eyes riveted, their mouths open, necks swiveling upward in unison as the beast rose from the water. The head of the thing, jaws gaping, teeth bared, approached the crow's nest. Its yellow, scaled body snaked through the air, slowing to a standstill as it reached the apex of its leap. Its tail, hooked like a shark's, was visible below the dark surface of the sea for any who cared to look. Its whole huge body was now in view, all glowing yellow. This beast was easily more than a hundred feet long.

The crewmen at the windlass forgot their duty. Their hands, like their jaws, went slack. The windlass spun wildly, unwinding the ropes to the longboat and dropping it to the sea.

Packer Throme felt the presence before he heard it, and heard the churning of waters below before he saw it. He dropped the telescope and looked down at the vision that rose to meet him, jaws wide enough to swallow a small house and all its inhabitants, teeth in row after row top and bottom, throat an open black pit, its scaly, slick snout a brilliant yellow, its scarred eye socket a permanent, evil wink.

Packer responded instinctively, from deep within him. Before he could think about it, before he could consider the absurdity of it, his sword was in his hand, and he had spun himself upside down again, this time poised to strike. The enemy was huge, powerful beyond reason, and bent on destroying him and the ship. Packer was small and powerless.

But in that brief moment, as time slowed to a crawl, Packer felt a supreme sense of confidence. He knew what he had to do. God had saved them from the Achawuk. If He wanted them to be destroyed by Firefish, then that was His choice, and He would do as He pleased. But this was not an attacking army; these were not other men created in God's image. Packer had no moral conflict here. This was a beast. This was a natural phenomenon, a storm at sea, a hurricane, a tidal wave, a thunderstorm, a bear at the cottage door.

Below him on deck were the men God had protected through the battle, men with wives and children and mothers and fathers and brothers and sisters who might still see their loved ones come home.

Even if it were a futile gesture, Packer would do all in his power to shelter them, to protect them, to cover them from the storm. And what he could do was draw his sword, and strike. What happened after that was God's own pleasure.

From deep within him came a war cry, certainly as much fear as rage, but more of victory than of defeat, a cry that intertwined the desire to protect and the desire to kill in order to protect. He thrust his sword downward at the rising beast, meaning, somehow, to stop it.

It was, of course, a ludicrous, impossible effort. A hundred swordsmen and a hundred swords couldn't stop a Firefish intent on its feeding. But Packer Throme could do nothing else. He saw the jaws closing, felt the hot, fetid breath, saw the teeth like knives, the Achawuk spear points. But he never saw what happened next. It was his last conscious effort before all went dark.

The windlass spun freely, and the heavy wooden hull of the longboat smacked the sea loudly, producing an instant spray of whitewater. The two huntsmen were knocked flat onto the floor.

The crew saw Packer Throme's sword, tiny and absurd, thrust downward toward the gaping mouth, heard him roar at the monster. But at that moment, as Packer's desperate lunge stabbed the air, as the beast neared its target and unhinged its jaw to engulf its kill—at that instant the Firefish felt and heard the smack of the longboat below and to its side.

An attack! The hard slap of water so near, and so close to the prey's body where its greatest strength would be, where its pincers or claws would be, was a startling and unexpected sign of a counterattack. And this came just as the Firefish was most exposed, most vulnerable, least aware, and least capable of maneuvering. The startled beast reflexively arced its body away from the sound. The flinch cost it its prey. The great jaws snapped shut with a rush of air that blew Packer's hair back. Its teeth missed his sword by inches.

But sparks leapt from the electrified teeth to Packer's blade, firing through his hand, his elbow, his shoulder. He was knocked unconscious, his burned hand unable to release the sword. He hung by the safety rope from the masthead.

"God above and devil below," Scat said aloud. It appeared, to all the crew, as though Packer Throme had turned the beast away with his sword. They all saw the electricity illuminate him, making him glow from within as the lightning jumped from the beast to the sword. Or was it from the sword to the beast? Had he stabbed it? They had all heard the battle cry. And they all saw the Firefish retreat. They were unsure how it had happened, but there seemed to be no denying that Packer's thrust had turned the beast aside.

A cheer rose from the sailors, guttural and instinctual.

It died just as quickly.

Furious now, its mouth and gullet still empty of the prey, the Firefish continued its arc, coiling back toward the longboat, already eyeing the new enemy. It had shot virtually straight up out of the water, but it fell forward parallel with the ship, its head turned toward her, attacking now, as it seemed to the crew, the *Trophy Chase* herself. When it smashed into the waves not fifteen feet from the longboat, everyone on board got a good look at its angry malevolent face.

And a thorough soaking. A huge wall of water followed the collision of scales and sea, drenching the entire deck and crew. Then the vacuum generated by the beast as it submerged created a black sinkhole in the dark ocean, a maelstrom that pulled hard at the *Chase* and laid her over on her side, on her beam ends. The deck pitched terribly, impossibly, at what felt like ninety degrees. The wind spilled out of her sails. There she hung, crew grabbing rails and lines and one another, all without taking eyes off the longboat.

Scat, the crewmen, Lund Lander, John Hand, all but the limp and unconscious Packer Throme watched in horror as the longboat and its occupants were dragged away from the *Chase*'s hull, stern first, down a slope of water so steep the entire boat disappeared in an instant, following the monster deep into the sea.

"Cut the bow line!" Scat yelled, suddenly realizing what would happen if they didn't. He reached for his sword as though he could do it himself, but it was gone; he'd left it on the quarterdeck with John Hand. "The line! Cut it!" he repeated, hoarse and urgent. But it was too late, would have been too late even if he'd had his sword.

Sailors standing by the whirring, spinning windlass were too stunned to move quickly. The waters closed over the longboat. The ropes stopped suddenly, the turning block groaned, the heavy, braided hemp creaked, and then the entire mechanism was uprooted from the deck, snapping away from the chains. Two crewmen who had the misfortune to be standing on the sea side of the windlass went with it, swept into the ocean so quickly they didn't have time even to scream.

And then the dark waters rose up as suddenly as they had sunk, the hole now a mountain. And from its top, like a small volcano, it disgorged the longboat and its cargo, casually flipping them to the surface with a modest spray of white saltwater, the boat upended, the occupants scattered. By now the longboat was twenty yards behind the *Chase*. Crewmen in the rigging saw Stedman Due surface, coughing, waving for help in the moonlight. Gregor Tesh did not surface.

The great Firefish spiraled downward in a fury, then turned over to see its attacker above, near the surface. It was a shellfish-like creature not much bigger than a shark. Or perhaps it was the pincer of the great beast. Either way, it must be destroyed. To the beast, the occupants of the boat, still near it and swirling in the waters, were legs or claws, pawing the water, still on attack.

This miserable little thing had caused the Firefish to miss its great prey, to lunge and miss? Rage moved the beast. It roared its message, holding the others in pursuit. It could not be bothered now to swim downward to gain speed, so it moved upward with a quick flick of its body, and lunged.

The mouth of the Firefish took the inverted longboat like a snake takes a mouse, crushing it easily. The flash lit the sea. As the jaws came down on it, the crewmen could see Stedman Due, his hand held above the water to fend off what could not be stopped. It was another Firefish moving in for its share. Another flash and he was gone. And then two more flashes took the crewmen who had manned the windlass.

Fear crackled through the crewmen like the lightning of the beast. They had feared for Packer and for the huntsmen. But now they feared for themselves. There were many, many more Firefish in this ocean. There was no way to stop them. The huntsmen and the longboat were both gone and no lures had been set. The yellow tracers would soon be upon them. Every eye scanned the seas.

But the ocean was black and calm. Scat's heart pounded furiously against his chest. An enemy like this needed to be in plain sight, and this one was suddenly gone.

"What now?" Lund asked in the eerie silence.

Hand looked up at the crow's nest, shaking his head. Packer was

moving again, struggling to regain both his footing and his consciousness. "I have no idea what just happened. Have you ever seen one leap like that?" he asked to no one in particular.

"And why the crow's nest?" Lund asked. He urgently needed the answer. They were like an army surrounded, with no idea what the opposing general might do. He knew now that for all he and his engineers had learned, he didn't know nearly enough about Firefish.

Mutter Cabe spoke. "The Firefish…they sense it."

"Sense what?" Lund demanded.

"The Ghost." Mutter was standing beside Captain Wilkins. He spoke with fear and trembling, so sure of himself he didn't care what the reaction would be.

"What ghost?" Scat demanded, eyes wide.

"Whoever that boy was when he came aboard," Mutter whispered hoarsely to the Captain, as though the words caused him great pain, "he's someone else now."

"What are you saying?" Scat asked, teeth bared, masking his terror with anger.

Mutter looked him in the eye, his certainty drilling his own fears directly into Scat. "He's a spirit, Cap'n. He's what Talon breathed into the dead boy's body."

Scat's chest tightened. His breath came hard. Talon had brought Packer back from the dead. She'd done that before, with men who had lost their own breath. But that wasn't what Mutter was saying. Mutter was saying that Packer Throme was a ghost, someone else's ghost, or a demon, walking around in Packer Throme's body. This was exactly what would curse the *Chase.*

John Hand saw Scat's fears but didn't know what to do about them, other than maybe to throw Mutter to the Firefish on the spot. "That's nonsense," he said. But Scat wasn't listening.

"We've still got two lures," Lund said with an odd calm. He had dismissed Mutter's theory out of hand, but he now had his own. He had that familiar faraway look in his eyes as he worked it out.

"What good are they now?" Hand asked.

Lund looked between the two lures and the crow's nest, but didn't answer.

"What? Tell me!" Hand demanded.

"Do you think he'll do it again?" Lund asked, blankly.

"I don't know," Hand said, shrugging. "Why don't you tell me what the devil you're talking about?"

But Lund was already gone. He strode to the lures. He put his arm through the brass ring of one of them and went straight for the ratlines with it. He began to climb.

"Where are you going?" Hand demanded once more, now a portrait of frustration.

Lund looked down as he yelled the answer. How could John Hand not understand this? "Wherever the bait is, that's where we set the lure!"

Packer slowly and painfully unfolded his hand from his sword hilt, the skin pulling and blistering as he did. The burns were excruciating, covering the entire inside of his fingers and palm. The base of the palm had a raw white circle the size of a gold coin, where the bolt of lightning had entered. His head buzzed, and his joints ached. But he managed to remove the sword and get it back into his belt with his left hand. The pain of it was unbearable. And the sword hilt felt strange. He tried not to think that it was covered with a layer of burned flesh.

He steadied himself, and then grasped the telescope with his left hand. It was hot to the touch, but otherwise all right. He looked behind them. Nothing but black water. He scanned the seas. No sign of Firefish. He looked in front of them.

"Oh God, no," he said aloud. "Please."

Scat went white, his forehead again soaked with sweat as he watched Lund climb. He looked at the water. Still nothing. Maybe they were gone? No, of course not! They were there, somewhere. But he couldn't see them. Suddenly, he had to know where the Firefish went. He had to know. He turned and sprinted to the afterdeck rail.

As Scat leapt up the steps, a pain shot through his left arm. He ignored it. He panted, wincing involuntarily, as he scanned the waters behind them, unwilling to be distracted. No dorsal fins, no chop in the water, nothing. They were gone. Had the ghost scared them off? Or were they beneath the surface…regrouping for an attack?

And then Scat felt the pain in his chest, sharp and full, as though he had been shot through with an arrow. He couldn't breathe. He clutched at his shirt, grimacing, and fell to his knees at the rail. His chest was in a vise. But he didn't take his eyes off the black water; he couldn't, he had to find the Firefish.

Under the waves, the lead beast had sent the signal. The others fanned out, diving, to surround and attack their prey.

Packer's breath rushed out of him as he looked through the telescope. There, dead ahead, directly in the path of the *Chase,* he could see them. Hundreds and hundreds of them.

Achawuk canoes.

And in them, warriors were lighting torches.

Chapter 17

Bait

The horseman rode up the beach, gray under the moonlit sky. He moved slowly now, riding north from Inbenigh, the sea on his right, the woods on his left. At one point he stopped, jumped from his horse, and studied the sand. From there he led the horse as he walked, his eyes constantly scanning the beach.

When he reached the gray tree trunk, he let go of the horse's reins. The animal stood motionless, obedient, as the man walked behind the fallen tree and knelt, touching the sand with a black-gloved hand. He brought a handful to his nose, smelling it. He dropped it; then he moved to the ashes of the fire, and poked at them. He stood again, surveying the scene one last time. He mounted his horse and rode south, back to Inbenigh.

"Achawuk!" Packer cried out from his perch.

John Hand closed his eyes. Surely he had heard wrong. The wind was blowing, the waves were spraying the deck. Surely he'd misunderstood.

"Achawuk, dead ahead!" Packer repeated.

Hand opened his eyes, set his jaw. He avoided looking at the crewmen standing at the rail as he walked by them to the forecastle deck at the prow of the ship.

Captain Hand looked out over the dark seas ahead. Achawuk, to be sure. This time they were in canoes, and this time they carried torches. As he watched, more torches appeared, and then still more. It was as though canoes were materializing from thin air. Well over a thousand, Hand guessed, maybe closer to two thousand canoes, carrying three or four warriors each, undoubtedly, and spread across the ocean less than fifteen hundred yards away. The *Chase* was racing full tilt from the Firefish and couldn't turn sharply enough to avoid the canoes without slowing enough to be caught. Hand wondered why these simple facts didn't create in him a sense of urgency, much less panic.

"It looks as though every last living Achawuk has come to pay respects," he said aloud to Jonas Deal and Andrew Haas, who now flanked him.

"Where in the devil's blazes did they come from?" Deal asked, sounding far more alarmed than Captain Hand.

Hand scanned the horizon, and could see the dark outline of what could be several islands in the distance. Somehow they knew about the recent battle, was all he could guess. Somehow they had come to avenge the loss. "Well, we haven't exactly been tiptoeing through their waters."

"But how did these find out so soon?" Jonas Deal asked, amazed.

Hand just shook his head.

Jonas looked up at the crow's nest, eyes narrowed.

From Packer's vantage point, the movement of the canoes was now evident. They were paddling from several small, darkened islands, which had come into view only in the past few minutes. They had paddled with unlit torches until they were positioned across the path of the *Chase*. Somehow they had lit the first torch, and then they began passing the fire from one torch to the next. More and more torches were being lit, giving the impression the canoes were simply appearing. It was a devastating vision. This was an enemy too great to defeat, too close to avoid. But Packer's emotions were numb. He knew this was a noose tightening around them, recognized that their chances for escaping intact had been reduced to zero. He closed his eyes, wishing it were all a bad dream. But the throbbing fire in his hand was all he could think about. When he opened his eyes, the nightmare continued.

Packer looked ahead, then behind, then ahead again. Something was very familiar about this. And then it dawned on him. He recognized this maneuver: The Achawuk were lined across the water like a trammel net, and the Firefish were driving them into it. The *Trophy Chase* was being snared.

The Fish had become the fishermen. The fishermen had become the fish.

Suddenly, Lund Lander's head appeared at the rail near Packer's shoulder, at the upper side of the angled perch. "Why did it leap?" the Toymaker asked intently, without any introduction.

"I…I don't know," Packer answered, startled.

"I brought a lure." Lund hefted the brass box up over the rail. Packer struggled to help him, using his left hand. His right arm remained hooked around the masthead, his burned palm open to avoid contact. "If it jumps again," Lund said, "set the lure and drop it into the beast's mouth."

Packer blinked. "How do I do that?"

Lund nodded grimly. He gripped the rail with one hand and opened the small brass door on the lure with his other. "That's a flintwheel. See it?"

Packer squinted through the moonlight. "I see it."

He looked at Packer, and now noticed his right hand. Lund took Packer's forearm firmly, turned the raw flesh of his palm up to the moonlight.

Lund looked down at the sea. His eyes grew distant.

"What orders, Cap'n?" Haas asked John Hand.

Hand answered with a sigh that housed a low curse. The Achawuk torches were now twelve hundred yards away. *What orders would help? Battle stations?* Then he looked around him. "Where's Scat?" If any man could rally the troops for one more fight, it was Scat Wilkins.

Deal and Haas both looked back to the main deck, amidships. Jonas Deal nodded. "I'll fetch him."

Scat lay on his side on the polished oak planking, his head by the rail, peering into the darkness behind them. His breaths were labored, cut short by the pain in his chest. Something was wrong,

he knew; something bad had happened inside him. His heart had given way, maybe. But he couldn't think about it. He had to think about the Firefish, think what to do. He closed his eyes, but was instantly greeted with the image of the towering yellow beast, its jaws snapping, lightning leaping to Packer Throme's sword. He opened his eyes again. He brought his knees up toward his chest, trying to find a comfortable position. He turned his forehead to the deck and closed his eyes again. But this time he saw Talon, her cold eyes inches from his, her voice a hiss…*His spirit has been among the dead!* He opened his eyes again, rolled onto his back, and looked up at the stars. He cocked his head slightly, watching the stars fade as blackness grew, seeping in from the edges of the sky. The moon's pale light grew brighter as all else slowly vanished.

And then a flag waved in front of the moon…a flag bearing the skull and bones, the battle flag of the *Chase,* rippling as it drifted across the dark sky.

He closed his eyes, sure now that he was dying.

Lund gritted his teeth and shook his head. Something had prompted the beast to lunge, and it wasn't a ghost. No superstition had yet held up to the Toymaker's scrutiny, and he believed none ever would. This lad was not a ghost, or how could he get a blistered hand? Mutter Cabe was wrong. It wasn't Packer himself that the beast was after. But what was it after? Lund looked up at the skull and bones above him. But he had no time to work it out. It was Lund who was supposed to know the Firefish, and it was Lund who knew the lures. It was Lund who needed to understand the beast's actions, explain them to the Captain and, hopefully soon, to a shipful of huntsmen. He pulled himself up over the brass rail. "Get down. I'm relieving you."

"There's no need," Packer countered. "I can do it."

"Your watch is over. That's an order." Lund swung himself around the wooden disk, and was practically standing on top of Packer in the small circle; there was no room or place for argument. "Andrew Haas has some salve," Lund stated flatly. "Go get some."

"Aye, sir." Packer heard nothing but coldness in the voice, and the man's face was a scowl, but Packer saw beyond both. The Toymaker wasn't angry about anything except the circumstances. This man had high principles, and a deep dedication to duty that could not be compromised simply because of personal danger. "There's Achawuk ahead, sir," Packer told him, upholding his duties as lookout.

Lund glanced in that direction and nodded. "I hope you can fight left-handed."

Packer smiled. "In fact, I can." Senslar was certainly thorough enough to demand ambidexterity of his pupils. Packer gave Lund the telescope and then maneuvered himself carefully, protecting his injury, over the lip of the crow's nest.

He paused to look up at Lund one more time. The Toymaker scanned the seas with the telescope, looking for Firefish, focused entirely and only on his duties.

Lund lowered the scope and looked down at Packer. "Well?"

"I…appreciate your taking the watch, sir."

Lund stared at Packer. "They change," he said simply. "Stedman Due was right about that."

"Sir?"

"The Firefish," Lund explained. "They change. They learn. Tell the Captain. Get down to the deck; your duty is there."

"Aye, aye, sir." Packer nodded, knowing that what had just passed between them was not something more words could add to. Lund Lander was content that his final words in this life should pertain to duty, and be spoken with calm assurance to an underling. Packer started down, feeling deeply honored and deeply saddened.

"The captain's down!" Jonas Deal's voice was an uncharacteristic yelp. He knelt by the unconscious Scat at the afterdeck rail. "I need hands!"

The crew on the main deck paused a moment, then rushed, every one of them, to their captain's aid.

The Firefish would not be denied this time. It had given the signal; the pack had spread out, the *Chase* was surrounded. In a matter of seconds the others would turn and streak for the sleek animal, striking the prey in a furious attack from all sides. But now, more than ever, the lead monster wanted the kill to itself. It was going for the throat again.

Packer stopped to watch the sailors run to the afterdeck. The great beast broke the surface again, now lunging with a fury and a velocity that exceeded even its first attempt.

Lund felt the sea open below him. A rush of energy went through him, and he grabbed the lure by the ring. He dropped the telescope, which he had not bothered to hang about his neck, and it bounced off the wooden perch, falling end over end toward the beast. He focused on the brass door, then on the flint wheel, but at the edge of his field of vision, the world below him was growing into a menace he could not avoid. The beast was rising, a growing yellow ring around growing blackness. He had the strange, dizzying sensation that he was falling into a hole.

The telescope struck the beast on the forehead and bounced away. The Firefish pressed the attack upward toward the sleek prey's neck. Nothing would distract it now.

Lund pressed his thumb against the wheel and turned it. A spark flew. But the Toymaker saw nothing more. The Firefish engulfed him, snapping its jaws down around the crow's nest, the masthead, the lure, and the lookout, its spiked teeth crushing them together in an explosion of electricity and yellow flame, illuminating a jack-o-lantern grin visible to no one but God and Packer Throme.

As soon as Packer saw the beast leap, he wished he had a safety rope. He assumed that the Fish would knock him out again. He hugged the mast and quickly looped his belt over one of the wooden foot pegs. As he did, he could feel the heat from the Fish's body. He was so close he could have put a hand on the glowing scales, or so it felt. But the electrical charge, when it came, passed through him without significant trauma, other than to make his right hand ring with increased pain.

But the crash of teeth on wood was quickly followed by the groan and creak, and then the crack and snap, of the mast just under the crow's nest, not twelve feet above Packer. He clung for all he was worth as the mast vibrated like a plucked fiddle string. Splinters flew, many of them burning. He lowered his head.

Packer opened his eyes in time to see the head of the Firefish fall past him. In the moonlight, the beast's single wet eye was angry, hungry, vicious...and the gaping, slashed eye socket was dark and empty as a bottomless pit. The Firefish whipped back and forth as it fell backward toward the sea, like a shark tearing at its meat. The flag, staff and all, was still gripped in its teeth, the skull and bones billowing full. The black cloth was ablaze at the bottom, nearest the Fish's mouth. The beast's tearing movements gave the impression that it was waving the flag as a soldier might wave a banner in victory.

Scat Wilkins saw the flag as it crossed the path of the moon, saw the Firefish fall.

The beast's yellow skin went dark as it hit the black water. It landed on its back this time, creating the same huge wall of white water on either side of it, the same hole in the ocean, the same maelstrom that pulled at the *Chase.* And then it disappeared in a plume of white foam and spray.

And now Packer could see the glow beneath the water, the blazing skin of sixteen other beasts streaking toward the *Chase,* converging on her hull, all less than a hundred yards away.

Packer looked up to see only black night sky and stars where Lund Lander and the crow's nest should have been. Where Packer had been only moments ago. He closed his eyes again, and hugged the mast.

The lead Firefish was not satisfied. It had reached the animal's neck, clamped down on it, and wrenched downward. The animal should have been pulled into the sea, wrestled under the waves, but the neck had been severed easily—too easily. Once more the sleek prey had not cooperated. The neck was not very meaty, and the beast was still upright. If it was a kill, it was not the satisfying kill the Firefish had anticipated, not the sating of its lust it had coveted.

The beast turned to join the others in the attack.

John Hand and Andrew Haas steadied themselves at the rail. The Firefish had pulled hard at the mast, levering the port deck well into the water before the mast snapped, rocking the entire ship and washing the last remaining lure overboard. They glanced at one another, unable to speak the extent of their amazement. That the Firefish had taken the crow's nest was dumbfounding enough, but that the *Chase* had survived—that she had twice in twenty minutes been on her beam ends and survived—was all but miraculous.

The bosun surveyed the damage to the mainmast above them.

"Did we lose any men?" Hand asked, knowing how difficult it would have been to hold onto ropes in the rigging.

"Only the lookout, I believe." Andrew Haas said it with more than a trace of sadness. He'd liked Packer.

John Hand looked out to sea, saw the glow, saw now the many Firefish attacking from all sides below. So much for the ghost, or the saving hand of God. The *Chase*'s remarkable engineering is what had kept her afloat so far, and some quick thinking, and a bit of luck. But now John Hand had no weapons, no maneuvers, no hope. Unless, somehow, Throme had set the lure…"Where's Lund?" he asked. He should have returned to the deck by now.

Haas shrugged, studying the rigging.

But even if Lund had gotten the lure to Packer, there would likely have been no time to set it. Even if it had been set, chances were it hadn't gotten into the Fish. Even if it had gotten into the Fish, so what? One Firefish might be killed; there were plenty more. And if by some miracle the *Trophy Chase* and her crew survived the Firefish, there was a small matter of a few thousand Achawuk.

"Orders, Captain?" Haas asked calmly.

Hand just shook his head. He couldn't think of a single order that would make a difference, even one that might give them something to do, something to keep them busy, trying, until the end. He looked at Haas and smiled. "I'm sorry, Andrew."

"Nah," Andrew answered with a gleam in his eyes wrought by both sadness and pride. He had never in his life heard those words uttered by John Hand. Nor had John Hand ever called him by his first name before. "It's been quite a ride, Cap'n. I wouldn't trade it. Not even now."

Hand nodded, then looked back out at the Achawuk. "It *has* been quite a ride, hasn't it?"

"He's gone," said Mutter Cabe, helping Jonas and the others lift Scat Wilkins.

"What are you saying, man?" demanded Jonas Deal, still shrill, still reeling from the collapse of his captain.

"The Ghost, I mean," Cabe answered quickly, an eye toward the rigging. "If he's gone, maybe those monsters'll leave us be."

"Forget 'em! Let's just get Cap'n Wilkins into his quarters so he can rest. That's what matters," Jonas instructed sternly, as though all would be well if they just cared for the Captain. "Careful there!" he scolded Delaney, who had stopped dead in his tracks, halting their progress.

"I believe they won't be leaving us just yet," Delaney said softly.

He was looking across the rail and downward, at the glowing streaks racing under the water toward the *Chase*.

"You pay attention to business, and that's an order!" Deal snapped.

The first Firefish to hit the *Chase* struck from directly below. It hit the keel, upper quarter astern.

It was a small Firefish, by standards of its companions, and while it took a dozen square feet of the keel with it, it didn't puncture the hull. But it hit hard, and the ship rocked so violently that even experienced, sure-footed sailors fell. This was not the movement of a ship at sea, even one as tight as the *Chase*. This was the movement of a ship under siege. Deal, Delaney, and the others, burdened with Scat Wilkins, could not keep their feet and fell together in an ungainly heap.

"Pick him up, men!" Deal bellowed.

Three sailors in the rigging also lost their footing, and had no deck under them to give them a second chance. Their knotted muscles and sweaty hands had kept them safe once, from the jolt of the mainmast breaking, but not twice. They could not hold the lines, and the rigging whipped them into the sea. They flew overhead with anguished screams, splashing into the water, the momentum of their fall carrying them deep under the waves.

Packer lost his footing on the pegs and, with only one good hand, he also lost his grip. He found himself dangling by his belt, which was still looped around the foot peg. His ribs banged painfully against the mast. When his feet found the pegs again, he gave up descending and chose to hug the rough wood of the mast and await the end.

He looked ahead. The Achawuk were within eight hundred yards.

The second Firefish to reach the *Chase* angled its attack at the hull, just above the keel. But rather than strike, it veered upward for the easy morsel, a crewman from the rigging who struggled furiously for the surface but would never find it. The next two Fish also veered off course for flailing sailors. Three quick flashes ended their struggle.

A dozen more Firefish zeroed in on the hull. The big Fish with one eye was back in the lead.

Lund Lander did not survive the jaws of the Firefish, nor did Stedman Due or Gregor Tesh, nor the unlucky crewmen who had been pulled in by the windlass or slung from the rigging. Their immortal Creator had not engineered them to withstand such use. But the lure did survive, engineered to do just that by its very mortal creator. The explosion was precisely timed from the moment the fuse caught fire. The lead Fish did not hit the *Chase*. Instead, it blew apart just below the neck, where the long passageway of its gullet began. The force of the blast sent a shock wave through the water. The impact of the shock wave smote all the attacking Firefish a painful blow, startling them enough to turn them off their course. Only two of twelve struck the underside of the ship, and both at glancing angles. Neither penetrated the hull.

The crewmen carrying Scat Wilkins dropped him yet again, what with the combined force of the explosion and the Firefish strike creating a series of even more extreme jolts. "Just stay down!" Jonas ordered this time, still focused only on his captain's comfort. "Hold him steady, boys!"

While Jonas Deal stripped off his shirt to provide Scat a pillow, the other sailors watched the sea roil, and then saw the white Firefish meat surface port astern. "We got one!" Delaney sang out.

"Shut up!" Deal ordered in almost a yelp, pained by the lack of respect, the inattentiveness such a shout of joy revealed.

Packer braced for more impacts, hugging the mast as tightly as he could. But there would be no more impacts.

He looked down, expecting to see the yellow streaks in the black water converging on the *Chase*. The streaks were there, all right, and he saw them, but they were no longer in pursuit of the ship. Instead, the yellow tracers led to a single focal point, the spot where the dead beast's remains bubbled up from under the water. The boiling sea where the lead Firefish had come apart had turned a bright yellow.

The Firefish, the entire pack, had recovered from their shock and, instead of returning to the hunt, they attacked the remains of their own dead like a flock of vultures diving for a single carcass, a school of piranha skeletonizing a hunk of meat. And the fury of their attack grew until the sea behind the *Chase* simply erupted. The sea turned to a fountain, black water and white spray and chunks of flesh, tails, teeth, jaws thrown high into the air, thirty, forty feet up, and at least twice that in width, all illuminated by the eerie electrical discharges of ravaging bite after ravaging bite.

Packer watched in growing horror. The extreme violence of their thrashing, the fireworks of their lightning strikes above and under the water was as spectacular as it was terrifying. It soon became apparent to him, as the grisly event went on and on, growing still in intensity as it drifted behind them, that these Fish were not simply feeding on the flesh of one fallen comrade.

They were fighting and killing one another.

And in fact, beneath the sea, the Firefish had begun a mindless, raging battle. It had started with feeding on the lead Firefish, but that was only the trigger. Almost immediately, one of the other beasts had bitten yet another, ripping a huge gash from its side. And that one turned not to attack its attacker, but instead to tear a ravenous hunk from near the tail of a third. And within seconds, others, attracted by the blood, began to feed, and then be fed upon. The beasts were destroying one another.

The crewmen helping with Scat Wilkins left him, and ran to the rail for a better look.

"Come back!" Jonas yelled after them. "The Captain needs us!" But now the sailors paid him no mind. Jonas Deal was as helpless as their Captain. He wasn't going to do anything but pat Scat's hand and whimper.

At the rail the sailors shook their heads in amazement, a wonder that slowly turned to relief. The hunt was over. The Firefish were devouring one another, and not them.

Packer tried to make sense of it. It didn't seem right; why would animals kill one another? Was there any other animal that would do such a thing? He thought grimly of the decks of the *Chase,* these very decks earlier tonight, where men had killed men with every ounce of strength they had. Then he remembered his father's insistence that Firefish were solitary hunters. *They are loners,* he wrote. *But something gathers them together in the Achawuk waters.*

Packer wrenched his eyes away from the glowing feast and looked at the ranks of the Achawuk ahead. The canoes were moving forward now, no longer waiting for the *Chase* to come to them. They were paddling hard.

If the Firefish were indeed solitary beasts, by nature and by instinct, it was for a very good reason, which was now being played out in this graphic display of brutality. They could hunt in a pack, but they could not connect with one another; they could not form a family. If God had created them to be loners, they had turned against their own natural instincts. But how? Why?

Packer wondered how long it would be before the Achawuk attacked again, when he noticed that the canoes were not paddling for the *Trophy Chase.* He stared for several seconds, for what seemed to him like minutes, before he could trust his eyes. But it was true, the warriors were ignoring the ship. They were pulling, with all their considerable might, toward the Firefish.

"Ready your arms, men!" John Hand cried as he too realized that the Firefish danger had passed. "Let's take as many of these butchers with us as we can!" He was energized by the sudden elimination of one virtually invincible set of foes. Only one more virtually invincible threat remained. The Achawuk canoes were hardly more than two hundred yards away, and the crewmen were outnumbered a hundred to one or more. But what was there to do but rally the crew one more time, and give it all they had?

Sailors still in the rigging quickly worked their way to the foresails for a better shot. Sailors on deck drew their pistols, loading and charging them even as they ran to the foredecks.

"Hey!" Jonas Deal shouted at the sailors as he still knelt by his Captain. "Come back, ye rat badgers!"

No one paid him any mind. It was as much as outright mutiny.

Jonas turned a sorrowful face toward his Captain, his leader, his master. Scat's skin was ashen, his breaths were short and labored. "Don't you worry now, Cap'n," Jonas said, cradling the pirate's head. "Jonas Deal won't leave ye. He'll never leave ye."

Why had the Achawuk attacked the *Trophy Chase* so ruthlessly, with such determination? And why did they now seem to be ignoring the ship completely, only to paddle toward the Firefish? Why did the Firefish start devouring one another, fighting each other to the death to do it? It wasn't until one of them died...

And then Packer understood. It all came together for him. He understood why the beasts gathered here in these waters. He understood the secret his father had learned about Firefish and the

Achawuk, why they were both here, together. There was a reason the Achawuk attacked ships like the *Chase*. There was a reason for the Achawuk numbers, a reason for their solemn faces, their almost superhuman strength. The reason was so simple, he couldn't believe he hadn't understood it before. Years before Scat Wilkins and the *Trophy Chase,* the Achawuk had learned to take the Firefish.

"Fire when ready!" John Hand commanded, his own pistol held out. He took aim, angling well up above the heads of the nearest canoes in order to ensure that the ball didn't drop too early, into the sea. Then he pulled the trigger. Very quickly some forty shots rang out. Half a dozen Achawuk slumped from their canoes. The men reloaded. By the next round, they would be well within range.

"Hold your fire!" came an urgent, fierce call from above. It sliced through the air like a spear. It was the voice of Packer Throme, the stowaway. The Ghost. Was he not dead, eaten by the Firefish? Hadn't they all seen it?

"Hold your fire!" Packer repeated urgently through the mind-numbing pain caused by using his bad hand as well as his good to get him to the deck quickly. "Hold your fire!"

All eyes turned upward, and finally located the yellow-haired stowaway as he came flying down from the dark sky, lowering himself hand over hand in the bosun's chair, the whine of the pulleys like a single note sung and held. He came into view below the mainsail on the starboard side. He was grimacing like an angry bear.

"Heave my soul to the grave," Mutter Cabe said aloud, his voice tortured. "He just won't die!"

Packer dropped to the deck, stepped out of the chair. "Hold your fire!"

John Hand stared hard at him. Packer looked around at the faces of the other sailors. He took a breath and strode quickly to the foredeck. "Watch them, Captain. Just watch," he said panting. "They aren't after us at all."

John Hand looked carefully at the boy, fought the urge to put a hand on him just to test the nature of his flesh and blood. Instead, he turned to look at the sea ahead of them, at the torches in the darkness where Packer pointed.

"By all that's above and below," Hand muttered, when the reality of it finally sank in. "By all that's holy, boy, you are right." The *Chase,* still bearing many of the spears left in her hull by brethren of these

savages, slid peacefully through and among the canoes. The warriors didn't pause, didn't look up, didn't pay attention to the weary sailors who stared down in wide-eyed and well-armed amazement, bone-tired and dazed and feeling as though they must be dreaming.

The Achawuk were paddling stone-faced toward the feeding frenzy the ship had left behind.

Hand finally looked at Packer. Packer turned to him and nodded, his blue eyes clear as noon. "That's why they attack. The Achawuk hunt the Firefish too."

Hand cocked his head, then looked back at the warriors.

"They've been doing it for generations, probably," Packer continued. "Storming our ship wasn't anything personal. Killing us isn't warfare, not to them. The Achawuk need bait to catch the Firefish. Lots of it. If we'd been a herd of cattle, they'd have killed us all and dumped us into the sea just the same. We mean nothing to them."

"But how do they kill 'em?" Andrew Haas asked. The Achawuk had no lures, no ships...

Packer gestured with his open left hand at the carnage behind them. "Once they get them feasting on blood, they turn on each other. It turns into what you see back there. They let the monsters kill one another."

"Then what?"

"I'm guessing they wait for the survivors to swim off, then move in and collect the remains."

John Hand was starting to see it. A smile crept up one side of his face. "You figured all that out?"

Packer shrugged, looking up at the rigging. "I just saw it..." He couldn't say why. He had looked into the eyes of the Achawuk, and had seen a lack of emotion he couldn't understand. He had looked into the eyes of the Firefish, and seen a lust that would not be sated. "They have to kill only one Firefish. Then the others do the rest."

"You mean they swim into the middle of them, armed with only spears?" John Hand asked.

There was a momentary pause of disbelief, before Delaney said slowly, "The spears are tipped with Firefish teeth." They all looked at him. "The spear tips are Firefish teeth. Cap'n Wilkins noticed it."

There was a pause as the ramifications sunk in. Hand nodded. "Of course. That's why they can penetrate the scales. They kill one, and they all turn on each other. Seems as though even Firefish can't resist Firefish meat."

"That's why the Firefish are here. The Achawuk feed them."

John Hand rubbed his face with both hands. The feeding waters. "But why do they kill Firefish? Just for themselves? Do they sell the meat, I wonder?" Scat had always said the Achawuk weren't interested in money.

Packer shrugged.

"It's religion," Mutter Cabe said. All eyes focused on him. The rumors of his Achawuk ancestry gave these words power. He looked down at the deck. "So I've heard." It was clear Cabe wasn't about to elaborate, having denied his ancestry for his entire life.

"It's over, then, boys," Hand said. "Everyone got what they wanted. Even Scat."

"Cap'n Wilkins!" Haas said, remembering their fallen leader. He rushed off, and Packer and Hand were drawn behind him toward the afterdeck, along with the other sailors. The Captain was resting in Jonas Deal's arms.

"Have we got a surgeon left?" Hand asked.

"We'll need a volunteer, sir. I sent a lot of men down to sick bay," Haas answered.

"Well, get him to his cabin," Hand ordered. "Make him comfortable, send a surgeon as soon as you find one." A group of them hoisted their leader once more, this time without distraction.

The feeding frenzy was a good four hundred yards behind them now, and retreating with every passing moment. Packer and Captain Hand stood at the railing, waiting and watching in silence. They wanted to see what the Achawuk would do, but the darkness and their speed would prevent it.

"Lund!" Hand exclaimed suddenly. "Where is he—he should be taking note of all this."

"Captain." Packer shook his head. "Lund's gone."

Hand looked quizzical.

"Lund set that lure, sir."

Hand studied Packer's solemn face, then looked up at the broken mast. He turned back toward the feeding frenzy. "He saved us, then."

"Aye, sir. He did." Packer remembered the hard-edged sense of duty in Lund's final moments.

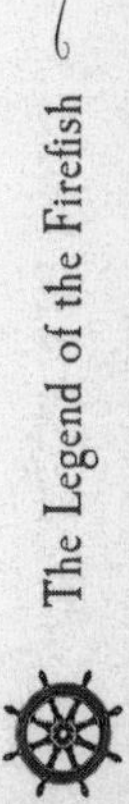

John Hand turned back toward the sea. "They're just waiting," he said, speaking of the Achawuk, watching their torch fires ring the melee. He turned away. He had had enough of Achawuk and Firefish for one day. "Well, Packer Throme," Captain Hand said with a weary smile, "what do you say we get on to port?"

"Which port, sir?"

"The City of Mann. We need a rest and a refit."

Packer nodded and set his jaw. "That sounds good, sir." But he was thinking of Talon, and of Panna.

Chapter 18

Bounty

Not long after dawn, Panna stepped up into a white one-horse carriage. She was attired in the finery of a young woman of great means. She wore a modestly cut but ornately embroidered dress the color of a robin's egg; it reached to the floorboards, puffed out with satin petticoats.

Her hair had been cut and dressed, wrapped high around her head and held with silver combs. Tallanna had insisted on the styling, and had supervised it personally. Panna's earrings and necklace were small, perfect pearls. She carried a dainty white parasol to protect her from the sun. She was perfumed and powdered and poised. She had seen herself in a mirror after the maidservants had finished with her, and she had been amazed.

Tallanna, the servant, wore a severe black dress that buttoned tightly from her throat down to her boots. She carried a black parasol, longer than Panna's, but slimmer—except where the ribbing fanned out at the handle. This accommodation allowed the black cotton material to cover the small bell of a hand guard. Talon's plan was to locate Senslar by noon, see him by mid-afternoon, and be back to sea by dark. She expected to be traveling quite alone by then.

Panna studied the hard features of her mistress-master. Her "lady lessons" of the previous day had not been difficult. They had worked hard, though, all day, in an elegant sitting room, under the tutelage of one of Madam Lydia's professional consorts. Panna found it quite easy, actually, to put on a show of elegance, once she knew a few simple rules. She just needed to move slowly, smile coyly, and not be afraid of long pauses in conversation. When in doubt, she learned, she could raise her chin, keep eye contact, and wait; others would quickly move to fill the silence for her.

Tallanna had been hard to please, but she had never let Panna forget their purpose: to find Senslar Zendoda. Twice, Panna had questioned the need for so much deception. Couldn't she simply go find Senslar as herself, and ask him to come to her aid, and the aid of a fellow native of Drammun? But Tallanna had been dismissive. They could not take the chance; Panna was an outlaw, and this would prevent even those who knew her from recognizing her and sending her straight to jail.

And Tallanna was clear that she wanted to look Master Zendoda in the eye to plead her case with him. "A Drammune warrior hidden somewhere out of sight is quite different than a fellow countryman who stands eye to eye, in need." Panna doubted whether their approach would have the desired effect, shrouded as it was in so much illusion. But Tallanna ignored her concerns as though they were mere naiveté, and Panna was bound to accept that judgment. Besides, Panna had made her bargain. She needed to find Packer, and if this elaborate ruse failed, at least she'd have found Master Zendoda, to whom she might confess all in exchange for his help. So Panna had accepted the role, and even learned to enjoy the play-acting.

But now, in the dusty and bumpy ride into the city, it all seemed too real, too dangerous. She was leading this unknown person to Senslar Zendoda, a very important man in Nearing Vast. And what if Tallanna really was a spy, sent to do him harm? She certainly was in disguise, like a spy would be. Panna wrestled with her doubts. What could go wrong, really? Tallanna was unarmed, Panna was certainly not a threat to him, and Senslar Zendoda was a great swordsman who could protect himself. Besides, they would be in and among many people, which was the whole reason for these disguises.

"You are concerned, little desperado?" Tallanna asked, startling Panna.

"A little, I guess."

"What worries you?"

Panna looked out the window. Then she looked back at Talon. "You do, I guess."

"Me, why?" Talon smiled, but all her instincts were immediately summoned to the potential that the girl would not go through with this, and if that was the case, this mission would need to be ended abruptly. In such a fine carriage, it would need to be a bloodless end.

"I guess I don't really know who you are."

There was a pause, then Talon softened. "What do you want to know?"

Panna thought a moment. "How does a woman become a warrior in your country?"

"It does not happen in Nearing Vast?"

"No, it certainly doesn't. At least not in the fishing villages."

"All Drammune are raised in the art of war. Those who show abilities are identified at a very young age. Boy or girl, it doesn't matter."

Panna blinked. It was a startling thought. "Who raises your children, then?"

"Oh, not all women are gifted as warriors. Most grow up to raise children, much as they do here. Female warriors like myself are rare. They have a name for us. In our tongue it is *Mortach Demal.* Warrior Woman." She smiled.

Panna looked out the window again at the passing countryside: a rolling green field covered with corn, an ox pulling a wagon loaded with hay, a round-shouldered farmer trudging in front of it. She took a deep breath. "Here, all women are assumed to be weak."

"You must find that a tremendous advantage."

Panna showed her surprise. "How?"

"It is deep in your mythology. The God who became man."

"Oh, that's not mythology. It's true."

Talon smiled again. "Yes, of course. But to take on a cloak of weakness, to appear weak, even to teach weakness to others, provides rich opportunities for the strong and fearless."

"I don't understand."

"This man you attacked...did he believe you were weak? I would guess you had an advantage, the advantage of surprise, because you were a woman and he did not expect strength."

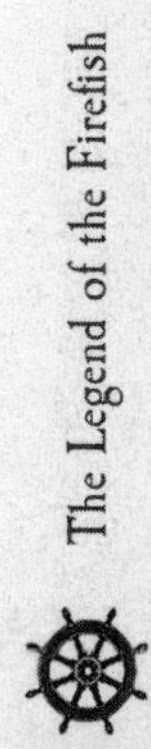

"Well, he didn't actually know I was a woman. But I think I see what you're saying. I was the one who surprised myself. I thought I was weak, so I attacked him really hard, like a man would, so he wouldn't guess who I was. And he just..."

"He what?"

"He kind of crumpled."

Talon smiled, a genuine smile now. "You see? The guise of weakness is a powerful tool. Just as your Jesus pretended to be weak, when in fact he was, as you teach, all-powerful."

Panna blanched. "No...he didn't pretend..."

Talon raised an eyebrow as Panna searched for some counterargument. When she found none, Talon continued. "It is all based on deception, your religion. In truth, power is power. You cannot be powerful if you are weak. You cannot be alive if you are dead. It is nonsense. Your religious leaders know this, and they use it to disguise their true intent, to cloak their drive for power."

Panna shook her head, feeling like the ground was quaking beneath her. "No. No, that's not it. My father is a religious leader. He doesn't do anything like that. He prays; he trusts God. That's what he truly believes and truly teaches." Her eyes blazed her certainty.

"And is he a powerful man?"

"What do you mean?"

"Does he do great things? Does he have great power to direct events, to change people?"

Panna swallowed hard. "No. He trusts God for that." She knew that God had not delivered on most of the things her father prayed for. At least, He hadn't delivered yet.

Talon smiled. "Then perhaps your father really does believe what he teaches. And perhaps he is really not a leader of your religion, but a follower, who teaches others to follow."

Panna turned away, looked unseeing out the window. Her heart was stabbed by these thoughts. Talon watched her. *Foolish girl,* she thought. This one had strength, certainly. But she was hopeless to use it, growing up as she had in the very nest of the Vast religion.

It didn't matter, of course. Panna had no cunning, and therefore no ability to recognize it in others. Here Talon sat in the guise of a servant, telling the girl in so many words that she was hiding her strength in order to deceive, but she couldn't see it. She couldn't piece it together, because the myth had seeped into her, she was steeped in it, her father taught her to be weak and to trust a powerful God. She had fought once, had experienced the simple power of power, but it was not enough to shake her confidence in the muddled belief that weakness is strength.

So before sunset she would be dead. Talon relished that thought. Senslar Zendoda would be dead. Packer's girl would be dead. No deity would protect either of them from Talon, and the religion of Nearing Vast would be shown to be the lie it was. And Talon would be free to return to Drammun. If only she could kill Packer on the way home, her mission would be perfectly fulfilled.

"Fret not, little desperado," Talon said gently. "It is my way to question these things. You have hope in the next world, and I do not. For that, I envy you. I wish I could believe as you do."

Panna smiled, and nodded. "But you can!"

Talon was satisfied that her lie had the desired effect. Panna would be compliant for the few hours Talon yet needed her. Of course, Talon would have to put up with Panna's attempts at evangelism in the meantime, but that was a small price to pay.

The horseman was tired; he had ridden all night to get back to the City of Mann, but there would be no rest now. He was in danger. He slowed his horse. He had been followed at a distance for almost three blocks, and now two men in dark clothing blocked the street ahead. Their faces were in shadow, but he could see the red glow of a matchlock pistol held by one of them. As the gray horse stopped, so did the echoing footfalls of heavy boots on cobblestones behind him.

"Hello!" the little man called out, close enough now to see the faces of the two men. His gentle voice was unperturbed, even friendly. His confident air and his immaculate grooming suggested that he belonged to the upper levels of Vast society, though he dressed in a style unusual for the streets of Mann. He wore a dark crimson beret over close-cropped hair; a gray suit buttoned to the collar; a black cape; boots above the ankle, then gray woolen stockings to the knees. His face was clean-shaven except for a generous salt-and-pepper goatee. He had a dark complexion, that of a foreigner.

"We'll be taking that pouch," stated the man on the right. His grizzled black beard grew through a heavily scarred face. "And that sword strapped to your side, and whatever coins you carry." The man who spoke raised his right hand into view so the horseman could clearly see the pistol aimed at his heart. The red glow came from the match, or wick, which was pinched in the pistol's hammer mechanism. Once lit, it burned there continuously, a red ember poised to ignite the powder when the trigger was pulled. By the standards of the wheellock, or even the flintlock, the matchlock pistol was a weapon of crude design. But it was effective enough and, so long as it wasn't raining, very reliable. It was a cheap weapon stocked by almost every street-corner merchant in the City of Mann.

"The pouch contains no valuables," the little man said, friendly and gentle, unfazed. "I carry no coins. And the sword is something you do not want."

The man behind him continued to move slowly closer, imagining he was undetected.

"Oh, really now," said the grizzled one.

"Yes," the little man answered with a smile. "Now if you'll kindly step aside, we won't be having any trouble."

The two men glanced at one another, then laughed. "He's a polite one, ain't he?"

The footfalls behind went silent, no more than six feet away.

The other man who blocked the street, lean and bony, produced a matchlock pistol from his cloak. He bowed and spoke. "Begging your humblest pardon, but if you'll kindly hand over the merchandise, we won't be rammin' a musket ball through your thick little skull."

Both men laughed again.

Senslar Zendoda shook his head. He wished now that he had not come this way. It was the quickest route to the palace, and he was in a hurry to deliver the contents of the pouch, but he knew these streets grew dangerous after dark. He chanced it because it was so near dawn; he hoped that even highwaymen would have packed up by now and gone home to bed.

Well, shortcuts are rarely short, he mused. The swordmaster took a look behind him. The man who had been following was a huge, lumbering thing, as Senslar had already determined from the sound of his boots, and he carried a blackjack in his right hand. He was clearly not the brains of the outfit. "Yes, I believe I understand you quite clearly." Senslar's tone was unchanged. "However, I must repeat that the pouch contains no valuables, I have no coin, and you do not want this sword."

The grizzled one grew impatient. "Hand 'em over, or die. Don't matter to me which."

"Please don't shoot. I'm dismounting." Senslar took half a second more to gauge their relative positions, then gripped his sword hilt. He pulled it from its sheath as he pirouetted off the horse's left side, slashing backhanded at the first armed brigand almost before he landed on the ground. By the time that highwayman's pistol had hit the ground, Senslar had spun under the horse's head, slashing a forehand at the second brigand. Both pistols lay on the ground as he remounted his horse from the right side, completing his task in one fluid movement. Then he backed the gray mount one step, to the side, and held his sword in the direction of the big man behind him, eyeing him alone.

"Ow!" each gunman cried in turn, shocked more than pained, amazed by the little man's lightning quickness, his agile movements. They looked at their bleeding hands and realized they were cut, but not badly injured. He had spun their pistols from their hands somehow, enveloped them the way a swordsman disarms another swordsman.

It took a moment to sink in. But there the weapons were, lying on the ground, and there the horseman was, back up on his horse. With a rush the two assailants picked up their weapons, aimed at him, and fired.

Both weapons clicked harmlessly. When they looked down, mystified, they saw the glow of two matches, severed and lying on the cobblestones at their feet.

"You have told me twice that you want this sword," Senslar said, still serene. "I have argued the point in vain. Tell me again that you want it..." Now his voice grew cold, and his eyes burned. "...And you shall have it."

The would-be robbers glanced at one another, unsure of their next move.

"What, have you changed your minds?" Senslar asked, his tone still deadly.

The grizzled one considered the glowing wick on the ground, realized a move toward it would result in the same kind of reaction

from the little man, this time with no guarantee of similar mercy. He cleared his throat. "In fact, sir, we have. I believe that I was...that is, we were...mistaken. We thought you was someone else."

Senslar looked at each man in turn. The danger passed, the horseman's good humor returned. "Fine, it was all a misunderstanding, then."

"That's all it was," the grizzled one said quickly. "A misunderstanding."

"Then kindly step back."

The two obliged, and Senslar maneuvered the gray horse between them.

"Good morning," he offered with a smile, and trotted off down the street.

"A misunderstanding?" the big one asked. "Who did you think he was, Dirk?"

"Shut up," Dirk answered.

To Mather Reynard Mason Sennett, Son of King Reynard Redcliff Odolf Sennett, the Duke of Nearingsford Alms, and the Crown Prince of Nearing Vast. The young man read the words pinned to the leather pouch and smiled. One day, and in the not too distant future, there would be a different title: *King of Nearing Vast.*

Mather Sennett sat on the warm stones by the fireplace near his bed, the blaze lighting the huge room, its ornate tapestries, its polished mahogany furnishings. He was up early, as was his custom, and the day as always started with mail and paperwork.

The pouch, just handed him by his valet, carried the stamp of Bench Urmand, the Sheriff of Mann. Bench was a good man. At thirty-eight he was nine years older than Mather, and one of the few people the crown prince considered competent. Most of the king's appointees were aged, doddering, and fat, much like the king himself. When the post of minister of arms had come open recently, Bench didn't get it, even though Mather had all but begged his father. Bench could invigorate a navy and an army that had both been in decline for a decade. But King Reynard had refused.

Mather pulled two scrolls of foolscap from the pouch. The first was a note written not in Bench Urmand's hand, but in a familiar, precise one:

B. Urmand brought the enclosed to my attention. As yet, it has not been posted. Bench granted me but one day to investigate. I have sought answers, but in vain. Please contact me at any hour so that I might gain your wisdom in this matter. Many thanks.

S. Zendoda

Then, as though the author believed it lacked urgency, two sentences were added beneath the signature:

Your life was in his father's hands. Now his life is in yours.

–Z.

The enclosed sheet was a likeness of Packer Throme, with these words printed below it:

PACKER THROME

of Hangman's Cliffs

Wanted for Murder

Reward: Five Gold Coins

Prince Mather stared hard at the likeness, and at the name. He remembered the shipwreck, the cold seas, as though it were yesterday. He remembered the warmth of the Throme home, the fires that burned there, bringing him life. He'd been whisked away to the Palace very quickly once he was well enough to inform them of his identity. But how the elder Throme's aid all those years ago had any bearing on the younger Throme's current troubles was beyond him.

Still, this was from Senslar, and Senslar was one of the competent ones who would help him rebuild his kingdom. To the swordmaster, the teacher–student relationship was lifelong. Mather knew this well, having labored many hours himself under Senslar's badgering. The crown prince went to his desk and dipped a quill, wrote a message back to Senslar at the bottom of the same sheaf:

Come to breakfast.

–M.

"Stebbins!" Mather called out as he sealed the document. The old valet creaked into the room.

"Sir?"

"Post this immediately to Senslar Zendoda, care of the Academy." Packer Throme's difficulties were undoubtedly of his own making, like so many of the supposed injustices perpetrated on the villages and their people. But he would indulge Senslar.

"Sir," the valet said languidly. "He's here."

"Who's here?" Prince Mather asked.

"Mr. Zendoda."

"He's here now?"

The valet pointed a bony finger silently, indicating that Senslar was positioned just outside the doorway, probably within earshot.

Mather smiled. The swordmaster was always prepared, and unfailingly persistent. A polite, careful, smiling man who locked onto a mission, or an idea, like a bulldog. "Well, send him in."

"Yes, sir."

"Oh, and...bring us our breakfast."

"As you wish."

Bench Urmand looked at the stack of handbills on his desk. He looked out the window, saw that the sun was on the ground, and sighed. He picked up the hammer, tucked it into his belt, and dropped the sack of nails into his pocket. Then he grabbed the handbills and headed out to the square to post the image of Packer Throme.

"Something else is afoot, Mather," the swordmaster said matter-of-factly, ignoring the breads and pastries before him. "These two murders are not the handiwork of Packer Throme."

"You think because you taught him to fight he's incapable of murder?" Mather asked, a cheek full of bread and marmalade.

Senslar shook his head. "His being my student has little to do with it, other than such is how I know him."

"The evidence seems to suggest the contrary, or the Sheriff wouldn't post the reward. Why not let justice take its course?"

"I do not fear justice."

"Then let the courts decide."

"That's a different matter. Justice is a goal to which courts aspire, Your Highness, but one they do not always attain. I have seen the two victims laid out for burial. I have visited the beach where the murders took place. I have spoken with the last man to see Packer Throme ashore. I am confident these murders were not Packer Throme's doing, but I need more time to find the sort of proofs required by courts."

"What makes you so sure?" Mather sat back, patting his dark hair to be sure it was still appropriately oiled and groomed. Then he sipped his tea.

"Two nights before the murders, Throme used his skills rather carefully to wound a man he could justifiably have killed. Reports are that Packer anguished over even this small act of aggression. The last man to see Packer alive was an innkeeper who sent him off to a ship, which is now at sea. The murders happened more than a day later, after the ship Packer was to board set sail. The victims were killed almost instantly, with no thought whatsoever for their lives, only for the quickest death possible."

"How were they killed, then?" The prince heaped more marmalade on his biscuit.

"One was shot through the throat, the other killed with a thrust to the heart."

"A sword."

Pause. "Yes. You see, in the first incident, you have a skilled but compassionate swordsman. Packer Throme. In the second, a trained killer, with no reluctance or compunction."

"But there was a witness to the murders on the beach."

Senslar nodded. "The man Packer fought and let live. A man known to hate Packer Throme. On questioning, he admitted to witnessing the murders from fifty yards away through a fierce rainstorm."

"Why does he hate Mr. Throme?"

The swordmaster grimaced, then spoke quietly. "There is speculation in Hangman's Cliffs that he is in love with Packer's fiancée."

The prince lit up. "Ah, the plot thickens!"

"Uncommon skill with a sword, twice in the area of the same small town, and a witness who will swear Packer's guilt. Our courts have convicted many on far less evidence."

"What does Bench say?" Mather asked, knowing the answer from Senslar's note.

"Bench is sympathetic. A day's pause in the machinery of his

justice is a great gift, which I appreciate. But a day is not enough. I have not found Packer Throme. And there is the small matter of the girl, who has now gone missing, a mystery I have as yet been unable to unravel."

Mather's eyebrow went up. "The plot thickens yet again. Who is she?"

"Her name is Panna Seline, at one time betrothed to Mr. Throme. She seems to have left home to follow him."

"The lovers vanish, bodies turn up on the beach...Say, it has some drama, doesn't it? Someone should write this down."

Senslar shook his head, not interested at the moment in his prince's literary aspirations. "A young man's life is at stake."

"As are the lives of innocent men and women. What will it hurt to have a suspect in custody? Then he and all others will be safe while the courts sort out the truth."

"I don't have to remind you of the debt—"

"Which has been fully repaid with his schooling," the prince cut in. There would be no more discussion along this line. "The law is the law."

"I have no desire to insinuate myself between Packer Throme and the law, Your Highness," Senslar said, hiding his disappointment. "The courts are far preferable to the bounty hunters Bench will involve by posting his name and likeness. If he is at sea, as I suspect, and arrives at some obscure port without knowing that he is a wanted man, he will be easy prey for their pistols."

Mather shrugged. "The money's the same if he's alive."

Senslar looked askance at him. "You know, Your Highness, how bounty hunters work."

"What do you want me to do?"

"Delay the posting."

The prince paused. "I must decline. I respect you greatly as a swordmaster, Senslar. But Bench Urmand is the expert in these matters. I trust his judgment, as should you."

"I trust Bench implicitly in such matters as these. He, however, does not know Packer as I do."

"Nor do I, I'm afraid."

Senslar stood and bowed. "Thank you for your time, my liege. And thank you for your tea and cakes." He had not touched the food or drink before him.

"But do keep me posted on how it turns out. It's quite an intriguing story."

Senslar nodded, but made no promises. He had to protect Packer from the bounty hunters.

A ragged troop gathered in the early morning light. The cool of the night was still felt in the breeze that drifted through the square. But the scent of dew and the promise of a new day were lost on this muster of half a dozen men—two Boweryton drivers with keen eyes and accurate long-rifles, and four others not much more than vagabonds and brigands. They worked the city's violent gray netherworld between law and order. They waited for Bench Urmand to post the day's work.

The Sheriff of Mann was a house of bricks, solid as a wall, his muscular shoulders square, his neck thick as a tree trunk. His dark eyes were crisp and full of purpose, his stride the same. He looked up the street one last time before posting the handbill. Bench knew how final an act it was likely to be. For confirmation, all he needed to do was to turn around and study the faces of the men standing behind him. He didn't have to look, however. He knew the scarred faces, the dirty clothes, the armaments they carried. He didn't much like the necessity of using thugs for the purpose of justice, but the royal coffers were low. If an outlaw was holed up in the city, the sheriff had enough manpower to bring him in. But a killer who roamed the villages and terrified the small towns required more resources than Bench had available. Five gold coins to bring swift justice and keep peace in the realm was a bargain.

As Bench looked, the familiar crimson beret rose up from the cobblestones. He paused, waited…but when Senslar's face came into view, Bench knew the answer. He nodded once, then tacked the poster to the wall.

The bounty hunters gathered in, studying and memorizing. Among them was a grizzled highwayman named Dirk. "Musketeer?" he asked.

"Swordsman," Bench answered.

"Last seen?" another queried.

"Hangman's Cliffs. Maybe Inbenigh, depending on who you talk to."

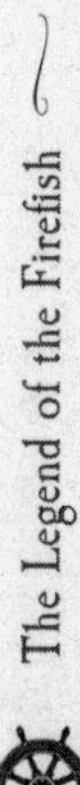

"Headed where?"

"To sea. Wanted to join up with Scat Wilkins and the *Trophy Chase*."

This stopped the questioning for a moment. "Must be a heavin' good swordsman," one said.

"Don't matter. Never knew a sword that could outduel a musket ball," another said, and the others laughed.

Senslar approached on horseback, his horse's shoes clipping the paving stones briskly.

"Still, if he's Scat's swordsman, five coins is five too light," the first said, unconvinced.

"That's the bounty," Bench said matter-of-factly.

"I know how you can double that purse," said a clear, precise voice. The horseman rode into their midst.

"How's that?"

"Bring him in alive," Senslar said.

"Whose money?" someone asked. Dirk slunk back, not wanting to be recognized.

"Yours if you bring him in alive, and well. From my purse to yours." There were sighs and whispers. Senslar looked at the men, eyeing their resolve, or lack of it. Then he noticed the man with the grizzled beard. "Ah, good morning once again, sir," Senslar said with a smile and a tap of his cap. "I see you're a man of many talents."

Dirk Menafee looked sour. "Who are you?"

"That's the Swordmaster of Nearing Vast," the sheriff said flatly. "If he says he'll pay it, he'll pay it."

Dirk swallowed, wide-eyed. He bowed his head slightly. "Sorry about…I…thought you were someone else, sir."

"Yes, I recall your mistake."

"So what's this Throme to you," he asked, "that you put up your own money to keep him alive?"

Senslar smiled. "He taught me a few things about swordsmanship."

Dirk blanched.

"Good day, gentlemen, and happy hunting." Senslar saluted Bench Urmand, who laughed and returned the salute, and he rode away.

"What's the story, Bench?" the others asked. "Is this Throme a pistoleer too?"

“I don’t know him.”

Dirk stewed. “Ten coins may be ten too light.” But in his heart, he was determined to find Packer Throme and bring him in. He would gladly take the little man’s money. But if he had to kill the man’s student, he’d take satisfaction in that too.

Chapter 19

The Gates of Heaven

The carriage stopped at the square just before noon, and Talon descended. The cool of the morning was long gone, the sun was high, and the day promised to be long and hot. Talon's hawklike eyes surveyed the city streets. All looked serene. She was looking for dangers in the form of swords and daggers, gunpowder and muskets, not in small line drawings, and so she missed seeing the one thing that would strike most deeply to confound her mission. She turned to help her young mistress from the conveyance.

"I'll pay the driver, ma'am," Talon said, and she left Panna standing on the cobblestones.

Panna looked around, breathing in the atmosphere. It was enough to make her forget who she was. She had been to the City only once, with her father years ago, and her memories were of dirty streets and multitudes of people, and the grandeur of the Cathedral, the solitude of the seminary. But here were more storefronts than she had known existed. This one square had two clothing stores, a haberdashery, a hardware store, a barbershop, the Sheriff's office, a bakery, a butcher shop, three taverns, and two inns. The movement of people was tremendous, with never fewer than thirty, maybe forty people in sight at all times. And their dress! All the lines, the colors, the bustles, the bodices, the knickers here and the tails there. She soaked it all in, inhaled it, the motion, the activity, the smells, and the sounds. For a moment she allowed herself to be a part of it. She knew she looked part of it.

And then her eyes fell on the handbill. From where she stood, from across the street, the picture was small. But she couldn't mistake the image. Her feet moved without her willing them, and she had to stop short to keep from being run down by a horse-drawn cart.

"Miss!" Talon hissed at her, following.

But Panna didn't hear. When she reached the parchment, she put both her hands on it, framing it, then touched it as though it were Packer's face and not a crude image of it.

Talon stopped two steps behind, considering the poster and its meaning, its potential to hurt her mission. She made a promise to herself that she would be more vigilant in assessing her surroundings, but wasted no energy in self-recrimination. She stepped in close behind Panna.

"So he is a murderer after all," she whispered.

"No," Panna implored, still staring at the poster. "No, there's a mistake."

"I will need much proof of that, before we continue with our bargain," Talon breathed.

Panna turned to Talon, anger and fear in her eyes. Would Tallanna abandon her now, here? "There's a mistake, don't you see? He's at sea. How could he have...how could he even be suspected of such a thing?"

"But when did he go to sea? And what did he do before he left? What might he have done after you saw him last?"

Panna's eyes jumped back and forth between Talon's, pushing away all thoughts of Packer's guilt. Talon knew Packer was innocent, and guessed rightly he was suspected of the killings on the beach, those she had committed herself. But Panna didn't know about those; she only knew about her own crimes. So Talon waited, knowing Panna's innocence and naïveté would once again work in her favor.

Panna turned again to the poster. Her resolve was iron. "He is not guilty of anything like this. He was not carrying the guilt of such a crime when I last spoke to him." His face, his kiss, his lips on her shoulders. She closed her eyes to return to that moment, in her dining room, on the bench. Then she opened them again. "It's a terrible mistake."

“He went to sea at Inbenigh,” Talon whispered, watching the girl, patiently waiting for the idea to slip through her defenses, like a cold mist through a locked door. “Perhaps something happened there before he left. Perhaps he fought someone, much as you did.”

Finally it struck her. She put a white-gloved hand to her mouth. “Oh, dear God. They think it was him!” She turned to Talon, who feigned bewilderment. “They think it was Packer who attacked that poor fisherman. He’s died, don’t you see? And they think it was Packer who assaulted him. But it was me! I should be on this poster. I have to tell them, I have to turn myself in!” Her eyes were unseeing as she imagined the grief she had now caused him, would yet cause him.

“Shhh!” Talon said, taking her by the arm and staring deep into her eyes. “You must listen to me now. Everything now depends on finding Senslar Zendoda.”

Panna’s eyes were wet with tears. “I have to give myself up. I can’t let this go on. I’m sorry.” Her bargain with Tallanna no longer mattered.

Talon squeezed Panna’s arm harder. “Yes, surrender—but surrender only to Senslar Zendoda. Him alone. He is Packer’s swordmaster. He can be trusted. Not some deputy. Not some sheriff. No one else will believe you. They will think you are lying to protect him. But the swordmaster will help you. He will help Packer. I know the ways of your people; I know the ways of mine. No one else will care about the truth.” Talon waited as Panna embraced this. “Do you understand?”

“Yes,” Panna nodded. She remembered the reverence with which Packer had spoken of Senslar, how he had defended his teachings to her father. “Packer trusts him.”

“Yes. You can trust Senslar Zendoda,” Talon said, cooing. She loosened her grip, glanced around to see what notice they had gathered from passersby. She knew their posture had not been one of a servant and her lady. No one seemed to be giving them more than a casual glance. Talon bowed her head, took a submissive pose. “Now, if you’ll precede me into the Sheriff’s office…”

“Yes, of course,” Panna said, wiping her eyes with a gloved hand.

The inside of the Sheriff’s office was dark and cool, and smelled of sawdust.

"May I help you?" a clerk asked, a thin man with wrinkled white skin that seemed to hang from his face and hands. He was wide-eyed, clearly not accustomed to dealing directly with ladies such as this.

"I have information about Packer Throme," Panna said, summoning her courage, trying to hide the redness of her eyes. Talon drifted far back, toward the small, curtained windows, where she stood with her head slightly bowed, as though out of place.

"Who?" the man asked, too loudly.

Panna smiled meekly, took her time. "Packer Throme. He's the one on the handbill just outside?"

"Oh, the murderer!"

Panna breathed in sharply.

"You have information about him?"

"Yes, but I will give it to no one but Senslar Zendoda."

The clerk frowned, then looked confused. Panna stole a glance at Tallanna, who was not looking at her, but who was smiling encouragement nonetheless.

"I don't understand. You're talking about the Swordmaster?"

"Yes, I must speak to Mr. Zendoda."

The clerk just laughed. "He doesn't come around here much. Why do you want to talk to him?"

"That is my business."

"Say, you know what aiding and abetting is?"

She shook her head.

"It means if you know something about a criminal, you need to say it, or you're a criminal too."

Panna glanced at Talon again, but she was looking at the floor, waiting submissively.

"I'm not saying what I know or what I don't know. I will speak only to Senslar Zendoda," Panna said, unapologetic.

"I see. Well. That's somethin' then." He scratched his head. "Wait here, would you?" The clerk left them, and went through a large wooden door into the back room.

Panna looked questioningly at Talon, who nodded her approval. Panna took a deep breath, relieved. She was glad Tallanna was here.

The clerk returned in a moment with Sheriff Bench Urmand, whose suspicious demeanor melted away quickly as soon as he got a look at Panna Seline.

"Good day. I'm the Sheriff of Mann, Bench Urmand. What can I do for you?"

"You can take me to Senslar Zendoda," Panna said firmly.

Bench stared at her for a moment. "This is about Packer Throme?"

"Yes."

"Are you after the reward, miss?"

"No," Panna said immediately, too emotionally. She imagined she felt the heat from Talon's eyes. "Packer Throme is a student of Mr. Zendoda's, and—" Tallanna's parasol slipped from her hand and clattered onto the wooden floor. Panna glanced around, caught the warning, and bit her tongue.

"So you know this Throme?" Bench pushed immediately. "From where?"

"I'm simply doing my civic duty," she added. "The reward is yours to give as you see fit."

He studied her closely. "I see. You wouldn't by chance be the daughter of that priest from Hangman's Cliffs?"

Panna's eyes went wide, and she felt her cheeks flush. She was caught, her disguise unveiled just that quickly. And then she realized she could not be caught, not yet. He had no idea who she was. And as she did in Inbenigh, when she refused to have her mission cut short, she turned on her attacker. "Do I look like a pastor's daughter from some backwater village?"

Urmand immediately backed down, holding both hands out in front of him. "No offense meant, miss. I just...I have to ask these things. So tell me, why didn't you go to his office at the Academy?"

Panna blinked. "Beg your pardon?"

"This is the Sheriff's office. Mr. Zendoda is Swordmaster. Why come in here and say you'll talk only to him, rather than go there?"

Panna felt another surge of panic. What did he suspect? She had no answer for this. She had no idea what to say, what the right answer was. She had come here because Tallanna said to come here. Remembering her training, though, she raised her chin, kept eye contact with a look of confidence, and waited. She couldn't believe this would work, but she had no idea what else to do or what to say.

Bench relented again. "I'm sorry," Urmand sighed. "I meant no offense. Whatever your reasons for wanting to speak to him, this is a legal matter, so you came to the right office." He held up both hands, conceding defeat. "I'll see if I can get a message to him."

"Thank you so much."

The Sheriff walked back through the great door, pulling on his earlobe and looking defeated, leaving Talon and Panna alone.

Talon had now studied the office thoroughly. The visitor's area, where she and Panna now waited, was relatively small, maybe fifteen feet across and twelve deep. The wall fronting the street featured two small windows, one on each side of the door, both heavily curtained. They were designed for defense; big enough for a gunman to use to protect the office, but too small for any person to climb in or out easily. Under each window was a wooden bench.

The front door was made of solid oak, hung on huge iron hinges, with an iron bolt as well as a keyed lock. The back wall, the one Panna faced as she spoke, was covered with yellowed handbills and wanted posters. A huge door hung in the center of it, solid ash, almost four inches thick. This door was hinged from behind. Four iron bars covered an opening high in the center of the door, a window measuring not much more than a foot square. There would be a jail, and likely prisoners, beyond the door. A great iron keyhole and lock mechanism provided security.

Beside the door, on the left, was the clerk's station, a small L-shaped desk. Behind it was a stool; in front of it was a single chair.

The white ash door now stood just slightly ajar, but Talon couldn't see past it. She heard voices back there clearly enough, however, and recognized the occasional rustle and slap of playing cards, the squeak of a burdened chair.

After what seemed an interminably long time, during which conversation could be heard in the back room, the Sheriff emerged, followed by the clerk. "I'll be back with an answer as quickly as I can," he said to Panna.

"Thank you."

"Assistant Deputy George will stay with you until I return."

"I appreciate your personal attention to this matter." She said it in a way that she hoped conveyed he might be rewarded. She was rather pleased with the way it came out, and knew Tallanna would be proud of her.

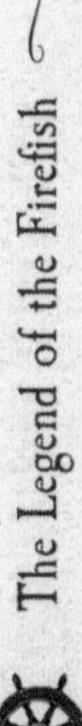

Urmand did not look terribly pleased as he bowed and grunted and left through the front door. He was carrying a leather mail pouch bearing the seal of the Sheriff of Mann; in it was a note he had quickly jotted for the Swordmaster.

Bench mounted his horse and headed up the street toward the Academy at a trot.

Assistant Deputy George invited Panna to sit across from him, and she did. But he did little more than watch the young woman wait, making her uncomfortable very quickly.

Talon moved the curtain back an inch and looked out the window, keeping her back to the clerk, trying to stay out of his thoughts as well as his sight. He seemed more than happy to spend whatever moments he wasn't straightening his paperwork looking at Panna.

The minutes drifted by interminably. The longer Panna sat, the deputy smiling and shuffling papers and then smiling again, the more she doubted the wisdom of this deception. It was fine with the deputies and the sheriff, but she needed Senslar Zendoda's help. She did not want to deceive him in any way. Yet how could she simply confess who she was when she had just denied who she was so thoroughly?

Panna waited in silence for what seemed like ages, though all told, it was less than a quarter of an hour. Two deputies came and went, exchanging paperwork with the clerk. Then suddenly, Talon stepped away from her spot by the window, closing the curtain.

"Excuse me, ma'am," she said to Panna. Both Panna and the deputy looked surprised. Talon bowed her head once, then walked right past them through the great wooden door at the back of the room. "I'll need the privy," she said as she went.

"Hey, you can't go in there!" Deputy George said, standing. "You," he ordered Panna, "stay put!" Then, shaking his head at the folly of women and of foreigners, he followed Talon, oblivious as a sheep in a slaughterhouse.

Panna saw the door close behind the deputy, and went immediately to the window. She heard noises behind the door, shuffling of feet, and she registered the single syllable of a spoken word, but she was unprepared even to imagine what was actually happening a few feet from her. Outside, she saw a short man with a black cape, a dark red beret, and a white goatee. He dismounted a very big horse. He wore a long rapier at his hip.

The *Camadan* entered the harbor of the Port of Mann just past noon. She limped along with shreds and ribbons where she should have had a mainsail, a topsail, a foresail, and a maintopgallant. The wind overfilled the sky sails, the jib sails, the spanker, and the royals, causing her to list precariously. She made port under the competent direction of the first mate, a cautious man who, after the storm, had been convinced by an overwhelming majority of the crew to make port here at Mann, risking the wrath of Scat Wilkins. It was the only city in which they could, with any reasonable certainty, find enough cloth to make repairs in short enough order that they could set sail for Split Rock, and perhaps make the designated rendezvous. But that's not why the crew wanted to come to the Port of Mann.

The crewmen and crew-women who worked the processing plant that was the *Camadan* all stood on deck and cheered the familiar sight as they pulled in. Scat Wilkins' driven need for secrecy had kept them from this port, home to almost all of them, for more than a year-and-a-half. It was a welcome sight.

Senslar Zendoda stepped into the office. He saw Panna, and walked to her immediately. He did not recognize her as Panna, of course, in spite of the descriptions he had gathered quite recently, and in spite of the descriptive terms Packer had used of her rather freely in his presence. He saw a beautiful, richly dressed, deeply concerned, almost fierce young woman; a striking, almost poetic vision of strength and need. It was easy for him to focus only on her, too easy for the last person on earth who could save her to be distracted by her.

Senslar Zendoda had sped here alone after a brief conversation with Bench Urmand, who had then left to visit the crown prince. He walked toward Panna and stopped a few feet away, his face open, friendly, warm; the bear to the bait, standing within the iron jaws that would trap him. "I am Senslar Zendoda." He bowed deeply.

Panna didn't speak. Her eyes were almost wild with a desire to spill all she knew, but she did not. Instead, she looked for Tallanna. The closed door did not move.

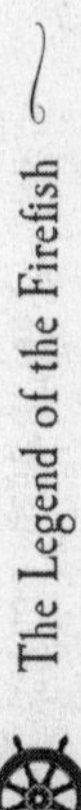

"What is your name?" he asked kindly.

She faltered, but only for a moment, and then, looking into his calm gray eyes, she remembered her own mission, not Tallanna's mission, not her bargain, but the true mission of her soul. She stepped toward him and put her hands out; he took them. "I am Panna Seline. And I need your help. I must find Packer Throme."

As Senslar's eyes narrowed with confusion, the door opened behind Panna. The swordmaster saw Talon, not Tallanna the servant, but a Drammune warrior. The servant's garb was gone, sheep's clothing shaken from the back of the wolf. Talon had been unwilling to confront her great nemesis in anything but her strength, and so she had removed the dress that disguised her. She stood now in her leathers, her knife at her belt, her bloodied sword in her hand. Her hair swept wildly around her shoulders. She had heard Panna abandon the carefully crafted pretense, but it didn't matter to her now. The deception had done its job.

Senslar's hands left Panna's in an instant, and his right hand went to his sword hilt. Panna spun around, following the sudden change that had come over the swordmaster, and saw Tallanna, with the fires of hell burning in her eyes. Through the open door, Panna could now see bodies, lying in blood on the floor, Deputy George and others. She knew instantly what this woman had done, understood in a moment what she herself had done.

The next few seconds were a blur to her. A hand, the little man's left hand, shoved Panna violently aside, with shocking strength, toward the wall. She tripped over the chair and fell backward, striking her head on the wall. The room buzzed and went dark. When Panna struggled up a few moments later, the room was spinning. She saw that swordplay had begun, the little man and the lean, dark woman both moving with a speed and agility, and with a fury, she had never witnessed before.

"Enochti rifal aziz," Talon growled. *You shall die.* She struck, again and again, lightning-quick thrusts and cuts, parried just as quickly by Senslar, his blade singing against hers.

"Nochtu rifala tremunsula," Senslar replied easily. *We shall all die.* He moved very little, letting the aggressor strike, and focused his mind on her swordsmanship. He paid no attention to where her blade was at any given moment; conscious action was useless at this level. He trusted his training, his experience, his own swordplay,

entirely. When she pressed, his sword was there, when she feinted, his sword was not. He was pleased to find that he was her equal, alarmed by the fact that she was his.

It took only a few moments before Senslar knew his adversary. He knew who she was, though he had never before seen her. Her skill identified her. The scar confirmed it. He had heard of only one woman with this level of skill, had heard the stories of a Drammune woman with both this ferocity and this felicity in battle. This was Talon, the chief security officer of the *Trophy Chase,* who sailed with Scatter Wilkins. But why was she here, attacking him, attacking deputies? What had she to do with Packer Throme, and Panna? And then he realized that this woman solved the puzzle of the two bodies on the beach. Here was the murderer.

When she disengaged, his blade went silent, poised to meet hers instantly. She didn't speak again, but attacked, engaged, disengaged again. Whatever line she chose to attack, he had the defense. While he acted and reacted, he studied her swordplay. Her position, her balance, even her conditioning were flawless. More impressive yet, he knew she was searching for weaknesses as she fought. She was studying him every bit as thoroughly as he studied her.

Finding no weaknesses, she began the most subtle of feints, inviting him to attack, leaving a slight target now, and the same target just slightly more obvious a moment later, a ruse handled so skillfully and with such subtlety that Senslar Zendoda was required to test it. But when he did, he was assaulted from it, a thrust from nowhere, from within the weakness, revealing the cunning that lay behind it.

Her swordsmanship was creative, intelligent, and masterful. He began to understand that he would not defeat her through mere superiority of skill. So he began to focus on her courage, her will to win, her temper. Her swordmastery.

He needed to know something more than her name and reputation to affect the outcome of this duel. He needed to know what drove her in this assault, this moment. Was it politics? He may have been lured here, but this was no assassination.

"Ema zien enmanteras," he told her. *I am not the enemy.*

"Enmateras aziz demincarcera." You are the enemy incarnate. Talon kept the core of her being cool, a flowing stream of simple willpower, letting her body follow the lead of her most immutable desires. She

was the bird of prey, unruffled in the turn, the dive, the kill. She was the Firefish, with no capacity for remorse, for fear, for pity or self-doubt. She was calm, even serene about her business. Perfect in design.

Senslar was struggling. Too many questions, too few answers, too little time. The Swordmaster felt the burn in his forearm, his shoulder. This opponent was younger, stronger than he, exceedingly ferocious, immensely talented, and extremely careful. He had ridden all night without rest; but even had he been completely refreshed, he couldn't outlast her. He began to realize he would lose to her. What drove her? In the answer to that question, behind that locked gate, was victory. He needed to find it soon.

"Una aziz?" he asked. *Who are you?* Her answer, if she would answer, would reveal how she identified herself. It was a direct thrust, rarely parried, into the heart and soul. If the answer was a name, then lineage was most highly valued. If a title, then honor. If a post, then occupation. If current task, then expedience. If any other answer came, then a greater revelation came with it.

She smiled. She understood why he asked. She knew his writings, his teachings—all of them. She had planned for this. *"Eyneg…ema…aziza." I am the darkness within you. "A rifal emo trumvala." And I shall be victorious.*

The sense of the words in Drammune was that she was somehow a part of him, she was one with him; but she was the ignoble part, that which lay buried deep within. *I am the darkness of you. I am the evil within you, and the evil within you has come to defeat you.*

Senslar was more puzzled yet. Everything he knew, all he could see, and now what he heard told him that she was driven in this moment by nothing more than the desire to defeat him, to mock him, to win against him; this was her identity, and now was her moment. It was a hatred born of culture, country, and competitive spirit.

But why? Why come so deep into the very heart of Nearing Vast? The Drammune were not stupid, and they were not suicidal. It occurred to him that she might be one of the Zealots of her homeland. They hated Nearing Vast and the Christian religion with a great passion. He had converted to Christianity, and would be their natural target. But she was a woman. The Zealots held no place of honor for females, and did not follow the ancient custom of the woman warrior, the *Mortach Demal.*

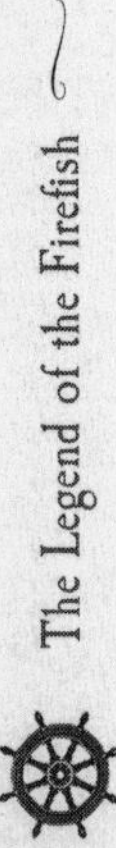

"Una aziz?" he asked again.

She was pleased with the urgency behind the question this time, urgency he did not intend to convey but could not help but reveal. She let their swordplay dwindle to a pause. She lowered her sword, let its tip hover a foot above the rough planks of the floor. He was panting. That was fine; he could recover his breath. Talon spoke in her native tongue. "I am the daughter of a Vast harlot," she said with venom, "and a young Drammune sailor, named..." and now her voice dropped an octave..."Senslar Zendoda."

Senslar felt his strength wither. Internal fires that burned in him hissed and steamed from this dousing. Was she lying? Surely she was. And yet, as a young man he had been as reprobate as any of his kind—sailors on leave, left to their own devices on foreign shores. Only in his mid-twenties had he responded to a higher calling and left his baser ways, along with his native land. If he had fathered a child by a prostitute, it would have been roughly thirty years ago.

A child born of his sins could be this woman's age.

As Senslar studied her face, searching for answers, she waited, prepared for the final attack, the thrust that would kill him. As the dawn of recognition broke over him, as soon as he realized the truth of her words and knew that before him stood his own daughter, at that moment she would attack. At that moment he would be changed, open, vulnerable, desiring suddenly something far different than a duel to the death. And at just that moment he would die. She had rehearsed it in her mind again and again, practicing his death in darkness and in silence. She waited for what seemed an eternity.

And then the moment came. His eyes opened, his face went slack. He could see himself in her, in the jawline, the nose. And in her eyes he could see...Lydia. He could see her!

Talon's sword was a bolt of lightning, a flash of powder, an electrical charge that exploded from nowhere and flew to his heart. He reacted too slowly, as she knew he would. But his movements were her movements, her lightning was his, born of his flesh, and he was able, at the last possible moment, to redirect the thrust. Talon's blade bit deeply into his left shoulder, just missing his heart but puncturing the muscle and tendon at its very strength. He pulled away, falling backward as he did. He spun to his left, landing on his knees with his back to her. Knowing his vulnerability, he rolled under the clerk's desk, then jumped to his feet on the far side of it, poised again.

Talon's eyes flashed at the missed moment, but he didn't see them. When he looked at her again, she laughed, her eyes merry. "Bleed," she said happily. "I have enough of your blood for the both of us."

His chest and shoulder throbbed. His left arm was almost useless; worse than useless, the pain of movement made just by breathing was difficult. She had wounded him badly.

"Who is your mother?" he asked, still searching. But he knew the answer.

She shook her head. "No one worth more than a fifth of a coin for half of an hour. But she had the black misfortune of being unable to forget you. And that misfortune she passed on to me. But I will destroy you and all you have built."

Senslar moved out from behind the desk, realizing that if he died, when he died, the young woman Panna would be in great jeopardy. He had to find a way to save her, if at all possible. He hoped Talon would forget about her for a moment. As Senslar circled, Talon's back was to Panna. Panna stood in agonized silence, and pressed herself back against the wall.

"I do not fall for your mind tricks, or the tricks of your religion, your pretense at weakness as you call on God to protect you. I am not weak. I am strong. And I am what you unleashed in the integrity of your youth. I have come to put an end to the deceit of your old age."

Senslar Zendoda was heartbroken. He understood now her purpose. It was to destroy him. That was all. And yet she was his daughter, a child he'd never known. There was something stirring in him, a paternal pride, and with it a great paternal sorrow. "Your strength is undeniable, Talon."

"Yes. Yes it is." Now she shunned her native tongue, so Panna could understand. "And your weakness is undeniable. Tell me your God will save you from me. Tell me He will save this weak girl. I will kill her, just as I killed her lover and your protégé, Packer Throme."

Panna's gasp was a convulsion. Black darkness made her head swim; nausea overcame her. She spread her hands against the wall behind her to keep from falling.

"And then I will return to the Kingdom of Drammun, and will not rest until the Drammune make war on Nearing Vast, that we may kill all the other puppets you have fashioned here in your deceptions."

She laughed again, but this time low and murderous. "Here we have the sum total of your life, Swordmaster of Nearing Vast." She paused to let the words bite deeply into the man before her. And then she said, "I, and I alone, shall be your legacy."

Senslar seemed to shrink. That Talon could or would carry out each of these threats was not only possible, it was likely. The physical wound she had inflicted was only to his shoulder, but in the context of this duel, it was fatal. She would kill him the next time their swords met. She had found his weakness and exploited it. She had turned his own teachings against him. He glanced again at the frightened young woman behind her. Perhaps he could still save her.

"Panna," he said softly, "I know you did not intend this. Do not give up hope."

Panna shook her head slowly, feeling hollow as a tree trunk. Tears flowed down her cheeks. "I...only wanted to find Packer."

"Yes, that's right," Talon cooed. "The poor little mouse was only following her heart." She spat out the next words. "This is the weakness you create with your lies. She has a strong back, but she could not see death and destruction though it rode with her in a white carriage."

Panna could not stop the sobs that came to her.

"You must leave, Panna," the little man said flatly, almost lifelessly. "I will give you the chance. It will only be a moment. But you must take it, and run. Do you understand?"

"Oh, no," Talon countered, "I think you will not have even a moment."

"Promise me, Panna. Promise not to give up hope. For me, for Packer. For God. Promise me."

Panna couldn't.

Talon cackled, and Senslar raised his sword, stepping toward Talon so that she could not afford to make a move toward Panna. "Find Prince Mather, Panna, at the Palace. Tell him all you know. Hold nothing back. Do you hear me?"

"Yes," she managed. Her head throbbed; she didn't know what to believe anymore. She understood his instructions, but didn't know if she could follow them.

"Go! Run!" Talon mocked. "Run to the Prince of Nearing Vast." She laughed again, the same cackle Panna had heard on the boat during the storm. "She's not going anywhere but where I send her. And I will send her to the bloody gates of your sterile heaven."

Will Seline had not eaten in three days. He had left his bedroom only to take some water, or to make some. He had slept little. His face, however, was not haggard or drawn, but calm. He had refused all visitors since Dog had brought him Panna's knapsack, her bloodied cloak. He had determined he wouldn't leave his room, or his knees, until he knew Panna was safe at home, either with him or with God.

The Spirit of God would have to work. God's power alone could right the terrible wrongs now plaguing his little village. If Panna was dead, then God had taken her. But if she wasn't dead—and he did not believe in his heart that she was—then God could still protect her. No man, good, bad, or in between, could stop the power of God. And Jesus himself had said that if you have faith as a mustard seed, a mountain could be thrown into the sea. He also said that some demons could not be cast out without fasting and prayer. Will did not know the extent of his own faith, or whether he could move mountains. But he could fast and pray.

Now, once again, he felt deeply the danger that Panna was in. He took joy in it; he knew she was still alive. But once again he cried out, offering himself up in her place, not just asking God if He would, but placing himself as an offering on the fiery altar of God, bearing her very burdens, her fears, taking the dangers on himself, if that were possible, so they would pass from Panna.

"Whatever mercy you have shown me, dear God, give that now to Panna instead. Let me take the pain, let me bear the fear, let me hurt, let me die, but let her live."

Talon did not turn, would not take her eyes from Senslar. The deep pain faded in Panna, and in its place grew something more full and angry and cold than she had ever felt before. She wanted to hurt this woman. She wanted to kill her. It took Panna a moment to recognize this pain for what it was. But then she was able to give it a name. It was hatred.

Talon moved in on Senslar, still smiling. When she began again, her strokes were quick as a sparrow, heavy as an oak. The Swordmaster's parries were slow, and weak. She nicked him on the forearm, then the ribcage. He stepped backward, trying to open a space for Panna to escape. But the swordswoman before him was too much, too great an enemy for him now. She saw what he wanted, and blocked Panna's exit. She cut Senslar's cheek, then sliced his thigh. She laughed again. She was toying with him.

Senslar Zendoda saw the approach of death as clearly as if the woman before him were robed in black and carrying a scythe.

His mind raced back three decades and more, to wild, pleasure-filled days on the shores of Nearing Vast. He had no doubts. There was only one woman who could have cared enough to carry his child, who could have carried such a fire for so long. She was a strong, quiet, intelligent woman who should never have fallen to prostitution. He had thought of her over the years with real affection, real yearning; not constantly, but now and then. He had even wished she were other than she was when he had met her.

He felt shame now. Shame like he had never felt, even in his darkest moments. His heart ached with the thought of her pain over so many years, ached with what might have been, with what had been, with what he had missed, what was his all along without his ever knowing. Home, family, wife, children—all things he had never known, and would have dearly loved to know. The weakness in him utterly overcame his strength. There was no way out.

But then, suddenly, there was a way in. Senslar felt the pounding of the waves, the salt spray, the current, the undertow. Like the sea turtle, Senslar had reached his sea. His time had come. In his heart, he gave himself up to God, regretting the depth of his sin, accepting his own death, accepting a forgiveness so extreme that only the crucifixion of an innocent man in his place could assure its justice. He knew what he must do.

Suddenly, Senslar pressed the attack with a determination and resolve that surprised Talon. He stepped toward her, countering all strikes that might cripple him, protecting only his head, neck, sword arm, and heart. She moved backward, perplexed at this sudden, iron resolve, fearful that somehow he had in fact found an inner strength that would turn the fight against her…fearful even, deep within, that perhaps the Vast God who lurked in weakness was real, and would somehow overcome her even now.

But Senslar looked for no opportunities to strike. That was not his plan. He left his midsection vulnerable, so obvious a target that even a novice swordsman would see the failure in his defenses. And still he pressed the attack.

For a moment, Talon believed it a feint, and stayed away, fighting for victory in all the places Senslar still protected fiercely. But it quickly became clear that he was truly exposed, immensely so, that he could not possibly parry even the simplest thrust to his centerline, as unguarded as it was. Once she accepted the truth of this weakness, she didn't think past her own victory, hers now for the taking.

The meticulous killer who had schooled herself to have no capacity for remorse or pity, who had taken the greatest of pains to sever from herself any of the weaknesses that might grieve her as they had grieved her mother, had also schooled herself away from any capacity for self-sacrifice, and therefore she could not see it in others. She was utterly blind to her opponent's purposes.

She thrust her sword through his belly, just below the sternum, burying her blade to the hilt. She followed it in so that her eyes, on fire now with victory, with the moment, were locked onto his, her face inches away. Now the rehearsals would pay off, and she would see what she had come to see. She would watch him die, watch him writhe in agony, watch for the very moment his light was extinguished forever. The Firefish, eyes and skin ablaze, watched her quarry, relishing the kill. *"Rifal...ema...trumvala."* She twisted the blade.

"Yes," he said, his breath leaving him in a rush of pain, his cheeks and chin quivering. Blood seeped between his teeth, outlining them in red. He looked into her face, but he didn't see the Firefish. He didn't see the killer. Senslar Zendoda, Swordmaster of Nearing Vast, being so near to heaven's bloody gate, was granted a vision, given a glimpse of his great, lifelong desire, now fulfilled. He did not see the swordswoman, the pirate, the predator. He looked past the witch and the wanton, and saw only the little girl. His own daughter. His heart leapt with joy, and his eyes stung with tears. His sword fell as he took her in his arms and embraced her. He pulled her head toward him with every ounce of strength remaining in him and more, with a supernatural power, and cradled her head between his cheek and his shoulder. His grip was iron and velvet, gentle and loving, impossible to resist, impossible to deny, as though she were an infant and he was her doting father.

"My little child," he said into her ear in Drammune, with a kindness beyond reason, a love beyond human capability, his cheek pressed tightly against her forehead. "Oh, how I have missed you!"

Talon was horrified. She struggled, but felt helpless to free herself from his grip. She fought it with all she had, but she could not escape the warmth, the sense of pure light and love that wrapped around her, that enfolded her in a way she had never felt, that reached into places she didn't know existed. Finally, when his last breath escaped him and his arms released her, she pushed him violently away, leaving her sword buried in his belly. She watched, still filled with horror, as his body pirouetted slowly downward, almost gently, as though he were being lowered carefully to the ground by unseen hands.

Senslar Zendoda lay on the worn plank flooring, on his side, with a forearm under his head and a calm expression on his face, as though sleeping peacefully. But her sword remained in him, piercing his very being.

Talon stared in anguish, in pain, her teeth bared like a wounded animal, her breaths panting and hard. And then something crashed around her, blinding her, knocking her to the ground. She staggered to her feet, growling aloud, and stared down at the dead man as though he could have struck her yet again. But he lay there peacefully yet. Then she wrenched her eyes away.

The girl! The chair, which the girl had fallen over, now lay on the floor beside Talon. The stupid little girl had hit her with a chair! And now Panna was gone, the door still ajar from her escape. And someone with heavy boots was approaching on the wooden porch. Talon kicked the door shut and shot the bolt closed violently with one hand.

She put a hand to her forehead, grimacing in rage. She looked down at herself, her black leathers wet with her father's blood. She cursed, then screamed aloud. This was not the victory, the death sting she had meant to deliver, the satisfying kill she had longed for.

And Panna had escaped!

Chapter 20

The Palace

Panna ran up the street, drawing stares, whispers, and attention. She was unaccustomed to being encased in such a great load of material. She felt like a huge porcelain doll. One block from the Sheriff's office she tripped over the hem of her dress and rolled into the street. She sat up, now smeared with dirt and mud, her dress ripped at the hem and her sleeve ripped at the shoulder. She stood, or tried to stand, and fell again, the toe of her shoe caught in the fabric. A small crowd gathered around her, watching her as she angrily pulled off her delicate white shoes.

"Can I be of some service?" an older gentleman asked.

She looked up at him, fighting back tears of anger and frustration and fear. She shook her head.

"Are you sure I can't help?"

"Do you have a wagon or a carriage?" she demanded.

"No," he responded.

"Then get out of my way." She stood, pulling at the front of her skirts to get them up off the ground.

"I have a carriage," a young man offered.

"Where?" she demanded, turning on him.

He was amazed by her demeanor, but pointed across the street at a small buggy, the seat of which might fit two people, if the two were small enough.

Without a word, she ran across the street to it. He followed, running to keep up.

"Where are you going?" he asked, mid-stride.

"To the palace. Where is it?" She didn't look back at him.

"It's that way," he said, pointing the direction from which she had come.

Panna climbed into the buggy. "I can't go that way. How else can I get there?"

He looked up at her, waiting for her to make room for him on the seat. She stared down, unmoving as a statue.

"I can take you around another way," he offered.

She studied him just a moment. He was a pudgy thing, not much older than she was. No threat, but little help. But she needed the little help he could offer. She slid over, handing him the reins. "Let's go. I'm in a hurry," she said.

"So I noticed," he gulped.

"The Captain wants to see you," John Hand said to Packer Throme.

"Me?" he asked, his hand on the helm. "The Captain?" he asked more intently, realizing what the statement implied about Scat Wilkins' health.

Hand smiled. "He's not well still." John Hand turned to the nearest sailor. "Son, take the helm. Steady as she goes."

The journey had been odd since they left the Achawuk waters. Bone-tired as they all were, and many wounded worse than Packer, they moved slowly from one duty to the next, but with an underlying buoyancy, a sense of, if not joy, then perhaps release. It was as if they had sailed through a nightmare and into a pleasant dream, and in the pleasant dream the nightmare was no longer real. Strangest of all, to Packer, was the behavior of the crew toward him.

Ever since he had taken the helm to steer them home, when they had occasion to cross the main deck or come near the quarterdeck, one at a time the crewmen would stop to speak with him at the wheel; but not just to speak, he noticed, but to touch him on the arm, or to pat him on the back, or to hold his wrist and examine the bandaged hand that had fought back the Firefish. Not one of these encounters seemed odd in itself, but every last man seemed to have a need to

touch him, to be sure he was alive and real. But it was almost more than that; it was as though they wanted to commune with him, to associate themselves with him, to side with him.

Packer followed the *Camadan*'s captain to Scat's quarters, through his saloon and into his private room.

"It's who?" the prince asked Stebbins, his valet.

"She says her name is Panna Seline. She's quite insistent that you'll want to speak with her."

Prince Mather stroked his thin beard a moment. Wasn't that the name of the girl Senslar had mentioned? "Does this have to do with the fishing village murders? With Packer Throme?"

Stebbins thin eyelids blinked. "She says she has news of Master Zendoda, and she did mention a Packer someone."

The prince's eyes lit up. "Yes, that's her, then. Excellent—send her in."

"It's a whole new world now." Scat was lying on his bunk, leaning back on pillows. Small beads of sweat stood out on his pale brow. "A whole new world." He had a cup in his hands, and he was slurring his words. He seemed a very sick, but very happy man.

"Aye," John Hand confirmed. "We'll need to start over, build a fleet capable of processing these Firefish and of staving off the Achawuk at the same time."

"Bull we will!" Scat countered, unduly loud. "We just need better sailors. Better tactics. A few new wrinkles to our defenses. And fast, fast ships."

Hand and Packer exchanged glances. Scat had apparently been drinking rum for quite a while before he'd summoned Packer. Scat was always ready for aggressive action, spoiling for a fight, but never more so than when he was in his cups. Hand smiled, smacked Packer on the back. "Well, I know we'll need more sailors like this one here," he said.

"Hmm, maybe," Scat said, with less enthusiasm, eyeing Packer through dramatically narrowed eyes. "Are you a ghost, boy?"

"Sir?"

Scat paused only a moment, then addressed the issue as he saw it. "Mutter Cabe thinks you died and the witch replaced your soul with a demon. That true?"

Packer laughed out loud. But he quickly realized that Scat was quite serious. "No, sir, whatever she did, she never did that. I'm me."

Scat eyed him carefully. "Can you prove it?"

Packer wanted to laugh again, but he knew this was a dangerous moment. Scat waited. "Sir, I'm afraid I'm not sure how to prove or disprove something like that."

"Nobody can," John Hand said, coming to Packer's rescue. "But the boy says he prayed to God, and God gave the wind. And that's what saved us from the Achawuk. How could a demon do that?"

"That true?" Scat demanded.

Which part? Packer wondered. "I did pray. And I can't summon the wind. Only God can."

Scat nodded. It seemed to him a convincing argument. "They say you turned back a Firefish with your sword. How'd you do that?"

"I'm not sure, actually. I wanted to stab it. But I think it just... missed me somehow. I only caught its lightning." Packer held up his bandaged hand.

"Let's see it."

"The wound?"

"Yes, yes—the wound."

Packer began unwinding the strip of cloth.

"Who bandaged you?"

"Mr. Haas."

"Hmm."

Packer couldn't open his hand fully, but held it out cupped. The entrance wound, where the electrical charge had hit him, was a white rimmed circle the size of a gold coin on the heel of his palm; the tissue within it was raw, refusing to scab over. The rest of his palm was a mass of scabbing sores.

"Look like a ghost to you?" Hand asked.

Scat grimaced. "Mutter's a muttonhead anyway."

Packer smiled. "He can fight."

"True enough. But can you?"

"I can. Aye, sir."

"You chose to stay in the rigging and watch."

"I came down to the deck. Then the wind blew, and I went back up. I saw what might happen if—"

"Yeah, I know, rolled 'em off our decks."

"Yes, sir. I came aboard to help any way I could..." He trailed off.

Scat nodded, convinced. "Which goes to our bargain."

"Sir?"

"Our bargain. As it turns out, we're going to need more sailors. A lot more. You think your fishing rabble is up to the challenge of taking Firefish?"

Packer took a deep breath. In fact, he now hoped they were *not* up to it. He did not want them involved in all this. But he couldn't speak for them, and in fact he felt quite certain they would be very willing, many or most of them, for a chance at some real money. "All we can do is ask."

"Ask?" Scat bellowed. Then he closed his eyes, put his head back. He was ill and in pain. It took a moment for the pain to pass, and then he took a deep drink, finishing what was in his cup. "You'll deliver them." He gestured for more rum, and Packer, who was sitting closest to the bottle, refilled his cup. "We have a deal, boy. I need that rabble of yours. We'll lose a good many, I'm sure, and we'll need a steady stream of replacements. A river of replacements." He took another drink.

Packer shook his head. Scat, he knew well, cared little for the life of his crewmen. Packer spoke more icily than he intended to. "If the pay is good, I'm sure you'll have as many as you need."

Scat laughed a laugh that ended in a cough. "Oh, we'll be lining your little mud streets with gold. Hangman's Cliffs, isn't it?"

"Aye, sir." Thoughts of Panna suddenly stabbed him deeply; her porch, her songs. But that village would never be the same once Scat turned his attention there. It was already changed, though how much, he shuddered to think.

"Well, you'll be a hero! Gold and glory, come to Hangman's Cliffs! All on account of Packer Throme."

There was a time, and it seemed like ages ago now, when this moment would have been tremendously exciting to him. This was the exact end for which he'd come aboard; this was how he had defined success. But now, no amount of gold seemed worth it.

Scat chuckled. "Aye, anyone in that town who survives the wrath of Talon is likely to get very rich. Very rich indeed."

Packer's eyes widened. "Talon?"

"Talon!" Scat said loudly, then winced, holding his chest again.

Packer exchanged a quick glance with John Hand. He seemed disappointed in the direction of the conversation, but not surprised. "You sent her on a different mission, to the City of Mann," Packer reminded Scat in a trembling voice. "Not back to Hangman's Cliffs. You didn't send her to Hangman's Cliffs."

Scat stared at him quizzically, and then seemed to remember the lie he'd told. "Oh, that. No, course not. If she's harmed a single soul, it's her own doing. Not mine. You can believe that, boy."

Packer's stomach churned. He hadn't believed it before, though he had hoped. He certainly didn't believe it now.

Scat stared at him. "Don't forget, boy, it was Talon who saved your life. Though she repented of it soon enough." The Captain grew suddenly morose. "If you care to know, I wish I had never sent her off the ship. We'd have lost far fewer men had she been fighting. And she can heal as well as kill. By the devil, if she were tending to me, I'd be up and about by now!"

"Or dead," John Hand offered.

Scat's eyes swung over to his compatriot. Drunken thoughtfulness. "You have a point there." He took another long gulp of rum. "Anyway, that's not what we're talking about. We're talking about turning the world on its ear! On its ear! Talon can't stop that. The Achawuk can't stop us, though they tried. Drammune can't stop us. King Reynard the Fat of Nearing Vast can't stop us. Nobody can. We've learned the secrets of the Firefish, boys! And that's thanks to the guts of Scat Wilkins and the brain of John Hand, and the…the spirit of Packer Throme!" He raised his cup and drank again.

Packer couldn't even pretend to smile. He closed his eyes, wishing he were anywhere else in the world. Then he opened them and looked hard into the face of Scat Wilkins, trying to understand what he saw.

"What's a matter, boy?" Scat asked, completely puzzled that anyone could be glum in such a circumstance.

Packer couldn't answer. What wasn't the matter?

"Ahh," Scat said with a dismissive wave. "You lose people. I know; it's hard at first. But you get used to it. I'm used to it. I'm used to everyone dying. Everyone but me!" He laughed.

"What does it mean," Packer asked coolly, "when the logbook

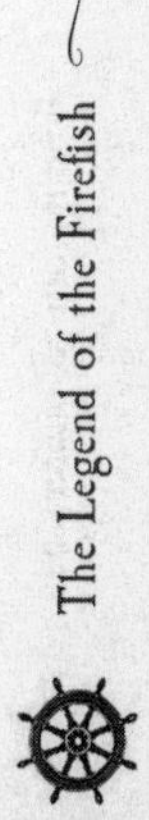

says that Marcus Pile was 'relieved of duty by Captain Wilkins' shot'?"

Scat sobered considerably. "What are you doing in the logbook?"

"I wrote the roll of the dead, and I saw it there. Lund Lander wrote it. What does it mean, Sir?"

Scat's demeanor darkened. "What are you accusing me of, boy? Shooting my own sailor?"

Packer nodded. "That's what I thought it meant."

"Oh, grow up!" Scat sneered at him. "You know nothing about sailing. Or business. Or life. You come here like you have all the answers—'Daddy told me this,' 'God did that.' When are you going to do something yourself? You gotta take life by the horns, and you gotta wrestle it to the ground with your own two hands, by your own strength! Or what are you? Weak. Crippled. Don't be a cripple, son. That's my advice. You understand me?"

"I do."

Scat wasn't hard to understand. He was a pirate, blinded by gold lust, calloused by bloodlust, drunk on his deathbed.

"You're dismissed."

Packer stood. He felt drained of every emotion but sadness. He glanced at Captain Hand, who raised an eyebrow cryptically.

As Packer left the Captain's stateroom and walked through the saloon, his eyes fell on his own sword, still in its scabbard and leaning in a corner. Without looking back, he walked over to it, picked it up, and took it with him.

"My dear, you do have a story to tell," Prince Mather said, standing too close and oozing too much charm for Panna's comfort. He eyed her torn dress, her exposed throat, the mud splotches, and the form beneath her blouse. "Come, sit down, and tell your prince what has been happening out in the hinterlands."

Panna had no time and no stomach for this. "Senslar Zendoda is dead," she said evenly, without moving. "The murderer is a woman who goes by the name of Talon. I can describe her to you. She is loose in the streets of Mann as we speak."

Prince Mather's affected airs showed only the slightest of fissures as he considered this woman and her news. "How do you know this?"

"I saw her kill him, not ten minutes ago, in Bench Urmand's office."

"Where was the Sheriff?"

"I don't know. Not there."

The prince nodded. "Go," he said to his valet. "Find Bench, and make sure he checks her story. Put the palace guard on high alert."

"Yes, sire." The old man disappeared. Panna felt a pang of distress about being left here alone with the prince.

"Sit down," Prince Mather said easily. He sat on a large sofa, patted the seat beside him. "You've had a rough day." His condescension was mitigated somewhat by the stark nature of her claims, but only somewhat.

"You'll soon know I speak the truth." Panna didn't sit.

"And this woman, who is she?"

"She is a Drammune warrior, I think. But now I don't believe anything she ever said."

"What did she say?"

"She told me her name was Tallanna, but Mr. Zendoda called her Talon. She washed ashore, shipwrecked, and said she only wanted safe passage back to Drammun. She talked me into helping her."

The prince nodded. He knew of the woman named Talon, who sailed with Scat Wilkins, but he didn't mention it. "And how did it happen that she killed Senslar Zendoda?"

"That was her purpose all along. She deceived me so I would take her to him."

"She surprised him?"

"Yes. And then they dueled." The image of Senslar's body spinning slowly to the ground, Talon's sword piercing him, came back to her unsummoned, unwanted. Panna closed her eyes against it.

"She fought him at swords?" The prince now looked slightly amused.

She nodded.

"Forgive me, but I think you are either imagining things, or you are mistaken about one identity or the other. Senslar Zendoda is a master swordsman, the greatest in the world, and would not likely be bested by a mere woman."

Panna stiffened. "This was not a mere woman."

Mather nodded, now doubting her story utterly. "Apparently not."

Panna shook her head in disgust. "Believe what you want. But right now she is escaping the city."

"We shall see about that." He chewed the inside of his cheek. "You do understand the seriousness of your charge, I hope. If a Drammune warrior infiltrated our shores to kill a Vast official, that is an act of war. Would you have me go to war on your word?"

Panna blanched. She had not considered the possibility that she had witnessed, had been part of, the beginning of a war between the Kingdom of Nearing Vast and the Kingdom of Drammun.

"I am your prince, Panna Seline, and this time I am ordering you to be seated." He again motioned to a spot on the sofa beside him.

Panna looked around, picked a small chair across the room, walked there, and sat.

Mather eyed her warily, but only sighed. She was beautiful, and had spirit. Who knew they grew such a thing in fishing villages? He stood, moved gracefully across the room, and sat near her, across a small table. He leaned forward, put his hands together as if in supplication. "Now. Tell me your story. Tell me about Packer Throme."

She studied the richly woven carpet for a moment, then looked back up at him. "Forgive me for being impertinent, Highness."

He waved a hand, smiling. She was so lovely. "Think nothing of it, dear."

"But tell me when you are prepared to believe me. Then and only then will I tell you what I know."

The wind changed as night fell, blowing cold from the north. Cold rain spattered across darkening streets and buildings. Women gripped their parasols like shields against the wet pellets, men pulled collars up and dashed quickly ahead, holding doors open for their companions. In the square, a light burned in the sheriff's office, but the door was closed. The poster of Packer Throme had been torn from the board.

Talon raced eastward toward the port just ahead of the rain. Her horse, stolen from among those tied in the alleyway behind the sheriff's office, was wild-eyed, foaming, at an all-out gallop. It feared and loathed, but obeyed absolutely, the fiery monster that had leapt with hissing strength upon its back.

"I have authority to put you in prison on a single word," the prince threatened. His easy demeanor seemed little changed, but the threat was real. He spoke slowly, with a voice like oil. "And worse. You do understand who I am, don't you?"

Panna was unmoved. She'd seen enough death today to be weary of it; her own imprisonment seemed a small matter. "I mean no disrespect."

"You have something to hide, then?"

"No. The contrary. Senslar Zendoda's last instructions were to run here, to you, and tell you everything that has happened, sparing nothing."

He pondered. That would have been a difficult quotation to simply invent for the present purpose. But then, what was her purpose? "And yet you refuse to do so? I don't understand."

Panna looked at him, saw nothing but the oily certainty of his rank, his lineage. "Mr. Zendoda must have respected you greatly," she said. "Surely you are a good man and a just prince, or he would not have put such faith in you. But you must understand that I speak the truth. If what you hear are only the wild ravings of a foolish girl…" she trailed off, not wanting her voice to crack. She swiped angrily at a tear in her eye.

Now the prince nodded, recognizing the backbone of the woman before him. This was principle, not evasion.

The valet strode back into the room, wide-eyed.

"Well?" Mather demanded, standing.

"It is…bad news."

"Speak it."

"I repeat only what I am told. Mr. Zendoda and at least three deputies, sir."

"What of them?"

"The report I have received—"

"Just say it, man, I will not hold you accountable."

"They are dead, sir."

"And Bench Urmand?"

"He's now investigating."

"Bring him here. Tell him I've got Panna Seline." Mather looked at Panna. Her expression was unchanged. He wondered for the first time if she might be dangerous. "And send a guard up here."

"Yes, sir." The valet left them.

Panna looked at him for just a moment, studying his face, and then said, "I am now prepared to tell you my story."

Talon finally reined the creature to a halt on a small bluff overlooking the bay. The docks spread out below her, two great piers angling out from a common boardwalk. Her horse trembled beneath her, blowing great breaths through its nostrils, dancing and anxious. There were half a hundred ships in port, in all sizes and shapes. She looked for one that seemed ready to sail. She would steal a small one, or commandeer a large one; it didn't matter to her. The wind was to her back; it had changed to her advantage. Any ship with a sail would head straight out to sea in this weather.

And then she saw it, a tall ship near the end of the northernmost pier, sails ragged, mast broken. "Idiots!" she hissed as she turned her horse and galloped at full speed down the bluff, across the boardwalk, and then right out onto the wooden pier, reining in the beast only as she approached the gangway and a single, terrified sailor who had been left on guard.

The horse's iron-shod hooves slipped and scrambled as it attempted to stop abruptly, and it almost went down. But Talon leapt easily from it, even before it regained its balance. She slapped the horse away with a single stroke to its hindquarters. The animal bolted, running blindly back the way it had come, escaping with its life.

The sailor stood wide-eyed, as if in a waking nightmare. He was still bent over a rusted kettle in which he'd been trying to light a fire. She recognized him immediately. Fenter was his name, but they called him the Weasel. He certainly recognized her, and in his panic forgot all protocol.

She didn't need to ask many questions. The *Camadan* had undoubtedly been caught in the storm, separated from the *Trophy Chase*. This was unknown to Scat Wilkins, of course, who never would have ordered one of his ships ashore here. This was John Hand's doing. She never did trust him.

"Where is your captain?" she demanded.

"On board the *Chase* last we saw him, sir. Ma'am." He was every bit as frightened as her horse had been, his Adam's apple bobbing and jerking like it had a life of its own.

"Where is the *Marchessa?*"

"Haven't heard from her either, sir. Ma'am." The sailor was growing alarmed at her intensity. Had anyone on board believed for a moment that it was remotely possible that Talon, the Chief Security Officer of the *Trophy Chase,* was ashore, and might find them tied to a pier in the Port of Mann, none of them would have considered docking here, not for all the ale in the city. "There was a storm, and we just came here to make repairs to the sails and the masts...refit, you know," he whined in explanation.

"Where are the crew?"

"On shore leave, sir. Ma'am," he croaked.

"All of them?" It was an accusation.

He nodded miserably. "Almost all."

"And they left you on guard." She said it with disdain. She knew the reason he was chosen. The Weasel didn't have the guts to stand up to the rest of them.

"Ma'am." He nodded.

Talon's eyes flashed. "And who was it, exactly, who gave orders to make port here?"

He shook his head. "It was the first mate who took command, Bemus Doherty." He left out the part about how the rest of the crew had threatened him, to force him to make the decision.

"Doherty is a mutineer. This ship is not to be in port! Those are Captain Wilkins' standing orders, and every last crewman on this ship knows it. So every last mother's son of you is guilty of disobeying a direct order. You are a mutineer."

"But I..." His fear turned to terror. Mutiny, as everyone knew, was punishable by death. She was perfectly capable of executing him here and now.

"Is anyone else on board?"

"One, in sick bay."

"Is he able? Can he sail?"

"I think so, but he was—"

"You will cast off and board this ship, sailor, and raise the gangplank. We will sail from here, now!"

"Yes, ma'am, sir!" he said, utterly relieved he wouldn't die in the next few seconds. "Thank you, ma'am." The poor sailor wasted no time obeying.

As he was releasing the mooring ropes, Talon went up the gangplank, casting her eyes up and down the pier for witnesses. She saw no one who seemed to be paying the least bit of attention. They were all scurrying to avoid the cold rain, which was just now beginning to fall. She watched as Fenter untied the great ropes and ran at a clumsy canter toward her, up the gangway.

The *Camadan* drifted away from the dock.

Packer stood on the forecastle deck, cold wind blowing through his hair. The rum kept a bit of the chill away, and the wet salt-sea air seemed like a breath from another world. The rain had stopped for the moment, but the familiar gulls were silent as they roosted on the yardarms and decks and wherever else they could avoid the weather. The rocking of the ocean, the sound of blue water slapping the prow, the mists blowing across the waters, the smooth movement toward home...If only he were home now. If only he could see Panna safe this moment. But he could not make himself believe that she was safe.

When the wind had changed, all able-bodied seamen had been sent to the rigging to adjust the sails. This did not include Packer, who had resumed his spot at the helm, where his injuries would not impair his duties. Minutes ago, Andrew Haas had offered to give him a break, and Packer had accepted it gladly. Now he stood above the face of the great cat on the prow, and watched the seas rise and fall.

If Panna were alive and well, then all was still possible. Anything might be true. If Talon had found her and...well, then there was no life for him and no place for him anywhere on this earth. He had no control over it. He knew he should be trusting God, absolutely. But knowing now that Scat had sent Talon for revenge, had let her loose ashore to fulfill her bloody promises, it was near impossible. God could stop her. But Packer couldn't imagine how.

"Nice night for a sail," a familiar voice said behind him.

"Not bad," Packer answered.

"May I join you?" Delaney asked.

Packer smiled. "Always." His friend, his brother.

"What are you thinking about so hard?" Delaney asked earnestly, as though this were an odd occurrence.

"Home."

"A' course. I don't have much of one of those, anywheres."

Packer stopped himself before he said, "Lucky you."

"I do think about people I know, though. I miss my mother, God rest her. And I had a girl once, Maybelle Cuddy. You probably wouldn't a' known her."

"No, I don't think so."

"And a' course Marcus."

Packer looked at Delaney, wondered if he should tell him about the Captain's log. But Delaney should know. "I believe now that Captain Wilkins shot Marcus down from the yard, in the storm."

Delaney blanched. "In that gale?" He thought a moment. "That's one heavin' good shot."

It was not the reaction Packer expected. "It was in the logbook when I wrote the roll of the dead."

Delaney nodded, looked out to sea. "It's a hard thing, then. I suppose Captain thought it was the only way to save the ship."

Packer stared hard at him. "He shot Marcus."

Delaney took a deep breath in through his nose, looked up into the clouded sky. "You know, I'm glad I don't got to face the judgment that Scatter Wilkins will face." He looked at Packer suddenly. "The men say he's feeling better. They reckon he'll pull through." He waited for confirmation.

"Mr. Haas told me the same," Packer said finally.

Delaney nodded. "Well, whenever he does die then. But I got my own sins to worry with." He looked at Packer. "You never killed a man in anger, probably."

"No."

"You're a good man. But there's a lot of bad men in the world. Like I was, though I'm trying to be good now. But when you carry that guilt around a while, what Captain did looks different. He didn't do it in anger. Marcus was a goner when he clutched, and Captain knew it. Don't get me wrong. I loved Marcus like a brother, and I hurt when he went, and I still hurt. I miss him. But it's the losing him that hurts, not the how it happened. That's God's doing."

Packer watched the waves. Was Delaney just finding a way he could justify serving Scat, or was there real wisdom in his words?

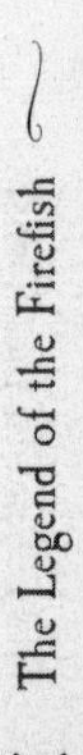

Either way, Delaney seemed comfortable, and Packer didn't want to trouble him further. "I guess God is in charge of life and death no matter how it comes."

"Like I say, I sure wouldn't want to answer for what Captain did. It was cold and heartless maybe, I'm sure it was. But what a terrified voyage this has been. And Marcus, he's been safe somewhere looking down. He was a good man too, but he didn't have your sword about him. I'd a' hated to see him get hardened like the rest of this lot. Which he would have—either that, or been dead by now. And that makes me feel peaceful about it."

Packer smiled. It was just possible—no, it was more than possible, it was quite probable—that for all Packer's wrestling with God and his calling, for all his anxieties about theology and about truth, about how to love and how to obey God, that Delaney was simply the better man.

In fact, Packer at this moment knew it to be so.

Chapter 21

Duel

"It's a ghost ship," Mutter Cabe insisted in a whisper. The crewmen standing on the deck of the *Chase* could see no lights, no people, nothing aboard the *Camadan* but darkness. The moon shone brightly; the wind flapped what few sails were unfurled. The *Camadan* moved slowly through the water in a southeasterly direction, but not a soul tended the sheets, nor the yards, nor the wheel, nor the crow's nest.

"Shut up, Mutter," Delaney said, but he stared hard with the rest, hoping it wasn't so.

"Ahoy!" Captain Hand shouted through the mist. The *Camadan* was certainly within earshot since the *Chase* was upwind of her. "Thunderation, who's got a voice that carries?" he asked. He looked around for Jonas Deal. "Where's Deal?"

"He hasn't moved from the Captain's door except to make water," Andrew Haas said quietly. Others laughed, but only those who thought he was exaggerating.

"Ahoy!" Andrew Haas yelled impressively.

No answer.

"The mainsail's gone completely. So's the foresail," Haas pointed out.

"Ring the ship's bell," Hand ordered.

Andrew Haas obeyed, but the clanging echo received no more response than had greeted the hails.

"Where in blazes did they all go?" Hand asked, seeming angered. They were far from Achawuk territory now. And if the Achawuk had attacked the *Camadan,* they'd have burned the ship. Wouldn't they? The *Chase* would sail past her within a few minutes, and while the great cat still had the muscle, Hand didn't have enough crew left to come about in short order, or with any measure of precision. He couldn't risk ramming her.

"I'll take a boat," Packer volunteered. "See what's aboard."

Hand grimaced. "No, it's my ship. I'll go."

"Begging your pardon, Captain," Andrew Haas said carefully, "but Captain Wilkins is ill. If you go aboard and find some danger...well, I believe we'd all rather the *Chase* had a captain than the *Camadan.*"

The other crewmen agreed quietly.

"I'll go with him," Haas then offered.

"Ahh, you can't go either, Haas. I need you to help me get this beast hove-to. Who will go with Throme?"

"I'll go," Delaney said immediately.

John Hand nodded his thanks. "Good. One other."

Silence.

Then, "Mutter'll go," Delaney offered. "He loves ghost ships." The men laughed as Mutter turned deep red.

Hand didn't laugh. "Fine. Throme, Delaney, and Cabe." Mutter's eye grew big, then narrowed on Delaney as the others chortled. "Go armed," Hand added. "Here, my pistol's loaded. Doesn't look like you'll do much good with a sword." He held it out to Packer by the barrel, but the young man simply drew his rapier, smoothly and easily, falling into a perfect fighting stance, left-handed. Hand smiled, returned his pistol to his belt. "As you wish."

Mutter Cabe got no sympathy. Ghosts were one thing, orders another. The men were happy to help him find his way to the jolly boat.

Within three minutes, Delaney and Mutter Cabe were rowing with Packer Throme across the rolling black water toward the tall, dark ship, their way lit with three lanterns. Their oars—little more than paddles, really—dripped, then dove into the cold green water, then dripped again. It was slow going. The jolly was the largest of the ship's boats, equipped with sails and rations for a long voyage. It was not the preferred vessel for a quick foray, but it was the only one left. The longboat had gone with the huntsmen, one shallop with Talon, and the other with Marcus Pile.

But they made headway, and as they neared the *Camadan,* their mood was overshadowed by the emptiness of the huge, rocking vessel. The silence, except for the creaking of masts and flapping of canvas, turned their blood cold. This was not right. This was not what tall ships were created for, to be alone, dark, and adrift.

Talon watched the jolly approach. She sat perfectly still, blending into deep shadows on the quarterdeck. It was an amazing thing to her, this sudden appearance of the *Trophy Chase,* and then, more amazing yet, the approach of Packer Throme. There was meaning in it, destiny. He was being reeled to her, or she was being blown to him. The horse that had carried her to the docks, the *Camadan* waiting for her there, the wind that had blown her straight out to sea, the *Trophy Chase* passing within a few hundred yards, and now Packer Throme paddling to meet her.

She hadn't really sailed the ship. She had let it drift. She was heading east, that was all that mattered for now. There was food and water aboard, enough for months of travel for a single person.

Fenter had abandoned her with a splash before they'd cleared the point at the Bay of Mann, jumping ship the first time Talon let him out of her sight. Apparently, he preferred to take his chances deserting his post rather than as the lone object of Talon's attention.

And this other crewman, the sick one Fenter had mentioned, had not shown himself, if he was on board at all. She had looked for him briefly, in the sick bay, in the forecastle, in the various officers' cabins. She had ordered him to show himself, but he hadn't, and she hadn't found him. She had little desire to hunt him down. If he was aboard, he was hiding. She'd find him eventually.

She watched the jolly boat approach, felt the rhythm of the sea, breathed in the thick, salt air. She had longed for another chance to kill the fair-haired boy, and now she would have it. But she felt nothing, no joy in the hunt, no seething anger. It puzzled her.

It was interesting to her that Packer had been sent out to investigate what danger might be lurking in a dark and silent ship. Cabe and Delaney she knew; they were but deckhands. So it was Packer who was performing the duty of a security officer. He had not only won acceptance aboard ship, he had replaced her. His sword had proven itself, undoubtedly. Scat trusted him. So much for her warnings.

And yet, even with that knowledge, she felt no deep or burning passion, no kindled desire for revenge. She would kill Packer, of course. She must. But this sense of calm, this resignation to the inevitable, was new to her.

Delaney was a good sword. Mutter Cabe, superstitious though he was, was also a fearless fighter. She would likely need to kill all three of them if she were to kill Packer. It seemed to her a waste. She wished these other two had not come along.

She pondered her own thoughts for a moment. Why did she want to spare Delaney and Mutter? Why did it matter to her? They were good men, sure, but she had killed many good men. Where had her rage gone, her focus, her deep fires? She was the Firefish, forever hunting, alight with electrical energy as she prepared to attack. But that energy seemed missing now.

It was because Senslar Zendoda was dead, she thought. That was the reason for it. There was a great relief in that. It was the end of a quest, the conclusion of a great hunt.

She tried not to think about his final moments, about his last words to her, his first and last embrace of her. Since it happened, she had refused to grant it any validity, refused even to consider it. It had been a mind trick; it had been his final, desperate attempt to use the Vast mythology to weaken her, and she would not allow herself to succumb. She would not allow him to prevail in his death, where she had planned for so long to prevail. Where she had in fact prevailed.

The jolly bobbed closer. She could see Packer's eyes as he turned to scan the ship; she could hear the water drip from the oars. Still she didn't move.

She felt a strong pull toward that moment, Senslar's last. There was a deep melancholy in it somehow; there was a deep pain she was not accustomed to feeling, deeper than physical anguish, like a deep, clean cut to the soul. Of course, she told herself, that was what Senslar wanted. He would want her to go back there and think about it, relive it, absorb the possibility that truth lurked within his words. Just the idea that light, comfort, and hope might be found there would be attractive to anyone.

But she would not go. She could not. It was a lie and a trick. And even if it were true, why would she want it? It was weakness, it invited pain on a level she could not begin to embrace, a kind of pain far more destructive than any she had ever inflicted or endured. She hardened herself against it. She was Talon; she was the predator. And she had work yet to do.

She lost sight of the jolly as it closed in on the *Camadan*'s hull. She heard its oars splash, then clatter against the gunwales as the men pulled them in, preparing to board.

Still she didn't move.

My little child. Oh, how I have missed you.

There. She had listened again. She heard the voice in her mind. It had no power. She felt nothing, nothing but the cold mist around her, creeping through her.

Delaney was able to throw a loop of rope around the anchor fluke, banging it against the hull as he did. Every noise seemed amplified and out of place in the mist. The jolly pitched and yawed and slammed into the *Camadan*'s hull, grating angrily. Mutter Cabe, despite his whispered misgivings, was now grim and determined. Packer again saw the warrior in him.

Before the three had time to discuss a plan, Delaney had started climbing the rope hand over hand. He reached the anchor and stood on it, then pulled himself up and over the rail. "Hang on, I think there's a rope ladder in the bosun's locker." They heard his footsteps drift away. After a silence that lasted far too long, they heard footsteps returning. The rope ladder came over the rail, and Packer and Mutter climbed up, Packer one-handed, Mutter struggling with the lanterns.

As they came over the rail they found Delaney standing with arms on hips, looking up at the sails blankly. "They been struck," he said. "Someone took 'em down, prob'ly to replace 'em."

Packer shrugged. "So?" Seemed logical.

"Who struck 'em? And why?"

No one answered. "Well, why don't we have a look around," Packer suggested. He held up his lantern. They had climbed over the starboard rail onto the main deck, so the quarterdeck was up to their left, the foredeck and the forecastle up to their right. There was no sign of anyone.

"I'll take the fore," Delaney offered, drawing his sword. He was thinking that the forecastle was likely to present the greatest danger.

"Fine. I'll go aft, and I suppose I'll meet you back here before we go below?"

"What about me?" Mutter asked.

"You stay on lookout," Delaney told him. "If one of us has trouble, we'll call out, you come to help."

John Hand and the crew worked diligently to turn the *Chase*. She had swept past the *Camadan,* and they would need to bring her about and catch up again with the drifting ship before an attempt could be made to heave to, matching the *Camadan*'s negligible progress through the water. But they would be several long minutes gone; it could take as much as half an hour to finish the maneuver.

Delaney swung his lantern through the darkness of the forecastle. Shadows played along the hammocks and hooks, but it was empty. "Ahoy! Anyone here?" he asked, his voice hoarse and quiet in the flickering light. "This is Delaney, from the *Chase.*" The forecastle had not been abandoned hastily, he noted. Most of the crew's gear was gone, and what was left was packed neatly away, as though its owners might reappear at any moment.

He thought he heard footsteps in the hall. "Ahoy! Anyone there?" He went to investigate.

Packer went through the officer's quarters aft before heading for the Captain's quarters, his sword drawn in his left hand, the lantern in his bandaged right. He realized after poking a lantern into three or four doors that whoever was aboard, if there were someone aboard, would most likely hole up where the comfort and the rum were most plentiful. That would be the Captain's cabin, which opened out onto the quarterdeck.

Packer looked around the decks as he climbed the companionway steps to the quarterdeck. Mutter stood where he had been left, holding the lantern and looking out to sea for the *Chase*.

The Captain's quarters were dark; no light came from around or under the hatch. Packer paused outside to listen. Hearing nothing, he slowly pushed on the door, swinging his lantern in as the hatch groaned. Nothing and no one. He entered. Captain Hand's quarters here were smaller than Scat's on the *Chase* by a wide margin. He had no saloon with accompanying table, no storage closet for wine and ale and spirits. Other than some additional square footage of floor space, little here recommended it over any of the other officer's quarters.

It had a bunk, which had been left unmade, the bedclothes in a heap at the foot. A map table stood in the center of the room, little more than a writing desk. A small wooden cabinet with a glass front containing two swords and a musket stood on the near side of the bunk. On the far side was a shelf of books, and a smaller shelf of bottles.

But Packer was drawn to the desk. He held the lantern over it. The chart of the seas still lay open, showing the course of the *Camadan* plotted into the Achawuk waters. Nothing since. The captain's log lay beside it, also open. The last entry read, "Docked safely at Port of Mann. Expect one to two weeks for refit. Crew given leave. Fenter left on guard."

It was initialed BD. It was dated yesterday.

Yesterday? Had the ship simply drifted out to sea? Or had it been stolen?

Then Packer heard a whining sound, followed by the deep thud of a heavy object plunging into the water. Something, or someone, had gone overboard. There was a creak, a crack, and a groan, and the ship shuddered. And then all was quiet and still.

Packer ran down the stairs to the deck. Mutter was gone. His lantern stood on the floorboards where it had been standing a moment ago. Packer's heart pounded in his chest. He ran to the gunwale, glanced behind him to be sure no one was near, then looked over the rail. The jolly was gone. How had it…? Then he saw the anchor rope, taut and trailing into the sea. Chunks of wood, planking and hull, floated behind them in the water.

Packer spun around again, expecting an attack. There was no one. "Mutter? Where are you?" he asked. Someone had let the anchor's windlass spin free; that was the whining sound he'd heard. The anchor had plunged into the ocean, and then the jolly, tied securely to it, had been pulled under by its weight, creaking and finally breaking as it went under.

Packer waited a few moments, during which he realized the full extent of his predicament. He didn't know where Mutter or Delaney was. If they were in trouble, he needed to go help them. If he went looking for them, he'd be inviting a sudden attack from almost anywhere on this dark ship. The *Chase* was now visible, but still

several thousand yards away, and anyway it had no more boats to send.

"Packer!"

He heard the muffled cry coming from below deck, perhaps from the forecastle. There were other words, but he couldn't make them out. He couldn't recognize the voice; it sounded like Delaney, but he couldn't be sure. He started for the forecastle deck, sword in one hand, lantern in the other. He left Mutter's lantern behind.

The darkness beyond the light of his lantern seemed absolute. He was easily visible to any foe; any foe was utterly invisible to him. But he didn't dare put his lantern down. He didn't know the ship; he didn't know the hiding places and the alleyways and the doorways where an attacker might conceal himself. He needed the light, it was his only hope, even though it made him completely vulnerable.

Something about his predicament seemed right to him, and gave him comfort, though he didn't have the time or the inclination to ponder it. He did ponder, at least briefly, what God had done in just the last few days. He did think about the power God had showed when Packer had put away his sword. He did think about his need to trust God now as he had in the barrel, as he had in the rigging, and not to take up the sword as he had with Delaney in the hold. He wasn't sure he could do that now. His heart was pounding and his blood was high.

He wanted God to do whatever God wanted. Packer prayed he would do no harm, unless that was what God intended. He prayed he would have the courage to do the right thing, the selfless thing, to sacrifice himself in order to help Delaney and Mutter, and not just to protect himself. But protecting himself right now was the overwhelming instinct of his entire being.

"Packer!" The voice was urgent, and though it was still muffled he felt certain now it was Delaney calling out to him.

"I'm coming!" Packer called back. He moved as quickly as he could to the forecastle deck, and then, swallowing hard, he started down into the forecastle itself.

"Packer, it's Talon! Talon is on board this ship!"

The words were icicles to his soul, putting every hair on end. But he did not slow as he moved through the cramped passageway toward the voice. He also did not cease to look both behind and in front of him, ready for the swordswoman to spring out at any moment.

"Where are you?" Packer called.

"In here! She's locked us in the brig!"

Both of them were alive when he found them, and for the most part, well. The brig was a dank eight-foot-by-eight-foot cell in a dank room of about twice that size. The cell was a panel of iron bars fronting a bench and a pot. The place smelled like urine. Mutter sat on the floorboards and leaned against the bench, holding the back of his head. Delaney stood at the bars, embarrassed and frustrated, but uninjured.

"What happened?"

"She surprised me in the dark," the sailor said glumly, and clenched his jaw. "I never had a chance. She led me here with a knife at my throat, threatening to slice me open if I even breathed loudly."

"Is he all right?" Packer asked as he shook the great padlock that clasped the iron bars together at its entrance.

Delaney shook his head. "She must have cold cocked him from behind. I don't think he knows yet what hit him."

"Did you see what she did with the key?"

"No. Took it with her, I think."

Packer swept the damp room with his lantern, but other than the two men's swords, which had been left on the floor just out of their reach, there was little here: a small writing table without drawers, an empty cabinet built in the wall, an empty peg above it that might have been where the key was kept.

Packer kicked the swords close so Delaney could reach them. "These will help if she comes back. But I'll have to find her."

"It's what she wants." He frowned deeply.

"She said that?"

Delaney shook his head. "She could a' killed us both. But she didn't, and she let us call you here. She *wanted* us to call you. She's waiting, Packer. Probably not far." Delaney was silent. "I'm sorry, brother. All a sudden, she was there."

"It's not your fault. The *Chase* will be back soon. I could just—" He heard a distant crack, or a pop. "What was that?"

They listened again, heard another soft pop, perhaps more distant.

"Sounds like gunfire."

"No, it's not." They both looked at Mutter Cabe. He did not open his eyes to look at them. He seemed to be speaking in his sleep. "It's fire. You can smell it."

Sure enough, Packer could now smell the smoke; very faint, but very real.

The ship was burning.

She sat and thought as the ship burned. She sat at the foot of the stairs to the quarterdeck. The quarterdeck and everything above and behind her was aflame. Across the main deck, the forecastle was also alight. She had set the fires. As soon as she saw Packer disappear below, she had gone to the ship's supply of lantern oil and poured it out fore and aft, leaving only the main deck for her final fight.

She thought about that, her final fight. It would happen here, now. She could have chosen deception; she could have put on the mantle of her old role, put herself at Scat Wilkins' service, made herself out to have simply returned from her mission. She could have hidden what she'd done to the Swordmaster of Nearing Vast, could have lied about how she came to be afloat here on the *Camadan,* alone. Scat knew nothing about her accomplishments of the last few days.

But eventually, she would be found out. She was an assassin. She had been seen, and could be identified. She was a killer, but not a coward. She would deceive to kill, but she would not deceive simply to protect herself.

So she was determined that this was the place, and now was the time, to play it out to the end. She did not think about what would happen when it was done. Somewhere in the burning ruin of the *Camadan,* when Packer Throme was dead, she would make her escape. A way would open up. It always had.

She felt now, deep inside her, that her mission was at an end. There would be a new mission, surely. But the ceaseless, ravenous desire at the root of her being was dissipating. She knew that now. She hadn't killed the two crewmen, hadn't even wanted to. The gale that had always blown hard into her sails had blown over. She did not know what it meant; it was not something she had anticipated. But there it was.

So she thought about how here, now, tonight, when Packer was as dead as Senslar Zendoda, she would prove, finally, the folly of believing that a weak God was somehow powerful. And proof, she had to admit, was now needed. The boy had escaped death at her hands. The girl had escaped her too. Her full intention in both cases had been to kill them. She had the will, she had the power, and she had had the opportunity. But both of them trusted in this broken God, and both were still very much alive. From one point of view, certainly from their point of view, these escapes would be seen as evidence that they did not believe in vain.

Senslar Zendoda had not escaped her, of course. But his death had not seemed entirely within her control either. It was not as she had expected it would be. And now, there was this twist of fate that put her directly into the path of the *Chase,* and brought Packer to her very feet. Did their God do this? Or was it simply a strange sequence of events, a coincidence? There would be one final test. She would kill Packer. Her strength would be shown to be far greater than his strength; that she did not doubt. But she needed to be sure that her strength was also far greater than his weakness.

As she prepared to test the very heart of the mythology of the Nearing Vast religion, she thought about their sacred stories. She thought of the ravenous lions that could not kill the prophet Daniel. She thought of the fiery furnace that could not kill three helpless devotees of their God. She thought of iron bars that burst open, that could not hold disciples when great forces were arrayed against them. And she thought of the greatest victory of weakness over strength in the mythology, the resurrection of the tortured and crucified weakling, the meek Prince of Peace.

These were all just tales, of course. They played their role in the mind control of Vast leadership. But if in fact there were, by some chance, a great God behind them, a Being stronger and more powerful than the Firefish, than the storms, than Talon, than death itself...if she were somehow wrong, and the fools and idiots were somehow right, she would like to know before she died. If the Vast leadership used such religion to their own ends, and yet in that religion was truth, which they abused, she would like to know that as well.

Even knowing, she would raise her sword in defiance to such a Power. Surely she would. But she would like to know with whom she had contended these many years.

The time had come. Packer descended the steps from the forecastle deck, his sword in his hand.

"Let the others go," he said as he approached. He unwrapped the bandage from his right hand. He would fight her in his strength. But ice seemed to wrap his heart as he watched Talon sitting there, watching him, waiting, the ship burning above her. Packer fought against an unreasoning fear. "You want me, I'm here. Release Mutter and Delaney. They're good and loyal crewmen." He put his sword in his right hand, felt the pain, fought through it. He moved toward her.

She just watched him approach. He stopped ten feet from her. She did not stand, did not draw her sword. Instead she reached into her jacket and pulled out a tress of hair, tied in a ribbon. She tossed it at his feet. She pulled out a red beret, with a dark stain on it, and threw it at his feet as well.

Packer picked up the items, keeping his eyes on Talon, and looked at the evidence she'd brought just for him. The long lock of hair was Panna's, pocketed while the girl's hair was being cut and styled. She had intended to put the girl's blood on its ribbon, just as she had bloodied the beret of the Swordmaster after his death. But no matter; Packer couldn't know what had or had not been her plan.

His fear melted instantly, replaced by deep pangs of grief. This was Panna's hair. No doubt. Touching it brought him back to her, brought him back to her bench, his fingers running through her soft, dark hair. It smelled of her. And Senslar's beret. Seeing it brought the swordmaster back, the smiling eyes, the calm demeanor, the gentle, firm command.

"I promised to find those you love, those who have helped you. And so I did as I promised. But I added one element, for my own satisfaction." She took a folded piece of parchment from her jacket pocket, and opened it up. She showed him the image on it, then tossed it toward him. The wind caught it, and he put his foot on it before it could blow away, leaned down, picked it up.

The fire now crackling above the duo burned hotter, illuminated the image of Packer Throme. *Wanted for Murder.*

She smiled as the full extent of her power rolled over him. "I did not kill them, you see? You did."

Packer looked at her. How could she have managed such a thing? But it all fell into place quickly, coldly, like a firing pin clicking within a well-oiled pistol. The scheme was masterful in its evil. Talon had arrived ashore and moved secretly. Whatever she did, whomever she killed, no one would know who did it. They would only know that some swordsman was on the loose at exactly the time Packer Throme, who had carefully proven to everyone his expert swordsmanship, had disappeared. Packer could imagine Dog swearing to everyone that Packer was the guilty one. He could imagine Pastor Seline's broken heart. He could imagine it all.

"I also promised to kill you. And so, now I will." She stood and drew her sword.

Packer just looked at her, tears in his eyes. "But why, Talon?"

She recognized the question. It came from the heart of his weakness. "Because I am strong, and you are weak. Because I am strong, and they were weak. Because there is no God who will fight for them, as there is no God who will fight for you."

He was crippled inside. He had no will to fight her. "I don't understand. You killed them only because they are weak?"

She stared back at him. "No. Because they pretend that their weakness is strength. Because they believe a God will save them in their weakness, and they teach others this stupidity."

"Panna was weak. But Senslar Zendoda was not."

She swallowed. "So it would seem." And yet Panna lived, and Senslar did not. Senslar had fought her, and Panna had fled. Senslar had fought her. And so far, Packer had not. The pattern was unmistakable.

And then Packer did the one thing that Talon didn't expect, the only thing that could send a shiver down her spine. He dropped his sword.

"You have killed me already, Talon." He was quite prepared to die. He did not want to defeat her, if that meant he would be required to live on to see the results of his own pride, his own sin: the names of Panna and of Senslar added to the long, brutal roll of the dead in the Captain's log, or on cold marble on some hillside...added to all the deaths, Vast and Achawuk, caused by his presumption, by his climbing into that barrel. Even if he could defeat Talon, then what? He would be tried for the murders of the two people he cared about most. No, he had no desire to fight, or to win. He was finished.

Talon stepped close, raised her sword, put the tip to Packer's chest. He did not notice the tremor in it as she did so. He could not see her heart race. He could not know the image that rose in her mind, the memory of an embrace that reached into places she did not want to be reached. "Fight me!"

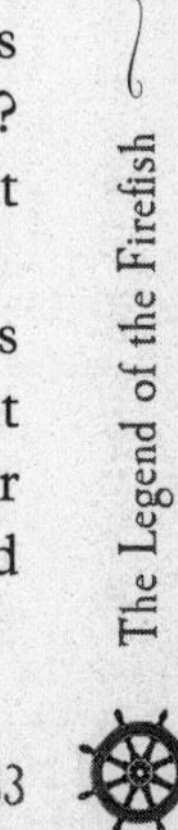

"No. I will die if God so wills it. If He wants me dead, not even you can keep me alive. If He wants me alive, you and a thousand Drammune warriors couldn't kill me."

She laughed. "I have killed, and I have given life. I have saved you, and now I will kill you. No God will do this. Just me."

He shook his head. "I put myself in His hands, Talon. Not yours."

And now the moment had come. A single thrust, and it was over. Proof would be hers. And yet, what would he do with a sword through his chest? What would he say? What look would be in his eyes? She saw in him now the same determination she had seen in Senslar Zendoda, the same fearlessness, the same focus, the same sadness, the same power. And yes, that's what it was. It was not the power to crush and kill; it was something altogether different. She remembered Senslar's iron embrace, that inescapable, overwhelming gentleness, that voice, soft as a lullaby in her ear.

Then Packer spread his arms wide, and opened his hands. Talon flinched. The image of the dying Christ, willingly giving Himself to death, was all she could see. Her eyes were drawn to his right hand, the damage there. He was helpless. But the power of God...She looked back at his face, unable to come to grips with what stood before her.

Packer saw fear. He saw terror in Talon's eyes. He didn't understand it. And then God granted him a vision, much as He had granted one to Senslar Zendoda. Packer saw within her the helplessness, the pain, the anguish that lived at the root of her soul. He didn't understand it, but he saw it. He knew.

For the first time, she appeared before him as something other than evil incarnate, something more than a soulless killer. She was a woman who was once a child, who had been hurt, who had hardened herself, who had lashed out in anger, who had schooled herself in vengeance, and who was not yet beyond redemption.

Packer smiled gently. "Your Father in heaven loves you." Packer meant to speak of her heavenly Father, of God, and couldn't know what meaning his actual words conveyed. But Talon reacted as though he had hit her in the stomach. Her breath left her, and she hunched forward, eyes wild. She shook her head, and backed up to the burning stairs. The heat of the flames, now licking down like the sun, was strong.

"No!" she said. She kept her sword out in front of her, to ward him off. This worried Packer, not for him, but for her. He stepped forward, back into range, back to where the tip of her sword touched his chest. His arms were still spread wide. He would welcome death. But even more now, he would welcome her, if she would embrace life.

"Whatever you've done, He loves you."

"No!" she cried again. It was as though Senslar, her father, had come to this boy and had told him all that had happened. But he couldn't have! Packer Throme couldn't know!

But her real fear was not that this was Senslar speaking to her, nor that Packer knew, and spoke the same. Her true fear was that this was the very voice of God. The God of weakness, the God of Nearing Vast, appearing before her, speaking through Packer. Her fear was that she was directly in contact with, directly in conflict with, the God of the universe.

If that were so, then she would address Him.

"Love is a lie!"

"No. Love is the power of God." He found himself aching for her, wanting desperately for her to understand. He dropped his arms to his side. "You've been blind. You've believed a lie."

"I have killed a thousand men, and You have not stopped me."

Packer now understood that she was questioning God, speaking to God, not him. But he also heard a question she didn't ask aloud. "He died to wash away the wrongs of the whole world. Even yours, Talon."

She shook her head, and stepped backward up the first two steps. The heat was unbearable, the crackling flames just behind her.

"Stop now. Put down your sword."

"I hate you. I despise your weakness." But there was a wince of pain in her voice.

"When I am weak, then I am strong."

"Lies! Yours is a religion for fools!"

"The wisdom of men is foolishness to God. Talon, the world is upside down. The powerful who seem to live at the top are really at the bottom. God's power is with the poor and the humble. And the meek."

"That is nonsense!" Talon climbed another two steps. The heat of the flames at her back was now painful, almost impossibly so. But the light in front of her was more painful yet.

"You abandoned me!" She grimaced, her face was contorted, her pain and anger now unveiled to the foundations of her being. "You never cared for me! I was hurt and alone, and you never came!"

"I'm here now."

Her eyes grew wild. That was Senslar's voice; those were his eyes that looked at her.

She backed up onto a step that was now in flames, still several steps from the top of the stairway, from the quarterdeck itself. Packer put out a hand toward her, wanting to pull her back, but she pulled away, and then in the blink of an eye, lost her footing and tripped backward. Packer climbed the three steps in a leap, and reached for her as she tumbled into the flames.

She dropped her sword, and reached out to him, a look on her face that was a simple plea for help. Her hair ignited; a blazing halo. Packer lunged forward, but the floor below her, already ablaze, gave way with a loud crack. And she was gone into darkness, darkness that suddenly erupted into flame and smoke that billowed upward like a cloud.

Packer looked up, following the flame and the circle of sparks as it spiraled into the night sky. "Talon!" For the first time, he felt the full intensity of the heat. It roared and billowed at him, forcing him back down the stairs. He looked around him. The entire ship was now fully ablaze.

Across dark water, visible in the light of the flames, he could see the crew gathered on the deck of the *Trophy Chase,* watching wide-eyed.

Something grabbed Packer's elbow. He looked down, saw a hand, looked up, saw Delaney's face. "Let's go!" Delaney yelled.

Packer let himself be led to the rail. The flames seemed to be all around them.

"Jump!" Delaney plunged feetfirst over the side. Packer followed. His sword he left behind him, resting on the burning deck.

Packer surfaced from the cold wet darkness, back to a world of fire and water, smoke and mist. Delaney was there, grinning as broadly as Packer had ever seen him.

Packer spit saltwater. "You're safe! Did you find the key?"

"Didn't need a key!" Delaney answered happily, pointing in the direction of the *Chase*. "Look!"

Not one but two heads bobbed in the water ahead of them. One

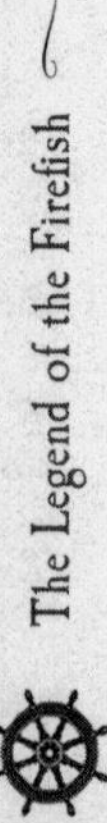

of them was Mutter Cabe; the other Packer didn't recognize. The man's head was plastered in a wet, white bandage.

"He's the carpenter's mate!" Delaney exclaimed, sputtering with delight. "He got the tools. Pried us out!"

And then the head turned to face him, and Packer recognized the boy. "Marcus? Marcus Pile!"

A broad grin came back in answer.

Chapter 22

Home

The red dawn promised more rain, but the air was as crisp and cool as a fall afternoon. Seagulls careened in circles, squabbling over scraps as though this were but one more morning in an endless sequence. Panna's chin was up, her face stoic. She stood among the crowds that had gathered to get a glimpse of the famous ship as she entered the bay in the pink and orange morning light. Surrounding Panna was a small force of armed men. The Sheriff of Mann was by her side, waiting patiently, his arms crossed across his chest and a flintlock pistol prominent in his belt. Panna's wrists were manacled together behind her back.

The main points of her story could not be corroborated by anyone in the city. Bench had found one or two witnesses who could remember seeing Panna enter the Sheriff's office, and with some prompting both men had said that, yes, she might have had a servant with her. Bench Urmand himself had seen the servant but could not recall her in any detail, and certainly had not found her remotely suspicious at the time. The Sheriff couldn't be sure the woman was even connected to Panna. It seemed a complete absurdity that she was Talon, a ship's officer on the *Trophy Chase*. Why should she be abroad in the City of Mann while Packer Throme, the son of a simple fisherman, was out at sea on that ship instead? Talon, it only made sense, was the one with the alibi.

A horse had gone missing from the Sheriff's office, belonging to one of the slain deputies, but no one had actually missed it until it had been found and returned. The biggest news was the disappearance of the ship during the rainstorm, one of the *Trophy Chase*'s escorts, but no one knew who had taken it or how it had set sail, or if it had simply lost its moorings. The single sailor who had been left on guard was gone, and no one had seen him for three days now.

Bench had dutifully investigated Panna's wild but certainly vivid story about stopping at a notorious inn out in the marshlands. Of the few people who could be induced to speak to him, none had ever heard of a woman named Talon. No one had seen any foreign-born women in weeks. The innkeeper was no help; she was blind and bedridden.

All in all, it was a much simpler story if Packer, who had a history of violent incidents, had turned criminal, fought and killed several people, and then turned on his old Swordmaster to prove his mettle. And Panna had simply lied to protect him. And as the Sheriff and every other law-enforcement officer knew, the simpler stories were more likely to be true. What Panna really knew, how much she was deceived and how much she willfully deceived others, all those were things the courts would sort out.

So Panna was put in irons, and kept safe in the Palace. Not in the dungeon, however. The prince had developed a soft spot for this hard-headed but lovely creature. She had been well-tended; occasionally better-tended than she thought proper, considering her circumstances, but neither the prince nor anyone else had laid a hand on her.

Panna stuck with her story. Talon had claimed to have killed Packer, but Talon had said a lot of things that were completely untrue. Panna swore to Bench and the prince and anyone who would listen that if the *Trophy Chase* ever docked again, Packer Throme, and thus she, would be vindicated. He had gone to sea, and had been at sea. Talon, the mercenary, had been behind every incident but one, the attack at Inbenigh, which for reasons the authorities couldn't fathom, Panna insisted was her own doing.

So when the rider came at a furious clip to the Palace, to tell the prince that the great *Trophy Chase* had been sighted far offshore, the prince granted the girl and Bench Urmand a fast coach to the docks. If Packer Throme was aboard, then she could be set free.

Bench didn't like it, but there it was. The prince had a flare for the dramatic.

Bench glanced at Panna now and then; it was hard not to. She seemed serene and confident and painfully vulnerable at once. As the ship drew close to the dock, Panna peered into the rising sun, straining to see Packer's face and form; her dark hair tangled, her elegant clothing rumpled and torn, her face and eyes puffy from lack of sleep.

Bench smelled familiar smoke, the incense of a matchlock pistol. His eyes scanned the docks in search of the source. He left Panna's side, crossed the dock to where a man with a scarred face and a grizzled beard stood leaning against a post, watching the ship approach. Bench stepped quietly into place beside the bounty hunter, Dirk Menafee. "Sorry, Dirk—this one's off the books."

The man with the grizzled beard was surprised, then angered by the presence of the Sheriff. But there was nothing to be done about it. Now that the Sheriff had stepped in, there could be no reward. Dirk raised his pistol, licked his thumb and forefinger, and squeezed the ember out with a hiss. No use wasting the wick.

The choppy seas were slate-gray, their foam caps pink, as the wooden prow cut through them, rising, falling, rising wet again as though the ship were breathing gently, sleepily. Packer stood again at the prow in the early morning, above the carved lion, watching the Port of Mann grow on the horizon. He feared that only the ruins of his life awaited him there. He wanted to hope, to find it in him to believe it was possible that Panna and Senslar were alive. But he couldn't. Doubt sat in his stomach like grapeshot.

"She might well have lied," Delaney told him. "Talon wasn't what you would call honorable."

Packer nodded. He didn't have any illusions about Talon. But he had thought often of that last look, the way she had reached out to him for help. Was she in fact reaching out to God? Or did she simply die in fear and anguish, after a lifetime of ensuring that others did the same? "But something happened to her," Packer said, "there at the end."

Delaney nodded. Packer had told him the story. "In the end, she feared God," Delaney said with finality, looking out over the sea. "But what good it did her, no man can say."

Packer smiled inwardly at Delaney's pronouncement, the grizzled reformed pirate speaking as a priest might, with somber ceremony and respect. He said it as an epitaph. Packer hoped it had done her great good.

But that was over. She was gone; he had to live with the damage she had already done. Talon had set out to destroy him and his world forever. It seemed utterly vain to hope for anything else. He dreaded finding out, learning with certainty Panna's fate, a certainty that drew closer to him with every passing moment.

Delaney saw the pale, plaintive look on his friend's face. "You never do know," he said quietly. "Look at Marcus. Everyone thought he was dead. But he only got a musket ball to the head, that's all. Didn't even kill him."

Packer nodded. They figured Scat's shot had ricocheted off the yardarm before hitting the boy. "No one's skull is thick enough to deflect a ball the way Marcus's did," Packer had told Delaney. "Not even yours." And Delaney had climbed out to the end of the yard to see, and sure enough had found a dent in the hardened oak timber, little more than a thumbprint in size. He marveled that such a little thing had made the difference in a life.

"That he came around in the ocean without drowning, and then found that shallop, and then that the *Camadan* found him, it was like he couldn't be killed no matter what. And why? Because God decides, and saves who He wants. If I'm not being too blunt about it."

Packer nodded. "No, you're not. You speak the truth." Packer believed what Delaney said, but he also felt that a man could walk into danger and end up dead so easily, it seemed to carry no greater mystery than the notion that one stupid choice will kill you. But it helped to hear it from Delaney, who'd seen far more untimely deaths than Packer had.

Even if Panna was dead, if the whole village was dead, and it was all Packer's fault, God had still let it happen. God was still in charge. God wanted Packer alive, certainly, though he had no idea why. Perhaps God wanted Panna alive too. And Senslar. Maybe Talon had lied about it all.

And then he sighed. It was too much. He remembered what Panna had told him when he promised to return and marry her.

"I'm not holding you to that promise, Packer...There's too much hope in it."

Not only was she beautiful, she was wise.

Panna watched the ship with anxious eyes, straining, hoping one of the small shapes moving about on deck might suddenly become Packer. At the same time, Packer scanned the shoreline, his stomach an empty pit, unwilling to let hope rise in him.

She spotted him first. Her heart swelled within her. She waited, fearing that the image she saw would dissolve into someone else as the ship drew closer. Finally she was sure, and a tear drained down her cheek. "That's him," she said, pointing.

"Which one?" Bench asked gruffly.

"The yellow hair. At the prow." She blinked away more tears that now rolled down her face.

And then Packer saw her. At first he couldn't believe it was her. She was dressed formally, richly, fashionably. For a moment he believed this woman only looked like Panna. But then he saw the tears, the warmth, the love.

There could be no doubt.

Packer's hand was bandaged. Panna's hands were chained. But with the miles between them dwindling now to yards, and the yards to feet, and the feet to inches, as the promise of a touch, and then an embrace grew larger and larger, the bandages and the chains were already falling away. Healing and freedom were at hand.

They kissed. Their arms wrapped around one another with gentleness, an almost airy touch born of love tested, hope tried and frayed and pushed to the very edge of black despair, and past, but now proven. In this gentle embrace, hearts were woven like a cord of three strands: Panna, Packer, and the invisible God who had delivered them to this moment, and to one another.

Panna was safe. Packer had returned. And they were together.

But there was sorrow within their joy, as they rode hand in hand to Hangman's Cliffs, inside a gleaming carriage finished in burl walnut, a plush coach furnished by John Hand, hired in thanks for the lad's many services.

Panna told Packer her story, one she had told and retold but would gladly tell once more, this time with the ending known, and with the kindled spirit of Packer Throme listening behind those sharp blue eyes, amazed.

The tale poured forth like a river, rushing frantically through narrows, widening through a quiet pasture, then plummeting over the edge into a boiling cauldron of white foam and terror, only to end in a glistening harbor, serene under a wide expanse of sky. The story flowed from the borrowed cobbler's clothes and Panna's flying fists to a gray tree trunk on a sodden beach, a stolen boat and a wild, wild storm, a darkened inn and a bright white coach that carried her toward a desperate hope, a hope dashed in the dying embrace of Senslar Zendoda.

And here Packer's eyes trailed unseeing out the carriage window, as he envisioned his swordmaster fighting his final duel, eyes bright and fierce, blade flashing, buying Panna's escape with his own blood.

And when her tale was told, they sat together without speaking for a very long while, the carriage swaying over the softened road, the horses' hooves plodding gently, step by step, closer and closer to home.

"He made it to the ocean," Packer said, from far away. "He's found the sea at last." And in his mind a great sea turtle swam beneath the sunlit waves, silent and peaceful and free.

And then he told Panna his story, as though reading aloud from memory the words inscribed there, as though describing images burned deeply there, seared into his heart and into his flesh.

Panna heard, and saw, Packer's soul and body torn and marred under the waves, dragged beneath a ship, torn and marred again at Talon's hands, cut deeply in a duel with Delaney, rent in an aching prayer as he descended from the rigging to a bloody deck, scarred badly by a beast that rose from the depths to devour him, striking with its lightning, only to die with Lund Lander's lure inside its belly, and with Lund himself. Here was a man Panna knew not at all, would never know, and yet to whom she owed the greatest debt.

And then she heard, and saw, Packer's spirit shredded with despair by a single tress of her own hair, a desolation that should have cost him his life but somehow instead cost their great adversary her soul. Or, perhaps, bought it forever. And then the marvelous return of Marcus Pile, a gift, it seemed, from the heart of God.

And this time in the following silence, amid the soft hoofbeats and blackbirds' caws and rustle of leaves in the wind, tears came. A single sob at first, from Panna, followed by Packer's glistening eyes. He put his arm around her. She nestled in close. And here he was! Packer himself, no dream this time, but real, warm, strong, and alive, returned to her at last. And he felt her warmth, Panna, alive and whole, sorrowful and thankful and lovely.

And when the storm had passed, Packer said, so gentle it seemed like words from a world far away, or from the sweetest dream, "Panna, will you marry me?"

And she answered, "Yes, Packer. I will marry you."

Summer passed. Winter came and went as preparations were made, as invitations were sent north to Mann, and far, far north to the Cold Climes, and as a small rundown cottage in the woods was rebuilt, restored, and made ready.

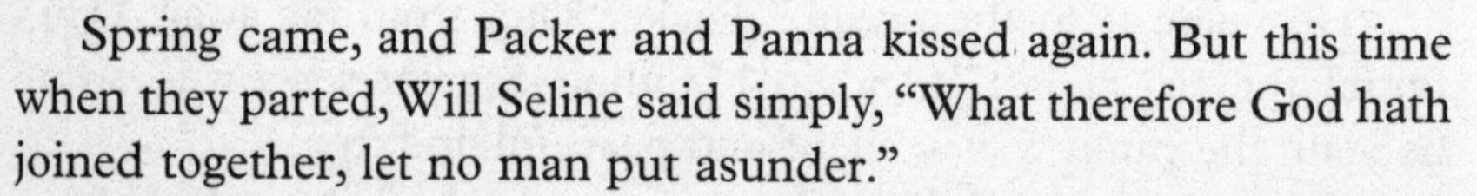

Spring came, and Packer and Panna kissed again. But this time when they parted, Will Seline said simply, "What therefore God hath joined together, let no man put asunder."

And Packer took Panna by the hand and, both dressed in white, they turned to face their friends, their family, all the faces gathered with them in the small, familiar church, now strewn with daisies, violets, and honeysuckle, sweet on an April breeze flowing through open windows.

Packer looked out to the many who had gathered to witness their vows. Here was Smith Delaney, grinning ear to ear, still more gum than tooth, pulling an offending collar with unthinking fingers. And beside him, young and lanky Marcus Pile, his shock of wild, wheat hair parted poorly in the middle and plastered flat with oil, so that he looked like an otter with a bad haircut. But he beamed a joy so unrestrained that Packer laughed out loud.

And here was Cap, red in face, jolly as he ever was, raising an invisible mug to toast the moment. A friend always. His Hen was here beside him, utterly unseeing for the tears that filled her eyes, rolled freely down her cheeks, and then found refuge in the folds of all her chins. She dabbed at them with a sodden cloth that had started out this day a dainty handkerchief.

And others were here too. Andrew Haas, and Fourtooth. Riley Odoms, nicely recovered from his beating, almost as nicely from the shame of being this young woman's punching bag. Panna had befriended him, and sent him cards and notes and breads and pies, until finally he succumbed to her heartfelt, culinary charms. "It was the rum cakes did it," he had said.

Dog Blestoe came, though he sat glumly in the farthest pew, lips pursed, holding out a vain and distant hope, now dashed, that someone would speak a reason that this couple should not this day be wed. And others from their village, from Panna's past and Packer's childhood, friends and family, old and young—all here, all sharing in this hard-won, long-delayed, delightful moment.

But some were not here. Packer's father, Dayton Throme—how he would have loved to be here—and to know that his stories of the Firefish were now proved true, stories that a year ago were fanciful as fairies and fierce dragons, and were now the latest news, spread far and wide. Packer looked up to the rafters, and beyond, hoping his father was here this day, somehow, looking down as his boy wed the only girl anyone who knew him could ever imagine would be his bride.

And Senslar Zendoda. Packer nodded upward, in silent tribute to his swordmaster, thankful for all he'd learned, grateful for the sacrifice that had given Panna her escape. What that good man had imparted would endure as long as Packer lived. And somehow, he felt his swordmaster would be well pleased with that.

Panna laced her arm in his, and the two began their walk back down the aisle amidst a warm sea of teary eyes, pausing only once when Packer took the hands of his frail mother, who had traveled the long road south from her people far away, to be here for this day. Nessa looked up at her son with shining eyes. And Packer kissed her cheek. And then he wrapped his arm around Panna's waist and walked her down the aisle.

Will Seline stood still, in his familiar place at the altar, watching. His smile was as bright as the sun.

The people poured from the small church, straight down the street toward the tiny pub. But this celebration would not be held indoors, not on a beautiful spring day like this. Tables were set out

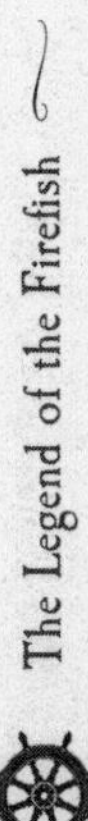

and ready, and nearly half the chairs were filled with well-wishers from neighboring villages, joined by the now-accustomed stream of visitors, strangers seeking Firefish, here to join the venture, or to simply bask in the bright ray of glory that shone down on the little village on the cliff. Doorposts dripped with white bunting. A fiddle and a bass viol, cymbals and an accordion rested casually on a storefront stoop, waiting for their turn to add their music to the day.

Cap ran ahead as best he could to serve his finest ale and freshest cider from his little pub's front stoop. Hen hurried after him, sweeping linens off the trays of bass and cod and duck, uncovering plates of fresh fruits and vegetables, laying out the modest feast that graced her serving tables. Children ran and whooped and laughed, little girls in Sunday best, but in their hearts each one a Panna in a white wedding dress, all chasing little boys who bore aloft their gleaming, sharpened swords, which to older eyes looked a bit like sticks.

The town's main street grew raucous with toasts and music, talk and laughter and plenty of good, good food. And in the center of it all the newlyweds sat quietly, hand in hand, watching, surrounded by so much goodwill, soaking it all in, humbled by their good fortune. And waiting patiently for the moment they could say goodbye and venture off to the quiet little cottage in the woods.

Dog sat with Fourtooth, also watching, but his talk was not of Packer or of Panna, or Firefish or the *Trophy Chase.* He watched the village priest. It still stung him that Will Seline seemed not the least embarrassed by his actions during Panna's trials. That the man had shown himself to be weak and pitiful, that he'd collapsed in the face of hardship, that he had given in to all his fears and hidden himself away—all this was undeniable, and hard for him and many of these rugged cliff dwellers to bear.

But little by little, a few more each Sunday, they had returned to hear him speak. And they had to admit, at least all but Dog, that the priest's sermons were perhaps more powerful than they had been before.

"Whatever he needs to tell himself to get to sleep at night," Dog said, having drained his mug. "That Panna, though," he wiped his mouth, "she's got real backbone."

"Aye." Fourtooth's grin turned quickly to a leer. "And it's in quite a pleasin' size and shape."

Dog gave Fourtooth a look that wilted his enthusiasm.

"You wait till those two have children," Cap Hillis fairly sang, walking by at just that moment with his huge earthen pitcher. He refilled Dog's mug cheerfully, if with less than stellar aim. Cap was blind to Fourtooth's mug, though the old man raised it hopefully. "Panna's children by Packer Throme," Cap said, looking over at the couple. "Won't they be something? Sons and daughters of the hero of the Achawuk battle, the conqueror of Firefish, the pride of the fishing villages—"

"All right, all right!" Dog cut him off, shaking the excess ale from his hand. "I was talking about the priest. We hear enough about that boy around here already."

"All I mean is, there'll be some bold traits passed on to Will Seline's grandchildren," Cap said, clearly pleased to be twisting the knife. "Sure enough, sure enough."

"Hmmph. We'll just see about that."

"That we will," Cap chirped. "Lord willing, that we most certainly will."

About the Author

George Bryan Polivka was raised in the Chicago area, attended Bible college in Alabama, and ventured on to Europe, where he studied under Francis Schaeffer at L'Abri Fellowship in Switzerland. He then returned to Alabama, where he enrolled at Birmingham-Southern College as an English major.

While still in school, Bryan married Jeri, his only sweetheart since high school and now his wife of more than 25 years. He also was offered a highly coveted internship at a local television station, which led him to his first career—as an award-winning television producer.

In 1986, Bryan won an Emmy for writing his documentary *A Hard Road to Glory,* which detailed the difficult path African-Americans traveled to achieve recognition through athletic success during times of racial prejudice and oppression.

Bryan and his family lived in Texas for a dozen years, then moved to the Baltimore area, where he worked with Sylvan Learning Systems (now Laureate Education). In 2001 he was honored by the U.S. Distance Learning Association for the most significant achievement by an individual in corporate e-learning. He is currently responsible for developing and delivering new programs for Laureate's online higher education division.

Bryan and Jeri live near Baltimore with their two children, Jake and Aime, where Bryan continues work on the Trophy Chase Trilogy.

Be sure and watch for the second book
in The Trophy Chase Trilogy,

THE HAND THAT BEARS THE SWORD

coming in July 2007.

The assassination of the great Swordsman has turned simmering animosity into open war between Nearing Vast and Drammun. Desperate for warships, Prince Mather sends Packer to sea aboard the *Trophy Chase,* hailing them as symbols of God's favor. But this war promises to be short and brutal, with all odds favoring the Drammune.

On one shore, Panna is caught in a treacherous web woven by a prince. Across the sea, vicious men angle for an emperor's throne. In between, Firefish stalk and cannons roar. But the true battleground is found within those who must choose between self-sacrifice, and selfish pride.

Another exciting tale in George Bryan Polivka's The Trophy Chase Trilogy.

Mindy Starns Clark

THE MILLION DOLLAR MYSTERIES

A Penny for Your Thoughts

Don't Take Any Wooden Nickels

A Dime a Dozen

A Quarter for a Kiss

The Buck Stops Here

Brandt Dodson

THE COLTON PARKER MYSTERIES

Original Sin

Seventy Times Seven

The Root of All Evil

Roxanne Henke

COMING HOME TO BREWSTER

After Anne

Finding Ruth

Becoming Olivia

Always Jan

With Love, Libby

B.J. Hoff

THE MOUNTAIN SONG LEGACY SERIES

A Distant Music

The Wind Harp

The Song Weaver

Susan Meissner

Why the Sky Is Blue

A Window to the World

The Remedy for Regret

In All Deep Places

Craig & Janet Parshall

THE THISTLE AND THE CROSS SERIES

Crown of Fire

Captives and Kings